Shield of Fire

Forged in Fire Series, Book 2

A L Evans

A L Evans

This novel is a work of fiction. Situations, scenarios, and characters in this book are a reflection of creative imagination and not representative of any specific person, group, situation, or event.

Cover art by A L Evans.

To my sons, you were my reason to keep going in the darkest season of my life.
I'm proud of you and the men you have become.

Shout out to Crowder for The Anchor, the theme song for this book.
If you haven't heard the song, please take a moment to listen.
https://www.youtube.com/watch?v=cve0AZtyU38

Contents

Content Warning

This book contains discussions that may not be suitable for all readers, such as: human trafficking, trauma, child abuse, sexual assault, rape, and the psychological aftermath.

There are NO graphic scenes, only an alluding to, but it may be enough to create a trigger for some readers.

"The Light shines in the darkness, and the darkness has not overcome it." John 1:5 (ESV)

This is Book 2 in a trilogy and must be read in order.
Read Book 1, Forged in Fire, before starting Book 2.

Prologue

Angel

Run!

Urgency yanks me awake, and confusion fogs my mind at the crushing weight on my chest. Swollen eyes flutter open against the glare of a bright bulb dangling from the ceiling. The all-too-familiar smell of sweat, mixed with something else, hangs in the air.

The weight hasn't moved, making it hard to breathe.

Wait . . . if he isn't moving . . .

I only hope he's finally dead, and this isn't a dream.

Run!

There it is again. More a feeling than a voice. I want to run, believe me, I do. I've tried so many times before, but nothing ever worked. And I always paid the price.

The weight on my chest pulls me from those thoughts. He still hasn't moved. With a desperate need to take a breath, I shove and scoot, shove and scoot, and slide out from underneath.

Finally, I can breathe. The deep breath I take carries the nasty smell that coats the air. With heavy arms, I push up, and my bleary eyes scan the room.

My room. What an awful thought.

A room that's been mine for too long.

A bed pushed against the wall. A small nightstand holding only a broken locket. The boarded-up window gives no light and no hope for escape. And the locked door. Always locked.

Run!

That feeling again, pushing this time. I lift my hands and rub my eyes, but the jingle I'm used to doesn't sound. I look down at hands no longer chained to the bed. My head spins around, wondering if this might be a trick.

I have to pay attention and not go back into the hazy fog. My bare feet slide onto the cold floor. The torn, dirty gown lies next to his clothes in a messy pile. I glance back at the still form on the bed. He hasn't moved, but that doesn't mean he won't. I don't have much time.

Shaky legs carry me forward to the pile on the floor as a shudder runs through me. I bend down, but decide to pick up his dirty gray t-shirt instead. It's cleaner than the gown he makes me wear, so I pull it over my head.

He still hasn't moved, but I sneak another peek at the man on the bed to make sure.

On wobbly legs, I bend down again and dig through his pockets. My hands shake so badly they're almost useless.

If I get caught, he'll probably kill me. And I'm okay with that because living is so much worse.

Run!

I'm trying, I am, but I can't move like I need to. It's so hard to shake off whatever he gives me. He said it makes me compliant, whatever that means.

I like it, whatever it is, because once he gives it to me, I feel nothing. I don't have to think about where I am or what he's doing to me. I even beg for it. I'm not ashamed to admit it. But right now, I'm moving too slow.

My hands move through his pockets till I find what I'm looking for . . . keys. I tighten my fist around them to keep them quiet.

Fear that he may attack at any moment shoots through me. I inch toward the door, not making a sound and barely breathing. One eye on the door, one eye on the still form. The doorknob is cold and smooth in my hand as I turn it, checking to see if it's locked.

I don't know why I bother. It's always locked. He locks the deadbolt on the inside when he comes in and the deadbolt on the outside when he leaves.

It's silly to try, but I do it anyway. Surprise runs through me as the knob turns in my hand, and the door opens.

He forgot to lock it. He never forgets to lock it.

I tiptoe into the hallway and push the door behind me, turning the knob gently so it doesn't make any noise. But a small sound from somewhere in the house makes me pause and hold my breath. I don't dare make another sound. Now, I stand in the hallway, out in the open, no longer hidden.

My fingers open, and I stare at the palm of my hand. So many keys. I need to choose the right one and lock the door so he can't get me.

It takes a few tries to find the right key, but I could cry when the key slides in and locks the door. I take a breath and relax, but only for a moment.

Someone else may be in the house, so I don't have time to waste. I slip down the hallway as quiet as I can, and look for a way out.

I'm only allowed to leave the room to go to the bathroom, and then, only while he watches me.

I don't know where I am. There's only this hallway with a couple of closed doors and then a messy room with chairs and a couch.

A door stands on the right. I peer around the wall and peek into the room, but no one is in here.

Run!

I sneak to the door and turn the knob, but it's locked. It doesn't need a key though, and with a turn of the latch it unlocks.

Darkness surrounds me as the door swings open, and I walk out wondering if any of this is real. I secure the door behind me, amazed at what just happened.

I take a deep breath of clean air for the first time in what feels like forever. I'm free. A breeze blows softly against my skin, causing bumps on my arms. But I won't complain. I'm outside at night for the first time in so long.

My head tilts back, and I gaze at the stars above in wonder. Stars, breeze, fresh air, so much I've missed. As wonderful as all of this is, I can't stay here.

But now what?

I always dreamed of leaving, but never made it this far.

As I step off the concrete to the ground below, rocks bite into the bottom of my feet, yanking me back to the task at hand. Soft light from the moon helps me see the dead grass that covers the yard. A large tree is on my left with a truck parked under it.

A truck. An idea pops up.

Don't know where I am or where to go; I just need to leave while I can.

Maybe I could drive a little and then leave the truck somewhere.

Tall grass crushes under my bare feet, making more noise than I want while I limp to the truck. When I reach the door, I pull on the handle, and the door lets out a loud groan into the quiet night. My hand freezes on the handle, and I jerk around, hoping no one heard.

With no time to waste, I hop in and glance around the dirty inside. Empty wrappers, cups and trash sit on the floor and seat.

There aren't many car rides I remember. It needs a key to start, and the pedal on the bottom right is to go and the pedal on the bottom left is to stop. The handle by the steering wheel makes it go forward or back.

Barely able to see over the steering wheel, I can only reach the pedals by sitting on the very edge of the seat. I hope I know enough to get out of here, and that's all I'm trying to do. After a few tries, I find the right key and with a horrible noise, the truck rumbles to life. Someone had to have heard that and will come for me any second. It's now or never.

I pull the handle down and push the pedal on the right. The truck jerks back so fast it scares me, and I slam my foot down on the left so hard I knock my head into the steering wheel when the truck jerks to a stop.

Okay, that could have gone better. Don't push so hard. Got it. I try again with much less force, and the truck backs through the grass. With a softer touch, I move the handle again a few times and press the left pedal until the truck wiggles forward. In slow jerks and stops, the truck bumps onto the rocky driveway. It's dark and I can barely see, but the moon shines just enough to light the way.

Somehow I make it to the road, but now I need to decide. Should I go right or left?

And for the first time, I get to decide. No one chooses for me.

I turn the wheel to the right and hope for the best. A flutter moves inside my chest.

Freedom.

Chapter 1

Elizabeth

Nausea makes a nasty appearance as tires bounce haphazardly onto the asphalt and let out a screech as we skid down the runway. Worst flight ever.

Mark reaches over to rub his hand across my back. "That was rough." He unbuckles his seatbelt and reaches beneath the seat to grab his satchel.

Body shaking as sweat caresses my brow, the breath I release trembles from my lips. Fingers ache from the death grip on the armrests, and it takes serious effort to pry them off.

"I don't think I ever want to fly again." Then I lean in to whisper, "We should have just teleported."

He grunts as he stands up and offers me his hand. I place a shaky hand against his warm and steady palm, and he pulls me to my feet. His touch is tender and strong. And right now I desperately need both.

"We are official! We get to be out in the field, no more sitting on the sidelines." Grace does a little shimmy down the aisle as Sloan tries to both pass and ignore her at the same time.

Not until my feet step onto the steady ground of the terminal, am I able to take in a full breath. Kissing the ground seems a bit much, but I respect the sentiment.

Grace bounces beside me. "Let's go, times a-wastin'." She slides her sunglasses on and strides forward.

"Oh, I think that's her," Roz announces while she walks beside me through the door. She throws her duffel bag over her shoulder, and we make our way to the pickup area.

With a mass of untamed, fiery red curls and a "Triton Security" sign, you can't miss Cressida. Standard Triton black pants and polo shirt, adorned with the Triton emblem. A pair of aviator sunglasses covers her eyes, and her skin glows from the Light within.

She pulls off the outfit better than I ever could. Mark laces his fingers through mine as we follow behind Dax and Roz. It's as if he knows I'm doubting myself. His hand in mine is his reassurance that I am enough, just as I am.

She lifts her hand in a wave when she notices our approach. "Hey y'all, I'm so glad you could make it. I'm Cressida." Her southern twang rings out, and she removes her sunglasses to get a good look at us.

"It's so good to meet you in person. I'm Roz, and this is our team." Roz waves her hand to the rest of us, trailing behind. Roz makes the introductions, but Cressida stops when she reaches me.

"So you're the one everyone's been talking about." Her gaze assessing. "Most of us don't encounter the heavenly realm during this earthly life. Maybe you wouldn't mind sharing stories from your time there. I've always been curious about the heavenly realm." It's a little unnerving to know I'm being talked about by people I don't even know. But I've got nothing to hide, and I'll answer any questions she has.

She eyes the rest of our group. "First, let me say, 'Welcome to New Orleans'. Before we get down to business, allow me to provide you with a proper introduction to southern cuisine. You'll never be the same." She pops her sunglasses back on her face and sashays out into the sweltering heat. "Let's get going."

We follow her path and run right into a brick wall of humidity. It's hot. So hot. My sweat is sweating. How does anyone live here? The last time we were here, it wasn't this hot. The cool air of the Pacific Northwest is very tempting right now.

On our way to the Southern headquarters, we stop to eat at a little out of the way seafood joint. And she isn't lying. Fried catfish smothered in crawfish etouffee, hushpuppies, seafood stuffed potato, green beans cooked down with bacon and potatoes, and bread pudding for dessert. Southern sweet tea, a syrupy concoction both strong and super sweet. Not sure I'm a fan. As wonderful as everything is, I don't think my cholesterol can handle eating like this on the regular. My arteries are begging for a salad with minimal dressing.

"Our headquarters are located just outside of New Orleans. Because we lie below sea level, we can't have anything underground. Our only options are up and out, which is why we're located just outside the city." Cressida pulls the nondescript white van up to a gated entrance with a guard station. The guard directs her forward.

There's not a hill to be found. Not even a small one. Vibrant green grass with trees in the distance surrounds the gated community. Large structures extend before us, disappearing into the distance. The compound is massive. Ours is as well, only it's mostly underground.

Once we've unloaded our things in the attached apartments, we meet back in the training facility. The setup here isn't wide open like The Cave. The rooms are enormous, but every area has its own separate space.

A beautiful middle-aged woman with silver streaks sliced through dark hair approaches as soon as we walk in. Her brilliant blue eyes offer hints of laughter and an easygoing spirit.

"I was wondering when y'all would arrive. Knowing Cressida, y'all stopped for food on the way."

"This is Sookie Guitreau, my Guardian. We'll be training you in human trafficking rescue. We'll go out in the field while you're here so you can experience what we encounter and how we work with local law enforcement." Cressida introduces our team.

Sookie falls in line with Cressida as they take us on a tour of the facilities. As we follow, Cressida fills us in on how this will differ from what we typically encounter.

"There's more to this than just battling demons and Fallen. Unfortunately, we have to contend with the humans who are responsible for human trafficking, and that means we work alongside local law enforcement. As much as we would like to eliminate every reprobate involved, that's simply not feasible. There's a delicate balance to dispatching demons and apprehending the humans responsible.

"Then, there's the task of saving innocent victims trapped by evil. The discoveries we've made are disturbing. Usually, victims return to their families or go with the authorities. Sometimes, though, Triton Security handles their care internally." Cressida's brief rundown leaves me feeling queasy as I picture the brutality these victims have lived through.

"How do you make that determination?" Sloan poses the question.

We turn the corner and enter the weapons room. A few people walk along each wall as they decide which weapon to take.

"That's a good question. You'll have to determine that based on the situation. Without a solid foundation of family and friends, some victims will end up right back in the same situation. We don't want that to happen. When they don't have a reliable foundation to go back to, we can offer a solution. We have the resources in place for that. It may be something you want to look into providing as well," Sookie responds.

It's more than just battling against demons; it's also being His Light to the lost and broken.

"We can't save them all, but we never give up." Cressida pauses and focuses on the guys headed our way.

Two men, wearing the typical Triton Security uniform, approach us. "I hate that Arden couldn't make it. I was looking forward to seeing him again, but I'm glad you could join us. I'm Reed Powell, the Head Director of Triton Security, and this is my Guardian, Brooks Bennett, the Assistant Director. Arden filled us in a little on what's happening in Miracle Lake. Unfortunately, we've had years to develop a good strategy to fight against human trafficking here. You're in excellent hands, and you'll learn enough to bring back with you to train others. I spoke with Arden moments ago, and we both agree that once you've trained here, we will send Cressida and Sookie back with you to help assess the situation you face and offer assistance in partnering with the task force you have there."

Reed Powell exudes the distinguished Southern gentleman with wavy, salt and pepper hair that curls at the end. His light brown eyes observe our team as he gives us a rundown of what to expect.

Brooks Bennett has skin the color of rich mocha. Deep brown eyes assess but give away nothing. His bald head shines, as if waxed, and the small gold hoops in both ears glint in the light. He hasn't spoken a word or cracked a smile. There is nothing gentle about this guy. I bet he would give Gage a run for his money. And I would pay to see that.

Sookie grins wide. "Oh, a trip to Miracle Lake. It's been a while since we've been able to get away."

Cressida nods her head. "It's a good idea to see what you're up against. We'll help however we can. But for now, it'll be good to train you on our turf. We'll have the advantage."

"We'll get Arden and Brenda down here soon for some good Southern hospitality, but for now, I hope you will enjoy all the South has to offer. I hear congratulations are in order for both of you." He nods his head in my direction and Mark's. "Don't work too hard while you're here. Enjoy the perks of being in the South. And if I know Cressida, she's already introduced you to our famous southern cuisine."

News about our upcoming nuptials spread fast. We decided on the date only a few days ago.

Mark responds, "Thank you, sir. So far, the food has been amazing, and we look forward to some sightseeing while we're here."

"I'll leave you to it, then." Reed waves his hand as he and Brooks walk back to the training area.

Cressida moves us through another set of doors. "You have about an hour before we leave. We've received intel of a mansion in one of the exclusive neighborhoods housing young women and girls for house parties. Tonight, we'll gather information the police can use to take down this organization."

"A mansion?" Grace asks.

Kind of what I was thinking. If I'm being honest, I'm not sure what I imagined we would be facing.

"It might be a nice house, in a nice neighborhood, but they're still held against their will, locked in rooms with no means of escape. They're sold by the hour or the evening, and they have no control over what's done to them. They've been so conditioned by fear that even when we offer a way of escape, sometimes they're afraid to take it."

Cressida shifts her stance, and her lips pinch together before she continues. "One thing we've learned, if someone doesn't want to be rescued, we can't force them. That doesn't happen very often, but it does happen. We set them free and give them a second chance. The younger girls are easier to rescue. Some find it harder to leave this life after spending any amount of time in it, either because they fear the consequences or because they've been taught to believe they are cared for. It's a hard line to balance. It can be frustrating, and it's not as cut and dry as you would think."

All of it is heartbreaking, and I'm not sure I'm up for this task. But crawling under a rock and pretending it isn't happening won't help anyone.

Cressida walks us back to where the apartments are located.

"That's enough for now. We have plenty of time over the next two weeks to provide more information. And now, you have a lay of the land to get around easy enough. You can explore or go back to your rooms to rest, and we'll meet back here in an hour so we can prepare to leave. There are a few things that need my attention before we meet up." Cressida pivots her stride, and Sookie throws out a wave as she follows.

"I wouldn't mind brushing my teeth and putting on fresh clothes before we need to leave," Roz mentions.

We divide up between guys and girls. The guys will stay together in one apartment, and us girls are in another. Toward the end of our stay, Roz and Dax will share an apartment, leaving Mark in a room by himself.

In just a few weeks, Mark and I will not only be sharing a room, but we will share a life together. That both excites and terrifies me at the same time. I'm accustomed to a life of solitude, and the last few months have thrown me into a mess of new relationships that I haven't had a chance to acclimate to.

Don't get me wrong, I'm grateful for these new friendships, especially what Mark and I have. My past does not get to dictate any current or future friendships. I want to do this right, and I just pray I don't make any horrible mistakes.

An hour later, we meet back at the training room dressed in tactical gear, even Grace. Which is surprising since I never know what she's going to wear.

"We'll be meeting with our police task force down the street from the location of the party. We need surveillance inside the house, and to do that, we have a Light Bearer that can camouflage into his surroundings. It's my understanding that Grace can do the same." Cressida's attention finds Grace. "Would you be willing to go undercover with him?"

"Absolutely not!" Roz and I both express at the same time as Grace responds with, "Absolutely!"

"I don't think we need a beautiful young girl walking into that situation," Roz explains her abrupt response.

"She won't be going in as a beautiful young girl. She'll be invisible. Besides, she won't be alone. Paxton will accompany her and will also be camouflaged." Cressida uses a gentled tone to offset Roz's worry.

Two young guys stride forward with a swagger that only the purely self-confident can pull off. Right away, my attention snags on the prettiest guy I have ever seen. Can a guy be pretty? Yes, yes, he can. He's so beautiful he could be a model.

Deep ocean blue eyes survey our team, then those eyes zero in on Grace. His smirk breaks out into a wide grin, with teeth so white they sparkle against the dark tan of his face. He's noticed Grace, who is only sixteen. Oh boy, we'll need to keep an eye on this one.

Standing next to him is a guy several shades darker with deep brown, assessing eyes. If I didn't know any better, I would say cold. A tattoo peeks from beneath his Triton Security polo on his large bicep. His gaze is intense as he watches and observes us.

"This is Paxton King and Tyler Ardoin. They will be with us tonight. Paxton is a great asset and has excellent observational skills. He is our eyes and ears in situations we cannot get into." Cressida makes the introductions.

So, Paxton is the surfer dude who has eyes for Grace. It's unwise to put these two in a dangerous situation together, given his potential lack of focus.

Tyler, on the other hand, exudes an aura of intimidation as he stands next to Paxton.

"How do you see this playing out?" Roz asks. "What's the game plan?"

Sookie lays it out for us. "Paxton and Grace will gather the necessary information and evidence for a police raid. We need to know about how many women and girls are being held, and we need proof of funds changing hands. The area will have demons and Fallen guarding their domain. We'll need to deal with that as well as any humans we come in contact with. The police force we work with has a general understanding of what we do, so they're aware of the supernatural forces at play."

Out of the corner of my eye, I watch Grace. The only thing that has her attention right now is Paxton. That girl had better get her head in the game.

Next to Grace, Sloan's scowl is firmly in place. Interestingly enough, it's aimed at Tyler.

Chapter 2

Grace

He is gorgeous, and his Guardian is attractive too. A touch broody with a bit of smolder. He may be exactly what Sloan needs. Judging by the way those two are throwing eye darts at each other, I may have to resort to some covert matchmaking. Oh, this is going to be fun. She'll never know what hit her.

But not a task for now. I need to focus. They're talking about what we'll need to do once we arrive.

"It's an invitation-only party, and the guest list is unknown. Once a guest enters, Grace and Paxton will slip in unnoticed. They'll camouflage into the surroundings to observe and record the events as they unfold. Our police team will receive it, gather any additional evidence, if necessary, and go in to make arrests and remove the girls. We'll eliminate any demons or Fallen we encounter to protect the area. Does everyone understand so far?" Sookie asks.

There are nods of agreement.

"Anything can happen. Things seldom go as planned, so expect the unexpected. We'll need to make adjustments as we go. Should a difficult situation arise, Paxton will guide Grace in proper protocol."

Roz lets out a growl. She wants nothing to happen to me, but she has got to give me some credit. I know what I'm doing. Sloan and I have trained for every possible scenario since we were kids. I'm thankful Cressida didn't hesitate to include me in this assignment. We only need a chance to get out and prove ourselves.

"We have two vans waiting to take us to the rendezvous point. Y'all load up and let's move out." Cressida nods her head toward the weapons room.

It doesn't matter what I wear tonight, but I want to be taken seriously with this first opportunity to really prove myself. Which means I dress in the same tactical gear as everyone else. Tonight, none of the wild outfits I'm known for.

Sloan looks over and raises an eyebrow. Yes, this is out of the norm, but I want others to know this matters to me. I give her my biggest goofy grin. She'll understand. Still myself, while I prove I'm more than a ditzy blonde to overlook.

We proved ourselves at the battle of the breach, but we snuck in and went against normal protocol. This time we're part of a team. It's different. There are expectations now.

I arm myself with whatever weapons I can carry. It's best to be prepared for anything. Besides, action is more my speed. I'm not a fan of blending in and doing nothing.

Paxton and Tyler load up in the other van with the guys. I planned to ride with them to get better acquainted before we got started, but that's not how it played out. I thought I sensed a bit of interest coming from him, but maybe he's trying to play it cool.

The police meet us at a vacant house for sale within the gated community. This will be home base tonight. If this thing goes sideways, we meet back here.

We gather inside the empty mansion. My boots echo on the pristine marble floor as I walk into the open kitchen area, where everyone goes over the plan.

Sulfur hangs heavy in the air. A clear indication demons are present. That I'm comfortable with, it's familiar ground. Hanging out in a mansion to gather info on women and girls who are being trafficked, not so much. That's something I haven't trained for, which is why we're here. While I'm familiar with it from news reports, I've never had first-hand experience with trafficking.

Cressida comes over and hands me an earpiece. "Keep it on. You'll hear us, and we'll hear you. Use this to let us know if you need help."

Paxton joins me as I secure the earpiece. "You ready for this?" he asks.

"Are you kidding? I'm so ready." I bounce a little on my toes, too excited to hold it in.

He chuckles and leans his arm against the counter. I haven't had time to be interested in boys, but I think I should find some time, and I think I want to start with this one.

"How many times have you done this? Gone into a trafficking situation undercover?" I ask.

"I've lost count at this point. It's one of the few ways we can get the information we need without being detected. The cops need to know where the victims are located, what the conditions are, and how many captors are in there before they go in. Unfortunately, it's as if we shut down one and three more pop up. It's discouraging. And the things I've seen? That will stay with me forever." He looks a little green as he shakes his head in disgust.

This won't be easy, but these girls need our help, and I'll do whatever I can to get them out of the situation they're in. We have an opportunity to train as a team and bring down this evil.

One cop addresses the room. "Based on our outside surveillance, people are arriving at the party. Let's get into our positions."

Cressida faces us. "Go ahead and shift. We'll have you walk to the house from here. Our team will leave out the back and make their way to the house. Use your comms device to stay in communication with us."

I nod my head as Paxton answers. "We will, don't worry. I know the drill."

Paxton and I both change our appearance right as Roz comes to join us. "Please be safe. I know you're perfectly capable, but don't take any unnecessary risks. Remember your mission – gather intel. Don't do anything to get yourselves noticed. I mean it."

She's perfected the mom look. "Thank you for caring. I love you, too. You be safe, too."

Even though she can't see me, she reaches out for a hug. Ever since the war at the breach, she's been extra cautious, and I let her. It's nice to be cared for.

I pat her back and release her. Lizzy comes up behind me as Paxton moves to the front door. "I know you'll be fine, and we won't be far away." She wraps her arms tightly around me.

I'm so proud of Lizzy. She stepped into this new world with no former knowledge of it, and she's finding her way. "Be safe, Lizzy. I'll see you in a little bit."

"They love you." Paxton mentions after we make it outside.

I'm uncomfortably aware we have the comms device on, and I need to be careful with my words while they listen. I don't want to say anything that would embarrass myself.

"They do. They're family, and that's the way it should be." And I mean it, they are my family. "Family is so much more than blood. I don't believe the saying 'blood is thicker than water'. Family is what you make it, not what you're born with."

"I agree." His voice turns contemplative. There's a story there, but that's for another time.

I've never worked with another chameleon. Even though we're both invisible, I can still make out his form. It's weird being on this side of it.

"I'm assuming you know where we're going." We walk along the sidewalk of the fanciest neighborhood I've ever been in.

"Yes, we studied the area before you arrived. It's not far. We'll stop talking before we get there." He remains alert to our surroundings as we approach our target, but my mind wanders.

"How old are you anyway?" I'm curious. Besides, I was going to ask at some point, so why not now?

"Both Tyler and myself are eighteen, but Tyler is about to turn nineteen in a few days." He doesn't ask my age or elaborate further.

He probably already knows my age. If he's any good at being a Light Bearer, he's done his research. My age makes things a bit tricky. Technically, they're both adults. I wonder how he would feel about dating a sixteen-year-old.

It doesn't take long to reach our destination. This place is lit up like a sparkler. And fancy, they even have valet parking. It would appear human trafficking pays well. Sickos.

A large man in a suit stands at the end of the driveway, stopping each car at the gate to verify the invite before allowing them to proceed.

We walk along the side of the driveway, out of the way of any cars. Only two have come through since we've been watching.

Paxton takes out his cell phone and starts recording. He captures the license plates first.

A voice comes across the comms. "We're in position. We had a few demons to dispatch, but nothing of significance. We're going to do a perimeter check for more demons and Fallen. As soon as you finish sending the intel, leave. We'll be waiting for you." The comms device goes silent.

Another car comes up the driveway. Paxton motions me forward as we approach the door. He wants to follow this person inside.

A well dressed portly man steps out of the fancy car and hands the keys to a valet. He's clothed in wealth and reeks of evil. It flows off of him in ripples. I itch to pull out my dagger and take care of him, but he's not a demon I can dispose of.

Until every person breathes their last, there's still hope of redemption. God can deal with this man.

We step behind him as the door opens, and someone checks his invitation before admitting him.

"Dr. Malloy, it's good to see you. Please come in. You're just in time. The ladies will be down momentarily. Enjoy the champagne and hors d'eouvres the servers are passing around."

He's a doctor? My hand twitches at the desire to make him suffer, but stave off the effort instead. We slide in right behind him. He's lucky I'm not as trigger-happy as Sloan.

The grand foyer holds a round table topped with an ornate vase filled with elegant flowers. A wide marble staircase curves to the right, reaching the second floor. Standard artwork hangs on the walls, but nothing offers any personal touches. No different from a high-end hotel. Fancy but not personal.

Bass from the music thumps in the background while lights pulse in time to the beat. Several people mill around in discussion as servers walk around with trays.

These "servers", teetering on high heels, are barely dressed with collars covered in crystals linked around their necks. I have so many questions, but can't ask Paxton right now.

We find an alcove out of the way we can tuck ourselves into and still see the great room where most of the activity is located. We need to get upstairs and look in the rooms, but they're probably locked.

Paxton pulls me closer and deeper into the alcove. His breath lands on my ear as he quietly whispers, "I'll be sending a live feed to the police. We'll leave before they come in and let them do their thing. Once they clear the house of the criminals, we can come back in and help look for any other girls or anyone that may be hiding. You can't imagine how many hidden rooms are in a place like this."

He lifts the phone again to record the room. Conversations of ages and preferences are made as they eagerly await the girls to arrive. It's no different for them than ordering a cheeseburger and deciding what toppings they want.

The music changes and the air shifts. Two demons appear on the stairs before a man dressed in a three-piece suit makes his entrance.

I pull two daggers out of their hiding place before I even realize I've done it. These demons need to be taken care of. But before I can contemplate my next move, girls appear at the top of the stairs. Young girls in fancy dresses and full makeup are presented to the men.

Young girls appear first. As more girls descend the stairs, their ages increase.

Men move around to get a better view. One girl tries to take a step back, but the man in the three-piece suit steps forward as she cowers behind another girl. He grabs her by the arm and shoves her toward one of the men. Her whimper is barely heard over the pounding music as she's handed off.

Paxton's hand lands on my arm and pulls me back as I move from the safety of the alcove. "Stay here," he barely whispers in my ear.

"What do you think?" the man in charge asks the guy.

"She's a little timid, but I can work with that. Ten thousand."

"Oh, come now, Max. I think you can do better than that. She won't go for less than twenty-five. Twenty-five, and we have a deal. I'll even let you take her upstairs before you leave."

The man pauses before conceding. "Fine, Quint. You have a deal." They shake hands, then the man pulls out a wad of cash from his jacket pocket and counts out twenty-five one thousand dollar bills.

"This isn't just for tonight, is it?" I whisper to Paxton.

"Doesn't appear to be. It looks like they plan to leave with these girls. If they leave here, they could disappear without a trace. Never to be seen again." His voice is difficult to hear above the music.

The scene plays out several more times as Paxton records. A demon walks by our alcove, sniffing. Before he even realizes we're here, I slice his throat as he comes near. The demon emits a screech, then obliterates into dust. Not a problem, no one but Paxton and I can hear or see the demons.

"Okay, we have enough evidence. You can leave. The cops are going in." The comms device squawks in my ear as Paxton puts away the phone and takes my arm.

"You can get the other demon later," he whispers as he leads me to the door.

No one can see us, so what are we going to do? Open the door and hope no one notices it opening on its own?

As we approach the entrance, the front door flings open and the front guard comes running past, clipping my shoulder and barely missing Paxton altogether.

The guard pauses and rotates our way but sees nothing.

He continues to the great room, leaving the door wide open for us.

"Boss, we have a problem. I just received word. There's a planned raid. We need to clear out." As soon as those words are spoken, everyone takes off.

I pull Paxton away from the door and our open exit. "We can't let them take the girls; we have to get them out of here," I whisper as quietly as I can.

Unfortunately, the comms device interrupts. "Get out of the house. We're on the way. Almost to the back door." Cressida's words come out clipped.

When I glance back to the great room, guys are grabbing girls and either finding exits or heading to safe rooms hidden in the house. Of course, they have an exit strategy in place.

"You can leave if you want, but I'm going to help them." Paxton needs to understand I will not leave these girls. I don't care what the protocol is.

I breeze past him, but he's right on my heels. "Let's help who we can, and let our teams handle the rest."

"I said get out of there!" I take the comms device out and place it in my pocket.

As we rush into the great room, Paxton asks, "You're a bit of a rebel, aren't you?"

"Not at all. But I will fight for those who can't fight for themselves, and no one gets to tell me I can't."

Some of the girls run back up the stairs away from the men, but most have already been grabbed. Moving at a much faster pace, I run up the wide marble staircase after the girls as Paxton takes off after one guy dragging a girl down the hallway.

I catch up to the first girl and gently touch her arm, which she immediately jerks away from. "Hey, I'm trying to help you get out of here. If I touch you, they can't see you." I speak as calmly as I can, but we need to hurry.

She pauses with fear in her eyes. I allow her to see me, but only for a moment. "Let me help you. We're here to get you out." She lets out a heart-wrenching sob and grabs onto me with a fierceness I was not prepared for.

"Stay quiet and let me help one more before we leave. My friend Paxton is helping, too. And we have more help on the way."

Unfortunately, a demon appears at the top of the stairs, taking up the entire space. The demon sneers as he shifts his weight to block our ascent. He's bulky and built for enforcement, but his grey mottled skin makes him look like he's been dead for centuries. It doesn't do him any favors.

He's assessing the situation, which means he's smart. Either he senses me, or he has the ability to see me. This may not be as easy as I thought.

If I let go of the girl I'm holding on to, she risks being seen. It won't be easy, but I can manage with one hand. "Whatever you do, don't let go."

I unsheathe a stiletto dagger and kick out with my right foot, hoping to distract the demon. It jerks from my kick, but the girl I'm holding on to throws me off balance trying to pull away. Something has her scared. One of the men is making his way up the stairs and right into our path.

Demon in front and predator behind. Only one of them can see us. I pull the girl to the other side of the staircase and out of the man's way. The demon uses my distraction as an opportunity to attack. His sword cuts deep across my back, and I let out a yell and stumble forward, losing my grip. Unable to hold the coverage, the girl and I are now fully visible.

The man looks up in surprise, his eyes focusing on me.

Uh oh. I can do this, but it's not ideal. We can't lose this girl. She can't go back into the hands of the enemy.

Paxton moves into my line of sight. He's coming back to help me, but I give him a shake of my head. He needs to help the other girls. I'll be fine.

"Run to him," I encourage the girl to keep going, pushing her toward Paxton. "He's here to help you get out." Paxton unveils his face so she can see him.

I place myself between this guy and her exit so he can't touch her.

By the smirk on his face, the man coming for me thinks this will be easy.

With the girl out of the way, Paxton can help her, and I can focus on both the demon and the predator. Both stalk toward me.

This calls for a sword. Thanks to Mark's instruction, I can pull one from the ether with ease.

Dagger in one hand, sword in the other. I allow both to approach me. The demon poised above me, and the predator a few steps below.

The man reeks of power, the demon reeks of dark, both are evil and need to be taken out. Only one am I allowed to destroy.

"Hey little girl, I think you missed the dress code for this party. Besides, I think you're outnumbered. Better give it up while you can, and I may let you live. For a little while, at least." The demon taunts as he takes a step closer.

The Light flares through me, and power surges. I'll never tire of that feeling.

"What's your name?" I ask the guy in the suit, ignoring the demon. Might as well get some intel out of him before I incapacitate him.

The demon won't let it slide that I'm ignoring him. It only serves to rile his anger, which pulses off of him in waves.

"You're in no position to ask questions. But since you won't be leaving here alive, I can indulge. Judge Nick Bryner at your service. You won't mess this up for me, whoever you are." He continues his ascent.

I can't help it, my eyes roll on their own. What an idiot. I'll enjoy taking him down.

He may be a judge, but he's fit. He definitely works out when he's not behind the bench.

He reaches behind his back, no doubt to pull out a gun, but before he can even blink I drop a few steps, swipe out my leg, and take him out at the knees before he completes his task. He tumbles down the steps in a mess of limbs and arms. The gun clatters to the floor, out of his reach. Ouch, I bet that hurt.

While he recovers from that embarrassing fall, I return my attention back to the demon. "How about I make you an offer?" the demon asks with an appraising gaze. "We could use someone like you on the inside. I can give you anything you've ever wanted. Everything you see here can be yours." He holds his hands out, gesturing to the mansion.

"Uh, no thanks. If you haven't noticed, I'm a little busy trying to take you out, not work on negotiating with you." I raise the sword and dagger in his direction. My stance at an angle to keep an eye on the judge as he regains his footing.

"You're dismissing an incredible opportunity of fame and fortune. But whatever, have it your way." He swipes his sword down, and I swing mine to block. The power behind the blow shifts me sideways, but I recover quickly. He moves to follow with another blow, but the dagger in my other hand slices across his throat as I block the blow with my sword. He jerks back in surprise, then I quickly swipe the sword at an angle, removing his head. Somehow, he nicked me in the side and I stagger. My foot misses the step behind me, and I land hard on one knee.

The judge is back on his feet, full of anger, but moving with a noticeable limp this time. While I'm down on one knee, I back kick him in the gut and he flies down the stairs once again.

"Police – freeze! Get your hands up!" Shoes pound against marble and echo through the house.

The judge spews out a few colorful words as he inches for his gun on the floor

The police can deal with that. What took them so long, anyway? Did anyone get away? Were we able to save the girls?

Paxton, with the girls, make their way toward me. "I didn't think you would want me to leave the girls to come help you."

"No, you did the right thing. If you had left the girls, I would have stabbed you."

He laughs as he passes by. He found two more girls while I was busy. I hold out my hand to the girl I helped earlier. She doesn't accept right away, and I don't blame her.

"What's your name?" I ask her. She shrugs and looks down.

"It's okay, you don't have to tell me. I would prefer not to call you girl, but I understand."

We walk past the stairs and straight to the police. I wince as the slice down my back pulls.

"Emma, my name is Emma," she tells me in a small voice. She can't be more than nine.

"Do you have family looking for you?"

"I hope so. I just want to go home."

A female cop comes up to us and speaks softly to Emma. I step back next to Paxton and allow the professionals to do their jobs.

Our team comes in to help search for any hidden rooms and also any demons that may be hanging around. There have to be more than the two I found. With this much evil in one place, there has to be more.

"What happened to you?" Lizzy asks as she rounds the corner.

"Eh, just a few scratches. Nothing much." Sloan slaps me on the back, barely missing the large slice across it.

Lizzy tilts her head. "That's not just a few scratches. We would have come in sooner, but we had a mess of demons and a Fallen to deal with." Lizzy places her hands on me. "Let me look." Her hands glow to aid my healing. I close my eyes and allow the healing touch to wash over me.

Chapter 3

Elizabeth

Concealed from sight, the demons and Fallen awaited our arrival in full force, hidden from view until the last second. They were prepared for a fight to hold the stronghold over their territory. While the police were gathering the evidence they needed, we were fighting off evil humans can't see.

The police thankfully apprehended the men attempting to flee with the girls, with a little help from us. It took us a bit to get inside the mansion, since we were preoccupied with what was going on outside.

Back at headquarters, we get checked out at the clinic for mostly minor injuries. Grace suffered the worst of it, but it hasn't slowed her down. And she is more determined than ever to fight against this darkness.

This is our routine for the next two weeks. Covert operations with the police to take down criminal and demonic activity in human trafficking. We learn what we can from the Southern Division and create a loose plan for when we get back to Miracle Lake. It will be a team effort between us and the police.

Tonight, we are out with our New Orleans team one last time. We leave early tomorrow to go back home.

Grace's voice cuts through my thoughts. "It's crazy. Just think, you'll be married in a week. How awesome is that?" She gushes as she takes a bite of pastalaya.

"Well, I, for one, can't wait to marry the love of my life. I know how blessed I am, and I won't take it for granted." Mark leans over to place a kiss on my temple and wrap his arm around my shoulders.

My body naturally leans into him. "Thank you for loving me, and for not giving up on me." Insecurities, for all of my shortcomings, creep in. There's this pull to do everything in my power to make sure he never regrets the decision to marry me.

"Awww" comes from several voices at our table.

"Thank you for inviting us to your wedding," Cressida says with a raised glass in salute.

Sookie raises her glass to join in. "I look forward to seeing this small town we've heard so much about, and getting out of New Orleans for a few days."

Glasses rise around the table. "Congratulations! To Mark and Elizabeth!"

***

Our plane descends just before dawn while darkness still has a stronghold over the night. Whoever thought it was a good idea to fly at this time was nuts. But there was no turbulence, at least. Not like last time. It was a smooth flight the whole way.

We each load our carry-on into the company van waiting for us in the parking garage. Mark takes the wheel while Dax rides shotgun. I slide onto the second row with Roz while the girls climb into the back.

Mark plugs in the address to Triton Security even though he knows where we're going, just in case there's any unusual traffic or a wreck that could delay our time. The app will move us around any problem spots, ensuring we get back home timely with no unnecessary delays.

I lean my head back and close my eyes. Everyone remains silent on the drive back, probably catching a little sleep.

"Why is it routing us this way? That's kind of odd," Dax comments to Mark.

"I don't know, but this is the route it's telling us to go. Maybe we should take it just in case."

My eyes blink open at the sound of Mark's voice, and I raise my head. Soft light filters through the windows as we travel down an unfamiliar road.

Several minutes in and I'm wondering where we are, even though the map is on the screen. According to the map, it's taking us on a route out of the way and looping back around.

I'm sure there's a reasonable explanation for it. There could be an awful wreck that shut down the interstate. Maybe an overturned olive truck spilled olives all over the interstate, making it too slippery to drive on.

What? It could happen . . . maybe.

Roz wakes up and looks over while Grace and Sloan still sleep in the back. "Where are we?" she asks.

"A random road taking us a back way to Miracle Lake," Dax answers while looking at his phone, probably trying to figure out why we're being routed this direction.

"Uh, Mark, there's a truck heading straight for us in our lane, and it's swerving all over the road." Roz notices it at the same time I do. An old rusty pickup is careening carelessly from one side of the road to the other.

"I see it. I'm slowing down in case I need to get out of the way. Let me flash my lights and see if that helps. Unfortunately, it may be a drunk driver."

Mark slows down and inches to the side of the road to avoid a head-on collision, but the truck is still driving erratically in our direction.

"Incoming! We've got two Fallen following the truck and a few demons on the ground. An angel in flight behind them." Dax pulls weapons from the ether and passes them around.

I lean over our seat to wake up the girls. "Girls, wake up!"

Mark stops our van on the side of the road just as the truck swerves off on the other side and crashes into the ditch.

I unbuckle my seatbelt as quickly as I can and scramble to get out. They may need medical help. "That looks bad. I hope they're okay." Roz follows me out the door, gathering the weapons Dax offers her.

The girls shuffle out, trying to shake off the haze of sleep. Mark and Dax meet us on the other side of the road, ready for the coming attack, while Grace and Sloan move to intercept the demons heading this way.

As they get closer, I recognize the angel in flight. Zuriel. He engages the two Fallen midair. We can manage the demons if Zuriel can take care of the Fallen.

"Maybe this is why we were routed out here. There hasn't been another car on this road." Roz glances down the road as we cross. She's right, there are no other cars out here.

"You may be right. What other explanation could it be?"

The rusty, grey truck is facing downward in the ditch with the driver's side door blocked by the incline of the ditch. We'll need to access through the passenger door to check on the driver. Roz covers my back as I open the door and peer inside.

"There's a girl in here, and she doesn't look so good." She's slumped at an odd angle against the driver's side window.

"Is she alive?" Roz asks as she peers around me.

I lift her wrist to check her pulse, but my eyes land on the scars running around her wrist. Deep scars that tell a story of a long history of abuse. "Yes, there's a heartbeat." But I don't tell her the rest. I won't need to, she'll see it soon enough.

The girl is young, very young, thin and emaciated. Old bruises mixed with new ones. Her blond, or what should be blond, hair is matted, dirty, and full of knots. Scars, wounds and trauma, not all of them from this accident. "She's definitely not old enough to drive."

Roz leans over my shoulder to get a better view and lets out a pained groan. "By the looks of it, my guess is, she saw an opportunity to escape and took it."

There's no one else in the truck, just this girl dressed only in a large stained t-shirt and nothing else.

"We need to get her out of here in case the person she's fleeing comes looking for her, but I'm scared to move her. I don't know if she has any neck or head trauma. Do we have anything in the van we can use to stabilize her neck?"

"Let me check and see." Roz rushes across the street to our van. Grunts and clashes fill the background, but I focus on the girl before me and her shallow breaths. I'm well covered by my team and don't need to worry about an ambush while I'm in the truck.

By the looks of her, this girl, barely more than a child, has experienced unimaginable horrors. "Lord, help me help her. Show me what you want me to do."

Roz slides in. "Here, Sloan was using this neck pillow. I figure we could use this to stabilize her neck. Grace had a ribbon tied to her bag. We can use it to secure the pillow. Found an emergency kit and a backboard under the backseat as well."

"That's great! Let me hold her head and neck stable while you wrap the neck pillow around and secure it. We need to find the right amount of tension with the ribbon. We don't want to strangle her."

It takes a few minutes, but we get her neck secure. Roz takes out her phone, no doubt to call the authorities, but something inside me seizes and the Light flares. Not understanding this urgency, I allow the Light to lead me.

"Roz, wait a second. I don't think we should call the authorities on this just yet."

She stops what she's doing and puts her hand down. "What is it?"

"I'm not sure, but we need to trust the Light with this. I think we need to bring her with us. We have everything we need for her at the clinic. She will get the best care possible at Triton." The Light flares again with encouragement.

Roz closes her eyes to check with the Light as well. This feels too important, we can't leave it to chance.

She nods her head and opens her eyes. "You're right, I don't understand it, but I think she needs to come with us."

Roz and I carefully move her to the backboard and lift her from the truck. As we get out, Roz checks to make sure we're clear to move her across the street to our van. Our team surrounds us, giving us cover to cross.

Zuriel hovers midair, watching over us. The demons and Fallen are gone, dispatched by Zuriel and our team.

Grace and Sloan put their weapons away and come to assist us. Roz and I lay the girl across the second row as we all get back into the van and head to Triton Security.

"What was that? Why was that truck being followed?" I ask no one in particular. Roz and I kneel on the floor in front of the second row.

Dax turns in his seat to face me, his eyes land on the girl lying on the seat. Pain etches his face. "They wanted to make sure the girl didn't make it, but Zuriel had no intention of allowing them to finish her off."

He shakes his head and stares out the window. "That GPS re-route was no coincidence. God's timing is perfect. He made sure we were in the right place at the right time. We could assist Zuriel so you could free the girl. Now she'll get the help she needs."

I pray for this precious life and ask God to help her. There are things she has suffered that we can't even imagine.

Roz lays a hand on the girl's leg. "It could be trafficking. We need to handle this situation carefully."

I study her features. Dark smudges under her eyes, track marks on her arms, a stained shirt made for a man covers her. And that's where my eyes stop. My heart drops, and nausea fills my gut.

"Roz, look at the shirt." Roz looks down. "Now look at her belly. There's a bump." I reach out and place my hand there. It's a definite bump and noticeable on her thin frame.

Tears fall before I even realize they've formed. *God, how are we supposed to help her? What do we do?*

As my hand gently rests on her belly, it glows. The tiny life inside flutters against my palm. A sob escapes before I can even hide it. As my palm continues to glow, pain consumes every part of me. Flashes of horror fill my mind. Not wanting to see anymore, I yank my hand away as fast as I can.

Did I just experience only a glimpse of what she's endured? Short bursts of breath puff out as I try and fail to catch my breath.

I rest my hand on her head and ask God to bring healing to her mind, body, and soul. My hand glows again, but this time it's helping ease her pain, bring some relief, and help her sleep.

We still haven't figured out exactly what I can do, and this goes to show that it's not one definite thing. What I just experienced was disturbing, and I don't think I want the ability to see or feel another's pain.

Grace places her hand on my shoulder as tears silently stream down my face. Tears line her beautiful face as well. No one can possibly be unaffected after seeing the condition of this child. It's heartbreaking.

Her skin is marked. Her past is brutal. Her wounds run deep, to a place none of us can reach. Only God can provide the complete healing she needs, and we can be the vessel He uses to help her on that path of healing.

Another instance where this isn't a coincidence. We just made it back home after learning how to fight trafficking. We've come back from New Orleans with the tools we need to help others who are in the same situation, if this is human trafficking.

Dax leans over to peer out the side mirror. "Zuriel is following us."

"He's making sure we have safe travels. We are carrying precious cargo, after all," Roz offers with a pained grin.

This precious girl, and the life she carries inside of her, will need all the help they can get. My heart weighs heavy with her reality. This girl, really only a child herself, is creating a life she can't possibly provide for. And here I am, a desire to have a family of my own, but no womb to carry a child.

How very unfair and cruel this life can be.

I wonder if she even understands what is happening to her, what this means for her – for her future. At least she has a future now. We will give her every opportunity to heal and thrive. If this is a form of human trafficking, maybe she has family out there and we can find them for her.

We make it to The Cave with no more demonic attacks. Dax dashes inside to get a gurney and bring it out since it's best we place her on something stable to bring her inside. We need to make sure nothing is broken. We took a tremendous risk in moving her.

The guys leave us to find Arden and fill him in on what happened. Dr. Lipinski meets us as we walk the gurney down the hallway to the clinic. "Dax filled me in briefly on what we have. Has she regained consciousness at all?"

"Not once," Roz answers.

Grace walks beside me as I stay with the gurney, and we arrive in an exam room. I'm thankful it's Dr. Lipinski that met us, she's one of the few female doctors on staff. A male doctor would not be appropriate in this situation.

I hate calling her girl all the time. Girl seems so impersonal. She deserves better.

I lean over to Grace. "Maybe we should give her a name until we know what to call her."

"Like what? What are you thinking?" She asks with interest.

"We can't keep calling her girl, and I don't want to refer to her as patient. We should give her a name that we can use until we learn her real name."

Grace nods her head in thought. "What about Angel?"

Roz smiles. "I think that's a great idea." Sloan gives a noncommittal shrug.

"Then it's agreed. Let's call her Angel, for now."

Dr. Lipinski addresses us while she examines Angel. "I have a call in to Alyssa. She'll be here soon and will scan her for internal trauma."

Dr. Lipinski's eyes land on the baby bump and her breath hitches. Even though this situation is disturbing, I'm thankful we were the ones to find her and not someone else. Like Roz said, God sent us a different route, so we would be the ones to find her.

Alyssa passes Sloan as she rushes in. She pauses next to Dr. Lipinski as she assesses the girl – no, Angel, on the bed. "Wow," she whispers.

Alyssa places her hands on Angel's shoulders to scan. We all wait in silence as she closes her eyes to focus on her task.

Sloan walks to the end of the bed, arms crossed, legs planted wide. Her gaze hardens, and nostrils flare. She looks like she's about to be unhinged.

Alyssa covers her face with her hands and breaks down, sobbing before us. I walk over and wrap my arms around her. She gets no judgment from me.

After a moment, she wipes her face before addressing us. "She's about thirteen years of age and maybe six months along. No current broken bones, but I see old breaks that have already healed: ribs, legs, arms, skull. You name it, she's had it. She has heroin in her body and has probably been given heroin for years. By now, she is fully addicted to it. If that's not enough, both she and the baby are severely malnourished."

She addresses Dr. Lipinski directly. "She's barely alive. If we don't help her quickly, they won't make it." Alyssa walks out of the room, shoulders shaking.

Dr. Lipinski rubs her hands down her face and releases a long sigh. "Okay. She needs nutritional support; we knew that by her appearance. We'll get a drip started right away to push fluids and do a liquid feeding."

She looks at me. "When you touched her, were you able to lend any healing?"

All the medical staff knows I can do something, we just don't know what, exactly. I've been able to assist with small wounds and injuries, but nothing on this scale. And I don't know that I want to lay my hands on her again in case I experience any part of her trauma again.

I shake my head. "Not really. When I placed my hand on her head, I was able to soothe her a little, but that was it." I tell her about the other situation, the ability to experience some of her trauma.

Dr. Lipinski shakes her head. "I don't know anyone else with that ability. The only thing I suggest is that you use caution when you lay your hands on someone. I can't imagine anyone would want to experience that."

She turns to walk out the door but pauses. "I'll get the staff to start on an IV for nutrition and start her on a course of methadone to relieve the withdrawal symptoms of the heroin in her system. She has a long road of recovery ahead of her." Dr. Lipinski sighs and shakes her head. "And a baby on the way – one she didn't ask for and probably doesn't want. We'll cross that bridge when we get to it. For now, we need both mom and baby healthy." She walks out the door.

I watch Grace and Sloan do that thing where they communicate with which other without words, and then they both walk out at the same time.

"We should keep an eye on those two. No telling what trouble they're about to get into." Roz takes Angel's hand in hers.

"I agree with you, but I don't want to leave Angel alone. I don't want her to wake up in an unfamiliar place with no one around to reassure her and calm her fears. She needs to know she's safe."

Roz nods her head in agreement. "We can take turns watching her, maybe set up some sort of schedule. Not the guys, of course, but we could include Grams and your mom. They would be great to sit with her and keep watch. Plus, it would keep Grams out of trouble. Who knew she would be such a handful?"

I shake my head and chuckle. "I think that would be great."

"But wait, you're getting married next week. You definitely won't be on schedule after next week." Roz sits on the bed next to Angel, still holding her hand.

Piper, one nurse I've worked with before in the clinic, walks in with the IV kit.

"Dr. Lipinski filled me in. This is just awful." Piper addresses me, "Do you want to help me get the IV started and get the fluids set up?"

A breath of relief escapes, now that I can do. I can practically do it in my sleep. "Absolutely."

Roz moves away from the bed to give us room to work. "I'll go find Grams and your mom, since they're both most likely together, and fill them in. Besides, I'm sure your mom will want to give you an update on the wedding plans she's been working on."

I give a shrug. "She knows I'll be happy with whatever they've come up with."

Roz shakes her head in dismay. "You would think you would be more excited or involved or something. How are you so nonchalant about your own wedding?"

"The wedding day isn't what's most important, it's the marriage that is. Besides, I've never been a girly-girl." I shake my head. "I never really dreamed of my wedding day. There's nothing that I absolutely have to have, not really. I know my mom and Mark's mom will make it beautiful. Honestly, I don't have time to plan any of it. We've been too busy."

Piper sets up the infusion pump as I tape down the IV to secure it on Angel's hand. The sooner we give her the nutrition she needs, the better.

Roz nods her head in acceptance. "Okay, I'll help make sure you have the best wedding day ever since Dax and I eloped. I'll be back in a bit."

Once Piper leaves, I sit on the edge of the bed and place Angel's hand in mine. I want to lend whatever healing I can, but I definitely don't want the memories. My hand glows in hers as a sense of peace washes over her. There's nothing further I can do for her beyond that, for now.

It's difficult to even think about our upcoming wedding with Angel's life in the balance. She'll need all the care we can provide, and it will be a long road to healing and recovery for her.

Guilt creeps in even at thinking about my wedding right now. How do I justify celebration amid such heartache? How do I hold both suffering and joy in the same hand?

Chapter 4

Mark

Dax and I leave the girls at the clinic to find Arden and fill him in on what transpired during our trip home. How do you come to grips with demons and Fallen following a girl who has been so horrifically abused, all to ensure she doesn't survive? That's nothing but pure evil. Without Zuriel's help, we would have been at a severe disadvantage, and we may not have been able to save the girl, much less make it home in one piece.

Dax sends Cressida a text, filling her in as well. She sends a text back to let us know she and Sookie will be here tomorrow, earlier than originally expected. They were going to be here for the wedding anyway. Why not come a few days early?

They want to scope out the area with us and meet with the officers who contacted us for help. Cressida advised us to establish the basics with them so everyone will know what their role is and how it will need to work for this to be a success.

I'm glad they're coming early. Elizabeth and I need to focus on our upcoming wedding. The rest of our team, along with Cressida and Sookie, can fill in for us while we go on our honeymoon.

We haven't even had time to discuss the honeymoon, so I took it upon myself to make all the plans. I hope she likes beaches because I booked us a romantic week away in Kahuku, on the island of Oahu. We can do anything we want - explore the island by Jeep, go to a luau, visit a coffee plantation, or never leave the room. I know which one will get my vote, but I'll take her wherever she wants to go.

She doesn't need more stress on her than she already has. I was hoping she could sit down with her Uncle Devon before the wedding and clear the air, get some answers about why he kept his life as a Light Bearer hidden from her, hiding her own identity as a Light Bearer as well. That betrayal runs deep. It crushed her in ways he can't comprehend. He needs to make it right, and I would love for that to happen before the wedding. We need a fresh start with nothing from her past hanging over us.

We also don't have a solid plan for where we will live. The house she lives in was her uncle's before he died, then it went to her, but now he's back and we don't have that minor hiccup worked out. And her mom moved in after Elizabeth came back from three months in the heavenly realm. It's a very odd situation. We need to get all of that figured out so we can get settled somewhere.

Sloan and Grace walk past us with determined strides. "Where are you two going in such a hurry?" Dax calls out.

"Weapons wall for training." Grace throws out over her shoulder.

"I don't trust those two. They're up to something," Dax whispers as he watches them.

"They do seem determined. Do you think we should follow them?"

"I think we should work on some training and grab some weapons from the weapons wall." Dax follows the girls.

So, that's a yes.

Before we make it a few feet, Arden calls my name. "Mark, can I borrow you for a moment, if you're not too busy?"

Dax waves me off as he follows the girls. At least they have someone to keep an eye on them.

"Sure, what do you need?"

"We need to see if the girl you brought in is in the missing children database, to see if she's a missing person. Maybe there are some age progression photos you could look through as well. We should do what we can to connect her with family, as long as this didn't happen in her home."

"I agree. I'll start doing some research and see what I can find. Oh, Cressida and Sookie will be here tomorrow. We'll meet with your contact at the local police and start a connection on that front. Get a plan in place as we move forward."

"I like that idea." Arden nods his head as he places his hands in his pockets. "You have a lot going on. So, the wedding will be at the end of this week. Will your parents be in?"

"They'll be here in two days, and the rest of my family will come in the next day."

His face breaks into a grin. "Best day of my life was marrying Brenda. She keeps me grounded. Do what you can before the wedding, then let your team take over. The two of you need to take a break and focus only on yourselves and your new marriage."

"Will do, sir."

My first stop is to see Elizabeth, check with her on the progress of the girl, and see if she's awake and can give us any answers. I'll also need a photo of her face to run through the system.

I text Dax to let him know what Arden needs me to handle. He informs me he's going with the girls to trace the probable route the girl came from. He doesn't believe the girl would have been able to make many turns or was able to drive very far. His hope is to find out where she escaped from, and take care of that situation. I wish I could go with them, but Arden trusts me to take care of this for him.

Hannah is walking down the hallway at the clinic as I round the corner. "Hey, Hannah. It's good to see you." I bend down to give her a hug.

"I'm glad you're back. I told Elizabeth I need her to try on the dress I bought. Don't let her put it off. If any adjustments need to be made, I need to do it now." She takes a step back. "I just left the room where Elizabeth and Roz are. Do you need me to get her for you?"

"Would you, please? I need to ask her some questions."

"Okay, give me just a moment." Hannah goes back the way she came and disappears into a room a few doors down.

Elizabeth emerges a moment later. As soon as her eyes land on me, she runs until she reaches me. I lift her in my arms, and she breaks down the moment my arms wrap around her.

She doesn't need words right now, only comfort. So, I hold her for as long as she needs.

"She still isn't awake. Mark, she's so broken, and I don't know how to help her." She leans back, her eyes finding mine. Grief etches lines across her forehead.

Her heart moves me with compassion. I wipe her tears with my thumbs and place a kiss on her forehead. "I'm sorry, my love. We'll do everything we can to help her, but with that much trauma, it's going to take time."

She sniffles and closes her eyes. "Sorry, I'm just struggling with this."

"You need to pray. You can't do this on your own."

"Oh, Grace came up with a temporary name for her. We're going to call her Angel." I let it slide that she just ignored my suggestion to pray. She'll figure it out.

Angel. A fitting name for a broken soul who will need every advantage to have a meaningful, well-lived life. "That's perfect. Arden asked me to help by going through the missing children database to see if she might match any of the descriptions or photos. Will you take a picture of her face for me? I'll do what I can to locate any family she may have."

"What if it was her family that did this to her?"

"Then, may God be merciful and help them because I'm pretty sure Grace and Sloan are going after whoever did this to her—family or not."

"You can't let them do that, Mark! We can't met out our own justice no matter how right it may seem." Her face contorts in frustration.

A chuckle escapes at her fierceness before I can stop it. "Don't worry, Dax is on it. But I understand how they feel. I want so much to make it right for her, for Angel. To make sure this never happens to her again."

"We can't promise that, but we can protect her. Now, I wish I were going with Grace and Sloan just to give this person a little taste of justice. That's all." She looks around as if she's trying to figure out if she can go.

I absolutely adore her. I place my hands on both sides of her face until I get her attention. Once her gaze rests on mine, I lean down and kiss her soundly. When I pull away, her eyes remain closed and a small smile rests on her lips.

And that's all I wanted, to quiet her mind and let her know she's loved.

She finally opens her eyes. "Thank you. Sometimes, I need help to get back on track. We all have a role, and I believe I can best contribute by being here for Angel and aiding in her recovery."

"Good. I'll be working with Arden on whatever projects he needs help with, and right now we want to see if we can locate Angel's family or at least see what happened that got her to this place." I pull my phone from my pocket and hand it to Elizabeth. "Will you take a picture of her face for me?"

She takes the phone from my outstretched hand. "Sure thing. I'll be right back."

Only a minute later, she returns with my phone in hand. "Here you go. She's still unconscious. It's best for her body and mind to rest right now. We found out she has heroin in her system. We've started her on methadone to wean her off of it. It's going to be such a long road of recovery, but we won't leave her alone for a second. She needs to feel safe."

"Heroin? Is there anything this girl hasn't been through?" I didn't think I could be more horrified by her situation, but this proves me wrong.

She shakes her head and wipes the moisture from her eyes.

"I know you and the girls will make sure Angel is taken care of." I place my hands on both of her arms. "I need to change the subject real quick. We haven't had time to talk about it, so I went ahead and booked our honeymoon. I hope you're okay with Hawaii."

A big, beautiful smile reaches her puffy eyes. "That sounds perfect. I've always wanted to go to Hawaii. Thank you for doing that. It's one less thing to take care of. Mom wants me to go by the house to try on the dress she bought for me. Once Grams comes to relieve me, I think I'll run do that and bring Roz with me so I can get her opinion."

She pauses. I give her a moment to gather her thoughts. "This is so hard. Here we are planning our wedding while Angel fights for her life. It feels wrong."

"I get it. There's this tension of living in both happiness for our new life together and sorrow for what someone else has experienced. But, like you said, it's going to be a long road for her recovery, and we'll be here for her when we get back." I push a strand of hair away from her face before continuing. "I need to try on my old suit tonight and make sure it still fits. If I no longer fit in the suit, I'll have to get a new one. There isn't much time." I pause, wondering what her reaction will be to my next question. "Are you ready? Excited? Having second thoughts?" Or questions.

Several emotions pass across her face before she responds. "I'm excited, maybe a little nervous. It's going to be different sharing my life with you. I'm not sure how to do that. What if I'm terrible at sharing my space or wanting alone time? Then again, maybe it will be easy and we won't have any problems adjusting."

She says the last part with a lot less confidence.

"I have no doubt it will take some time to adjust, but I can promise you, I pick up after myself. I'll do my own dishes and feed the dog when we get one." I throw that last one in there to see her reaction.

"Did we talk about getting a dog? I don't remember that." Her face scrunches and she tilts her head to the side.

"No, we haven't, but I hope we get one, eventually. We always had a dog when I was growing up. It's one of my favorite childhood memories. I had a golden retriever until about a year before I moved here. She was a great dog and a fantastic companion, but unfortunately, she died of old age. I miss having a dog around."

"Okay, maybe once we get settled, we can look into adopting a pet. I wonder what Tiger would think about that. Then again, she's not my pet."

I let out a laugh at the mental picture that just popped into my head of bringing a dog home and Tiger rounding the corner to meet it. "Oh, she's going to hate it."

There's one more thing to discuss before I let her go. "I know standing in the clinic's hallway is not the best place for this conversation, but have you given any thought to where we will live? My temporary lease of the house is ending. I have an apartment here at The Cave, but that's not exactly ideal for a newly married couple."

She shifts her gaze behind me before landing on mine again. "I haven't discussed it with my uncle, and I need to. That's something else I need to take care of. Not only get the house situation figured out, but clear the air and get some answers. I don't want to be angry and bitter, but I'm struggling with what he did. I can't just sweep it under the rug and forget about it. He kept this part of my life from me, and I don't think he had any intention of filling me in. I honestly don't know if I can ever trust him again."

"You won't get all of those feelings sorted until you talk to him." I rub my hands down her arms, giving her space but also letting her know I'm here.

She lets out a frustrated sigh. "I know."

"Have you seen him today?"

"No, I haven't, but I'll look for him later. I love him, and that's part of the struggle. How can you trust someone you love so much after they hurt you so irrevocably? He can't go back and fix it. What's done is done." She slashes her hand through the air.

"That's true, but you can move forward. Your relationship may just look a little different this time around. You may not be able to go back to the way it was, and maybe that's a good thing. You're an adult with your own life, and you found your calling all on your own, even without him. It may need to be a mutual respect for one another until you can find your new normal."

"I know, you're right. After I get back from trying on the dress, I'll find him. I'll talk with him, I promise." She nibbles her lip, and all I want to do is kiss it.

Pulling her close, I lay one hand on her hip. "Sometimes adulting can be hard. I'm here for you. I love you."

"I love you, too. Let me get back to Roz and Angel. We're going to leave in a few minutes once Grams arrives."

She goes back to Angel's room. I watch until she waves and walks through the door.

It's time to do some research and see what I can find. Maybe I can get some answers where Angel is concerned.

***

Several hours later, I have no more answers than when I began. There is no information on our Angel, at least not that I could find, anyway. She's either not a missing child, or it's been so long and she's so malnourished that the photos aren't matching. I'll get one of our IT people to run it. They may have better luck than I've had.

It's time I ran home to try on my suit and make sure it still fits. I also need to check on Dax with the girls, since I haven't heard from him. There's no telling what they could have gotten themselves into.

I slip inside my temporary home and walk to the large windows along the back wall facing the lake. It's been a great place to stay, but the lease is up and the owners have it rented out for the summer. It's time for me to pack up and move my things to the apartment at The Cave until the wedding. I dig through the closet for my nicest suit. I pull it out and hold it up. And let out a laugh. There's no way this is going to fit.

Since becoming a Guardian I've filled out and gained muscle. The only thing I wear these days is the standard Triton uniform of cargo pants and a polo. Anything I've needed, I've been able to get at The Cave. Guess I'm hitting up a men's store for a new suit.

Before I leave, I send a text to Dax, but don't get a response right away. Not surprising. He'll text me back when he can.

***

New suit bought and paid for. I'll pick it up tomorrow after they make a couple of alterations on a rush request.

Dax pings me his location as I walk out of the store. I pull up the directions on my phone and hop in my Jeep to follow.

As the GPS app maps out the directions, I call Elizabeth. She answers the phone as I pull out of the parking lot.

"Hey," she answers, a little out of breath.

"Hey, what are you doing?"

"Dax just pinged his location to Roz, so we're on our way to meet him."

"I'll see you there then. I was walking out of the men's store when he sent me his location, too. I'm on my way."

"So, your suit didn't fit?"

A chuckle escapes at the thought. "No, apparently I've filled out quite a bit. I had to get a new one, but it looks better than the one I had. I think you'll approve."

"You in a suit? I definitely approve. I'll see you soon."

The call disconnects, and I follow the app to the road we were on earlier today. The directions lead to a rundown home on the outskirts of town. A chain-link fence surrounds the overgrown property, and a sad excuse for a house sits out of sight from the road.

Roz and Elizabeth pull in behind me as I park behind Dax's SUV. We exit and meet at the back of my Jeep.

"Have you heard from Dax? Is he inside?"

Roz shakes her head. "He didn't answer my call. I'm not sure where he is."

Elizabeth walks up to me and leans against my side. I put my arm around her. "Let's do a perimeter check. I'll take the back, you girls take the front."

We split up, and I walk around the back of the house through tangled grass that hasn't seen a mower in years. No movement outside and no sounds coming from inside. A dirty window reveals an even dirtier kitchen, but I see no one until Roz walks past the kitchen and out of sight.

At the back door, I try the handle, and it turns with ease. As I walk inside, Elizabeth passes the kitchen to follow Roz down a hallway. The house smells dank and sweaty, as if no one has aired it out in years. The darkness inside grows as daylight fades.

Loud voices, originating from somewhere down the hall, draw me in their direction.

Chapter 5

Sloan

Watching Angel lie on that bed causes my blood to boil, and my mind travels to places it shouldn't, bringing back too many unwelcome memories. She's an innocent. Beaten, abused, and treated worse than trash. Treated as an object of possession and nothing more.

As Guardians, we aren't supposed to deal with the human side of justice, our primary fight is with the darkness. But there are times we have to manage the human side. Like when there is no other alternative in a life-or-death situation.

As much as I would love to wipe the world clean of those who are responsible for what happened to Angel, I can't. But what I can do is make their little, pathetic lives miserable, and that's exactly what I intend to do. When I'm done, they'll wish for death or beg for mercy. And I can guarantee they will never do this again.

With one look at Grace, she knows exactly what the plan is. With an imperceptible nod of her head, the objective is in place. It's time to locate the person who did this to Angel, and create a little justice of our own.

We leave the room and go straight to the weapons wall to gear up. Unfortunately, Dax and Mark notice our trajectory and question us. The fewer questions we have to answer, the better.

"What's the plan?" Dax's voice startles me as I'm counting out weapons and strapping them on. I should have known we wouldn't be able to just slip out unnoticed.

He throws his hands up. "Look, I have no intention of stopping you, but I want to come along. Plus, I can legally drive and you can't. Not yet, anyway."

The man has a point. Even though I can't legally drive, that has never stopped me before, but he can get us a set of wheels much easier than I could.

"We're going back to the site where we found Angel and try to retrace her route. It's doubtful she drove very far, but you never know. When someone is desperate enough, they are capable of just about anything."

Grace leaves the weapons wall while strapping on a weapon and joins us. "Dax, you coming with?"

Dax nods his head. "I thought I might join you, if that's okay."

Grace bounces on her toes. "The more, the merrier." I roll my eyes and walk away.

Grace is all sunshine and rainbows, she gets along with everyone. Me? My distrust of people is well deserved. No one gets close. Grace is the only one who knows some of my secrets, but she doesn't know them all. If she did, she would treat me differently, and I won't live my life like that.

Grace is the light to my dark, and I never want what's inside me to taint her. She balances me and keeps me from going over the edge.

Sure, there are days her perkiness makes me want to punch her, but I'm sure there are days she feels the same about me. It can't be easy being around me all the time.

"Alright, let's go. We can take my SUV." And just like that, Dax is now part of our ride for justice. I could be annoyed, but I'm not. He's one of the few who's always supportive of us and never once tried to hold me back.

Sunset paints the trees a deep orange hue, and stars flicker to life as Dax stops at the site of the wreck from this morning. There's just enough light to see the old truck partially in the ditch with the passenger door still hanging wide open.

Grace and I get out and walk across the street to search the wrecked truck. I lean in on the passenger side and open the glove box to dig around for the registration. Nothing in there except restaurant napkins and an old strip of condoms that have seen better days—doubt they would even work. I toss them out into the ditch. The truck is a mess with trash on the inside, but a quick check reveals nothing of importance.

"Nothing useful in here to track down the owner." I walk past Grace as she leans against the back of the truck waiting for me to finish. Dax stands next to his SUV, scanning the sky for an attack.

"Let's go," I call out to Dax. Grace follows me back to the SUV.

Dax starts the vehicle. "Let's continue down this road and check out the direction she came from."

"I'm surprised no one has come for the truck. Doesn't that seem strange to you?" If my truck was missing, I would have been looking for it.

Grace speaks up from the back seat. "Nothing about any of this is normal."

"Just keep your eyes open. We're vulnerable to another attack while we're out here." Dax scans the sky as he drives.

He's right. The darkness is all over this.

"What are we looking for?" Dax drives like an old man with no destination in mind. Which suits me just fine.

"Just give me a second, I need to look at the area."

Dax shakes his head. "There's no way you can tell when a home hides abuse, or human trafficking, just by looking at it. You saw the mansion in New Orleans. It was the perfect setup for a crime. No one would have suspected a thing."

"I need you to trust me on this." We come to a road on the left, while the one we are on continues straight. "Turn left on this street."

Dax shrugs his shoulder. "If you say so." A car pulls behind us, and Dax moves off to the side of the road so it can go around. Once the car passes, he continues at a slow pace, allowing me to scope out the surroundings.

There's no way to explain it, but I'll know it when I see it. There's this connection I have with Angel, and it's not anything I care to divulge to anyone.

We pass a few houses set back off the road, some dilapidated mobile homes mixed with a few two-story houses that boast of wealth and luxury. A strange mix of homes on this stretch of the road.

And then, I feel it. My head swivels to the left. An overgrown yard surrounded by a chain-link fence. The house is not visible from the street, but it's there.

"Turn here."

Dax gives me a sidelong look. He doesn't believe me. Whatever.

"Trust me."

He pulls onto what should be the driveway. Even overgrown, it's easy to tell that something has traveled down this path recently.

A slight turn to the right brings the house into view. Or what should be a house.

"Ew, this place is so gross." Grace leans forward between the seats to peer out the window. "I really do not want to go in there."

"Remember why we're here." She may act like a princess sometimes, but she's far from it.

She nods her head and locks down the emotions. We will bring Angel some form of justice today.

Dax pulls the SUV out of the way under a tree. If anyone is in the house, they already heard us. I don't bother to close my door quietly.

"This was your idea, what's the plan?" Dax asks as we move to the front of the house. Someone boarded up the windows, and one side of the roof sags. It looks abandoned, but it's not. This is the place. I know it.

"We walk in and take care of business — no plan needed." I cross my arms over my chest and challenge him to disagree.

"You sure about that? You don't want me to walk to the backyard and cover the back for you?" He responds by placing his hands on his hips.

"I don't think he's the type of person to run for it. I bet he's looking for a fight, but if you want to check the back, go ahead."

Grace palms her Glock and approaches the front door. I position myself in front, to shield her from what may appear on the other side, and swing the door open.

Grace and I have developed a system; she lets me take the lead when I need to. She understands there are some things I need to handle myself.

She doesn't ask questions, and I'm thankful for that.

The door bounces as it hits the wall. Then the smell hits.

"Oh my gosh, it smells awful. Seriously, if this weren't for Angel, I would not walk into this house." Grace covers her mouth and nose in the crook of her arm.

I roll my eyes. "You're a Light Bearer, so why is this bothering you? You've been in nasty situations before."

"I don't understand why people choose to live like this. Look around." She tosses her hand around the space. "This place could have been halfway decent if they'd just picked up after themselves. There's no telling what that smell is. Most likely garbage that has piled up. Or a dead animal because it's buried under piles of trash. And it smells like some serious BO up in here. A shower will not kill you!" She yells out the last part into dead silence.

"Is anyone even here?" she asks as she steps over mounds of stuff.

I walk to the back of the house and unlock the door for Dax. He walks in and covers his nose. "This is awful. How does anyone live like this?"

Grace throws her arms up. "That's exactly what I was saying!"

"Let's keep looking." I move to the hallway with Grace and Dax following close behind. So far, no signs of life. If I weren't confident, this is where Angel came from, I would turn around and walk out.

Every door in the hallway is shut. Seems unusual. What are you trying to keep out? Or what are you trying to keep in?

Two doors across from each other have deadbolts. "It's not normal to have a deadbolt on a bedroom door. "

Dax draws closer. "Let's check the other doors first. If they're locked, they should be easier to get in."

The first door on the right is locked, but Dax kicks it in with ease. Shards of wood fly as the door flings open. Piles of junk obscure the remnants of a former bedroom. Like most of the windows in this house, this window is boarded up on the outside.

We back out and move to the door adjacent to this room. The knob turns easily in my hand, which I wasn't expecting. A bathroom, that has seen better days, comes into view. No surprise that it's grimy, rust-stained with broken and missing tiles. I would go outside to use the bathroom before using this one.

Two rooms are left, and deadbolt locks secure both doors.

"Okay, how do you want to approach this?" Dax is letting me take the lead.

"Look at the doors. If these are bedrooms, the hinges should be inside the rooms, but someone flipped these doors so the hinges face the hallway. Let's check the door first to see if it's locked. If it is, I can't pick a deadbolt, but we can remove the hinge pins, pry the door from its frame and remove it. I'm not worried about causing any damage."

"I'll watch the entrance to the hallway in case we have any visitors while you do that." Dax walks back down the hallway and turns his body so he can survey the house from every angle.

Grace knocks on the door. "Anyone in here?" We wait a beat, but there's no sound. She turns the knob with ease, but the deadbolt is latched and the door won't budge.

"Okay, let me get my toolbox. I'll be right back." Dax walks out, leaving us in the hallway.

I keep my back along the wall to watch the hallway while Grace moves to check the other door. The knob doesn't turn in her hand, revealing that it's locked as well. She knocks on the door. "Anyone in here?" Again, there's no response.

We really may be in an empty house, but something niggles at the back of my mind that we aren't alone.

"Do you remember what I showed you?" Recently, I showed her how to pick a lock. She's tried a few times, but she takes little longer to pick a lock than it takes me.

"Yeah, let me try it." She removes a tiny pick set from the pocket of her cargo pants.

Dax walks back in as Grace works on picking the lock. "I see you've been training her." He sets the toolbox down and digs through it.

"That I have. Every girl needs to know how to pick a lock. You never know when it will come in handy."

He nods his head in agreement. "Especially in a life or death situation. Watch the hallway while I work on this door." He must sense it too.

We each remain vigilant.

"I got it!" Grace does a little bounce. It didn't take as long as last time. Definite improvement in time.

I move next to her while still watching the hallway. She turns the knob, and the door opens with ease. The door swings open to a dark and silent room.

"Hold up," I call out to her. "You don't know what's in there." I pull a flashlight from a side pocket and flip it on. "Use this to check first."

My gaze covers the hallway as I guard Dax and Grace while they work on their own tasks. Whatever lies on the other side of those doors will provide the answers we're looking for.

"The room is empty, but it's sparse, unlike the other one." Grace flips the switch on the wall to illuminate the dark room.

"Just a bed and a side table. It was used to hold someone because there are handcuffs attached to the bed frame."

My heart stutters a beat as anger roils inside. How could someone treat another human this way? Especially a child.

I nod my head back to the room she just exited. "Check under the bed and make sure no one is hiding." She examines the space under the bed and verifies that it's empty.

Grace exits the room. "I hope we find whoever did this. You're not the only one who gets to exact justice. I want a piece, too."

My head nods as Dax removes the last pin.

"Here, help me with this door." He uses a crowbar to create space between the door and the door frame. Grace pulls, and the door moves away from the frame with ease.

My eyes go between them and the entrance to the hallway. I'm expecting someone to jump out any moment, but so far, I have seen no movement.

"Alright, here we go." Dax and Grace maneuver the door out of the way, revealing another bedroom. Dax props the door against the wall and nods his head for me to follow Grace inside. He's going to stand guard.

He really is letting me take the lead on this. A man who's confident enough in who he is as a Guardian, that will allow two sixteen-year-olds to take the lead. He will never know how much this means to me.

I follow Grace inside, and my eyes go to the bed. More specifically, to the naked man sprawled face down on the bed. Grace sucks in a sharp breath and reaches for her dagger.

"He's dead." She doesn't need to stab him, he's no longer a threat.

Grace pivots away from the dead body to survey the room. He's been dead for several hours by the looks of the purple hue of his skin.

"There's a dirty gown over here, along with the rest of his clothes on the ground." Grace motions to the haphazardly discarded clothes.

My eye catches on the empty syringe lying on the nightstand. This is the room Angel was held in.

So, he not only held her hostage, he beat her, raped her, and drugged her for who knows how long.

The muscles beneath my skin quiver as my heart pounds an unsteady rhythm. I want to kill him . . . slowly. That he's already dead has me ready to explode. There is no outlet for this hatred. No way for me to exact revenge. I can't beat him within an inch of his life. I can't threaten him the way he did her or anyone else he abused. There's no satisfaction in this.

What am I supposed to do with this energy coursing through my body? I need an outlet.

"Dax, you can relax, the guy is dead." I yell out into the hallway so he can hear me. "And before you even ask, no, I did not kill him. He's been dead for a while."

Dax walks into the room and takes a sharp breath. "Uh, the guy's naked, maybe you shouldn't be in here." I narrow my eyes and cross my arms. This isn't anything. He has no clue what I've been through. No one does, and I intend to keep it that way.

Grace walks away, lips pinched, shaking her head. I can relate.

"I pinged our location to the rest of our team. This feeling that things are about to go sideways won't leave me." I'm glad he senses it, too.

There isn't anyone alive in the house, but something is about to go down.

Chapter 6

Elizabeth

Roz and I both get an alert on our phones at the same time. We both just finished trying on our dresses that Mom picked out for the wedding.

She picked out a beautiful, simple white gown with a lace-covered bodice, satin buttons up the back, and a slight train at the end of the gown. It's something I would have picked out for myself. My mom knows me better than I thought she would.

She also picked a lovely off the shoulder gown in deep violet for Roz. The color brings out her eyes and complements her skin tone.

Both dresses require only a few minor alterations to get the fit just right. Mom said she could take care of that for us later this evening.

We jump in Roz's cobalt blue convertible, and she plugs in the address on the GPS. Her car navigates the roads like a boss. The ride is smooth and fast, and we make it to our destination in no time. I don't bother to check her speed, pretty sure she isn't anywhere near the speed limit.

After greeting Mark at the back of his Jeep, we walk inside to an obnoxious odor and raised voices, but none that I don't already recognize.

Sloan's raised voice indicates she's irritated about something, while Grace stands in the hallway watching her, arms crossed.

Roz walks into the room where Dax tries to calm Sloan. "Hey, what's going on?" I nudge Grace with my elbow. Mark slides his arm over my shoulder after he stops beside me.

Grace peers up at me with those gorgeous blue eyes of hers. "Good news is, the guy is dead and he can never hurt Angel again. Bad news is, he was dead before we got here. We can't get any information from him, and Sloan didn't get to scare him within an inch of his life. She's beyond ticked."

I lean inside the room. The guy lying on the bed is stark naked, clothes thrown on the floor. It doesn't take a genius to figure out what was going on here.

Did Angel kill him before she escaped? How did she get out?

"What's with the door?" Mark asks as he nods his head at the door leaning against the wall.

"The deadbolt was locked. We had to remove the door to get in."

"So, Angel escaped and locked the deadbolt so he couldn't get out. That was smart thinking on her part." Mark bobs his head in thought. "I'm assuming you searched the truck. Did you find the keys when you searched it?"

Grace shakes her head. "I didn't even think about the keys." Her shoulders sag. "That would have been helpful about thirty minutes ago. I bet the keys to the deadbolts are on that keychain. My guess is they're still in the truck."

Dax and Roz walk out of the room, making the narrow hallway crowded. "Let's all step outside. We need to call the authorities. And I need some fresh air." Roz fans her face with her hand.

Sloan storms out of the room, expression tight, nostrils flaring.

We walk out of the house into a soundless night, an eerie feeling hovers. Not even a breeze to stir the air.

As we gather in the front yard, away from the horrors lingering in the house, the darkness surrounds us and presses in.

"Now, this is what I was expecting." Dax pulls out a couple of weapons and hands them to Roz while Mark pulls Defender from the ether, handing it to me. He then arms himself. The girls already have their weapons out.

Demons and one Fallen descend on us with a swiftness I was not expecting. The Fallen lands in front of me. "We can't seem to get rid of you. Maybe it's time I took care of you once and for all." So this is about me? I thought it was about Angel. I'm so confused.

About ten demons fan out behind the Fallen. Mark angles his body in front of mine while Defender ignites with fire. The Light within flares as Mark and I face off with the Fallen while the demons surround us.

With no angels in sight, we have no choice but to battle against the Fallen. I don't like the odds. There's no way for us to kill a Fallen, only wound it and dispatch it. They are immortal. Even removing its head is not a death sentence like it would be for us.

The Fallen snickers as his size morphs into a giant. Now towering above us, he pulls out a mammoth sword and wields it with ease. But that's okay, with Defender, it looks like I know what I'm doing; only Defender gets to do all the work.

The Fallen makes the first move, his sword moving so fast it blurs through the air, giving the appearance of more than one blade. He's fast, faster than any other Fallen I've encountered. Mark and I are both moving as quickly as we can to avoid his sword, Defender, blocking it at every turn.

Somehow we have got to get on the offense. Trying to stay out of the way won't work for long. He won't give up and just let us walk away.

Defender blocks a strike aimed at my midsection, but not before the blade slices through tender flesh. The burning sting catches me off guard, and I bounce off of Mark as he spins to avoid the blade coming at him. He grabs my arm to steady me, but it's a distraction he doesn't need. That split second his eyes are off the Fallen is the moment the Fallen takes to swing his sword and aim for Mark's head. Defender intercepts at the last moment, causing my body to vibrate with pain as our swords collide.

Mark uses the distraction to swing his sword at the Fallen's midsection, then twists and runs the sword straight through. Defender uses the opportunity presented, turns up and across, slicing through the neck and removing the head. The Fallen drops and turns to dust, swirling away on the breeze.

"You're hurt, let me look." Mark tries to lift my shirt to survey the wound, but I slap his hand away.

"We don't have time for that. Let's help our team finish this so we can get back to The Cave." Mark acknowledges my request with a tight smile. He's worried, but it's not a mortal wound. I'll be fine for a little while.

In the time it took us to dispatch the Fallen, our team has reduced the number of demons down to four. Mark and I join the fight.

Sloan is getting all of her aggression out as she goes head to head with a demon twice her size. I leave her to it. She's most likely playing with him anyway. With the six of us fighting against four demons, it doesn't take long to get rid of them.

Exhausted and with pain spreading through my side, I'm ready to get back to The Cave. And I want to check on Angel. I have no idea what I can do to help. I just need to be there for her.

"We need to get to the clinic. Elizabeth needs stitches. Anyone else need medical attention?" Mark looks over our team and waits for a response.

Roz glances around. "Nah, I think we're okay." She addresses Dax. "The girls can ride back with me if you want to wait for the authorities and fill them in on what happened."

"I can do that, but how do we explain how we found this guy out here?" Dax hooks his thumb at the house behind him.

Roz offers a bemused smile. "We're working with the task force on human trafficking. Let them know we were following up on a lead, and this is what we found."

Dax bobs his head. "Okay, I think that should work." He gives her a smoldering smile. "That's why I married you. You're the brains in this marriage." Dax saunters up to her.

"And I married you for your body. I think we both win." Roz slides up to him and wraps her arms around his neck. A smile breaks free in the midst of my pain. I love how they can tease each other.

"Please . . . just stop." Sloan groans and walks away.

Mark leans over and gently kisses the side of my head. "Let's go get you stitched up."

I lean against his side. "I'm glad you still have your head, that was a close call."

"I wasn't worried. That's why we're a team, we have each other's backs. My only regret is that you suffered the injury."

Grace sways back and forth and places her clasped hands under her chin. "I just love, love." She lets out a breathy sigh and follows behind Sloan.

Roz kisses Dax soundly on the lips and then lets him go. "I'm taking the girls with me. I'll meet you back at The Cave."

"I'll see you guys in a little bit." Dax walks to his SUV to sit and wait for the authorities to show up.

Mark leads me to his Jeep with the palm of his hand on the small of my back. Gently leading. He's understandably upset about the wound, but it could have been so much worse. Defender did what needed to be done and kept us safe.

He's quiet on the ride back. No doubt analyzing this latest fight and finding holes in his performance. I wish he wouldn't beat himself up over it.

"Hey, it's not your job to keep me safe. Only God can do that." I let that sink in before I continue. "You know, there's no one I would rather do this life with than you. I never thought I would get married and have a family, but you're giving me the dream I had given up on."

He gives me a side smirk. "I know what you're trying to do, but it *is* my job to keep you safe. I'm your Guardian. That is literally my one job. If anyone is going to get injured, it should be me."

"Pfft, now that's just silly. The very nature of our job is going to get us into some messy situations, and wounds are inevitable." It's funny, I never thought I would say that about my job.

The burning in my side grows, and I'm too terrified to look at it. It's a good possibility that it may be worse than I thought. My shirt and pants are soaking up a lot of blood, but I don't want Mark to see it. He would get upset all over again.

I fiddle with the hem of my shirt and notice a couple of chipped nails. "I'm eager to get back to Angel. There isn't much I can do, but somehow I feel responsible for her. That it's my job to protect her."

"The Light will lead you as long as you listen, and it might be leading you in that direction. But make sure you're following the Light and not your own path. If you do this on your own out of some sense of obligation, you could make the situation worse if that's not what God has for you. I just don't want to see you get hurt."

My head nods in acknowledgment. He doesn't want me to take on a role in Angel's life that may not be mine to take, but it's a risk I'm willing to take. She needs so much love and healing, and it's going to take all of us. "I hear what you're saying. I'll pray about it and seek clarity from God regarding what He wants me to do in this situation." Tears prick my eyes as I lean my head back against the seat and close my eyes against the pain.

Back at The Cave, the nurse lifts my shirt, and I get a good look at the wound. It's definitely worse than I thought. The slice through my side is about eight inches long. It's deep, right under the ribs on my left side.

Mark glares at my side, jaw tight, arms crossed. He's furious, mainly at himself. If his eyes could shoot daggers at himself, I'm sure he would try.

As the needle pierces my side, I try to hide the wince, but it hurts. It doesn't take long to get stitched up. The bloody clothes are sticky and uncomfortable. I had better change clothes before I go check on Angel.

Mark gives me a quick kiss and leaves to go find Arden. It's late, and I need to get some sleep, but not before I lay eyes on Angel.

"Elizabeth, I was hoping to run into you." I stop mid-stride at the sound of my uncle's voice.

"Uncle Devon." All I want to do is fall into his embrace just as I've done all of my life, but his betrayal simmers just beneath the surface and keeps me from doing what my heart longs for. I waffle between anger and love. I never know which will creep to the surface when I'm around him. Apparently, today it's anger.

"I heard about the girl you found this morning. How is she?" His eyebrows draw together, and he tilts his head in concern.

"When I saw her last, she was still unconscious. She has a complicated road of healing ahead of her, and she's going to need all the help she can get."

"Is it true? She's pregnant?" He almost whispers the words, his eyes pinched.

I lean against the wall for support. "Yeah, she is. Until we can talk to her, there's no way to know if she's even aware of that fact." My voice comes out soft.

He gives a slight head nod as he looks off to the side. "I had no idea this was happening so close to home. You're working with the human trafficking task force, and I want to help. Let me assist your team."

"You can check with Arden and see what he says. Has he even released you yet?" Uncle Devon has been under constant supervision since his return under Leviathan's imprisonment. I doubt Arden has cleared him for work, which I know is driving Gage, his Guardian, crazy.

He looks down at his shoes. "No, not yet. But I can't keep sitting around here doing nothing. I have to do something."

"It's only been a couple of weeks. We don't know what Leviathan has planned, and you aren't out of danger yet."

For the first time during our conversation, he takes in the blood-soaked clothes I'm wearing, and his face pales. "What happened to you?" His voice quivers, and he clears his throat.

"We had a little run-in with a Fallen and some demons at the site where Angel was being held." I shrug my shoulder, which only pulls the stitches, and I wince before I can cover it up.

"Wait, who's Angel?" He gives me a frown, no doubt noticing the wince.

"The girl we found this morning. We gave her a name until we know what her real name is."

And now I realize that Uncle Devon is standing in the hallway by himself, with no supervision. "Where is Gage? Isn't he supposed to be watching you?"

"He's getting stitched up after a training mishap, and I needed to use the men's room. I was just on my way back." He places his hands in his pockets and leans back on his heels. "And maybe I was hoping to run into you. I can't live with you being angry or disappointed in me. I need you in my life. I know I have a lot to answer for, but I will do anything you ask. And I mean that."

"Yeah, I know." I close my eyes and let out a breath. "I miss you, too. But I don't know how to deal with this." The wounds are fresh, the betrayal is real, and the damage he created won't be an easy fix.

He takes a small step toward me but then stops. "Would it be okay if I walk you down the aisle? I know I'm not your dad, but you're like a daughter to me. I guess I always assumed I would be the one to walk you down the aisle and give you away."

He's right. That's the way I envisioned it, too. After he died, or at least I thought he had, I accepted I would walk myself down the aisle. Of course, that's when I thought I was marrying Lucas. But Uncle Devon is back, and my old dream now has a chance of rebirth.

"We need to clear the air, and as hurt and angry as I am with you, I still want you in my life. Need you in my life. And yes, I would like you to walk me down the aisle. It's that, or I walk myself."

He shakes his head and crinkles his nose. "No, please don't walk by yourself. It would be my greatest honor to walk you. Besides, I need to make amends, and this is the best way to start, don't you think?"

"I don't want to start my new life with your betrayal hanging between us. I promise we'll talk more before the wedding, but right now I need to get out of these clothes." I pull the bloody shirt away from my body. His smile dims at the truth of my words, or maybe it's the bloody clothes. He steps forward to give me a hug.

Gage interrupts as he walks up. "Francis would not stop talking."

I take a step to the side, not ready for his hug just yet. The light in Uncle Devon's eyes fades as he realizes I've shut down his embrace.

I point my thumb behind me and shift my feet. "I should go. I need to change my clothes before I check on Angel."

"Who's Angel?" Gage asks as I walk away. I don't bother responding. We aren't on good terms either.

After putting on a fresh pair of Triton Security joggers and a polo, I step into Angel's room. Mom is sitting in the chair next to the bed sewing the finishing touches on my wedding dress.

"Any improvement?" I try not to scratch the stitches that are pulling. It's already healing, but it still hurts.

Mom looks up from her sewing. "Oh, hey baby. No, nothing has changed. She hasn't even moved." She tilts her head. "You look exhausted."

I am exhausted, and I haven't eaten. "Do you know who is staying with her tonight?"

She sets aside her sewing to stand and stretch her back. "Grams will be back soon to stay with her for a few hours, then one of the nurses will finish the rest of the night."

"Okay, as long as she's not left alone. They know to call me if she wakes up?" My hands fidget with the hem of my shirt.

"Yes, the staff knows. Now, go home and get some rest. I won't be far behind you. There's stuff for sandwiches in the fridge if you're hungry."

"Thanks, Mom." I bend down to kiss her cheek and leave the room.

Back at home, I survey the stitches before I step into the shower. One large bruise surrounds the wound. I'm careful to stand with the wound facing away from the water.

Today did not go at all like I thought it would. I figured we would come home, give Arden a brief on what we accomplished in New Orleans, and work on wedding stuff.

No, this day veered hard left and careened into a brick wall.

After the shower, I fix a sandwich and then head up to bed. If I don't get some sleep, I'll be no good to anyone, especially Angel.

Something wakes me in the middle of the night. A soft noise, maybe. I can't put my finger on it. It's not really a sound. Maybe a feeling. But what?

I wait to see if anything happens, but nothing comes. The clock on the side of the bed shows it's three in the morning. Only four hours of sleep.

I roll out of bed and place my feet on the floor but scream when my foot touches something furry.

"What are you screaming for?" Tiger asks as she moves out of my way.

"Are you kidding me right now? I thought you were a rat or something." Heart racing, I flop back against the bed. Now, I really need to pee.

Tiger hasn't been around much, which is why her presence startled me. There's no telling what she's been up to.

Since it's obvious I won't be going back to sleep, I can go stay with Angel and relieve the nurse that's with her. No sense in neither of us getting any sleep.

"She's going to need you." Ah, is this the message she came to deliver?

"I'm not even going to ask who you're referring to. I assume you mean Angel. And yes, I know she needs me."

"Even more than you realize." She follows me down the stairs.

No point in asking what that means because she won't tell me, but I'll tuck that away for later. It means something. I just don't know what yet.

***

As I approach the door to Angel's room, a voice trickles out into the hallway. Someone is speaking softly, and as I listen, I'm surprised at the voice.

"I know better than anyone else what you've been through. But you're free now. You'll be okay, I promise. It's going to take time, but I'll make sure you have a good life. You'll never go back to that again. You're safe, and you can rest now." The heavy weight of those words sinks into silence.

I don't know whether I should stay or leave. I'm pretty sure I wasn't supposed to hear that. Not that there was anything wrong, but it was very personal, and she would be furious if she knew I was standing out in the hallway listening.

After several more minutes of silence and me standing out in the hallway like a weirdo, I figure it's safe to go in.

I tap lightly on the door and peek my head in. Sloan swivels her head, but makes no move.

"I couldn't sleep and wanted to check on Angel, maybe sit with her for a while. How long have you been here?" I ask.

She gives a barely perceptible shake of her head. "Not long. I couldn't sleep either." She puts her feet on the chair and pulls her legs to her chest, wrapping her arms around them, signaling she doesn't plan to leave.

"Do you mind if I stay?"

She watches me for a moment before answering. "You can stay."

I settle on the edge of the bed and face Angel. There may not be much I can do to help her, but I place my hands on her head and close my eyes. She may be resting, but I sense her turmoil. My hands glow, and peace descends as I pray over her. For healing. For peace. Only God knows everything she needs.

The glow fades, and I remove my hands, placing them in my lap while I watch her sleep.

The IV drip is still going and will be for as long as she needs it. Especially while she's unconscious.

Before I even realize I've done it, my hand finds her swollen abdomen and the tiny life growing inside of it.

Emotions well up, and try as I might, I can't hold them back. A sob escapes, and what comes out is volcanic. The sobs explode and heave as my own pain bubbles to the surface. I have no right to feel shattered. Not compared with the horror she's experienced.

It's a blending of her pain and mine. A mess of tangled emotions. How could life be so cruel? Her innocence stolen, my future to carry children—gone.

I'm a snotty mess before I'm able to quell the tide. A box of tissues appears in front of me, Sloan holding out the box.

"Thank you," I rasp out as I take the box and grab a wad of tissues to clean up the mess I've made.

"That was . . . unexpected," Sloan murmurs as she takes her seat.

"Yeah, I wasn't expecting that either." But somehow . . . it was cleansing. I never grieved over my barrenness, not like I did just then. I had quietly accepted it, shed a few tears, and pulled up my big girl panties and moved on.

I didn't realize I needed to release it. Grief has stages, and it won't always go in the order or in the time frame we think it should. There will always be a part of me that will mourn never having kids of my own, even if I've come to terms with it.

I blow my nose and toss the tissues in the trash, careful not to jostle the bed too much.

An awkward silence fills the room. I'm not sure what to say, and I grasp for something to fill the void.

"Cressida and Sookie will arrive sometime today. We'll be able to meet with the police task force, get some intel, and hopefully get out in the field and do some work."

Her eyes narrow. "Shouldn't you be getting ready for the wedding?"

My fingers tap out a rhythm on my lap. "Uh, yeah, I guess so. With everything that's going on, I sometimes forget that it's the end of this week."

"Don't you want to get married?" Her brow furrows.

Uh oh, that's not at all what I meant. "Yes, of course. I love Mark and want to spend my life with him." Maybe a little honesty is needed. "It's the whole sharing of our lives together I'm coming to terms with. I've been alone for a long time, and I'm not sure how to share my life with someone else."

I palm my face as another thought hits. "And there's the little issue of where we're going to live." I should have talked to Uncle Devon about it, but I completely forgot.

Sloan doesn't respond, but the look on her face tells me she's not convinced.

"Marriage isn't for everyone. There's no shame in that. Me? I have no intention of ever being in a relationship, much less getting married. It's not something I want for my life. Being a Guardian is my life and always will be." Sloan's honesty throws me. She's not one to share her thoughts, especially not with me.

"You're right. There's no shame in that. It's important to know what you want for your life. Me? I never thought I would get married after I caught my ex-fiancé with my best friend. I had come to terms with remaining single. You didn't know that about me. In fact, there's a lot you don't know, but I didn't think marriage would ever happen for me. I guess in a way, I'm waiting for the other shoe to drop. Mark seems too good to be true. I guess there's a part of me that's waiting for him to look at me and say, 'You're so not worth the trouble'."

Those old insecurities creep in unbidden, trying to steal any joy and peace I may have.

Sloan shakes her and lowers her feet to the ground. "You shouldn't think that. I've seen the way he looks at you. He loves you. It's obvious to anyone watching."

"Thank you. Sometimes I get sucked in and need to quiet those lies." Sloan is always observant, her mind constantly working.

Exhaustion weighs in and my eyes grow heavy. No doubt from that little cry fest I had moments ago. "I think I need some rest. Why don't you pull the extension out on the couch so you can lie down and rest? We can both stay with Angel until Grams comes in to relieve us later."

"I think I will." She adjusts the couch and lies down facing Angel. I move to the recliner next to the bed and lift the footrest.

Angel has a family to look after her and care for her. A family that will fight for her when she can't. She just doesn't know it yet.

Chapter 7

Mark

After leaving Elizabeth, I meet with Arden to fill him in on what we encountered where Angel was being held.

"In light of this, I want you and Elizabeth to stay close to home base. Your wedding is in less than a week, your family is coming in, and you've been trying to move out of your rental. With Cressida and Sookie coming in, they can fill in for you until you get back from your honeymoon. This will be one of the best times in your life, and I don't want you so busy that you can't enjoy it."

"Thanks, there's a lot going on. I've packed most of my things, but the housing situation is still up in the air. Elizabeth still needs to speak with Devon about it. We may need to move into one of the apartments here."

"You can if you need to, but I have faith it will all work out. Devon can't stay alone right now, anyway. He needs to remain under Gage's watch, and I don't know when that will change." He sighs and rubs his hands down his face. Fatigue evident in the dark circles under his eyes. "Gage is one of my best fighters, and it's not ideal that he's been relegated to babysitter. We have got to get this situation with Devon resolved. And soon."

"I agree, but we don't even know how to help Devon. On top of that, Elizabeth is still struggling with his betrayal. She doesn't know whether to be angry with him or overjoyed that he's still alive. Right now she's both and very confused."

Arden nods his head. "The sooner Elizabeth deals with it, the better. I trust she will. In the meantime, I would like your help with the administrative side of things, and it will keep you out of any dangerous missions. Griffin always helped me manage, but with him gone I can't balance it all. You've been a big help already."

That he would consider me for such a role is an honor. It hasn't been easy for him with Griffin gone, to have the weight of the northwestern division to carry on his shoulders alone. "I would consider it a privilege to help you in any way I can."

"Thank you. I'll let you go so you can get some rest. You and Dax will pick up Cressida and Sookie from the airport tomorrow. Then, your team has an appointment with the police task force at noon in the Triton boardroom. You and Elizabeth are not to take on any new missions, but I want you in on the meeting. Allow your team to handle what needs to be done without you for the time being."

"Thank you, sir, I will. Have a good evening."

***

We arrive at the airport before the plane lands. We make our way to the information kiosk near the entrance and wait for their arrival. Hoards of people shuffle about with their luggage while we find a safe place out of the way.

"You ready for the big day?" Dax asks as he leans against the wall. He looks like any other traveler to those who walk past. Hands in his pockets, sunglasses on his face, but his eyes constantly roaming and surveying the area.

"I've been ready. Elizabeth is still struggling, though. She's been burned in the past. Badly. And thanks to her uncle, his betrayal is still fresh. So, yeah, she's holding back. Scared to believe it's real. I need to prove to her I'm not going anywhere and that my love for her is genuine." Yeah, I know all about her jerk of an ex with her best friend, and what Devon did doesn't help.

"Man, that's tough. I'll be praying for you." His head jerks to the left.

My head moves in the direction he indicates. Cressida and Sookie descend on the escalators, but my eye catches on someone behind them. No, make that two someones. Paxton King and Tyler Ardoin follow behind.

"I didn't know they were coming," Dax murmurs as he moves from his place against the wall.

"I didn't either." We approach the escalators as they step off.

"Good to see you again. I didn't know we had more company coming." I stretch out my hand to shake Cressida's as Dax greets Sookie.

I give a fist bump to Paxton. "Good to see you, man."

"Good to be here. Looking forward to a small-town getaway." Paxton lifts his duffel bag onto his shoulder.

I greet Tyler with a fist bump as well. He's a man of few words with a permanent scowl on his face.

"It's a good thing we brought the SUV. Let's get your luggage and head back to The Cave. We have a meeting with the special task force at noon. Lunch will be delivered in case you're hungry." Dax leads the way to the parking garage after we gather all their bags.

"I'm always hungry," Paxton says as he rubs his flat stomach.

Once we make it back, we get everyone settled into their rooms and then head to the Triton boardroom to meet with the police task force we will be working closely with.

We've been told they understand we deal in the supernatural, and of course, they're naturally curious and want to learn more.

The girls walk in first, with Elizabeth and Roz trailing behind.

"Oh good, food. I'm starving!" Grace makes a beeline for the table set up with gourmet sandwiches and sides. Drinks and cups fill another table.

Sloan makes a hard stop, and Grace bounces off her back. "Dude, what did you stop for? There's food."

Grace walks around Sloan, giving her the side-eye until she realizes we have company. Of the boy kind.

"Oh, hey. I didn't realize you were coming with Cressida and Sookie." Grace walks up to Paxton as she gives Tyler distance.

Paxton hands Grace a bottle of water from the food table. "Sunshine, how are you?"

Sunshine? He already has a nickname for her? You have got to be kidding me.

She beams a bright smile his way.

"Yeah, it was a last-minute thing. Cressida wants us to have more training, so here we are." Paxton lifts his hands out as if to say 'ta da'.

Grace slides in next to him and places one of each item on her plate, taking time to analyze the food while she engages him in conversation.

I place my hand on the small of Elizabeth's back and motion for her to go ahead of me, but we have to wait for those two. All I want to do is fix a plate before we sit down for our meeting. My stomach takes that moment to grumble in complaint.

Sloan gives Tyler the death stare at the back of his head while he fills his own plate with food. She grabs a few items, not even looking at them, and throws them on her plate.

Sloan rolls her eyes and walks to the other side of the room. Probably to get as far away from Grace and Paxton as possible. Tyler tracks Sloan with his eyes, but gives no other indication that she exists.

Of course, wherever Sloan goes, Grace goes, and Paxton follows behind her. Sloan isn't getting away from them no matter where she goes. Tyler finds a seat at the opposite end of the table.

Dax raises his eyebrow. Way too much teenage drama going on between the four of them. We're going to have to keep an eye on these guys.

Roz and Elizabeth are speaking with Cressida and Sookie at the table when the task force walks in. A task force of only two guys. Kind of disappointing. Not sure what I was expecting, but I figured there would be more. No wonder they need our help.

"Hi, everyone." A large, fit man with skin the color of deep, rich chocolate walks in as a shorter, stocky guy with auburn hair walks in right behind him.

"I'm Officer Dannon, but you can call me Wesley, and this is Officer Miles Carter. We're missing our female officer, Athena Hamilton, today. She had an emergency and sends her apologies."

Elizabeth lets out a small gasp. "Wesley?" Her smile shines with recognition.

A huge grin slides into place. "Elizabeth, I was wondering if that was you. You look great." He walks over to give my fiancée a big hug. His massive arms engulf her smaller frame.

I'm not jealous. I'm firmly confident of Elizabeth's love for me, but watching this exchange knocks me down a peg or two.

They both start talking at once, trying to understand how each came into their respective roles. Apparently they worked together some in the ER, and he moved to this task force recently.

"Come and meet my fiancé." Elizabeth walks Wesley over.

"Wesley, this is my fiancé Mark. Our wedding is at the end of this week."

Wesley extends his hand, and I reach forward to shake it. "It's nice to meet you, Wesley."

"And you as well. Do you mind if I fix a plate before we get started? I'm starving. Didn't have time for breakfast this morning, and donuts aren't going to cut it." Elizabeth nods her head for him to go ahead.

The stocky guy walks over after making introductions to the rest of the group. "Miles Carter."

"Miles, I'm Mark, and this is my fiancée Elizabeth."

With a handshake and a head nod, he asks, "Is this everyone?"

"Yes, Cressida, Sookie, Paxton and Tyler are only here to help us train together since they've been doing this for years. The rest of us will be the core group you will work with."

"Okay, good to know." He nods his head as he scans the crowd one more time. A man of few words.

"Alright, everyone, let's get started. Grab some food if you haven't already done so, and let's get down to business." Roz directs the room.

Cressida steps to the front of the table. "Wesley and Miles, what made you reach out to Triton Security in the first place?"

Wesley puts down the fork to answer. "We don't have the resources larger departments have to tackle human trafficking. Miracle Lake is a small town, and we're stretched thin as it is. We need help, and what better way to get that than to reach out to an established firm that handles a wide range of security issues and threats?"

Roz speaks up. "And what do you know about us exactly? We were told you understand we have special abilities."

Wesley clears his throat before responding. "Ah, well, yes. As a Christian, I'm very familiar with the scriptures on demonic powers and spiritual warfare. A friend confided you fight demonic forces, and honestly, we need all the help we can get. What is happening in our small town is definitely demonic. That we are here discussing this is proof of that."

Dax nods in agreement. "Anytime there is any form of stealing, killing, or destruction, it's most definitely demonic. 'The thief comes only to steal and kill and destroy . . .' And because of that, we stay very busy."

Wesley gives a slow nod, his voice tinged with a hint of emotion. "I think it's divine providence we're able to partner together."

"That it is." Cressida's smile brightens as she leans on the table. "We have a great working relationship with the New Orleans task force. They understand how we operate, and we're able to balance each other's strengths and weaknesses."

Cressida and Sookie take over and explain the practical side of working together and even share some of their funnier stories. Not every operation has gone smoothly, but they haven't lost anyone. They share some of their close calls, but also the joy in defeating the darkness.

"There are things we can do that you may not understand, but trust us, we won't do anything to jeopardize your mission," Sookie shares.

Wesley tilts his head in thought. "I'm not worried—I'm ready to get started. I'm aware there are things happening all around us I can't see. Can you share some of what you do? Elizabeth, what about you? What can you do?" His attention moves to the left, where Elizabeth is sitting.

Grace snickers, and Roz elbows her.

Pink blossoms on Elizabeth's cheeks. "Well . . . we aren't sure what all I can do. We're still working on that. It's all very new." She clears her throat and fiddles with her napkin. I long to smooth the lines that appear on her forehead.

Grace is trying not to bust out laughing, Sloan looks like she would rather be anywhere but here as she sharpens her nails into fine stabby points, and Tyler and Paxton have bored expressions on their faces. This isn't a very exciting meeting, but it's important to lay the groundwork.

It's time to get us back on track. "We received a tip about a girl being abused and held against her will not too far from here. We went to the house yesterday. It was empty except for one guy, who was already dead." Not untrue, just not all of the information. "All the signs point to a human trafficking situation, but we can take you to the house and have you look around. Give us your thoughts on the situation."

"Yes, we received the information this morning and have plans to ride over there today. The coroner will do her job and give us the findings once she has them, and that will give us a little more to go on. But it could be some time before we have that back." Miles folds his hands on the table and leans back in his chair. Probably the most words I've heard from the guy.

Wesley braces his hands on the arms of the chair and lifts up. "Well, I say let's head on over there. I want to look around, and you can let us know what you observed before the scene was processed."

It's decided that Elizabeth and I will stay back since Arden gave us orders to stay close and focus on our upcoming wedding. He has some assignments he wants me to take over, which will help relieve some of his workload as well. I'll help him with that until the wedding.

As we prepare to leave, Tyler gives a side glance at Sloan, which she completely ignores, Paxton and Grace pick up where they left off, and Dax leads the others out of the conference room.

Our team leaves for their first mission with the police task force while Elizabeth and I are relegated to the sidelines.

"I want to check on Angel's progress. See if there's been any change." Elizabeth leans against my side as if I'm what's holding her up. And I want to be that for her. For her to be confident enough to know she can come to me anytime for anything, and I will be here to hold her up. *Thank you, God, for every day with her.*

I wrap my arm around her shoulders and hold her close. "I'm so angry on behalf of Angel and what she's been through. I want to right all the wrong that's been done to her, but I have no idea how to do that. Hopefully, this new team we'll be working with can find something else to give us a lead on anyone else that may have been involved. I kind of feel like Sloan on this one. There was nothing satisfying about finding that guy already dead."

She peers up at me and smiles that beautiful smile. "I know what you mean. I don't know how, but God will make it right. He will make sure Angel gets justice, but more importantly, He will bring the healing she needs."

She pauses while she gathers her thoughts. "You know what's crazy? We're getting married in just a few days. It seems like it's all happened so fast, and I'll admit I'm a little nervous."

My heart stutters at her words. "Are you having second thoughts?"

She doesn't answer right away, and my thoughts race with all the ways she could tell me she wants to call it off.

"No, it's not that. I have no doubts about you and your love for me. That's not it at all. I'm scared I'll let you down. What if I'm not marriage material? I haven't exactly had the best role model for what a solid and successful marriage is supposed to look like. Our marriage should be secure and united no matter what comes our way, but what if I'm just not any good at it?"

Okay, this I can work with. I see where she's coming from, and understand her fear. "Well, if it makes you feel any better, I've never been married before either, and we can learn together. My parents were a great example, but they weren't perfect and they didn't always get it right either. Sure, we'll make mistakes, but as long as we communicate and don't shut each other out, we'll be just fine. Maybe even have a little fun along the way."

I place my hands on her shoulders and kiss her forehead as she giggles. "One thing I do know, if I prefer you and your needs over mine, and you prefer me and my needs over yours, we've just mastered the formula for a successful marriage. In fact, the Bible tells us to do just that, to prefer others over ourselves. That's not to say it will be easy. We're all born selfish by our very nature, which is why it's never easy to prefer someone else over our own needs and desires."

She lets out a little snort. "Pfft, and how are we supposed to do that if we're all born selfish?"

"Oh, it's utterly impossible. We can't do it." My shoulder shrugs as if it's no big deal.

She squints her eyes and wrinkles her nose. "Now, you're just not making any sense."

A laugh escapes at the confused look on her face. "If God doesn't help us and the Light doesn't lead us, we can't do it on our own. Not for very long anyway."

"Okay, that makes sense." She bobs her head. "I was worried about you for a second."

"Are you feeling any better now?" I sure hope so because I'm ready to get married. But if she's not one hundred percent on board with this, we can postpone the wedding. It's not what I want to do, but I will.

"Yeah, I think so. Sorry about that. I get stuck inside my head sometimes." A shy smile tips the corners of her lips.

"It's all good. You can always talk to me about anything, I hope you know that."

She lifts up on her toes and kisses my lips. The kiss is entirely too short for my liking. "I do know that. And I need to find Uncle Devon and get the whole house situation sorted out. It would be good to know we have a place to live after we get back from the honeymoon."

My arms draw her close. That little kiss won't cut it. My lips meet hers, and the kiss deepens, like a man who is passionately in love and wants his woman to know it. I back away, and she sways toward me, a little off balance. Good. That should keep any doubts away.

"We can live in an apartment here if we need to. I'll be fine as long as we're together. But for now, I need to find Arden and see what he needs help with. Can we meet for dinner later?" I take her hand in mine as we leave the conference room.

"Yes, that sounds good. Do we want to cook something, or eat here?"

"Why don't we get some food from here to go and bring it back to your place?" As much as I enjoy her cooking, we both need to relax.

"Oh, that's a good idea. Food that we don't have to cook, and we get some alone time. I'm in."

I give her a quick hug and release her. "Alright, I'll see you later. I love you."

A satisfied smile graces her face. "I love you, too."

I watch as she walks away. The next few days can't pass fast enough.

CHAPTER 8

EIZABETH

I'm surprised to find Brenda, Arden's wife, in the room with Angel when I walk in. We were introduced recently, and I know nothing about her other than she's married to Arden.

"Brenda, hi." Her head jerks up at my greeting and closes the book she was reading.

"Elizabeth, it's so good to see you. How is the wedding planning coming along?" She lays the book next to her on the tiny hospital couch.

"Our moms have pretty much handled everything. It helps that we wanted something simple."

Brenda pats the seat next to her on the couch before scooting over to make room for me. "I'm glad you're here. We haven't had an opportunity to talk, and I would like to get to know you better. Arden has had nothing but good things to say about you." That's a relief to hear because I'm pretty sure it could go either way.

I take the seat next to her, thankful for her kindness. "Thank you for sitting with Angel. We don't want her left alone. I'm assuming Arden filled you in on how we found her."

"He did. He wants to make sure she has someone who can help her when she wakes up. I'm not sure if you're aware, but I'm a child psychologist. I've recently cut my hours back to be available for Arden more now that Griffin is gone." Her face glints with a hint of sadness, acknowledging their recent loss. Losing Griffin would have affected her too.

"I didn't know that. How is it you have time for a regular job?" There's no way for me to work at the hospital and be a Light Bearer at the same time.

"Oh, I'm neither a Light Bearer nor a Guardian. I've been able to work as a child psychologist while Arden is busy with his duties. It works for us. We've never had kids, and we're able to devote ourselves to what God calls us to."

I thought everyone here was either a Light Bearer or a Guardian. It never occurred to me that wasn't the case. "Okay, please forgive me, but I didn't know that was even possible."

"What? There are others here besides Light Bearers and Guardians?" She asks with surprise.

"Well, yes, but how does that work? You're married to Arden, but you're not like us. I thought we had to keep that part of our lives separate from others."

She gives a soft smile. "That's right, you weren't brought up in this life. There's plenty of us that know about Light Bearers and Guardians, even raised with them. The only difference is we can't see the Spirit Realm like you can."

"Wow, I feel like I should have known that. We have a special police task force working with us who know a little about us, but what you're telling me is different from what I was thinking."

Brenda pats my knee. "Give yourself some grace. You're still new to this. And it's good the police came to us for help. Your team will be an asset in this fight. God will use anyone who is willing, and it works best when we can come together as a team."

I'm learning something new about this life every day, and it makes me angry all over again at Uncle Devon. I don't care what his reasoning is, he should never have kept this life hidden from me. There's so much I don't know, thanks to him.

The rising anger isn't helping anything. I need to get off this train of thought. "Have there been any changes with Angel?"

She hesitates for a moment before speaking. "Nothing new. It's good that her mind and body are resting. I'll stay close by for when she wakes up. I believe it will take all of us working together to help her through this."

She shifts and faces me, a serious expression on her face. "Arden and I have been talking. Until we know her home situation, I would like her to come stay with us once she's released. If she has a stable home to go back to, I can offer my services to the family, but if not, we want her to stay with us permanently. It may mean that I would need to retire, but I'm willing to do that."

"You're right. She needs a stable, loving home. A safe place. I'm thankful you're willing to do that for her." Angel needs every advantage if she's going to make it.

A light knock at the door halts our conversation. Uncle Devon pokes his head through the door. "Do you have a second?" he whispers as his gaze finds mine.

"Sure. Thank you, Brenda. I'll see you soon."

I gently touch Angel's hand as I pass by the bed.

Uncle Devon is in the hallway waiting for me as Gage stands nearby.

"Do you mind if we take a walk? I was hoping we could talk." He motions his head down the hallway.

I know we need to talk, but I don't know how much good it will do right now. Anger is burning fresh right now, and I can guarantee I won't be able to hold my tongue.

I follow him out into the heart of The Cave as Gage follows at a respectful distance. I'm glad he's sticking close. As livid as I am, I still love Uncle Devon and want nothing to happen to him. Like getting sucked back into Leviathan's lair.

"I've been praying, and I need to make things right with you." He shoves his hands into his pockets. "I've apologized many times already, but I'm sorry. I went about all of this the wrong way."

My head jerks to the side, and before I can process the words, they fly out of my mouth. "Ya think?" Yep, no filter right now.

His head lowers, and he lets out a long breath. We stroll along a path that will eventually bring us to the lake. "You're angry, and you have every right to be. Honest, I was only trying to protect you. There was never any intention of keeping you from this life permanently. I was only trying to protect you from the prophecy. Unfortunately, my plan was taking way longer than I had expected. I also didn't plan to go missing for three years and have everyone presume I was dead. It's really turned out to be a big mess."

Such a big mess. "Yeah, and all of that mess was dumped on me."

He lifts a shoulder. "I really was just trying to protect you. Keep you safe until the prophecy passed, then bring you in. I tried to be the fill-in for you. That's why Gage and I went after the Sword of Heaven. I figured I could force the prophecy forward since we are of the same lineage."

I stop mid-step at the absurdity of that statement. "That doesn't even make sense. Everything I've been told is that the prophecy will always be fulfilled exactly as it was intended. There's nothing you can do to change it."

Now facing me, his look is somber. "When you become a parent one day, you will understand. You'll do anything in your power to protect your child, even if it doesn't make any sense."

Oh, the irony. "Well, that's not gonna happen. So I won't be making the same mistake as you." I fold my arms across my chest.

His brow furrows in confusion. "What do you mean? You don't want to have kids?"

I shake my head sharply and start walking again. "No, that's not it at all. I physically cannot have kids, so that will never be a problem."

He catches up to me, but I refuse to look at him. "When did you find this out?"

"That last mission you went on to retrieve the Sword of Heaven? I had to have emergency surgery. You never knew." Only two people knew. My best friend at the time and my now ex-fiancé. My mom doesn't even know. That's another fun conversation waiting to happen. See what happens when you put something off?

We walk in silence for a while. When he speaks, his voice is shaky. "I don't know what to say. I am so sorry, Elizabeth." He reaches up to wipe away a tear. "How can I make any of this right? I can't stand this distance between us. This isn't us. We've always been close."

As we near the lake, I come to a stop. The view is always a soothing balm to my soul. Taking a deep breath, I hold it, then release it slowly. "I don't hate you. I don't like you very much right now, but I've never once stopped loving you. The distance between us is tearing me apart, but you've got to give me some time. I don't know how to move forward from this."

My gaze moves away from the lake, and I face him fully. "There's a part of me that wonders if I'll ever be able to trust you again. Only time will tell. I've been praying and asking God to help me forgive you. Not so much for your sake, but for mine. Scripture tells us we are to forgive others just as the Lord has forgiven us. It's not an option. And I know I need His help to do that."

He nods his head, and a tear slips from his eye. He doesn't bother to wipe it away this time, only focuses on the lake ahead.

This rift between us is physically painful. With every fiber of my being, I long to wrap my arms around him, but I can't. Not yet. My heart isn't ready.

I walk away, but before I get too far, I realize I have one more piece of unfinished business to discuss with him.

"Uh, I'm not sure how to bring this up, but with the wedding only a few days away, Mark and I are trying to figure out where we will live. Do you mind if we stay in the house for a bit until we find a place of our own?"

Surprise crosses his face, and he relaxes his stance. "Elizabeth, the home is yours. I want you to keep it. I don't need it. I can live anywhere."

That's more than generous considering how I've shunned his affection. It's his house, but I won't argue with him. I've fallen in love with the place. "Thank you. That's very kind of you."

A sorrowful smile flickers across his face. "Elizabeth, I want you to be happy. You matter to me so much more than any house. Besides, Gage has a nice place, and I have enough room of my own that we don't get into each other's space."

"Okay, but only if you're sure." I bite my lip, wondering if he's trying to earn my affection.

He nods his head and smiles. "I'm sure. Please stay, it's yours."

My posture deflates. I may be angry, but I miss Uncle Devon so much. Or the old Uncle Devon I thought I knew. He may be right here, but he's not the man I once thought he was, and that hurts. The pain of betrayal will fade with time, and one day I'll realize it no longer hurts like this. But that day is not today.

"Alright, thank you." I leave him at the lake with his thoughts.

Yeah, he may have been trying to protect me by completing the prophecy on his own, but all he did was make a colossal mess. And it still played out the way it was supposed to. And the biggest hurt of all, he kept me from the life I was supposed to live all along. No, it doesn't make me feel any better.

***

Mark's parents arrive for the wedding ready for some family fun. Now it's time to switch gears and focus on our upcoming nuptials. It was easy to let my mom and Mark's mom take over all the wedding details while we were in New Orleans. They didn't have a lot of time to do anything too over the top, and they know the most important thing for me is that it remain simple.

It didn't take much for our moms have become fast friends. They quickly developed a warm friendship while pulling together this wedding on short notice.

Mark and his dad are in the backyard cleaning the gazebo and hanging up twinkle lights. Mom has me trying on the dress one last time to make sure the stitching is perfect.

Roz, Dax, Uncle Devon, Gage and Mark's siblings with their families are coming over for dinner soon. There's roast with potatoes in the oven, along with salad and garlic bread.

"Oh, sweetheart, that dress is beautiful on you." Mark's mom, Charlotte, puts her hands to her mouth as her eyes fill with tears.

"Thank you." She's right, it is beautiful. "Mom, you picked the perfect dress." My gaze finds hers in the mirror.

"I only did what you told me to. You asked me to find something simple. Simple can also be beautiful."

"I think it's ready. Let me slip out of the dress and hang it up so nothing happens to it."

Now, to make it down the aisle in one piece.

***

Bright eyes stare back at me—familiar, yet different. I almost don't recognize my own gaze. The reflection is beautiful in a way that reminds me of an old painting. My hair is styled in a sophisticated yet casual updo, adorned with delicate pearl pins.

Grace and Sloan created the masterpiece in the mirror. I was a little worried about turning all control over to them, but it came out perfect.

The wedding dress lay on the bed, its delicate lace a symbol of future hope, ready for me to step into.

Grams places her hands on my shoulders as we both stare in the mirror. "Girls, you've outdone yourselves again. Let's leave Elizabeth and her mom to finish up. It's almost time."

"Thank you so much. You've done an amazing job." I give Grace and Sloan a hug as they leave the room.

"I'm so excited for you!" Grace gives one last squeeze as she bounces out the door.

"They really are amazing." Mom wraps an arm around my shoulder. "This is it. My baby girl is getting married."

My eyes get misty at the tender tone, and I blink rapidly to stop any tears. "I know. I'm excited and nervous and everything in between."

Mom places her hands on my shoulders. "Could I give you one piece of marriage advice? Not from my own personal experience, mind you. It's something I've learned as I've walked with the Lord."

I give her a nod, and she continues. "Mark is not your source of joy or peace. He never will be. That comes only from having a relationship with Jesus. Allow Mark to be Mark, and allow Jesus to be your everything."

She's right, I know she is. It's easy to have certain expectations for the one who pledges their life to you. Certainly, some they will never be able to meet. I'll need to be careful not to place unrealistic expectations on Mark.

A knock at the door interrupts our mother-daughter moment.

"Wait right here. I'll see who it is." Mom pads to the door and barely cracks it open since I'm still in my satin robe. No reason to put the dress on too early. So, I'm waiting until the last minute to put it on—just in case. I don't want anything to happen to it.

"Would it be possible to have a moment alone with Elizabeth? I promise not to take too long." Uncle Devon's voice filters through the door.

"Of course, Devon. I'll leave you two alone for a few minutes while I make sure everything is ready downstairs."

I watch him through the mirror as he steps in and walks past Mom. A strange look passes between them, one I can't put my finger on.

The door shuts quietly with a click.

His face softens as love radiates from his gaze. "Elizabeth, you look stunning. You've always been beautiful, but there's this contentment about you now."

"Thank you. Please have a seat. We still have a few minutes." He takes the chair near the window.

The gazebo, with its twinkling lights and vibrant flowers planted around it, is a beautiful sight through the window. The joyous dance of the afternoon rays glisten across the lake. The few rows of chairs remain empty as guests stand around mingling before the ceremony.

How romantic is a sunset wedding near the lake? That was Mark's idea. I know, I stink at planning a wedding. Simple, without a lot of fuss, is all I asked for. He had more of an idea of what he wanted than I did.

Mark is the complete package. He loves God, loves people, and loves life. He's gentle and fierce, strong and polite, gorgeous and unassuming. Maybe all of his exceptional traits will rub off on me. Hashtag life goals.

A soft sigh escapes my lips. "Everything okay?" For a moment, I completely forgot my uncle was in here with me.

"Yes, just thinking about Mark."

He grins and bobs his head. "I really like him, Elizabeth. You couldn't have done better if I had picked him out for you myself."

A smirk escapes. "I didn't pick him. I think God did that."

"He's good for you. He'll help you find balance in life." His shoulders lower before he speaks again. "I still can't believe I've missed the last three years. So much has changed, and I struggle to keep up with it all. In my mind, I'm still here but three years in the past. Days like today remind me that life moved on without me."

He stands up, and I wait as he gathers his thoughts.

"I can't thank you enough for allowing me to be a part of your wedding. You could have told me you didn't want me here. And I would have honored your request, but it would have broken me. You would have every right, and I would understand, but I want you to know how much it means to me."

Pain etches the small lines around his eyes. "You are my daughter. Even if I'm not your biological father, you are in every sense of the word, my daughter. It physically pains me to know I hurt you. You must know that was never my intent. My goal was only ever to protect you. And I didn't even do that."

He leans his shoulder against the window frame and folds his arms across his chest. Defeated eyes stare back at me. "How do I make this right?"

I stand up and walk to the other side of the window opposite Uncle Devon. I match his stance as I lean against the window frame.

"I understand you were only trying to protect me, and I love you for it. But you went about it all wrong. What I struggle with the most is that you prevented me from being a Light Bearer. My destiny. My whole reason for existing, and you kept that from me. That kind of betrayal," I shake my head and look away. "I can't just get over it. How could you do that to me?"

A visible shudder runs through him as he exhales. I'm not trying to hurt him with my words, but this is all his doing. To make this right, he needs to fully understand what he did, so he doesn't do anything like this ever again.

"You have to believe me, it was only supposed to be until I could make sure the prophecy was fulfilled and you would never have to be a part of it. I was arrogant in thinking I could alter it, but I felt like I had to try. To protect you. I couldn't live with myself if something happened to you and I didn't do everything in my power to prevent it. I was wrong, and I am so sorry that I kept being a Light Bearer from you."

He shifts and unfolds his arms. "I've been watching you. You are made for this life, Elizabeth. I wish I could go back and change it so you would grow up in this world. My prayer is that God will redeem the time you missed, and my mistakes, and give you the life you were always meant to live."

It's heavy - the weight of holding on to the anger. I don't want to hold it anymore. "I keep praying and asking God to help me forgive you because I don't know how. I don't know how to let this go. I don't know how I can trust you again. It's all so exhausting." My shoulders slump under the weight of it all.

My defensive stance drops. I long to rub my hands down my face but don't want to ruin all the lovely work the girls did.

The ball is in my court. The next move is up to me. There's nothing else Uncle Devon can do to fix this.

My spine straightens with resolve. "Let's move forward and start fresh today. I can't forget what happened, but I do forgive you. God will have to help me work through my anger and trust issues."

His shoulders relax, and he lets out the breath he was holding. "I don't deserve your forgiveness, but thank you."

He ambles toward me and holds out his arms for a hug. We need each other – father and daughter. He's right. He's more of a dad to me than my own father.

We all make mistakes. Some are much bigger than others, leaving behind a legacy of pain in their wake. But he loves me and would never intentionally hurt me.

I meet him halfway and open my arms. As we embrace, my heart settles. With my head on his chest, I close my eyes, and his arms envelop me in a hug only a father can give. I've missed this. I've missed him. It feels like coming home.

Darkness moves across my eyelids, and before I can open them, the ground beneath me tilts. The world swirls around us, and my stomach spins.

Uncle Devon whispers, "Oh no." He holds on and doesn't let go. The ground beneath us falls away, and we free-fall. I grip Uncle Devon tighter and hold on with everything I have. End over end with nothing to stop us. The air shifts as we enter another realm.

How did this happen?

Somewhere along the way I lose hold of Uncle Devon. My hands are the only things that prevent my face from smacking into the ground when I land.

My hands hit first and absorb most of the impact as the rest of my body hits hard. Pain radiates from my hands up my arms. Ringing in my ears does not help the nausea rolling through my stomach. Both hands are scraped and bloody, and my wrists throb with every heartbeat. Probably sprained from the impact. Hopefully not broken.

Beneath my face, the uneven ground is covered in dirt and who knows what else based on the sickening smell. Dingy light filters through a hole in the top of a high stone wall marked by years of abuse, with no way of escape.

A strange noise has me jumping to my feet, ready to fight off whatever is coming, but my shoulders relax when I realize the noise is only Uncle Devon as he climbs to his feet.

"Where are we?" I glance around unfamiliar surroundings.

All color drains from his face as awareness takes hold.

"I remember. I remember . . . everything. How did this happen?" The same thing I'm wondering. "Elizabeth, we have to get you out of here." Eyes wide, his breath quickens as he lets out a moan.

"Where is here, exactly?" My robe hangs off of one shoulder, and the sash around my waist has come undone. I adjust the robe and tighten the sash, securing it with a knot. This is not ideal fighting gear.

Uncle Devon's harsh whisper startles me. "This is Leviathan's lair. We're in his dungeon. All the years I was stuck in this place, I never found a way of escape. Your sacrifice at the breach was the only way I made it back home."

Okay, not ideal, but I knew something like this was going to happen. Eventually. Not like this exactly, but did it really need to happen on my wedding day? And without Defender?

Why today of all days? It's my wedding day. I'm supposed to be getting married right now.

How do I get a message to Mark, or to any of the others? My cell phone is back at the house, charging on the nightstand.

Now is the time I wish I was more like Sloan. She would have a weapon strapped somewhere.

Shifting my focus, I check in with the Light. The flutter reassures me that all is not lost. As long as I have the Light, there is hope. *Okay, what do I do? How do I get out of here?*

Wait. It's the only response I get. And I don't like that one.

Glancing over at Uncle Devon, I realize he hasn't moved. Still as a statue - frozen in fear.

He needs to snap out of it, but I don't want to startle him out of whatever nightmare he seems to have lost himself in.

"Uncle Devon." I place my hand on his arm with the softest touch. "I'm right here. You're not alone."

It does the trick. He comes back to me and blinks at our surroundings in dismay.

"Elizabeth, I don't know how this happened. I'm so sorry. This is all my fault." He places his hands over his face and leans against the wall.

"It's not your fault." I shake my head and look around at what appears to be a dungeon. Dark, creepy, cold. "Leviathan was coming after me no matter what. It was only a matter of time. I knew it was coming."

As if speaking his name conjured the dragon himself. Evil tinges the air and precedes his presence. He takes a deep inhale before uttering the words I've been dreading on a hiss. "My sssweet. You finally arrived. How I've longed for you, but the timing had to be jussst right. How poetic that it would be on the day you were to wed your betrothed. It'sss right, don't you think? Jussst as my plansss were coming together, you tore them apart. I thought it only fitting I ssshould return the favor."

As much as I thought I could be strong, fear pings around inside of me searching for a place to land. Our last encounter was not a pleasant one. I survived, but barely.

Sound narrows, and my extremities tingle as fear slithers and coils its way through me. It wraps its bony fingers around my throat like a vice, shutting off life's very breath. Lights dance through my vision as I fall to my knees trying to claw away whatever squeezes me tight. Desperate for a breath, I struggle to breathe, but nothing makes its way through.

"Let her go!" I barely make out Uncle Devon's words as everything grows dim.

The squeezing fades, and I choke on air as it passes through my lungs. Violent coughs wrack my body as I struggle for breath, sprawled out on the ground.

"Ah, my pet. How I've misssed you. We had fun, didn't we?"

Anger and fear roll off Uncle Devon in waves. He wants to protect me, but he's powerless to do so.

How are we going to survive this?

CHAPTER 9

MARK

Standing around talking to the guys, I'm killing time until I make Elizabeth my wife. I rub my hands together in anticipation of watching her walk down the aisle to stand by my side. Not just for today, but for the rest of my life. My partner and my other half.

I couldn't have ordered better weather if I tried. Today is absolutely perfect. A pleasant breeze filters off the lake, and not a cloud in the sky. A deep inhale of tranquility and exhale a layer of excitement.

The guys and I finished setting up the gazebo and nearby trees with lights while the ladies placed flowers and greenery all around it. Elizabeth wanted simple with no fuss. I believe we delivered.

My sister Mags pads over and brushes a kiss on my cheek. Barely showing with baby number two, she's had severe nausea and even looks a little green.

My arm settles along her shoulders. "Why don't you go sit down and rest? We have a few minutes before it starts."

She shakes her head. "It doesn't matter what I do, the nausea is still there. I can't wait to move out of this phase, it's absolutely miserable."

"I'm sorry, sis, but the end result will be worth it." I kiss her head, careful not to mess up her hair. Grace and Sloan have been busy getting all the ladies ready for the wedding, and I do not want to get in trouble for messing up their hard work.

Holding my sister close brings thoughts of Elizabeth, and the fact she will never experience all the highs and lows of pregnancy. I want to give her everything her heart desires, but some things are out of my control.

Henry, Margaret's husband, looks a little green himself as he stands hunched over next to Mags. I recently came across a story about how some men experience sympathy symptoms right along with their wives. It's called Couvade Syndrome and can be caused by empathy or even stress. It's fascinating that some men can experience what their wife feels right along with them. I bet Henry would prefer he didn't right about now.

I walk Mags over to the outside sofa on the patio. "Sit here, and I'll be right back." With a wave of my hand, I grab Henry's attention and motion for him to sit next to his wife. He doesn't have to be told twice as he makes a beeline for her.

In the kitchen, I grab a ginger ale from the fridge, and pull two glasses from the cabinet. Grace and Sloan are busy putting the finishing touches on the wedding cake. After filling the glasses with ice, I pour the ginger ale and mix in some frozen ginger cubes Elizabeth keeps in the freezer to cook with. This should help settle their stomachs.

Hannah descends the stairs as I reach the back door. When she notices my hands are full, she rushes in front of me to open the door.

"Let me get that for you." She opens the door, and I step onto the back patio.

"Thank you."

I pass Henry and Mags the glasses of cold ginger ale. They both give me a grateful smile as they sip the drinks. Mom is busy keeping their three-year-old son Luke entertained in the backyard, rolling a ball back and forth.

"Devon wanted a few minutes alone with Elizabeth before the wedding, and I thought I would come check on everything. Is there anything else that needs to be done? Is everything ready?" Hannah fidgets with a floral arrangement on the table.

"I think we're ready. The timing will be perfect. The sun will set soon, and it will bathe the lake in a golden glow."

Her lips quirk in a smile, and she pats my arm. "You're such a romantic."

Hannah gazes out across the backyard. "Elizabeth wanted simple. That definitely made things easier."

Elijah, my brother, steps up and slaps me on the back. "It's almost time, brother. How are you feeling?"

The big, cheesy grin escapes, and I don't bother trying to hide it. "I'm ready to start the first day of the rest of my life." I rub my hands together as those butterflies flutter around my stomach.

"I can't think of anyone who deserves this more than you. You've waited a long time for the right one, and I'm glad that day has finally arrived." Elijah puts his arm around my shoulder, and we do the brother hug, back slap thing.

Surrounded by those who love us, I reflect on how good and gracious God has been to me.

Grace and Sloan step outside and join us on the patio. Everyone is here, including the New Orleans team.

I check the time. We should start any moment now. I lift my hand and motion for everyone to move to the gazebo.

But just as I do, the air shifts, and the hair on the back of my neck stands on end. The dip in my stomach has me on edge. Something happened. By the looks on everyone's faces, I'm not the only one who felt it.

I holler to Dax, who's standing at the gazebo with Dad, Gage, and Arden, "I'm going upstairs to check on Elizabeth." He gives me a head nod, and they move closer to the house.

Even taking the stairs three at a time still takes too long. Before I reach the door, I already know she's gone. The void is there. A feeling I've only felt once before, and I despise it. She's left this realm, and Devon is with her.

The empty room only confirms my suspicion. Her wedding gown still lies on the bed untouched. Nothing is out of order in the room. No struggle.

What happened was supernatural.

The tinge left in the air carries a sinister intent and can only mean one thing. My hands curl into fists as they shake.

Dax pokes his head in the room as I stare at the dress. "She's gone," I mutter. "Leviathan has her." The words are like gritty sand in my mouth. My body vibrates with anger.

Dax mutters out a curse and runs back down the stairs. Exiting the room, I pull the door closed behind me. We need to come up with a plan and quickly.

Elizabeth doesn't have much time. Leviathan made it known he was coming for her. My guard was down, and I was not prepared. And that cost her dearly.

Everyone is in a huddle in the backyard waiting for me. By the worried looks on my loved ones' faces, they sense something is wrong, but they don't know what. How much should I tell them? How much am I allowed to tell them?

As I join the circle, I give Arden a questioning gaze. He gives a slight head nod, the decision is up to me.

Mom speaks first. "Do you mind telling us what is going on?"

All eyes zero in on me as they wait for me to fill them in.

"Okay, Mom. You know how there are angels and demons, but we can't see them?" My nerves are a jumbled mess as I try to explain this. Sweat breaks out on my brow.

She frowns at my question. "Of course. What does that have to do with anything?"

"Well, that's not entirely true, some of us can see them." Tension runs through my body, and I rub the back of my neck to release it.

"Yes, I'm aware of that, too. Son, what does this have to do with what's happening on your wedding day?" She's getting huffy and losing her patience with me.

A breath escapes past my lips as I brace my hands on my hips. "This is probably going to sound weird."

"Son, try me. I've been around for a long while, and you're taking too long, so just spit it out." She senses the seriousness of the situation and wants to get down to business.

Here goes nothing. "All of us at Triton Security," I wave my hand around our group. "We can see the Spirit Realm. We battle against demons and banish the darkness that threatens all of humanity."

Elijah bobs his head. "Yeah, it does sound weird."

Mom gives him the look. The one that tells him to shut it.

She shifts her attention back to me. "What does that mean for right now? What has happened?"

Her reaction to this news is surprisingly nonchalant. "Elizabeth has been taken, and we need to get her back."

Dad speaks up next. "Then what are you standing here for? Go get her."

He's right, we've got to move. "Will you please pray? We'll be back as soon as we can, but time moves differently in other realms. I don't know how long we'll be gone."

"I may not understand it, but you've got it, bro. We'll be praying." Elijah slaps me on the back, and Mom gives me a tight hug as if she's trying to infuse me with her strength.

"Let's go." Gage takes the lead.

Back in The Cave Arden steps into his role as leader. "You know for a fact Leviathan has Elizabeth?"

"Yes, sir, he has her." There was no proof, but I know that's where she is.

Arden rubs his palms down his face. "I really do not want to cross over. The darkness is relentless; there's no break from it. We need to get her out quickly. I'm assuming Devon is with her since he's not here."

"Yes, that's my assumption as well. My best guess is Leviathan created a portal using Devon, and at the right time Leviathan was able to pull the trigger and cross them over. According to something I recently discovered in one of the family journals, an object or a person can serve as a portal. I thought nothing of it at the time, but I wish I had paid more attention. I should have known Leviathan would do something underhanded like this." I cannot believe I allowed this to happen. Why wasn't I paying more attention?

Arden studies me. "That's an interesting theory. So, you believe Devon was the portal that was used to bring Elizabeth to Leviathan? I can say I did not see that one coming."

Gage paces as his anger wafts over us in waves. "This is my fault, and I take full responsibility for it. I'll get them back."

Arden folds his arms across his chest. "First, it's not your fault nor your responsibility. Second, there was nothing you could have done even if you were standing right next to him." Gage doesn't look convinced.

Arden addresses the rest of us, including Cressida and her team. "There's no way to prepare for a trip to the underworld. The terrain moves and shifts around constantly, and you can't map out a plan for that. Hell is a place of no escape for a reason. We will trust the Light to lead us home, but we need to leave now. The more time we waste, the smaller our chance becomes of rescuing her. We need to get there. Let's get dressed and load up on weapons. We leave in five. Meet up at the portal, and we'll leave from there."

Four minutes later, we're ready and waiting at the portal. A wall covered in what looks like an overgrown mirror, but once activated, turns into a substance that allows us to cross into different realms, or move to different parts of the world quickly.

Cressida's team stands at the ready, and I'm thankful for their commitment to come with us. They don't have to join us and risk their lives to bring Elizabeth home, but they wouldn't be deterred.

"This is a little tricky. We have no way of knowing exactly where we will end up when we arrive. Do your best to stay together in teams. I don't want any of us to get separated. Whatever you do, follow the Light, that's our only way back. I pray we all arrive back safely. Let's go and Godspeed."

I link arms with Grace and Sloan so the three of us will stay together. We follow right behind Arden and Gage through the portal. As soon as we cross the threshold, fierce winds tear against us, and I struggle to hold on to the girls. They are being ripped from me, but I wrap my arms tighter around them and pray I'm not squeezing too tightly.

When we land, it's hard and face first. We jump up quickly, prepared for an attack. After a few moments of standing on guard, no one else from our team arrives. We're on our own, but I like my chances with these two. We are separated from the rest of our crew, and I hope we find them soon.

Waves of heat roll around us and through us. The air is dense with the smell of death and desolation. Sulfur, a sure sign of evil, invades every breath. There's no getting away from it. No way to find relief from the onslaught. No doubt, we do not belong here.

After Grace has a look around, she asks what we're all thinking, "Where are we? And where is everyone else?"

"Excellent questions. Let's check in with the Light and see if we can get some instruction. We can't stay here. We need to move." There's no time to delay, and I ask for discernment.

The Light flares. *Go right.*

"Go right," we all say in unison. We walk across charred ground with nothing in sight. Random fires pop up as we trek across barren land but dissipate just as quickly.

Darkness weighs us down as we trudge forward, trusting the Light to guide us.

Sloan makes a hard stop. "Incoming." She whips out a mace and swings it above her head in a circle.

I wish I could pull Defender out and use it, but it doesn't belong to me. Grace and I both reach for a sword as Sloan lets the mace fly. At what, I don't know because I see nothing. Literally nothing.

The mace hits the desired mark. As it does, a mammoth-sized Fallen materializes where it was invisible before. The mace, deeply embedded in his forehead, dispatches him on contact. He falls backward and dissipates as the others with him materialize.

The Light had us go this way for a reason, but right now it feels like this was a bad idea as several demons and Fallen surround us. This is not how I pictured my wedding day.

The only thing that matters right now is finding Elizabeth and getting her home, and these demons are standing in my way.

A nasty demon, foaming at the mouth, lays its sights on me. Fine, let's do this.

I approach him with sword swinging. The demon jumps up as I run for him, and he rises above my head.

I step back to reorient and swing across as it descends, slicing clean through the midsection. The top half lands on my head, foaming mouth and all. I flip it over as it turns to ash.

Grace and Sloan do their thing and dispatch several to my one. I take the last one as they finish with two.

The demon lumbers my way on stumpy legs, and I lift my sword. He snickers and pulls out flaming arrows. I've trained against these, but have never had to actually use that training until now. That training needs to pay off today.

Faster than I can blink, the arrows fly at me. Quick as I can, I drop and roll as the arrows sail past my head. Jumping to my feet, I pop up right in front of the demon as he prepares to hurl another set of arrows. My sword slices off his wrist, and the arrows fall.

He roars in anger and leaps on top of me, tackling me to the ground. The sword gets knocked out of my hand as I wrestle the demon, working desperately to keep his teeth from my neck. Why is he so desperate to get at my neck?

He gouges my arm with a clawed hand as I flip him off me. Pain shoots through my arm as toxins from the demon pulse through my veins. Barely able to move my arm, I grab the sword with my non-dominant hand.

He stumbles to his feet as I arc the sword and slice off his head. He vanishes to dust right as I collapse on the ground.

Pain ricochets and races to every extremity. This is a new kind of agony, one I'm completely unfamiliar with on this scale.

Grace glances in my direction as she finishes off one of the damned. As soon as they're clear, she rushes over with Sloan on her heels.

"You're not looking so good," Grace says and reaches into a side pocket of her pants. "I'm guessing that was a venomous demon. I have a small vial of antivenom that should help until we can get back."

Oh, thank you, Lord. I want to say it out loud, but don't think I can. My jaw clenches tight against the pain.

"You need to drink this, but you're gonna have to open your mouth." Grace places the miniature bottle to my lips, but I can't seem to open my mouth. Every muscle clenches tight at the surge of toxins trying to kill me.

Pounding feet approach from the distance, but I'm in no condition to fight. Sloan jumps up and flips around to face off with whoever is coming, her sword poised to strike. "It's the rest of our team. They're here." She drops her arm but remains alert.

Grace squishes my cheeks together with one hand to part my lips and pours the contents from the vial with the other, determined to get the antivenom in. I work my tongue to swallow down the liquid, praying it gets where it needs to go. The horrid substance burns as it goes down.

The clatter of feet gets closer as our team arrives.

"How bad is it?" Roz asks and drops to my side.

"A venomous demon got him. Grace had some antivenom and just gave it to Mark." Sloan provides the answer while keeping an eye out for trouble. I couldn't respond even if I wanted to.

"We need to get you back to The Cave. We can split up. I'll take you back while the rest of the team finds Elizabeth." Roz places her hand on my shoulder.

A gurgled reply is all that comes out. I try to shake my head in response. Roz better not transport me back.

"Ungh, unt oing ack," is all I can manage with a jaw unmoving like granite.

"I think he just said, 'No, not going back'," Grace translates for me. I knew I liked her. That's why she's my favorite.

"ess." I try a head nod. It doesn't work.

"Mark, you can't be serious. You can't even move. We can't carry you around." Roz narrows her eyes.

Gage folds his arms across his chest. "I don't care what you do, but I'm not carrying you. If you can't walk, I'll leave you here." That I believe.

Arden steps into my line of sight. "I know what you're thinking. You want to be here for Elizabeth and bring her home, but Roz is right. You can't move. You're a liability."

"us, ive e a inute." I glance at Grace for her to translate.

"He said, 'Just give me a minute.'" Grace pats my shoulder in solidarity. Everyone stares at me like I'm crazy. Sloan stands guard with Tyler and Sookie next to her.

Once I'm able to relax for a moment, I realize my muscles aren't as tense. Testing out my fingers and toes, I give them a wiggle. Finally, I can move.

My jaw loosens just enough so I can reply on my own. "I'm not going back without Elizabeth. I abandoned her once, and I'm not doing it again." My voice gurgles, but it's working. Sort of.

"You did not abandon her. We were all knocked out by a supernatural detonation. There wasn't anything you could do." Dax tries to reason with me.

"It doesn't matter. It felt like I abandoned her, and I won't do that again." My words come out a little slurred, but I'm doing much better than I was a few moments ago.

"And Gage, I don't want you to carry me. I'd rather crawl through hell."

"You just might get your wish," Gage snickers and walks in the direction we were going before our fight with the demons.

Good, as long as he doesn't get any ideas.

It takes a few more minutes, but I manage to get on all fours and then wobble to a standing position. Arden and Dax stand on either side, ready to brace me if I need it. I think I can get by on my own as long as no more demons attack us right this minute.

Sloan and Arden take the lead, following after Gage. "Does he know where he's going?" Sloan asks Arden.

Arden nods. "This is the direction the Light was leading us when we found you."

"The Light was leading us as well." Grace twirls a sword and walks with me at a slow amble. She doesn't seem to mind. Paxton slows his walk and comes alongside her.

Dax and Roz, with Cressida and Sookie, follow behind us to be our cover. It's not great, but I'm up and walking. It's progress, and it's getting us that much closer to Elizabeth.

We tread through intense heat along scorched land. The light here is dim, making it hard to see. A dead tree, with its broken arms, leans to the side as if abandoned and long forgotten.

There's no sign of where Elizabeth could be, but until the Light gives us further direction, this is the path we follow.

Grace studies me as she twirls her sword. "You're looking better. Still a little green, but you're not dead. So, definite improvement."

"I didn't thank you for saving my life back there, but thank you. I'm glad you had the antivenom." My arm hangs uselessly at my side as I limp along.

She shrugs a shoulder. "I figured one of us should carry Elizabeth's first aid kit. It's a good thing we have it. Hopefully, we won't need it again." She pats the pocket carrying the medical kit.

"I agree. We need to find Elizabeth and get out of here. This is not where I want to spend my wedding day."

"That's right, I totally forgot that was today. It feels like it was yesterday. Man, that sucks to be stuck in hell on your wedding day." Grace giggles, and I can't help myself, I laugh with her. Dax and Roz join in, but it doesn't last.

The Light flares in warning before the nightmare continues.

Chapter 10

Eliabeth

The foul stench of hell scorches my nostrils and churns my stomach while I gasp for breath. Uncle Devon hangs suspended midair, his face turning red. Nothing visible holds him, only the presence of evil. There's nothing physical to attack. Leviathan isn't even in here with us, only his manifest presence. His form, or what I can make of it, lies beyond the cell doors.

"I have no need of you. Your usssefulnesss hasss run out." Leviathan tosses him like a broken toy against the dungeon wall. He slides to the ground, limp and unmoving.

A groan escapes as I place one hand underneath and push myself up. Everything hurts.

There has got to be a way to get us out of here. I have no intention of staying here to be used as target practice. Not that I think Leviathan plans on keeping me alive for long.

He's made it clear he no longer needs Uncle Devon. Can I buy us enough time to come up with a plan?

No, I can't. I have no way of getting us out of here on my own.

I need the Light.

Lord, I know you see me, see us. Please help us get out of this mess, or show me the way of escape. Help me keep Uncle Devon alive long enough for us to get out of here. And thank you I'm not alone, You are with me. Don't let me forget that.

Peace washes over me. As I look around, my situation hasn't changed, but a flicker of hope has taken root. I refuse to die here.

Leviathan's attention shifts to me. "I'll be back, my sssweet. I have big plansss for you."

He vanishes in a puff of smoke, leaving us to choke on it.

No longer distracted by Leviathan, my attention shifts to Uncle Devon. He's deathly still, and I can't tell if he's breathing.

Leaning down, I gently place my hand on his chest. It moves but barely, and his breathing is shallow.

"Uncle Devon, can you hear me?" He groans, and his eyes flutter open. He attempts a deep breath but coughs violently instead, his whole body shaking with the effort.

"We need to get out of here." I help him into a sitting position and lean him against the wall.

"There's no way out. Believe me, I spent years trying." He shakes his head and weeps. I don't know that I've ever seen him cry. There's a brokenness in it that leaves me feeling vulnerable.

I can't imagine the despair he must be feeling, but I can't afford to think that way.

The iron bars in front of me mock our position as prisoners and taunt our helpless state of affairs. Darkness, nothing but darkness on the other side. No sound. No light.

If there are other prisoners here, I can't see or hear them.

I place my hands against the bars and then leap back with a yelp. The bars are scorching hot and leave a red line in the center of both palms. Blowing on them to relieve the pain, I wonder if Defender could slice through them. It doesn't matter. I don't have Defender with me, and I still don't know how to pull it from the ether.

"Hey, Uncle Devon, do you think you could pull Defender from the ether?"

His gaze finds mine. "I can try. For you. But it never worked for me when I was here before. I couldn't transport myself out, and I couldn't pull anything from the ether. It was as if a force was blocking all my attempts."

"Can you walk me through what I need to do? I've never done it before." This is the time that particular skill would come in handy.

He takes a careful breath before responding. The way his breath hitches gives me concern. I pray his ribs aren't broken. "Close your eyes." I follow his instruction.

"Now picture Defender in your mind, floating in front of you. Once you get a solid vision of it, reach out and grab it."

I close my eyes and picture Defender, the blade already aflame. A smile lifts at the corners of my mouth as I picture my saber. God knew what He was doing when He paired me with the sword.

I reach out to touch it but grab only air. It's so strange; it was right there, right in front of me, but I couldn't grab it. My eyes pop open.

"Don't be upset. I was never able to pull anything from the ether while I was here either." He leans his head back against the wall and closes his eyes.

It seems easy enough, which makes me wonder why Mark never tried to teach me how to pull Defender from the ether.

I'll keep working on it. I'm not giving up hope.

"Were you able to connect with the Light while you were here?" I ask him. Thinking of how I connected with the Light just a moment ago. I'm not cut off from it.

He regards me, his face a reflection of embarrassment and shame. "I never tried to connect with the Light. I figured it was what I deserved—winding up here. It was all my fault, every bit of it. I couldn't pray because I knew I didn't deserve God's help."

"Wow, that's pretty harsh. I don't believe for a moment it was God punishing you. You cut yourself off from Him and from any help."

He shakes his head as a smile plays on his lips. "And He still rescued me . . . through you. And He used the very thing I was trying to save you from. I was foolish and stupid. Thought I could do it on my own. All I proved was that I need Him more than the air I breathe, and I can't do a thing on my own, even to save myself."

"At least you figured that out, and you're not trying to do it on your own now." I tilt my head and narrow my eyes. "Or are you? Have you connected with the Light?"

He looks down at his hands in his lap. "Not yet, but not because I don't want to. I'm going to do that now." He closes his eyes, and I look away to give him a moment.

A scratching noise comes from the corner of the room. A dark-gray fur ball scurries from a hole. Before I let out a scream, I recognize the sarcastic sidekick that's supposed to be my guide.

"Well, you sure got yourself in a pickle this time." Tiger glides her body next to mine and rubs against my legs, then sits at my feet.

"Uh, Elizabeth? When did you get a talking cat?" Uncle Devon's eyes are wide with shock.

"Oh, you can hear her? Good, that will make this easier. Uncle Devon, meet Tiger. She's my guide." She regards him with what looks like boredom, but who knows what she's thinking right now.

"I've never seen an actual guide. I've read about them but have never met one. Didn't even know they still existed." His mouth falls open, and he stares at Tiger as if in awe. He shouldn't be. She's sarcastic and not as big of a help as one would think.

Her being here could go either way.

But she's here. If she got in, she should be able to get us out. "Can you help us get out of here?"

She stares at me for several moments before responding. "You'll get out of here, but it might get a little dicey."

She just arrived, and she's already testing my patience. I take a deep breath and let it out slowly. So basically, she'll help, but not directly. This I'm familiar with.

Can we just get out of here? I have no desire to learn another lesson. Mark is waiting for me, and I need to get home to him so we can get married and live our lives.

"We will get out of here. I have a wedding to get to."

Uncle Devon takes his eyes off of Tiger. "I'll do whatever I can to help you. You've proven that an impossible situation is never hopeless."

Footsteps echo off the stone walls and cause a shiver to ripple down my spine. I don't think for a moment it's a crew to rescue us. If this is our rescue, I would hope they would be more stealthy than that.

Several Fallen appear on the other side of the bars. One peels away from the group and approaches with a key as Uncle Devon struggles to his feet. If we have to fight our way out of this, he won't be much help.

Subtly, I place my hand on his back and force healing to flow. We don't have much time as the Fallen unlocks the door. Uncle Devon gasps as power surges from my hand into his body, providing healing and strength.

"Follow me." The Fallen who unlocked the door swings it open and motions for us to step out. I look back for Tiger, but she's already gone.

"Are you our escort out of here?" I know the truth, but it doesn't hurt to ask. "I'm sure this was all a case of mistaken identity, and we are now free to go." I give him my best smile.

He looks in my direction but doesn't answer. The rest of the Fallen surround us to prevent our escape.

I'm not stupid. On my very best day, I'm no match for a highly trained assembly of Fallen.

My shoulders slump, and I follow without making a scene. We make several turns down one darkened corridor after another. I try to memorize the turns at the beginning, but I think they're going out of their way to confuse me.

Everything looks the same – dark stone walls, dark stone floors, dim lighting. Probably makes it easier to camouflage the blood.

Nervous anxiety settles in my stomach and bounces around like a tiny toddler on a sugar rush. Whatever is coming next will most likely be horrifying and will border on the line of painful.

The Fallen in front of me opens a large wooden door and walks through first. I'm shoved from behind and lose my balance but catch myself before face-planting on the floor. Uncle Devon moves to help me up, but he's rammed from the side into the wall.

With a grunt, Uncle Devon rights himself and follows behind me, not wanting to leave my side for a second, no matter how much pain he may be in.

We're led into a large open rotunda. Unlike the dungeon, the veined marble floor shines, and the dome ceiling, several stories high, features light blue paint with gold accents. I'm not sure what I expected, but this wasn't it.

A female Fallen, something I've never seen before, yanks my arm and moves me to the center of the room. The two remaining Fallen who brought us here are holding Uncle Devon back.

Not liking the way this is playing out, I yank my arm back trying to remove her hold but get shoved to the floor. Not sure why I thought that would work.

I manage to catch myself with my hands before I hit the floor with my face. My wrists scream out in pain as they catch my fall again.

She yanks me up by my hair as a panel in the wall opens and an attractive man wearing a navy suit swaggers into the space. My jaw clenches against the scream that threatens to escape, but I refuse to give her the satisfaction of hearing me cry.

The instant his deep blue eyes meet mine, a chill snakes up my spine. I stare back, every instinct screaming danger. This is no ordinary man. His eyes, devoid of all humanity, pin me where I stand as he assesses my frame. He blinks, and for a moment his eyes change to those of a predator. Another blink, and they go back to blue. A shiver runs through me.

He adjusts the sleeves of his jacket and straightens his tie. "This will not do." His deep timber reaches my ears and snakes through my head. His voice glides like oil laced with poison. "We must have something she can wear."

I look down and realize I'm still in my white satin robe, now stained with dirty smudges. I'm completely underdressed for this meeting in my bare feet.

"Eliana, fetch her the battle leathers. After all, I'm nothing if not fair." That dark smirk says differently.

Fair is not a quality that will ever describe him.

Standing before me is Leviathan. He shed the monstrous dragon form and reshaped himself to appear human. It doesn't change who he really is or how deadly he can be.

I have no weapons. Nothing to defend myself with. Nothing to fight with. Whatever he has planned will be anything but fair.

Eliana returns and strides forward with a bundle in her hand. She drops it on the floor in front of me and focuses her attention on Leviathan, completely ignoring me.

"That will be all. You may go back." Leviathan dismisses her with a slight nod, and she retreats to the wall to stand guard.

My gaze lands on the bundle lying on the floor. "Where should I change?" I won't lie, I'm glad I can get out of this thin robe and put some clothes on. I am entirely too exposed.

Leviathan's eyes fill with unmistakable hunger. "Right here, of course."

Yes, of course. I should have seen that one coming.

"Don't tell me you're shy. You have no reason to be embarrassed. Come now, don't you want to be more comfortable?" He raises his arms as if he's harmless.

Fully clothed? Yes. Undress in front of everyone? No.

I lift the ensemble from the floor. Buttery soft leather glides along my fingertips. Silky soft. Not gonna lie, this is nice. I take hold of the pants and slide them on underneath the robe. Every eye watches in rapt attention.

The smooth pants fit loosely, but I won't complain. Loops and pockets line each side of the pants. Maybe for storage, hiding weapons, or snacks. Pockets just don't get the recognition they deserve. I pat the pockets to check for any hidden items I can use, but unfortunately they are empty.

The shirt has leather ties, but I have no idea whether the ties are for the front or the back. I shrug my shoulder. It doesn't matter.

I slide the shirt on over my robe and lace it in the front. The bottom of my robe hangs over the pants, making it look like I layered a skirt over the pants.

I'm not mad about it. I'm not here to make a fashion statement. Battle leathers with a satin skirt. It could work.

I face Leviathan and throw out my arms. "Okay, I'm here and I'm dressed. What do you want?"

With a slight shake of his head, his gaze caresses my hip, and it's as if his own hand touched me. I cringe in disgust. "That was highly disappointing," he says with a mock scowl.

He continues to stare as I shiver uncomfortably in the middle of the room, every eye on me.

"Right. Yes, let's get on with it. I have a gift for you."

"You have a gift for me?" Pretty sure his idea of a gift and my idea of a gift are two very different things. "Why? Your ultimate goal is to kill me."

"My goal is to stop your interference in my agenda, and I intend to have some fun with you before I end you. I'm in no hurry. You could be of some use to me." He glides around me in a circle with the grace of a predator stalking its prey.

Not good. I need to figure out how to get out of here, and fast.

Leviathan lifts his hand in the air and as he brings it down, an orb materializes and descends in front of me. The orb expands, smoothing into the form of an oval-shaped door. It settles on the ground, and a picture appears from within the orb.

Before me is the scene of a house, I'm all too familiar with, and my stomach drops as old wounds resurface. The front door holds a cheery wreath, and colorful flowers sit nestled in the flower bed. None of which was there the last time I was. The home is cozy and inviting . . . perfect for a family.

The door opens, and two young boys run out onto the front yard chasing each other. A chocolate lab bounces close behind, giving chase.

A beautiful woman with red wavy hair, wearing a button-up shirt over blue jeans, steps onto the porch. She glows as she watches the boys, and places both hands on her rounded bump, absentmindedly caressing it.

Samantha. My breath hitches.

Long-buried feelings emerge and well up to suffocate the beautiful life I now have. The pain of betrayal inches its way out of the tightly sealed box hidden in the crevices of my mind and threatens to swallow me whole.

The story before me is such a beautiful reminder of what I can never have. Two relationships irreparably damaged by betrayal. The pain of wasted years with nothing to show for it except tragic heartache.

As if the picture before me is not enough of a reminder of everything I lost, Lucas steps out onto the porch with a kitchen towel slung over his shoulder. He steps behind Samantha and wraps his arms lovingly around her belly. He bends down to kiss her neck. She tilts her head to give him better access and laughs as he kisses his way up her jaw.

Bile rises in my throat as I watch the life I was supposed to have unfold before me. That's my life. She stole my life.

I thought I dealt with all of this. Thought I had moved on. Thought I had forgiven them. If I did, then why does this feel like I'm being boiled alive?

Something drips onto my hand. When I look down, I realize I'm crying.

"You know, revenge is always sweet. Want to level the playing field a bit?" Leviathan's velvety voice cuts into my tormented thoughts.

I jerk around, having completely forgotten I'm not alone. Every single one of my emotions has been laid bare, exposed to everyone's scrutinizing gaze.

I swipe my hands across my face, furious at Leviathan for showing me this. I was perfectly fine not knowing what their lives are like.

"What are you talking about?"

He tilts his head toward the story that continues to play out in front of me. "I have the power to change their course. Don't you want to pay them back for what they did to you? A little vengeance always makes me feel better." He slides a hand down the front of his suit.

"No, I just want you to turn this off!" I wave a hand at the scene. "They can have whatever life they want." I shift my gaze away from the orb filled with crushed dreams. That's all it is. A bitter reminder I don't need or want.

Facing away from the orb, I don't see what happens next as a scream cries out and echoes through the room. I jerk around and watch as Samantha doubles over while Lucas tries to help her back into the house. The boys come running at the sound. They begin to cry and race inside.

The orb dissipates as Samantha's screams pierce the air.

"What did you do?" My anger at Leviathan takes over as I flip around.

"Oh, just a little gift for you. A welcome present to help settle your nerves." A smug look settles on his face, and he peers down at his shiny gold watch. "Well, I hate to cut our meeting short, but I have somewhere I need to be. I trust you will find your way back to your room." He vanishes as I lunge for his throat. The rest of the Fallen disappear with him.

I bend over and empty the contents of my stomach onto the gleaming floor. My body shakes as I heave again. Backing away from the mess I just made, I scan the room.

Uncle Devon is the only one left.

As I take a wobbly step in his direction, I shake my head. "He annihilated me without using a single weapon. There was no way for me to defend myself against that. We can't stay here. We have to find a way out." Exhaustion seeps through my pores, and legs like spaghetti noodles refuse to hold me. I collapse at his feet and fall apart in a messy puddle.

His arms wrap around my shaky frame as I purge the torment of this latest encounter with Leviathan.

Uncle Devon. I've missed his hugs, and I've missed his friendship. Arms so familiar it's easy to fall back into the habit of allowing him to provide comfort.

I'm not angry with him, but I don't know how to get past this broken trust between us.

Regaining my composure, I look up at Uncle Devon and see concern in his eyes.

"Thank you. I'm okay, I promise." He helps me to my feet and keeps his arm around my waist until I'm steady on my own.

He motions to the empty room. "They left us here with no guards."

Yeah, the space is empty, but why? "Either we're trapped with no way out, or he knows we have no chance because the exits are locked. Either way, I have no intention of staying put."

But as I walk to the spot where we entered, the door isn't there. I turn around in a slow circle and look for any door, but there is none. Only smooth, solid stone walls surround us.

"Do you remember where we entered?" I ask Uncle Devon as he lays his hand against the wall.

"It was right here." He motions to the space in front of him.

I close my eyes and rub my forehead. There's a way out. I just don't know what it is.

I rub my hands along the wall in front of me, looking for some sort of hidden door, as Uncle Devon does the same.

"Elizabeth, you know that was never supposed to be your life." His voice echoes across the room. "This is where you were always meant to be. Well, not here in this room exactly. But you know what I mean."

I face him as he stops looking for a way of escape. There must be a confused look on my face, so he continues. "You said, 'That's my life. She stole my life.'. But I wanted you to know that it's not."

"I didn't realize I said that part out loud. That entire scene was unexpected, and I guess some of those old feelings are still there. I don't regret for a second where I'm at right now. Well, not here right at this moment but here in this part of my life as a Light Bearer."

He meets me back where we started. "As long as you know you're worthy of so much more than that. Your life is so much bigger than that life would have ever been."

"I know it is. I love Mark and our life together. Sometimes I wonder why he loves me and wants to be with me, but I'm not stupid enough to walk away."

Uncle Devon places his hand on my shoulder. "I've seen the way he looks at you. He loves you and would do anything you asked him to."

"Yep, and that's why we need to get out of here. Knowing him, he's probably killing himself to get here and rescue me."

Tiger pops in front of me, scaring me so badly I almost tinkle. "Ugh, a warning would be nice!"

"Where's the fun in that? Never mind, don't answer that. Come on, follow me." She presses her paw against the wall, and a portion depresses and pops out. A size large enough for a person to fit through opens up. "I've found a way out."

Without question, I follow her out of the dome-shaped room that now smells like vomit. The floor isn't so shiny anymore. A small smile escapes at the thought of Leviathan losing his marbles over the mess on the floor.

Chapter 11

Mark

Everything else fades away as she strides confidently in my direction, golden hair blowing behind her as if in slow motion. It's like watching one of those shampoo commercials. She's a beauty dressed in battle leathers, my warrior bride. Her golden light glows brilliantly against the darkness.

As soon as she spots me, her grin blossoms and she races toward me. Thankful to have found her so quickly, my pace picks up to meet her. Still a little slow after that round with the demon, but I move as quickly as I can.

Now we need to find a way out, and I only pray we can return home safe.

Her eyes shimmer as she nears. In fact, all of her shimmers. My smile grows into a laugh as I reach her. If God is the very air that I breathe, she's my heartbeat.

Almost to her, she pulls out a dagger as I close in. I flip around to catch the threat behind me but see nothing except our team.

Confused, I turn back to face her, intending to find out where the threat is coming from.

The smile on her face morphs to a sneer as she plunges the dagger into my chest.

It doesn't register at first. The smile I so proudly wore slips in disbelief. I peer down at the dagger in confusion, then back up to Elizabeth and see the sneer still firmly in place. Pain blooms outward from the dagger still firmly planted in my chest.

"Oh, I'm not done yet." She draws out a sword, spins around, then swings it at my head with all the finesse of a ballet dancer.

Before I even comprehend what I'm doing, I grab a sword from the ether and block the blow before she detaches my head.

Finally, coming to my senses, I yank out the dagger and let out a yell. "What are you doing? I'm here to rescue you!"

She hisses in disgust, "I don't need to be rescued. As a matter of fact, I don't need you at all. You are nothing but a distraction, and I don't have time for distractions."

Her rejection hits its mark. My heart stutters in my chest, and a different sort of pain takes over. I know she doesn't need me, but I at least thought she wanted me. Thought she wanted us to spend our lives together.

Doesn't she know I would do anything for her? Give her anything she asked?

She takes another swing with the sword that I manage to block, but barely. I have no intention of causing her harm, but she has got to stop trying to kill me. Why doesn't she understand I'm here to help her?

The Elizabeth I know would never act like this. She's not cruel or unkind.

Suddenly, understanding hits me with stunning force, like an anvil dropped from above. This isn't Elizabeth. She would never do something like this.

In the distance, a frantic yell cuts through the air. "It's an illusion! Open your eyes!"

The Light flares to gain my attention as the scene vanishes before me, and it's one of the Fallen that stands before me. Not Elizabeth. "I see you finally figured it out. I was convinced I could finish you off before you realized what was happening. Nothing stings quite like the sting of betrayal. Am I right?"

Anger at the distraction preventing me from finding Elizabeth flares hot and rages inside me.

Anger that I'm here instead of kissing my bride at the altar.

Anger at Leviathan for taking her from me.

Anger at the Fallen standing before me.

Hotter and brighter it burns until it's all I feel. Rage seizes me tightly in its grip with each passing heartbeat.

I grab another sword from the ether and face off with the Fallen. One sword in each hand. "Enough!" I shout as I twirl the twin swords like Sloan.

With a flick of his wrist, the Fallen's sword bursts into flames, reminding me of Defender.

My fingers tighten their hold, and the Light within flares.

The Fallen's sword arcs through the air and whips across, but I block with one sword and plunge the other in his midsection. It's not enough to dispatch him, but it catches him off guard.

And that's all the opening I need to swing the other sword, but he's quick and blocks it before I make contact. I kick him in the abdomen, right where I stabbed him. He lets out a howl that vibrates right through me, making my very bones shudder.

He's angry and wounded. I can work with that. I've trained angry and wounded, so I anticipate his next move.

He lunges forward with his foot while he swings the sword, aiming for my neck. I duck as the sword flies past. Both swords held firmly in hand, I jump up and cross them to remove his head. The slice is clean, and his head falls to the ground as the Fallen turns to ash.

I spin around, and each of my team members are in various stages of their own fight. All holding their own. I slide in next to Arden, who is closest to me, and help him finish the Fallen he battles against.

As a pair, we defeat the Fallen, and he vanishes. The others dispatch each enemy they are fighting, putting an end to this latest attack against us.

No, the Fallen aren't destroyed forever. They are immortal after all. But it will take time for them to regenerate and get back to fighting force.

Covered in gore, exhausted, and shaken, but not defeated. I'm not the only one sporting fresh wounds. My legs quiver and give out as I collapse to the ground. The adrenaline of seeing Elizabeth has worn off. The anger has subsided, and now I sit in a heap feeling hollow and spent in every way.

I'm no closer to Elizabeth than I was when we first arrived. Time we don't have is being wasted. Leviathan won't lose any time ending her life. Every moment that ticks by brings Elizabeth closer to her last breath, and I can't let that happen.

“Here,” a voice says, and the cool metal of a canteen touches my palm. Grace holds it out for me to take. "You need to hydrate. Your body is still trying to heal itself."

"Where did you get the water?"

"Stashed it in my cargo pants. That's what all these pockets are for." She pats the various pockets, and they jingle with whatever else she's stuffed in there.

"We'll find her. We didn't come all this way to leave empty-handed." Dax crouches next to me as he guzzles his own water. "Here, let me look at your chest. We need to make sure the wound isn't too deep."

He moves my shirt to the side and takes a cloth from Grace to wipe away the blood. "I'm no doctor, but I've seen worse. It looks shallow enough, but you can't stay here much longer. You need medical attention."

"I'm fine." My jaw clenches as I take the cloth he's holding and press it against my chest. I have to be fine. I'm not leaving without her.

Arden remains off to the side, separate from the group. He's visibly shaken and trying to pull himself together. I roll onto all fours and push myself off the ground. Dax gives me his arm and helps me to my feet.

"Give me just a moment," I whisper to him, then nod my head in thanks.

Stepping next to Arden, I place my hand on his shoulder. "You okay?"

His head swivels in my direction, eyes filled with indescribable grief. "It was Griffin. He was back from the dead, or so I thought. For a moment I had him back, and he was with me—until he tried to kill me. It took me longer than it should have to figure it out." Shaking his head, his gaze drifts to the desolate landscape stretching before us.

I can't imagine the turmoil of emotions he's experiencing right now. The overwhelming heartache of losing Griffin all over again. The reminder that he isn't coming back, and there's nothing Arden can do about it.

"We need to keep moving." Sloan's voice slices through the pain to our present reality, and Sookie's gaze scans the horizon watching for another attack. "These distractions are meant to undermine our resolve and prevent us from being vigilant. Leviathan wants us to second-guess our actions and not trust our instincts. We can't afford to fall for his traps. We need to keep going in the direction the Light instructed."

Arden and I join the rest of the group, ready to finish this.

"Did everyone see someone they love?" Cressida's voice rings hollow. Heads nod all around. Except for Sloan, she looks away, jaw clenched.

She stalks off and marches on with Grace by her side. If she was shaken by what she encountered, she won't show it.

We follow on like good little soldiers, stuffing down the swell of emotions that rocked each of us to our core. No amount of training prepares you for what we just experienced.

Arden and I walk side by side in companionable silence. Paxton leaves Tyler at the front of our group and joins my other side. He doesn't say a word, simply stays by my side. A silent figure of strength.

I'm mentally and physically drained. The stakes are high, and there's a real possibility we won't make it out of here alive.

We press onward with no other encounters, and my thoughts slowly drift away. I'm not sure whether I'm awake or dreaming. Every muscle in my body aches, making it difficult to do anything at all.

"I like what you did back there with the double swords. It's a good move." Sloan's voice startles me. I don't know when she started walking next to me, or when Arden moved in front to lead with Cressida and Tyler. I must have zoned out.

"Yeah, thanks for showing me that. It came in handy."

Grace slows down and moves to my other side, next to Paxton. "You don't look as green as you did. That's an improvement." That may be a compliment. Paxton nods in my direction, leaving me with Grace and Sloan, and joins Tyler near the front.

She gives me a closer look. "And you're sweating. That's a good sign. Your body is getting rid of the toxins."

Of course I'm sweating—we're all sweating. The heat is killing off brain cells the longer we stay here.

Arden holds up his hand for us to stop. When we do the Light flares.

Lord, please help us find Elizabeth and get out of here. I don't think I can handle another encounter with the Fallen.

Before us looms a dark, foreboding mountain, its shadow stretching out ominously. Somehow, I failed to notice the mountain that stands directly in front of us.

Sharp, pointy peaks reach into nothingness as barren as everything else. Every place on the mountain has razor-sharp points, and there's no crossing over it.

Arden pulls out his sword as an object emerges from the base of the mountain. A shape that looks oddly familiar.

A groan escapes as I withdraw my sword.

God, you have got to give me a break here. How am I supposed to do this?

With sweaty, shaky hands, I watch as Elizabeth's form materializes like a dream. Or what appears to be her form. No way am I falling for that again.

Blinking my eyes and shaking my head, I attempt to clear my vision and focus on the Light. A warning doesn't come, but I can't let my guard down even for a moment.

Nothing is as it seems in this place. Or maybe I'm disoriented with the venom still running through my system. It's as if it's a living thing trying to destroy me from the inside out. It's clawing and scraping away from the surface, desperately trying to hang on and complete its task.

I'm thankful Grace had the foresight to bring the medical kit and include the antivenom. Death would have been a guarantee otherwise.

Normally, it would be Elizabeth carrying the medical kit, and that thought brings a tightness to my already aching chest, making it hard to breathe.

With unsteady movements, I brace myself for the attack that's coming. Planning to go on the offensive and not wait for it to come to me, I step past Arden. He reaches out to stop me, but I shake off his hand.

"Mark, stop! You need to wait just a moment. Let's assess the situation before making any moves."

Elizabeth spots me as I step around Arden, delight and relief on her face when her eyes meet mine. "It really is you. I thought my mind was playing tricks on me."

She runs for me, but I lift the sword ready for the attack. Her steps falter as she catches my expression. She glances around our team in confusion. "What's going on?"

Devon emerges behind her with Tiger on his heels. This vision is more elaborate than the last one.

"Anyone else seeing what I'm seeing? Or is it just me?" I ask my fellow teammates.

Grace tilts her head to the side. "I see Elizabeth, Devon, and a cat. Why would her cat be here? Is this another counterfeit creation?"

They don't know Elizabeth has a guide. They assume this is just an ordinary cat.

If Tiger is here, maybe this is real. But how can I be certain?

Elizabeth takes a tentative step forward as Devon walks beside her. "Seriously, guys, what is going on? Why are you looking at me like that?"

Roz motions her arm around. "Let's just say that our last encounter was not a pleasant one. We're a little wary this will be another attack."

Elizabeth shakes her head. "I know what you mean. What I just went through was unpleasant at best. I have my doubts that we were simply permitted to leave on our own. It's too easy."

Arden nods his head. "It's probably a trap. Let's form a circle facing out to protect our backs. Everyone arm yourselves as we attempt to transport out of here."

"We don't have any weapons," Elizabeth says as her gaze pierces mine.

The last thing I want to do is hand her a weapon, especially Defender. We must prevent the Fallen from getting their hands on that weapon.

I still don't trust she's not part of the trap. Since I can't trust my own thoughts right now, I look to Arden for guidance.

Tiger walks up to me. "This is real. I was able to show them the way out, but I can't get all of you back home on my own."

Sookie stares at the cat, then looks at me. She moves her hand back and forth between us. "What's this? What's going on here?"

The sigh escapes me before I can rein it in. Everything is exhausting. "Elizabeth has a guide. This is her guide, Tiger." I pinch the bridge of my nose to prevent the oncoming headache I can feel building.

Sloan steps next to me to get a closer look. "You mean to tell me she's had a guide this whole time and none of us knew? Do you know how big that is? Not just anyone gets a guide. Only a privileged few ever get to see one." Sloan rarely exhibits anything but restrained hostility. That she's in awe over this is substantial. I should take note of this moment, I may never see it again.

With an air of excitement, Sloan steps toward Tiger. "Don't even think about it." Tiger sticks her tail in the air and raises her head.

Sloan stops her advance, but the excitement doesn't leave her face. She and Tiger stare off with each other, completely oblivious to their surroundings and that we need to find a way out of here. Now.

"This is so dope. I want one." Grace bounces beside me.

"Can we please get out of here? I'm trying not to pass out, but it's getting harder to stay upright. And can someone give Elizabeth and Devon a weapon? I still don't trust that this isn't a trap, and I'm not handing over Defender to just anyone."

Elizabeth tilts her head and observes me. "What happened to you? Why are you about to pass out?"

Grace points her finger in my direction. "Demon venom."

She lets out a groan and steps toward me. I step back, away from the intended embrace, just as she reaches for me. Her eyes widen, and she blinks rapidly.

If this really is Elizabeth, it's not my intention to hurt her. Never my intent, but how do I know she's real? Everything is jumbled in my mind, and I can't think clearly.

Sloan passes over a weapon to both Devon and Elizabeth. After they have their weapons firmly in hand, we form a circle facing outward.

"I want everyone to focus on transporting back to The Cave. We need to get out of here as one unit. Don't let your guard down until we've made it back home."

And because I know it won't be that easy—Fallen descend in front of us. A man wearing a suit shrouded in darkness steps out to address us. Evil drips from his pores, and for just a moment his eyes give a glimpse of the predator that lies underneath.

"Now, now, why are you in such a hurry to leave my humble hospitality? You haven't seen all I have to offer. The fun is only just beginning." He lifts his hands out to his sides in mock humility.

As one, the Fallen launch into the air to attack our small group. We are hopelessly outnumbered and no match against the force they wield. We have no choice but to face off against their assault.

Realizing it's going to take more than what we have, I heave a sigh as I reluctantly pull Defender from the ether and hand it to Elizabeth, all while using my dominant hand to fight off the Fallen. This gesture could completely backfire, but what choice do we have?

Anything less than all of us getting out of here alive is not an option.

She slides next to me and focuses her attention on the man who strides forward. Wrong. Not a man. Evil incarnate.

With a flick of her wrist, Defender flares to life as flames engulf the blade. Drawn to the desire of wanting a flaming sword of my own, it's not until I feel the sword slice through my skin that I realize my eyes were on her and not on the fight in front of me.

The Fallen leaps into the air as I raise my sword, slicing clean into his midsection. Elizabeth directs the flame of Defender at the man in the suit, who deftly moves out of the way, laughing at her attempt. He's completely unfazed by the threat she wields.

One of the Fallen steps in between Defender's flame and Leviathan and gets fried, turning to ash. The Light flares, bringing my attention back to the other Fallen right before he thrusts his sword clean through my heart. I evade the blow and counter with one of my own. Power from the Light surges, lending me strength. That burst of power is all I need to finish the Fallen before me, and he vanishes in a puff of smoke.

Keeping one eye on the Fallen and another on Elizabeth, or who I sincerely hope is Elizabeth, I plead for divine help. It's the only way we're going to make it out alive.

Pulling out another sword, I fight off two of the Fallen and soon find myself overwhelmed. My strength, which I've come to rely on, is waning.

A Fallen catches Elizabeth unguarded, slicing his sword across her middle. And I'm not even paying attention to the two Fallen in front of me as they both swing for my head.

Chapter 12

Elizabeth

Leviathan steps out from behind the Fallen when they take flight, giving us a brief reprieve before the attack. His gaze devours my courage, and I shrivel in fear under his scrutiny. That one sneer leaves no question–he wants me to suffer.

We're completely outnumbered, and my only job is to incapacitate Leviathan. But without Defender, I'm at a tremendous disadvantage, and the fight is futile.

With only the short sword Sloan handed me, I barely block the blow aimed for my head as a Fallen descends directly in front of me. Without Defender, my defensive moves are sloppy at best and will most likely get me killed. I block a sword to the chest, but it still slices my arm. A yelp escapes, and I drop the sword. With another sword swinging for my head, I drop and roll away.

As if Mark finally understands the severity of the situation unfolding, he reluctantly withdraws Defender and hands it to me. His stiff demeanor leaves me confused. It's so unlike him, and I can't help but feel the influence of Leviathan at work.

He's taken the sweet man who loves me and turned him into someone who looks at me as if he doesn't know me. Almost as if he's afraid of me. And I'm not sure how to respond to that, but it's a problem for later . . . if we make it out of here alive.

The immediate need is to take down Leviathan long enough for us to find a way out, then I can get to the bottom of whatever happened with Mark.

He needs medical attention. I'm no expert on demon venom, but I know it's a significant threat, and Mark is operating far below what he's normally capable of.

Defender blocks a sword aimed at my head, but another slashes across my midsection. The slice cuts through the leather shirt, and pain blossoms through my middle. Any distraction in this situation is going to get me killed.

Leviathan's human shape wavers, then morphs into his dragon form, taking up all the real estate in front of me and knocking several Fallen out of the way. He crouches before me, nostrils flaring, as they billow out waves of smoke.

"Let'sss have a little fun, ssshall we?" he hisses into my mind before he launches off the ground and into the air on his massive wings. We all duck as his barbed tail whips out above our heads.

Already injured, pain ricochets through my body as I throw myself to the ground. Breath escapes my lungs on a hiss as I push myself back up to face the coming assault.

Leviathan swoops through the air, flipping in a spiral above us, while Fallen continue their offensive strike.

This isn't sustainable. We can't fight off Leviathan and the Fallen. None of us possesses the gift of flight, and we don't have the benefit of the heavenly angels fighting alongside us this time.

Leviathan swoops down and glides low. An idea forms in my mind. It's a terrible idea, most likely will get me killed, but it's the only one I have.

I quickly tuck Defender into the loops on the side of the pants. Even if that's not what they're for, it works out perfect. As my team drops to the ground again, I duck only long enough to jump up and latch onto a scale on his side as he passes. It's not a perfect grab, but I hold on.

He lets out a long blast of flame aimed for my team. They deftly roll out of the way as I scramble onto his back, desperately hanging on through his twists and turns.

Tiger appears next to me and climbs over the smooth scales. I'm concerned for what she's about to do, but I can't let her throw me off balance. "I'll distract him while you aim for his heart. If we don't get out of here soon, we will never leave. There's not much time. Our window is closing," she says, climbing the scales past me.

She continues up his back as I follow at a much slower pace. The wound to my midsection makes my movements sluggish. Leviathan dips to the right and curves his body. My right hand loses its hold, and I slide. A yelp escapes as I swing myself up and latch my right hand onto a scale, while my feet flounder to gain leverage. Pain sears from the wound, igniting fire in every part of my body.

Stars flicker through my vision, and I breathe through the pain. This is no time to pass out.

It's almost impossible to get a firm hold on the scales while Leviathan flies through the air. My hold is precarious at best, but it's the only shot I have at ending this long enough to find an escape.

"It'sss sssweet you think you will get out of here alive," he hisses into my mind. "You don't have your preciousss angelsss here to sssave you thisss time."

An image of myself, along with my entire team, lying slaughtered on the ground, appears in my mind. I shake my head to clear it. He can't have my thoughts.

He won't get a response from me. My focus needs to be on moving closer to his chest. The ground nears as he dips into a dive, and I crawl directly under his arm. I need only a moment to aim Defender at his heart.

He moves his arm to dislodge me, but I hang on. Hos scales slide smoothly over the battle leathers, and I'm thankful for the outerwear. Not deterred, he uses his other hand and latches hold of me, ripping me away from my secure spot. A scream of frustration escapes as I'm gripped beneath his sharp talons.

"How dare you try to weaken me in my realm!" he shouts out, his grip tightening around me, but it doesn't crush me.

"Hey, I didn't come here willingly! This is your fault!" I return the shout, kicking out against his hold on me.

"You will sssee what I'm truly capable of," he hisses into my mind.

He barrel rolls and dives to the ground fast as a missile. My stomach drops. My team, fighting for their lives, is the last thing I see before I close my eyes.

"You will have a good vantage point to watch as I dessstroy your friendsss." It can't end this way. I won't let it. Held prisoner in the enormous cage of his hand, I reach for Defender, and it flares to life, releasing its hold from the loops of the pants. Between two talons, I aim the sword where the heart should be.

"Who ssshould I kill firssst?" A stream of fire shoots forth, but I don't watch where he aims. I can't. I have one goal.

Tiger jumps between Leviathan's eyes and latches on with her claws. Leviathan lets out a mighty roar and jerks to a stop midair, tail thrashing wildly.

My aim slips at the abrupt shift in flight, but Defender doesn't need perfection, only an opportunity to shoot fire aimed straight for the heart. Leviathan didn't count on Defender. I may be incapacitated, but Defender is not.

Leviathan's roar shakes the air, and sound waves ripple past me. He flails wildly trying to get free of the flame and Tiger's claws. Defender's flame does not falter even as he thrashes his arms around, shaking me like a rattle. There's no one to come to my rescue this time. My team fights valiantly against the ground assault, but we are losing this fight.

Leviathan rolls his body to escape the flames, but Defender will not be denied. The flames wrap around his body, tangling him in a blaze that converges at his heart. Not just a flame, but it acts as a rope constricting his movements, disabling his wings and arms.

His enormous dragon body tumbles. Wrapped in a rope of flames, he screams out a ball of fire and thrashes his tail wildly as the fire from Defender finally disables him.

Unable to maneuver away from the flames aimed at his heart, his dragon form disintegrates piece by piece. His hold on me loosens, and I fall.

The ground approaches in slow motion while I observe my team and Leviathan's crumbling form. I watch helplessly as Uncle Devon jumps forward to intercept a blade meant for Mark. The blade pierces Uncle Devon's chest as Mark falls to his knees. Any strength he had, now completely gone.

What's left of Leviathan's body fades on a final roar as my body tumbles to the scorched real estate below. Mark and Uncle Devon fall motionless to the ground, just as a powerful explosion rocks the air.

Suspended mid-air, it's as if time stands still. Silence falls, ash hovers in the air. A picture of devastation frozen in place beneath me.

Blinding light burns through the atmosphere, leaving nothing but embers in its wake.

The brilliant light turns, fading as darkness takes over. Inky blackness tugs and pulls me under. This situation is eerily familiar, and I'm powerless to stop it.

***

Noise filters through the buzz flying around my head. My hand lifts to swat it away and strikes a furry object.

"Stop hitting me. You can open your eyes now," Tiger fusses as she climbs off my chest.

Not feeling very confident in her encouragement, I blink one eye open, and harsh light filters in. I quickly shut the eye again. Voices flow in and out of focus.

What was I doing, and why am I lying on the floor?

I don't enjoy waking up like this. It's not fun. Maybe I was dreaming of coffee because all I want right now is a glorious cup of the good stuff.

With the thought of a cup of coffee now firmly planted in my mind, I bravely open my eyes to chaos as a nurse rushes past me.

Rolling to my side, I lift myself up and look around. We landed in The Cave. My team lies around me in various stages of consciousness.

It trickles into my mind like a slow-moving brook, in no hurry—the tumble into the underworld when I hugged Uncle Devon.

Solace runs through me at the realization we made it back alive. Maybe not completely in one piece, but we made it back.

Tiger walks off, but before she gets too far, I stop her. “Hey, thanks for what you did back there. If it weren’t for you, we wouldn’t have made it out alive.”

"I'm only glad I could help." She walks away without another word.

A nurse approaches as I finally get myself into a sitting position on the floor. She squats next to me until we're at eye level. "Are you injured?"

Not feeling any pain, I shake my head.

"Are you sure? You're covered in blood." She stares at my midsection, and I look down and watch as my blood soaks the leathers I'm wearing.

"Now that you mention it, there may be a wound." The pain that was nonexistent flares to life with a vengeance.

"I figured there might be. Do you want to lie down so I can assess the damage?"

Fire courses through my abdomen as I roll to my side, then to my back. Not good. My teeth clench together tightly as she lifts what's left of the top to assess the damage.

Barely breathing through the pain, I try to listen as she talks me through what she's doing. Being unconscious is preferable.

She wants me to wait a day or two before doing anything strenuous. She cleans and stitches up the wound and then applies a bandage covered in medicine.

"It missed all the vital organs. It's deep, you were lucky. You could have been sliced in two." She packs up her bag and leans down to help me up. "Anything worse and you would have had to go in for surgery."

The burning is mild, thanks to the medicine. I rise to a standing position, even if a little hunched over.

She turns to leave but stops. "Hey, weren't you supposed to get married today?"

I had completely forgotten about that. "Uh, is that still today? I have no idea what day it is."

"It's almost midnight, so still today. I'm guessing, based on the carnage, it didn't happen."

"A little delayed, but it will happen." Definitely not today.

"Well, good luck." She kneels next to Sookie, who is speaking with Grace.

A couple more medical personnel attend to our group, but Mark and Uncle Devon aren't among them.

One nurse notices me looking around. "If you're looking for Mark, they rushed him inside the clinic. Both he and your uncle had the most significant and life-threatening injuries that needed immediate attention. When your team landed, we did a quick triage assessment of the worst injuries."

That makes sense. "Thank you. I'll go check on them."

"And take care of yourself. You need to take it easy. Don't forget, you're wounded, too."

Yeah, I don't need a reminder. The pain is reminder enough not to do anything stupid.

Hobbling on unsteady legs, I make my way to the clinic. When we landed, it was in the middle of the training area of The Cave, so I don't have too far to go.

There's no one at the front desk when I walk in. A steady hum of voices and a few beeps from machines fill the air, but nothing else.

After a few minutes, no one arrives at the desk, so I decide to look for him myself.

First stop is the emergency area, kind of like an emergency room. I follow the sound of voices to the first bay. Uncle Devon lies on a gurney as a team works on him.

His face is ashen, and he looks so frail on the bed. At least, what I can see of him, which isn't very much.

"Will he be okay?" I ask anyone in the room not wanting to interfere in the work they're doing.

A doctor turns at the sound of my voice. "We're doing everything we can for him. We're about to rush him to surgery. It's too soon to tell, but prayers are recommended."

He releases the brake on the bed, and they wheel him past me down the hall. The gurney disappears behind a set of doors.

Left alone in the hallway, the fear of never seeing Uncle Devon alive again twists like one of those corkscrew roller coasters. I double over, heaving at the thought that he might not make it.

It takes a few moments, but eventually I rise and wipe the tears. A deep breath, and I pull myself together to find Mark.

Shuffling on wooden feet, I move a couple of rooms down until I hear more voices. Mark is laid out as a team of professionals do what they can for him.

He's silent and unmoving. His every breath is labored.

Silently, I slide into the room to watch and wait. My prayers turn to pleas as my heart cries out to save Mark's life. Today was supposed to be our wedding day, but nothing turned out the way it should have.

I need to let his family know what happened, but I have no idea how to approach the supernatural and the Spirit Realm with them. I'm not sure what they know, or if they know anything at all.

They're probably worried and wondering what is going on. That's okay, I'm in the same boat. I need an update on Mark's condition so I'll at least have information to share with his family.

The flurry in the room settles as they finish what they're doing.

"How is he?"

The nurse next to me startles, not realizing I snuck into the room.

With a hand to her chest, she gives me a small smile and nods toward his bed. "You can speak to him if you'd like. He's in and out of consciousness right now. We've given him another dose of antivenom and a sedative to help him rest. We believe he'll make a full recovery, but it may take some time for him to regain his strength."

I heave a sigh of relief I didn't realize I was holding. "Yes, I would love to speak with him."

"We're just finishing up here." She goes back to cleaning up and follows the others out the door.

I step up to the end of the bed and watch him for a moment. He's breathing a little easier, but his pallor is still off.

I could have lost him today, and Uncle Devon, too. Both are still very ill, but very much alive.

My hand closes over Mark's as I sit next to him on the bed. His hand is cool in mine, and I lift it to my mouth and press a gentle kiss to his fingers.

His eyelids flutter, but they don't open.

"Hey, I'm here. Just rest and get better. We still have a wedding to get to, and I'm not letting you get out of it this easily. I need to leave in a bit so I can fill your family in on what happened. I know they've got to be worried."

I love him, this man of mine. He made me believe in love again. He showed me how good life can be. He showed me Jesus.

I didn't realize how lost I was, how much I needed grace. How much I needed His love.

"Thank you, Jesus, for bringing Mark into my life. Without him, I wouldn't know You."

I give Mark's hand a squeeze. "I'll be back as soon as I've spoken with your family. I love you more than you know."

I almost run into Grace and Sloan on my way out of the room.

"We wanted to check on Mark. How is he?" Grace motions to Mark's still form lying on the bed.

"They're optimistic he'll make a full recovery. He just needs to rest. I need to let Mark's family know what happened, but I'll be back to stay with him until he recovers."

"I'll stay with Mark until you get back. That way he won't be alone," Grace says, and she steps more fully into the room.

"Thanks, Grace. I appreciate that. What about you girls? Any injuries?"

Grace shrugs a shoulder. "Some stitches, but we'll make it. Glad to be home. If I never take a trip to the underworld again, it will be too soon."

Sloan nods her head in agreement. "I'm going to check on Angel and sit with her. I'll catch you later." She tucks her hands in her pockets and walks down the hall.

"Seriously, thank you for staying with Mark. I won't be long." I give her a hug, taking an extra moment to squeeze her tight. They risked their lives for me and didn't leave me in the underworld. I can't thank my team enough.

I'm not sure how we made it out, but I'm glad we did.

When I walk through the door of my office, I realize how I must look. I can't face his family like this. Still dressed in battle leathers, now shredded and covered in blood, I look like I just left the set of a demented, medieval slasher film.

Coming up with a new plan, I decide to slip quietly upstairs unnoticed and change clothes before anyone realizes I'm back. With a solid plan in place, I sneak out of the hidden door to the office and tiptoe down the hallway. I move toward the stairs on silent feet and take the first few steps.

A scream from the living room and the shattering of glass scare the stuffing out of me, and I let out a yelp in surprise. There's no way I can sneak upstairs unnoticed now.

"What in the world happened to you?" My mother's horrified voice comes from below me.

I face her fully, and she covers her mouth in horror as her gaze travels from the top of my head to my feet.

My hands raise. "It's not as bad as it looks."

"Not as bad as it looks?" Mom's raised voice brings the others to the bottom of the stairs.

And now I stand on display with all of them crowded around. This was not how I pictured this going.

I glance down and amend my approach. "Okay, that may not be exactly accurate. Maybe it was that bad, but we made it back alive." Aware of what I'm saying in front of Mark's family, I try to figure out how to explain this.

Understanding dawns on my mom's face, and she nods her head. "They already know. Mark filled them in briefly, and Grams and I covered the rest, or some of it anyway. What we don't know is what happened."

I scrunch my face and rub my forehead. My fingers touch dried blood and sweat crusted on my brow. Not the best way to have this conversation.

"It's a very complicated story, so here's a brief rundown. I was sucked into the underworld, and Mark, along with our team, came to rescue me and Uncle Devon. We sustained injuries in the process, but we should all make a full recovery. I am so sorry about ruining the wedding. As soon as Mark is feeling better, we will have the wedding as planned, just a little late." I wipe my sweaty palms across the leather pants.

Gross. Everything is gross, and I need a shower.

"Where is Mark? Why isn't he with you?" Charlotte's voice trembles as Silas wraps an arm around her shoulders.

Mark's brother and sister, with their spouses, wait for my response. The only ones missing are the kids, and I'm glad they aren't awake right now.

"Uh, yes, Mark is back at the clinic. He's received a second dose of antivenom and is still pretty out of it, but will make a full recovery. I came to fill all of you in and to take a quick shower before going back to sit with him."

"Antivenom?" she asks in horror.

Seriously, how am I supposed to explain demon venom? I just nod my head.

Realizing she's not getting anything else from me, she switches gears. "Is there any way we can see him?"

"Honestly, I don't know the answer to that. I'll need to find out and let you know. The clinic is part of a secret facility, and I don't know what the rules are for that. I'm still new to all of it."

"I understand, dear. I'm just eager to see him. Give him my love." She pauses before continuing. "Maybe clean up a bit first before you go." She gives me a warm and comforting smile.

"Thank you, and I will. Let me run upstairs, and I'll be right back."

I rush up the stairs to my room. It's not until I stand in the bathroom that I remember how bad the wound is. The stitches. Ugh, I can't take a shower.

I put soap and water on a cloth and clean up the best I can. It takes several times of rinsing and repeating before I'm halfway decent.

There's a knock at the door as I slide a clean shirt over my head. "Can I come in?" Mom calls through the door.

"Sure, I'm almost finished." She walks into the bathroom as I'm brushing my dirty hair, and I pull it up into a messy bun.

"How is everyone really doing?" She crosses her arms over her chest and leans against the door frame.

Setting the brush on the counter, I look at her in the mirror. "Uncle Devon's prognosis isn't a definite full recovery, Mark will heal with time, and I have stitches across my stomach. Everyone else on the team is pretty banged up, but are doing much better now that we made it back."

"How in the world did this happen?" she asks.

"Uncle Devon." I shake my head. "Leviathan created a portal within him, but we had no idea." I raise my arms out to the sides and drop them. "I don't know what that means for Uncle Devon, or if it could happen again."

"Oh, baby, I don't know what to say." She reaches over and pulls me into a hug. "No matter how upset you are with him, I know you love him."

"I do, but I don't know if I can ever be around him again. If he was used as a portal once, couldn't it happen again?"

She releases me from the hug and steps back. "You should go downstairs and talk to Mark's family before you go back to the clinic. I'll meet you there as soon as I finish up here." She bends down to pick up the bloody clothes. Hopefully, she burns them. I don't want to see them ever again.

Every step down the stairs is weighted with uncertainty. When I enter the living room, Mark's family stands up to greet me with a hug. Each one lingers as if I can transfer every hug back to Mark. Maybe I can.

Charlotte grabs my face and peers into my eyes. Silence stretches as she stares. After several moments, it gets a little uncomfortable, but she finally speaks. "I love you. You are precious to us, and I'm thankful you arrived back safely. I'll be praying for Devon for a full recovery and for complete healing for each of you. Come back when you can, and give us an update on Mark."

Tears swell in my eyes as I choke back a sob. "Thank you so much. I'll try to be back soon with an update and to let you know if there is a way for you to go to the clinic."

"Wait, before you go." Mom shoves a mug in front of my face, and the beautiful fragrance of freshly brewed coffee wafts up, causing the tenuously held back tears to flow. "Drink this before you go. You look like you're about to crash. I can't have you passing out because you're un-caffeinated."

The sob escapes as I accept the mug from her hands. "I don't think that's a word, but thank you. I really needed this."

It's bean one of those days. The words on the mug cause me to smile. It's a watery smile, but it's the best I can manage under the circumstances. I'm a blubbering mess.

The crashing wave rolls over and drags me under. Uncle Devon may die, and I will lose him all over again. Mark is sick. Very sick, and it could take him a long time to recover. The darkness will never stop coming for me.

Arms wrap around me from every side. Mom removes the mug from my hand as I unleash the torrent of tears that I've held at bay.

Mark's family lends me their strength even though they must be sick over everything that transpired today. They haven't blamed me for any of it, and that's such a relief.

One by one they release me, and peace takes over, wrapping me in a warm embrace.

"Drink this before it gets cold." Mom places the mug back in my hands. The warm brew goes down smooth. It's lovely, and whoever said that coffee was a hug in a mug knew what they were talking about.

Finished with the coffee, I hand the mug back to Mom and kiss her on the cheek. "I need to get back. Thank you all so much for your love and prayers. It means everything to me."

***

Grace rises from the chair when I walk into the room. She gives me a hug on her way to the door. "I'm going to check on Angel and Sloan." She glances back at Mark. "He's going to be okay." She nods and walks out.

My gaze shifts to Mark. His still, prone form on the bed gives no hint of the vibrant man I fell in love with. The poison has wreaked havoc on his body, leaving Mark a faded version of himself.

I shuffle to the side of his bed and bend down to kiss his cheek. The coldness surprises me. Where I expected warmth, there is none.

What has this poison done to him? What if he doesn't fully recover?

I press both of my palms to his cheeks to provide some warmth. Closing my eyes, I lift up a prayer.

When I open my eyes, I find my hands glowing against his cheeks. Inky blackness swirls through my mind and tries to pull me under. I yank my hands away and gasp.

Chapter 13

Mark

The soothing warmth of Elizabeth's hand in mine beckons me as I battle against the shadows invading my mind. Slushy thoughts, weird dreams, visions of Elizabeth trying to kill me-none of it makes sense. If I could only escape this unrelenting torment.

Using every ounce of strength I can find, I get one eye open. Light filters in and stabs the overly sensitive orb. It slams shut, cutting off any hope of finding an answer to these mysterious dreams.

"Mark, can you hear me? Are you awake?" Her voice pulls me through the muddle of confusion. Gentle fingers stroke my hand, eliciting a barrage of unwelcome tremors that ricochet through my body.

That foolish eye blinks open again, allowing the cruel light to penetrate my muddy brain. The other eye joins in feeling left out. More light careens through, pinging against the four corners of my head.

A groan from somewhere, the squeeze of a hand, a gentle kiss on my forehead — it pulls me out and lands me on a hard bed in a sterile room.

Beautiful brown eyes meet mine, and a relieved smile crosses her face. "You're awake. We've been wondering how long you would be out."

The will to answer is there, but the strength is not. All I can do is blink in response. Such a helpless feeling.

Elizabeth smiles but tugs her lip between her teeth, and worry creases her brow.

Her nearness prompts conflicting feelings. I love her. I do. But there's something else, something I'm supposed to remember. But whatever it is, remains just out of reach.

Everything remains just out of reach.

A thought emerges from a dark corner of my mind: *she's not who she appears to be. Don't allow her to deceive you.*

What? That doesn't make any sense.

A shadow appears in the doorway and moves closer to the bed. I want to run but can't. There's no way to escape its reach.

"Arden, how are you?" Elizabeth's voice cuts through the panic. Arden? The shadow is Arden?

"As good as can be expected after escaping from the underworld. How are the two of you?"

She nods her head. "My stitches are almost healed. Mark just woke up, but he seems a little groggy. It's taking him a bit to come around."

"Demon poison is nothing to mess around with. It could be a long road of recovery, but that doesn't mean it will be. Grace's quick action saved his life, but it was longer than recommended before he received the second dose. Have you heard anything about your uncle?" Arden leans against the wall as he crosses his arms over his chest.

"Yes, the surgery was a success, and he's in recovery now."

The tightness around Arden's eyes eases. "That's good to hear. Why don't you go visit him and I'll stay here with Mark?"

Her face pales, and she shakes her head. "I don't think that's such a good idea. If he was used as a portal to the underworld once, it could happen again. That's not a risk I'm willing to take."

Arden unfolds his arms and straightens as he considers Elizabeth.

"I see your concern. You're right to be cautious. I should have thought of that. Maybe you should stay away from him for now until we can get confirmation that it's safe for you to be around him. Why don't I go check on him, and I'll come back and give you an update?"

"Thank you, I appreciate it." Her shoulders relax, and she visibly sighs in relief.

"You two get some rest."

Arden walks to the door, but Elizabeth's words stop him. "Hey, Arden, is it possible for Mark's parents to come visit him? They're worried and would like to see him."

"Yes, of course, let them know they are welcome. They will need to use your office to enter The Cave. If it allows them entrance, then it's safe for them to proceed."

"Thank you, Arden. And don't forget to get some rest yourself."

With a nod in Elizabeth's direction, he exits the room and leaves us alone.

"Do you need anything? Is there anything I can do for you?" Elizabeth leans over to fluff my pillow.

A croak comes out when I attempt to speak. Water. I would like some water, but the words won't come.

Elizabeth's gaze shifts to understanding, as if she can read my mind. "Water. Is that what you're trying to say?"

With a slight nod of my head, she gets up and pours water into a cup and shifts the straw to my mouth. The cool water soothes my parched throat.

"Slow down. You don't want to choke on it." She removes the straw and sits next to me on the bed.

There's a part of me that doesn't want her so close. My eyes close at the intrusive thought. What am I missing?

"You're still tired, so I'll let you rest. Let me get your parents and bring them here so they can see you. They'll be relieved to know you're awake." Another kiss on the forehead and a squeeze to my arm. I keep my eyes closed until I hear her steps retreat down the hall.

Relief washes through me at her departure, and I breathe a little easier.

I shouldn't be relieved she's gone.

Sleep pulls me under before I can dissect this strange feeling.

"Arden said you were awake." Grace's voice filters through the haze of sleep as she walks into the room.

My eyes open when she approaches the bed. There's a slight limp in her step, but she's wearing a bright smile. And a shiner that looks brand new.

I try to manage a smile for her, but I'm not sure anything is working properly.

"Not looking too bad, Mr. Armstrong. Not looking great, but you're getting there."

My head nods in response. I'm not sure I feel any better.

She tilts her head. "Are you not able to speak?"

I clear my throat and attempt a reply. "Ughhh, nuh mush."

She scrunches her nose. "Was that 'not much'?" I nod my head again, thankful she can understand.

Why is everything so difficult? It's like I'm swimming through tar. It's frustrating.

"Wa'er, ease." That's all I can manage.

"Water?" She reaches for the pitcher and fills the cup. "Here you go." She lifts the straw to my lips so I can take a few sips.

"Better, thank you." It comes out as a horse whisper, but it's something.

"You just lie there, and I'll fill you in on what's been happening." She hops onto the edge of the hospital bed I'm stuck in.

"What's going on?" It comes out raspy. Making progress.

"Angel woke up!" She bounces with excitement.

My eyebrow raises in encouragement for her to continue.

"It wasn't exactly what we were hoping for. I thought she would be excited to be free, but she was freaking out, kicking and hitting anyone that was near her. Hence the black eye." She points to the dark smudge under her eye that's already fading since she walked in.

"Sloan and I were the only ones in the room with her when she woke up. We were both on our phones and not paying attention. We realized she was awake when she started to get out of bed. Sloan talked to her in a soft voice while I got up to help her. I was not expecting the right hook. First time I've been taken by surprise in a long time. Sloan isn't going to let me live that down." Grace lets out a long sigh as she leans her head back.

"Anyway, she had to be sedated. It was awful. She was so scared, screaming and hitting anyone that came near. After Angel was sedated, Sloan made everyone leave the room, so I decided to come see you. I thought you might be bored and figured I would fill you in on Angel. The nurse said they would slowly bring her out of the sedation. We hope she'll be calmer the next time she wakes up."

"She doesn't know she's safe yet. It's going to take her some time before she realizes you're only trying to help," I croak out. Angel has a long road of healing ahead of her. It will take time before she even remotely trusts anyone near her.

Grace looks around the room. "Where is everyone? I thought Lizzy would be here with you."

"Ahem," I clear my throat, and a horse whisper emerges. "She went to get my parents and bring them here."

She nods her head. "How long are you stuck here for?"

I lift my shoulder and let it drop. Who knows? I doubt I could get up and walk out of this room right now. My eyelids droop in response to those thoughts. Even thinking about getting out of this bed is exhausting.

She pats my arm. "You rest. I'll stay until your parents get here." She moves to the chair and pulls out her phone.

The heavy cloak surrounding me pulls me under.

***

Whispers wiggle around and through my unconscious state. Sleep drifts away as awareness dawns, bringing with it the desire to awaken. My brain doesn't feel as foggy and my body not as heavy. Sometimes, rest is better than any amount of medication.

Eyes still closed, I stretch my arms and legs to get the blood flowing. I don't intend to stay in this bed for long.

"Oh, honey, you're awake." Mom's voice travels from the other side of the room. Footsteps approach the bed, and my eyes open when she touches my arm.

Her smile is a gift. She has a special grin reserved for anyone who needs gentle encouragement. Her light shines brightly in this dark world. Though she isn't a Light Bearer or Guardian, her Light from within is unmistakable.

She exudes warmth and light in everything she does. She's the best mom anyone could ever ask for.

I grab her hand and give it a squeeze. "I love you, Mom." My voice is still a little raspy, but stronger.

She laughs and cries, throwing her arms around my neck. "I love you! I'm so glad you're okay. My knees need some recovery time, so how about you give this heart of mine a rest?"

She grabs my face and gives me a kiss as Dad slides in next to her.

"Hey, you think I could get a tour of this place? I may never get another opportunity like this again." He leans over Mom to peer around her so I can see him.

Mom glares at him. "Seriously, that's what you're thinking of at a time like this?"

A blank look crosses his face. "What? The boy's fine. They train with angels to battle against demons in a hidden underground . . . " he waves his hand around, "whatever this is. I want to check it out."

A laugh escapes as I watch the exchange. I love them both. "I may be able to give you a tour if you can help me get out of this bed."

She swings her head in my direction, the glare now extending to me. "You cannot be serious right now. You barely survived whatever this demon venom is. You're not going anywhere."

"Oh good, you're awake." Elizabeth rounds the door into the room. "I was checking on Angel. They still have her sedated."

My breath hitches and shoulders tighten at her appearance. She stands next to Mom with a smile on the face I fell in love with, oblivious to the distress she's causing.

Mom, ever vigilant, must sense the unease. She reaches over and gently lays her hand on my arm. "What's wrong? Are you in pain?"

Elizabeth bites her lip, and her eyebrows draw together as she watches me.

Mom's gaze lands on Elizabeth and then back to me. "Elizabeth dear, would you give us a few moments? Maybe you could show Silas around. He's itching for an adventure."

Elizabeth nods with lips pursed. "Of course, I can do that. Take all the time you need. We can explore for a bit."

Dad jumps from his spot and makes a dash for the door, grabbing Elizabeth's hand along the way. "Don't wait up, we might be gone for a while!" He throws out a wave as he exits the door, dragging Elizabeth with him.

"Sweetie, what's going on? I know you love that girl, but I watched as a look of panic crossed your face, then you looked like you wanted to run as far away as you could get." She pats my hand as she sits next to me on the bed.

I shake my head and stare at the ceiling. How do I explain what I don't even understand?

The love of my life petrifies me, and I don't want to be in the same room with her, but I don't know why.

"Something happened, but I can't remember what. Every time Elizabeth is near . . . " I shake my head. "I don't want her around me."

Mom scrunches her eyes as she watches me flounder. "I wish I understood what was going on in that head of yours."

"There's something I'm forgetting. If I could figure out what it is, I think that would help."

"Why don't you ask one of your teammates what happened? Maybe they can help you figure out what's causing this distress and how to fix it?"

"Yeah . . . yeah, that's a good idea. Here, help me out of this bed." I give her my hand, a request for her help.

"I don't think you should get up just yet. Shouldn't you wait to be cleared by someone first?"

I shake my head and wiggle my fingers at her. "Just help me up, and don't let me fall over."

"That's a tremendous responsibility you placed on my shoulders. I hope we don't get in trouble."

She stands up and braces her feet as she takes my hand and helps me out of bed.

It takes every bit of strength I have not to fall over. Mom lifts my left arm across her shoulders to help carry some of my weight.

"Alright, you're standing up. Now what do we do?"

"I need to find someone from my team. But I don't know where anyone is. I didn't exactly think this through." I sway a little, but Mom holds me steady. "Maybe I should sit down for a minute."

She helps me back to the bed. "Why don't you just call or text one of them?"

"I don't know where my cell phone is. Can you check the side table and see if it's in there?"

She pulls my phone out of the drawer and hands it to me, but the battery is dead. Resigned to my fate in this bed for now, I let out a deep sigh. I don't handle being idle well. Sick or not.

"We should pray." Mom grabs my hand and starts praying. Not a minute later, there's a rap on the door and a head pokes through.

"Arden." Relief washes over me as he walks in.

"It looks like you're on the mend. You're looking much better than the last time I saw you." He stops next to Mom as he appraises me.

"I'm ready to get out of this bed, but my body has other ideas." I lift my hands and let them flop back down.

"It's not easy letting your body get the rest it needs when you're used to action. Don't be too eager to get out of here. You don't want to crash and burn later."

Mom motions her head in Arden's direction, encouraging me to let him in on our discussion.

Arden watches the exchange with curiosity. "What is it? What am I missing?"

"Something went down while we were in the underworld, but for the life of me I can't remember what happened. I'm irrationally afraid of Elizabeth, and that doesn't make any sense. Whenever she's near, all I want to do is get away from her. Do you have any idea what could have happened to cause these negative feelings toward her?"

Arden pulls up a chair and sits down. "A lot of things happened." He rubs both hands down his face.

He's exhausted, yet still trying to take care of everyone else.

"At one point we were all confronted with a nightmare. Which, by definition, is the underworld. But more specifically, it was an illusion that was unique to each of us. I didn't see what you had to face, but I know it was Elizabeth. Or more accurately, a demon that looked like Elizabeth, until the illusion fell away."

And it all comes crashing back as the memories flood over like a tidal wave, taking my breath away. Elizabeth, or who I thought was Elizabeth, tried to kill me. No wonder I'm terrified of her.

And Arden had to witness Griffin back from the dead.

"Yes, I remember what happened now." The image of Elizabeth as she stabbed me with that sneer on her face, wars with the reality that it wasn't actually her. How do I reconcile what I saw with what is true?

Even though we've made it back home, we are still dealing with the repercussions of that experience.

And here, Arden is left with the reality that Griffin will never come back. "Arden, who do you have to help you? When it all gets to be too much, who helps you?" He's drowning in all he has to do, and with Griffin gone, he can't manage it all on his own. I do what I can to help, but I'm not Griffin.

He gives a tired smile. "Brenda. She's a godsend. I don't know where I would be without her. She can't take the place of Griffin. No one can. And I pray. A lot. But you help fill in when I need it. So, get rested up so you can get back to work." He laughs as he rises from the chair and turns to Mom. "And don't let him overdo it."

She lets out a snort. "I'll do the best I can, but no promises."

Before he walks out the door, I call out to him. "Hey, Arden. Get some rest. Take care of yourself."

"I will." He waves, then leaves the room.

"So, that's what happened. Baby, I'm so sorry. Tell me what I can do to help you." Worry mars her face.

A somber smile crosses my lips. "Just pray. Somehow, I need to convince my brain that it wasn't Elizabeth who was trying to kill me."

Chapter 14

Elizabeth

Silas is a trip. The weapons wall was his undoing. He begged Sookie to spar with him, and with a twinkle in her eye she obliged. She gave him some defensive moves he can use if he ever finds himself in a situation that would require a quick takedown. She let him have his fun, and I think she even enjoyed the momentary diversion it created.

We're still reeling from our time in the underworld. Each of us needs to deal with and heal from what happened there in order to move forward and not be hindered by our own internal demons.

Oh, how the enemy likes to play the long game. The battle waged in the mind is a strong one. An enemy not seen but just as deadly.

Mark is a shadow of himself in that hospital bed. A sickly shade tinges his skin. He seems distant, but he's also very sick from the poison pulsing through his system. This could be a long mountain to climb before we find ourselves on the other side.

He's definitely not well enough to get married. Which means our wedding is on hold. Besides, this isn't the right time to bring it up. His body needs to heal.

Uncle Devon's recovery is slow as well. I asked Arden to keep me in the loop on his recovery progress. According to the doctor, he had died, but they brought him back. When I heard that, I lost it. I can't go through losing him again. Not when I just got him back.

The prognosis is good. He will heal with time. The question that remains is whether I can ever be around him again.

Will there be a way to have him in my life without the fear of being sucked back into the underworld?

Leviathan will never stop coming for me. That is my reality. He wants to destroy me, but more than that, he wants to watch me suffer. I will always have a target on my back.

Silas and I make it back to Mark's room in one piece. He is beaming. Charlotte may have to drag him back home.

The way Silas and Charlotte took to the news of the supernatural world was surprising. They didn't miss a beat but accepted it as reality because of what they already know of God and the Bible.

They understand that angels and demons are very much a part of our world, they just can't see them. I was afraid they would think we're all crazy, but that's not what happened. If Silas has his way, he'll join us as an honorary Light Bearer or Guardian.

"Silas, what in the world happened to you?" Charlotte rises from the chair and moves to Silas, gripping his arms so she can get a good look at him.

Bruises and scrapes are an everyday occurrence, so I thought nothing of it on Silas. I give him a quick once-over while Charlotte fusses over him. A few bumps and bruises, but nothing serious.

He grabs her face and plants a kiss on her lips that deepens into dangerous territory, having forgotten they are not alone. Mark closes his eyes and leans his head back against the pillow, but at least he's sitting up in bed. A marked improvement from earlier.

Silas leans back but keeps his hold on Charlotte. "Baby, they have this weapons wall. I've never seen anything like it. Any weapon you could imagine, they have it. And I sparred with Sookie. She showed me these moves that an attacker will never see coming." He pats her arms. "This is what I want to do. We can move here and help Mark and Elizabeth."

Silas bubbles with excitement, and Charlotte smiles brightly at his enthusiasm. She pats his cheek and steps back. "I'm glad you had fun, dear, but we can't pack up and move here. The rest of our family lives in Tennessee, the grandkids, our church family. I promise we will visit often and stay for a while."

Silas beams as if he'd won a victory. "I'll take it."

A smile finds its way to my lips as I watch the exchange. Those two are adorable.

"What's new with you, son?" Silas ambles over to the bed and slaps Mark on the shoulder. An imperceptible wince slips, but Mark recovers quickly.

"I can almost get out of bed on my own. It won't be long, and I can ditch this room altogether." The sickly shade of grey is fading, and color is returning to his face. It's a relief to see he's on the mend.

My steps are hesitant as I approach the bed. "That's good to hear. Is there anything I can do for you?"

"No, I don't need anything, just resting a bit until I can get around on my own. Thanks for showing Dad around. It will be the highlight of his trip." The timid smile he gives me is so unlike him. He's always been confident.

"It was fun watching him. We had a good time."

The door opens, and Grace pads in. "Lizzy, Angel is coming around. I thought you would want to be there when she wakes up. Mama C, you can come, too. We need all the prayers we can get."

I raise my brow at Mark, making sure he doesn't need me for anything before I leave again.

"Go on, I know you've been worried about her." He motions with his hand to the door.

"I know, but I've been worried about you, too." I hesitate to leave so soon.

"I'm fine, I promise. It won't be long before I'm back to normal. Besides my dad is here." He motions to Silas, who is now dozing off in the chair.

Even though I'm hesitant to go, I follow Grace to the door. I turn back to Mark before I walk out. "Okay, I won't be long."

Charlotte loops her arm with mine. "Are you sure it will be alright if I'm in the room? I don't want to overwhelm her with too many people."

"It can't hurt. Maybe kind faces will help. And we definitely could use your prayers." Grace nudges Charlotte's side with her elbow.

Grace slips the door open, and we step into the silent room. Apprehension unfurls as we wait for Angel to become fully aware of her new surroundings.

She moves with a restlessness born of agony. Before I can give it too much thought, I move to the bed and place my hands on her head, praying I don't experience any of her trauma this time.

My hands glow, and peace settles her mind. Her body quiets as calm takes over.

She needs every advantage she can get. For far too long, the odds have been stacked against her.

She doesn't know it yet, but she has a family waiting for her. Waiting to help her. Waiting to love her.

Sloan sits next to the bed in the uncomfortable chair, Grace stands at the ready, while Charlotte hovers near the door, eyes closed, praying.

I lift up my own prayer for help and peace.

Angel stirs again, but this time there's not a frantic energy to it. Just a peaceful coming awake.

Her eyes blink open against the light streaming in from the window. She squints and turns her face toward it. For a moment she stares in complete rapture of the light.

"Sun," she whispers in awe.

How long has it been since she experienced sunshine?

She closes her eyes and breathes deeply.

Sloan rises from the chair, drawing Angel's attention. She jerks in surprise but doesn't move. Eyes wide, she regards Sloan with curiosity.

"You're safe now. No one here is going to hurt you. You have nothing to be afraid of with us." Sloan's voice is soft. A gentleness that is in complete opposition with the person I know.

Angel notices the rest of us in the room. Uncertainty mars her brow but not fear. That's a start.

"Are you in any pain?" I ask.

She looks at me but doesn't reply. A slight shake of her head is all I get.

"Would you like something to eat? Maybe something to drink? Perhaps some warm tea?" Charlotte stands at the foot of the bed, a kind, motherly smile on her face.

Angel's eyes widen, then a single tear trickles down her cheek. A slight nod of an answer is all Charlotte gets in response. She doesn't know what to do with such kindness.

I swallow hard and lower my head to keep the tears at bay. My hand clutches my stomach as pain for what she's been through slices through me.

Starved of basic decency. Starved for friendship. Starved for kindness. Starved for love. And just plain starved. My heart breaks for this child.

Charlotte leaves the room, I assume to get the tea.

Not wanting to overwhelm her, no one makes a move. We watch Angel as she takes us in, wanting her to set the pace.

She doesn't show any signs of distress. That's all thanks to God and His peace in this situation.

"We found you on the side of the road in a pickup truck. Based on your sustained injuries, it was clear you couldn't go back where you came from. We have plenty of questions, but for now, we want you to rest and heal." My hope is to put her mind at ease. She needs to know she's not going back.

She only stares, not saying a word.

"Would you like to sit up more? We can raise the head of the bed a little higher for you." Grace motions to the bed.

She gives a slight nod, nothing more. Almost as if she's afraid to say anything.

I don't imagine she's just going to accept us as friends and everything will be fine. She's in a strange place, with strange people, even if she is safe with us.

All she's known for so long is fear and pain. She has to start over. To know what it is to feel safe. That she can speak freely without fear.

She doesn't know it yet, but she can trust us and trust that we will take care of her and protect her.

Charlotte bustles into the room with a cup in hand. She places the tea on the side table and adds a few ice chips from the ice bucket to cool it down.

"It's a combination of lavender and chamomile. I hope you like it." Charlotte hands the cup to Angel with a delicate touch.

She reaches for the cup with shaky hands and wraps her fingers around it.

"Now take your time, dear. Small sips. If you like it, I can fix you some more." Charlotte treats her as if she will bolt at any moment.

"And I let the nurse know you're awake, so there will be a couple more people coming in soon." Charlotte's tone is gentle.

Angel sips the tea, spilling a little when her hands shake. "Don't worry about that. It's okay." Charlotte gets a tissue from the box on the table and dabs the sheet.

Dr. Lipinski walks in followed by Brenda, Arden's wife. "Angel, I'm Dr. Lipinski. It's good to see you awake. We know Angel isn't your real name, but that's what we've been calling you since we don't know what it is. How about you tell me your name while I check your vitals?"

Dr. Lipinski reaches for her hand, but Angel snatches it away and scoots to the edge of the bed, spilling tea. It's a normal reaction considering what she's been through. She doesn't want to be touched.

Brenda places a hand on the doctor's arm. "Dr. Lipinski, maybe we should give her some space. Let her get acclimated. She just woke up, and all of this is foreign to her. There's a lot we need to discuss with Angel, and she's the only one who can answer our questions. But for now, let's settle on getting some liquids in her and see if she will eat some food."

Brenda's attention moves to Angel. "I see you have some tea. Do you think you might be up for some food? We can start out small with something light and see how you do."

Angel sets the mug of tea on her lap and gives Brenda a cautious nod.

Brenda smiles at the response. "Let's get you some food. Ladies, let's all step out into the hallway and give Angel some breathing room." Brenda holds up her hand before Sloan can protest. "Everyone except for Sloan."

Brenda ushers us out of the room and closes the door behind us. "Look, we all want to help, and we all want answers. It will come . . . with time. She's experienced a level of trauma most will never know. We need to be patient. I don't think anyone should approach her or touch her without her permission. She needs to feel like she has control of something in her life. We will show her respect."

Dr. Lipinski deflates a little. "You're right. I should never have approached her the way I did. I'll need to monitor her and the baby, but I can do that when she's asleep."

"And Grace, see if you can round up some soft foods for Angel. A few different things she can try. Let's see if she can hold it down. We can increase to more solid foods later." Grace turns to leave, but Brenda is not finished. "And Grace, don't bring back a lot of food. She may try to eat all of it, and that will only make her sick. Get a spoonful of each item and no more. That way we can also learn what she likes and what she doesn't."

Grace salutes Brenda and marches down the hallway.

Brenda's gaze finds Charlotte. "Charlotte, thank you so much for letting us know she was awake. The warm tea was a nice touch. She could use a bit of mothering, don't you think?"

Charlotte beams. "Absolutely, that precious child needs to know she's loved and safe. And I can help for as long as we're here."

Brenda nods in agreement. "Grace and Sloan should be the ones to stay with Angel, just as they've been doing. I think Angel will relate to them better than to any of us. I'll talk to her when I can and hope to discover some answers. But for now, let's give her breathing room."

Brenda's face turns somber, and she puts her hands on her hips. "We need to find out if she understands that she's pregnant. It won't be a simple discussion, and definitely not one to be had with a room full of people."

Brenda is the most qualified to handle Angel's care. She needs a delicate touch and not cold, intrusive medical care.

Grace comes back with a tray filled with two plates, a bowl, and three Styrofoam cups with lids. Each plate has several small bites of food.

"I did what you said and also picked up apple juice, orange juice, and coffee." Grace beams at the accomplishment.

"Excellent! Maybe not the coffee. We should probably hold off on that for now. Why don't you bring it in to her?"

I hold up my hand to stop Grace. "Which one is the coffee?"

She tilts her head to the right. "The one on the end."

I snatch up the cup and lift the lid. She already added cream, and I assume sugar. Sweet girl. I take a sip and savor the brew. It's not great, but it will do. The caffeine will at least keep me going.

How many days has it been since I've had sleep? Or any of us?

The emotions of everything we've been through hit all at once. And like a wave crashing over me, I'm overwhelmed with gratitude that we all made it back home alive. Tears track down my cheeks before I can even stop them. I'm exhausted and grateful and all the things in between.

Charlotte wraps an arm around my shoulders and leans her head near. "I know exactly how you feel. It's been a crazy couple of days, but we're all here and we're together. I think Brenda has this covered. Let's go check on our guys."

Brenda gives a wave as she moves back into Angel's room. Dr. Lipinski leaves with a smile as she goes to check on another patient.

Silas and Mark are both sound asleep when we enter the room.

I lower myself onto the bed next to Mark and take his hand in mine. I rub my thumb across his knuckles. His chest rises and falls with each breath, a reminder he's alive. I could have lost him. I almost did.

Each breath he takes is a gift. He risked his life to rescue me from the underworld.

As well as the rest of our team. They thought nothing of it. They willingly risked their lives for me, and I love them for it. How can I possibly thank each of them for their unselfish sacrifice?

Mark's brow furrows in his sleep, and I reach up to smooth out the wrinkle.

His eyes fly open and land on mine. But instead of the soft, tender smile I expect, his eyes widen in panic before he schools his features.

But I saw it.

There's something he's not telling me.

Chapter 15

Mark

They gave me strict orders to return to the clinic if any complications arise. Apparently, any number of side effects could appear after demon poisoning. It feels like this healing is moving at a snail's pace.

Don't get me wrong, I'm thankful to be alive, but I have no desire to return to the underworld. Ever. A shiver racks my body just thinking about it.

Elizabeth's house is filled with family, which I would normally love. However, today it leaves me with a sense of emptiness. My siblings return home today. They can't wait around for a wedding that won't happen anytime soon. And no one wants to sit around and watch me recover. I don't even want to do that.

They have their lives to get back to, and the kids need to go back to school. They haven't left yet, but I'm already feeling their absence.

And the wedding. No one has brought it up, but for obvious reasons the wedding is on hold. Aside from my slow physical recovery, I can't even be in the same room with Elizabeth without wanting to run the other way, so there's no point in rescheduling right now. Besides, I need to come clean with her about what happened in the underworld. I'm afraid she'll think I'm being ridiculous and may incorrectly assume I'm trying to come up with an excuse not to marry her.

She was betrayed before, and I'm afraid her mind will go back there again. How do I reassure her I still love her and still want to marry her?

But I can't marry someone who throws me into a panic every time she locks eyes with me. My mind understands it wasn't really her that tried to kill me, but PTSD is real. There has got to be a way to get past this, but I don't know how to move forward.

And no, I haven't discussed any of this with her. We haven't been alone since I was released.

To compound everything further, I don't think she has slept at all. She was bouncing between my room and Angel's trying to be available for both of us. She needs to rest, but if she's been mainlining coffee to stay awake, like I think she has, she may not be very rational at the moment.

Elijah steps into the living room where I'm reading, suitcases in hand. He sets them down as Sophia, his wife, follows with their kids Greyson and Hope.

"Well, brother, it's been interesting. You definitely have a talent for getting attention. Kind of like throwing a perfectly good cheesecake into a koi pond." He tilts his head. "We came for your wedding, but found out you have the ability to see angels and demons instead. Not exactly what we thought would happen."

I place the book down and stand up as Sophia wraps her arms around me. "Mark, I am so sorry about the wedding, and everything else that's happened. Ignore your brother." She gives Elijah the side-eye. "You let us know when it gets rescheduled, and we will be here."

I wrap my arms around her in return and hold her tight, not wanting them to leave. Greyson and Hope take her place. Maybe I squeeze them a little too hard and hold on a little too tight, but I miss these guys so much. It's harder being away from my family than I thought it would be.

"Uncle Mark, do you think I could be a Guardian like you?" Greyson asks with hope-filled eyes.

"I want to be a Light Bearer like Aunt Elizabeth." Hope follows and twirls in a circle.

"Honestly, guys, anything is possible. I'm not sure how it all works, but pray about it and see where God leads you. But make sure you follow His plan and not your own." I tousle their hair as they step away.

Elijah gives me the typical guy hug with a back slap. "We'll be praying for you. I'm just glad you're alive. It would have been a real bummer if you hadn't made it back."

"Gee, thanks for that." I punch him in the shoulder. Hard. He falls onto the couch clutching his arm.

"Ow, that was uncalled for. That's gonna leave a bruise." I laugh as he struggles to sit up.

"Seriously, boys. I raised you better than that," Mom huffs as she comes into the room with my sister Margaret and her husband Henry trailing behind her. Mom is carrying Luke in her arms, getting those last hugs in before they leave.

Mom and Dad changed their plans, extending their visit to stay with us a little longer.

"Sorry, Mom," we both say at the same time.

"Mags, thank you so much for coming. I know the flight here was rough. Hopefully, you'll be past the morning sickness next time you come back." I give her a long hug. I love my kid sister. As the older brother, I felt it was always my job to protect her when we were growing up.

She was so small and delicate, unlike me and Elijah. We would beat each other up just for fun. Mags only wanted to play with her dolls and to have dress-up tea parties. We could not relate, but I loved her something fierce and still do.

"Henry, be safe getting home. It was good to see you." I stretch out my hand, and he grasps it firmly in his.

Dax walks in. "The van is ready." He offered to drive my siblings and their families to the airport in the company van.

Sophia glances around the living room. "Where's Elizabeth? We want to tell her 'bye' before we leave."

Mom answers, "She went upstairs to take a shower after we got home. She wasn't able to take one before because of the stitches. She said she was 'gross' and needed to get clean. I'm sure she'll be down any minute."

That's the first I heard of this. I had no idea she had stitches because I never thought to ask her how she was doing after we returned from the underworld. Aside from surviving demon poison, the only thing I was concerned about was avoiding being left alone with her. In thinking only of myself, I neglected her needs, and that is not the man I want to be.

If it's taken her this long to heal, it must have been serious.

"Aunt Elizabeth, I want to be a Light Bearer like you." Hope jumps in her arms as Elizabeth walks down the stairs. Elizabeth catches her with ease even though Hope is almost the same height. She hugs her and places her at the bottom of the stairs.

"Then you should probably talk to Grace. She knows more about all of this than I do. I'll give her your number, and you can call or text each other." Elizabeth gives her a squeeze, and she hugs the rest of my family.

She's beautiful in jeans and a Henley. No makeup, wet hair thrown in a ponytail, barefoot. I absolutely adore her.

And then the irrational fear takes over. I know it's irrational, that's what's so frustrating about it.

She doesn't want to kill me. I know this. But when I close my eyes, all I see is the smirk on her face as she plunges the knife into my chest.

I wave from the front porch and watch the van pull away as my family leaves to go back home. Melancholy sets in as the van drifts from view.

This weekend was a complete disaster. Nothing went according to plan.

As we walk back inside, Elizabeth heads left for the kitchen, and I make a right for the living room. My parents follow me and sit on the couch as I go back to the chair where I was reading.

I should go upstairs and pack my clothes. Again. My head falls back against the chair, and I stare at the ceiling, not motivated to do anything.

We moved all of my things into the house the day before the wedding. Now, I'm once again searching for another place to live. I'll have to get with Hannah and have her locate an available apartment for me at The Cave.

It's exhausting to think about moving again. Everything is exhausting. I hate being this tired.

"What's wrong?" Mom asks.

"I'm trying to find the energy to go upstairs and pack my clothes."

"Do you really need to do that? There are two rooms upstairs you could stay in, and you still need someone to keep an eye on you right now." She scrunches her eyes in concern.

She means well, but I need some time to myself. And time to pray.

"Mom, I can't stay here. We aren't married, and it wouldn't be right. I'll be fine, I promise."

Elizabeth walks into the room, coffee mug in hand. "There's coffee in the kitchen if anyone wants some." Purple smudges under her eyes reveal the true state of her exhaustion. She plops down in the chair opposite mine on the other side of the fireplace.

I've come to know it as her comfy chair. She's been known to fall asleep in it a time or two.

She pulls her feet up under her and faces my parents as she takes a sip from the mug. "I'm glad you decided to stay for a while. You'll have to let me know if there is anything you need."

"Oh, you don't need to worry about us, sweetheart. We're here to have a little vacation of our own and to help you and Mark, of course. I think I'll take you up on that coffee. It smells too good to pass up." Mom gets up as Dad lets out a snore. The man can literally sleep anywhere.

"I'm going upstairs to pack, and then I'll be out of your hair in a minute so you can get some rest. You look exhausted."

She actually deflates before my eyes. Her gaze doesn't meet mine but looks out the window to the backyard as she nods her head.

An unintended sigh escapes past my lips as I get up and walk upstairs. It doesn't take long to pack since I don't need much.

Roz is in the living room when I come down the stairs. She and Elizabeth look like they're about to leave.

"What's going on?" I place the suitcase at the foot of the stairs.

"We got a call to assist with a rescue. We're heading out." Roz points to the door.

"I don't think that's a good idea. Elizabeth is exhausted." I face her. "When was the last time you slept?" Elizabeth drinks the last bit of coffee as if to prove my point but not meaning to.

"I'm good. I got my caffeine fix." She lifts the empty mug as if it fixed everything that is wrong. The smile she gives me doesn't reach her eyes. And she didn't answer the question.

"Roz has a full team ready to go. Cressida, Sookie, and the guys are still here. You can let them fill in so you can get some much-needed sleep." I try to reason with her logical side.

She shakes her head in frustration. "Have you forgotten that I worked for years as an ER nurse? I didn't always get consistent sleep. I'm used to long days with little to no sleep."

I lean my arm on the banister and shake my head at her. "You don't need to go. They have this covered."

Roz doesn't intervene, only watches.

"I have my phone. Let me know which apartment you'll be in, and I can come check on you when I get back." She places the empty mug on the side table.

She's completely ignoring me. "Roz, I think it would be in everyone's best interest to have Elizabeth sit this one out. Just this once."

Elizabeth's head whips in my direction, eyes blazing. She places her hands on her hips, ready for battle. "I'm standing right here. I don't think it's your place to make decisions for me. I'm perfectly capable of speaking my own mind and determining my own actions."

She's so frustrating. Why won't she listen to reason? "Are you? Because you're not acting like it. This is an unsafe decision for your team. You're tired and not thinking clearly. They don't need you on this mission. You can stay back and rest up for the next one." Why is she so determined to go?

Roz just stands there watching the exchange, her head pinging back and forth between the two of us. Thankfully, Dad is still snoring during this heated discussion while Mom is in the kitchen.

Elizabeth's eyes narrow, and her voice lowers to a depth I've not heard from her before. "I don't know who you think you are, but you don't get to decide what I'm going to do. You are in no condition to say anything." She waves a hand in my direction. "You can barely stand up."

Her words find purchase. Sweat beads on my forehead, and I drop my chin to my chest and focus on the ground. I need to get out of this room. Thoughts from the underworld race through my mind, and my pulse speeds up. The memory of the sword she so callously drove into my chest replays on repeat with phantom pain radiating from the wound, as potent as the fury etched on her face.

She's my perfect dream and ultimate nightmare all rolled into one. There's no way I can be in the same room with her right now. And as much as I want to go with her and protect her, I can't.

Raising both palms, I back away. "You can do whatever you want. I was only trying to help." The last part ends on a whisper as tremors wrack my body. She can't see me like this.

I never want her to see me as weak. But she is my ultimate weakness. I would do anything for her, but I can barely stay in the same room with her.

I drag the suitcase behind me and put one foot in front of the other. My only goal is to get to the office before I collapse. I only need to make it to The Cave, then I can fall apart there.

***

Hello, old friend. I'm back.

Same one-bedroom apartment I stayed in when Elizabeth was missing for three months. At least Hannah hadn't listed it as vacant yet. I lower the suitcase to the floor and fall onto the couch. Everything hurts. I rub at the ache in my chest.

My head falls against the back of the couch cushion, and I close my eyes. Things could not be going any worse.

Emotions from the last couple of days flow past the banks of self-restraint, evident in the lone tear that leaks out and glides down my cheek.

There's nothing I want more than to pull Elizabeth close and hold her as her nearness settles me. But right now, there's nothing about her that soothes me. Nothing about her right now brings me peace.

There's only One who can calm this crashing swell that threatens to overwhelm and drag me under.

I slide off the couch and hit my knees. The living room becomes an altar, a place where I can bring it all and lay it down.

Lord, please help.

It's all I've got.

Chapter 16

Elizabeth

"Girl, what is going on with you? I've never seen you talk to Mark like that." Roz stares at me like I've lost my mind as I watch Mark back out of the room, suitcase in hand.

Maybe I have. I'm drained, and I don't want to admit it, but maybe Mark is right. I'm not needed right now. They can do this without me, but part of me doesn't want to be alone right now.

And something is off with him. He can't seem to get away from me fast enough.

He needs to rest, and I need to get out of here. I don't want to dwell on all that's going wrong right now. I need a distraction, and a new mission will do just that.

My hand flies in the direction Mark just walked. "He's being ridiculous. I'm fine. I'm going to fix a travel mug of coffee. You want one?"

"Sure." She shrugs and follows me to the kitchen. "You know you can stay behind and rest. He's right, you know, we have a full team. I only stopped by to let you know we're leaving. I didn't mean for you to come with us."

"There's nothing for me to do here except watch Mark ignore me. No, thanks." I busy myself with making more coffee.

"What's going on with the two of you, anyway? Both of you seem a little out of sorts." She leans a hip against the counter, watching my every move. Entirely too observant.

"I have no idea." I slam the mug onto the counter harder than I intend. "Ever since we've been back from the underworld, he's been distant, not himself. He's incredibly sick, and his body is weak and fighting to heal itself. I need to give him time and maybe some space."

I hand her a travel mug emblazoned with, *Coffee is a part of my daily grind.*

After placing the top on mine, I take a sip from the mug that reads, *Sorry, my work isn't complete, I was pro-caffeinating.*

"Okay, I'll let you come with us, but I don't want you involved in any combat. Maybe you can hang back with the officers and help if we have anything medical related." She takes a sip from her mug. "This is fantastic. I see why you like it so much."

She lifts the mug in salute. "Cute mug."

"Let's go." I lead the way out of the kitchen on wooden legs and with a heavy heart.

Instead of sipping some fruity drink by the beach on my honeymoon, I'm stuck here where Mark avoids me. This is not what I envisioned for my life. Part of me is wondering if we will ever get married. Best to leave that thought for another day and lose my worries in a rescue mission to help someone who needs it.

***

As the sun dips below the horizon, we meet the rest of our team and the officers at a rendezvous point near our target, a house in the suburbs.

The brilliant colors of the fading sky give way to twinkling stars. The sky is clear, lending us pleasant weather for the task at hand.

"Our team will surround the building and eliminate any demonic threats before you advance. We will give the all-clear when it's safe for you to proceed." Dax takes the lead for our team and addresses the officers.

A lone female officer joins our group. This must be Athena, the female officer who was unable to attend our first meeting with Miles and Wesley. Her brow furrows in concentration as she listens intently to the conversation.

Her skin is the decadent color of smooth milk chocolate, and her hair is styled into a fierce bun. She's a little shorter than my height, but she's solid. I would not want to have a run-in with her in a dark alley.

As my team fans out across the property, Wesley slides next to my hiding spot behind a tree. "Why aren't you going with your team?"

"I'm staying back to help you in case a medic is needed. Hopefully, there will be no need." The caffeine is wearing off, and the past couple of days are barreling straight for me at top speed. The crash is going to be brutal. Or as Grace would say, "It's going to be epic." And not in a good way.

I should have listened to Mark and gone to bed, but I didn't want to be left alone with these nagging thoughts running through my head. Looks like I'm about to pay for that very irresponsible decision.

We each have a comms device, and I listen in as my team approaches the house. We're in a typical residential subdivision on the outskirts of town. All is quiet. Maybe too quiet.

"Incoming," crackles through my earpiece. I peer up at the sky and barely make out dark forms on the horizon.

All I can do is stand back and listen. I say a prayer for protection over all of us and for a successful mission.

In the distance, a battle rages as I stand on the sidelines. It's not long before we're given the all-clear to proceed to the house as my team stands guard for any demonic attacks.

I follow the small task force team through the quiet neighborhood, alert to every sound. Evil lies around every corner, especially in the most unlikely places.

We approach a beautiful house with a lovely garden filled with flowers. Light shines through the windows, indicating someone's inside.

"Grace and Paxton are inside under camouflage, neutralizing any demonic threat from within. We'll remain outside to keep everyone covered." Dax's voice comes through the earpiece.

Athena approaches the front door as we spread out behind her. She bangs on the door while Miles stands off to the side, out of sight from the door. Pounding feet against the floor comes through from the other side of the door.

"We have a runner," Roz calls out. Wesley takes off for the backyard.

Athena bangs on the door again. "Police! Open up!"

No response.

The door unlocks and opens as Grace removes the camouflage that kept her hidden. "They took off while we were dispatching a demon."

Paxton walks up behind her. "A few demons were on the hunt, but we took care of them. We walked around the place, but didn't find anyone else. We should be clear."

"Yeah, but there's a bookcase that doesn't sit right. We weren't able to move anything around, but now that the place is clear, we can check it out." Grace motions for us to follow her.

A beautiful bookcase, painted white, sits against the wall in the living room, but Grace is right. It feels off in the space. It's far too large for the small living room.

Miles, as usual, makes no comment. Just nods his head as he studies the bookcase.

"Well, let's take a look." Athena strides forward and starts moving things around. When I pull out a stack of books, the bookcase swings out, bumping into me.

Miles pulls on the side to move it farther away from the wall. Behind the bookcase lies a thin door set into the wall. Really, it's just a panel and not a door.

Grace places her hands along the seam. "How do we open it?"

Miles steps up. "Try pushing it."

Grace presses around the edges and it finally pops open outward, leaving a narrow opening. Athena steps in, shining her flashlight through the open space.

"I'll go first. You watch my back." Athena moves into the dark space and calls out, "There's a set of stairs. I'm going down."

I stay behind with Miles as the three of them descend the stairs. As we wait, exhaustion sinks its claws in deep, penetrating to my very breath. Holding up my own weight is a burden, and I'm aggravated with myself for insisting I come on this mission. I've got nobody to blame but myself.

I am not fine. But at this point, I've made my bed. If it were a literal bed, I would lie down on it.

I glance around the space. It's a cute house, but there are no personal touches to distinguish this house from any other. No family photos adorn the walls. No kids' artwork on the refrigerator. Nothing that makes it a home.

"She got away," Roz's irritated voice comes through. What surprises me is that it was a she and not a he in the house. I shouldn't let preconceived notions cloud my thinking.

And if she did nothing wrong, then she would have no reason to run.

Voices rise from the open hidden door. "Liz, get down here!" Roz calls out.

I glance at Miles. "Will you be okay here by yourself?"

He folds his arms across his buff chest and raises one eyebrow.

"Right, never mind. Just holler if you need . . ." The look he gives me sends chills. "Uh, never mind, you know what you're doing. Carry on then." My mouth and brain are no longer working together.

Wooden steps greet me as I run down into the basement. Nothing but concrete walls and floor, with a washer and dryer tucked in the corner. The space is surprisingly clean. It takes me a moment to figure out where to go.

To the side stands a narrow opening now fully visible, freed from the shelf of cluttered boxes that blocked it.

"In here," Grace calls out.

I take a deep breath before I walk in, knowing that whatever lies beyond that opening must be awful. She wouldn't have called for me if it wasn't necessary.

And it is so much worse than anything I could have imagined. Several severely malnourished children of various ages huddle together in the tiny room.

Fear etches each face, and their eyes reflect silent terror. Their clothes are torn and covered in dirt.

The sight is unimaginable, and the smell is even worse. As I take in the scene, my gag reflex kicks in. Why would anyone do this to children?

"Liz, over here." Roz motions me to the corner of the room. Paxton and Grace try to coax a few of the children to leave with them, but instead they huddle closer against the wall. Either they don't understand we're here to help, or fear prevents them from trusting us.

"These two are the worst. I don't think they're breathing. If they don't get immediate medical attention, I don't think they'll make it. We have an ambulance on the way, and the team is heading in to help Paxton and Grace get the rest of the children out."

It won't do anyone any good if I fall apart now. My legs give out as I kneel next to two small children lying on the floor. Neither one is moving, and she's right, it doesn't look like either is breathing.

Lord, please help.

There is nothing I can do to help them in my own ability, so I cry out to the Lord for help and place a hand on each child's matted head. My hands warm, and I can feel the Light weave through my body.

My eyes blink open, and I watch as my hands glow, but only one child is getting the Light. The Light doesn't move through the child on my right. Nothing is happening.

No! This has to work.

As breath moves through the child on the left, my attention turns to focus on the child to my right. I place both hands on the child turning blue before my eyes. No life or breath remains.

Please, God, this child cannot die.

Nothing happens. My pleas are met with silence. The glow from my hands fizzles out. This can't be happening. Not now.

The response is automatic. I perform CPR, but frail bones crack beneath my hands. This brittle body can't handle it.

My arms wrap gently around this fragile soul. With the utmost care, I pick up this child, holding him close to my chest and cry. A keening sound flows past my lips, and gut-wrenching sobs emerge.

If I could give this child my life, I would, but there is nothing I can do to save him. All of my best efforts are not enough. I am not enough.

A tiny life, that didn't have a chance, lies lifeless in my arms.

Voices swim in and out of focus as the floor tilts beneath me.

A face hovers above me when I come to. Grace has one of my eyes pried open. "I think she's waking up."

I swat her hand away and attempt to sit up but lean to the side. "I'm fine."

She helps me sit up but stays by my side. I'm surprised to find I'm at home in my own bed.

"You're not fine. You finally crashed right as we were rescuing a room full of children. We had to help you, too. The timing of your crash and burn was terrible." Roz's voice comes out sharp.

"Are they alive? Did they make it?" She can fuss at me all she wants to, but all I want to know is if the kids are alive.

Roz gentles her tone. "The only one that didn't make it was in your arms. He was already gone, and there was nothing anyone could do to change that. Not even you. You did what you could. The rest of them were sent to the hospital where they will be cared for."

My breath hitches, and a wave of despair washes over me. I wasn't able to help anyone. "It was all for nothing."

Grace looks at me in confusion. "What are you talking about? We saved a room full of children."

"And one of them died before we could save him."

She squeezes my hand and gives me a weak smile. "And he is no longer on this earth suffering. He is at peace, finally free from his pain and rejoicing in heaven. We follow the Lord's lead and do what we can, and we let Him handle the rest."

Roz shakes her head and gentles her tone. "Liz, we were right where we needed to be at the right time. Look at the good we did today. Even though the task given to us as Light Bearers can seem too great at times, saving even one person is everything to that one person."

"I'm sorry, you're right. I guess I'm feeling out of sorts." I shift on the bed, uncomfortable with their searching gaze fixed solely on me.

Roz folds her arms over her chest, jutting out her hip. "You're officially off duty. No more missions, and no more helping in the clinic until you get some proper rest."

"Is that why I'm in my bed?" I lift the blanket and drop my hands.

"Yes, stay here and recover until you are well-rested. And don't come back until you and Mark have worked everything out." She gives me a pointed look.

"Wait, what's wrong with you and Mark?" Grace grabs my arm in concern, worry marring her face as she sits next to me.

"Don't worry, Grace. Nothing is wrong. We are fine." Of that, I am not completely certain. Her concern may be granted, but I'm not telling her that.

I give Roz a hard stare that hopefully she can decipher. I don't need her to share any of what is going on between me and Mark with anyone else.

Roz carries on as if she didn't just expose my worst fears. "The police have reason to believe the kids were smuggled into the U.S. It looks like this is an underground ring with tentacles that spread far and deep. We're helping the police track down the two that got away. Then, we're going after the Fallen and demons behind all of this."

Roz points her finger in my direction. "And you are staying put."

Both hands go up in surrender. "I'm not going anywhere."

She squints her eyes. "Not even to the clinic to check on Angel. Not until after you're fully rested."

"Fine, I get it. Rest. Don't go anywhere. Got it." Yes, I'm pouting.

Grace leans over to give me a hug. "Rest. We've got this."

"You just got back from a mission. Shouldn't you rest, too?" I ask her.

Roz walks to the door. "We were resting when you weren't. Tonight we help the police. We won't be gone long. Stay put."

She turns back before walking out. "Spend time with the Light. You need more than rest. When we try to do things on our own and don't have God's direction, we can make a real mess of things."

Grace wiggles her fingers in a wave as she follows Roz out the door.

The door shuts, and their footsteps retreat down the hall. I fall back against the pillow and breathe out a harsh sigh.

Why do I feel like I've just been grounded and sent to my room?

Chapter 17

Grace

They aren't telling me everything. Something fishy is going on, and I intend to find out what it is. Not that I think they would confide their deepest secrets to me, but I can keep a secret in confidence.

It's obvious Mark and Elizabeth need my help. I'll work on that as soon as we get back.

We meet the task force at some random location outside of Seattle in a deserted warehouse district. The neglected street hosts an outdoor market of the bizarre and demonic. Witches, tarot card readings, mystic crystals, and vendors of the dark arts beckon seekers and followers alike. It's like an outdoor farmers market, but for the demonic.

It's no surprise the darkness will exploit anything.

Shadows settle over the area like a blanket as fog rolls in to cover the market in a cloak of disguise. I'll give them kudos for the special effects.

"I've heard about these pop-ups, but how did you find it?" Roz asks Wesley as she surveys the area.

"We received a tip. Honestly, I wasn't sure it was legit, but we have to follow up on each call-in no matter how absurd it may seem. It appears this one held some merit. It may mean nothing to this particular investigation, but it may prove to be a good source of information." Wesley watches in fascination as the vendors set up their booths and display their goods.

Sookie lifts a shoulder. "This is nothing for New Orleans. We see this stuff all the time." It comes out in her Southern twang, and I love it.

I've grown fond of our new friends from the Southern Division. They fit right in with our team. I have to admit, I'll be sad to see them leave.

Paxton has been a terrific partner, but it has caused a slight rift between me and Sloan. She has nothing to worry about. She's my Guardian and best friend, and that will never change. But I can definitely see more in the future with Paxton if he were to stay. Not that I think he would, and he definitely won't stay without Tyler.

Tyler, now that one is a mystery. He's such a closed book. Even more than Sloan, and that's saying something. He doesn't talk—like, ever. Not because he can't, because he chooses not to. That's a book I'd like to crack open and read. I bet there's some hidden skeletons running all around up in there.

"Wesley, your group can do its thing. We'll keep an eye out for any Fallen or demons that might cause you trouble. There are already too many here for us to go after, but we'll keep you covered. Let us know if you run into any issues and need some help." Roz taps the comms device in her ear.

Wesley, Miles and Athena peel away from our group to do whatever it is they do. They're dressed in street clothes to blend in. They gave us photos of the suspects from the house. Not sure we'll find them here, but hey, who knows. Stranger things happen every day.

More vendors arrive to set up their wares as demons settle in for an evening of mischief. A few Fallen hover in the skies watching over the area.

It's not ideal — a dark market for humans surrounded by demons and Fallen. We can't run around hacking away at demons around the average human. No, they can't see them, but it would sure look strange to see us fighting off an invisible force. Kind of hard to explain. Besides, we are seriously outnumbered.

"I'm curious to see who shows up tonight. Let's split up and do a perimeter check, get a feel for the place." Dax nods his head to the side of the building to our left.

Sloan takes off to the right of the building, and I follow, but so does Tyler. Interesting.

"Guess we're going this way," Paxton mutters as he falls in step beside me.

"Something wrong with going this way?" His steps match mine, like a choreographed walk. But without the dance music.

"No, of course not. It would just be nice if I could make some decisions once in a while." He jams his hands into his front pockets, scanning the buildings next to us.

"Trouble in paradise?" I snicker and peek in through a broken window to my left. A bunch of abandoned office equipment.

He gives me a sidelong look, one brow raised. "No." He pauses and exhales loudly. "I didn't sleep well last night, soI might be a little grumpy. That's all."

"I get it." I do. Sleep deprivation dampens my usual perkiness.

The darkness grows around us, causing the hair on my arms to stand on end. In front of us, Sloan and Tyler survey the buildings on either side. Anything could be lurking in any number of places. Shadows hide the most unsavory things.

The market is on the next street over on the other side of these warehouses, but it's deserted over here. Not a bad idea to search for hiding places. It's also an out of the way area to lead and dispose of any Fallen or demons that we may need to get rid of. Good to know.

The warehouse walls become a playground for the demons, who flicker in and out of view like shadows. It's time for a few of them to go missing.

A slash of my sword as one passes by my left leaves a trail of ash in the air as it vanishes.

We perform a little stab and seek during the perimeter check, dispatching several demons wafting through the air, drunk on the growing darkness. They don't even realize we're on the hunt.

But it won't last long. One of them will catch on soon.

Sloan and Tyler work well together. Both of them watch each others back and work in tandem without a word spoken. I bet they don't even realize they're doing it. If I didn't know any better, I would think they're perfect for each other.

I could just swoon. But I can't, don't want to lose my head.

Literally.

A Fallen lands soundlessly in front of me and Paxton, cutting off my view of Sloan. And I am not happy about that. I was enjoying watching them. It's like a Hallmark movie, but with a darker twist of broody individuals as they battle demons. Okay, so maybe not so much like a Hallmark movie after all.

Wings flare out on either side of the Fallen angel in a cascade of feathers. Gorgeous, but deadly. An Adonis on steroids with a smirk on his face. I smile back.

What? It's the polite thing to do.

Sloan's anger radiates from every pore and slides across my skin like water.

You would think four against one Fallen would be a piece of cake, but Fallen are tricky. And this one? The tips of his feathers are razor sharp. Makes things a little problematic.

"What makes you think you can come onto my territory and pick off my demons? There are consequences for that." The Adonis flexes its wings and spins.

We drop and roll away from the path of hundreds of blades. Paxton and I phase to make ourselves invisible.

That leaves Sloan and Tyler visible, but I trust they can handle themselves. Invisibility only gives us a slight advantage over this powerful Fallen.

Ripping my sword from the ether, I move like gangbusters to slash across his Achilles tendons as he turns. He screams and drops to the ground. We jump back and out of the way of those deadly wings.

He lands on his knees and covers anything vulnerable with his wings. We don't have a second to waste. He'll be in the air in the next moment. The only reason he's down now is that he wasn't expecting such a quick attack, or for his tendons to be sliced in two.

Sloan and I stare at each other across his back, and the plan is in place.

We both take a running leap. As soon as we launch up, his wings shoot out, and we barely miss the slice of those blades. But before he can take off into the air, we land on his back with swords drawn, impaling them into his spine at the same time. Paralyzed and with no way out, he vanishes without a trace. Sloan and I land on the ground.

"We were going to take his head off." Paxton has his sword raised right where the Fallen was just a moment ago.

"I'm glad that's over. Razor-sharp feathers are no joke." I scan the alley between the buildings. We won't be alone for long; we need to get out of here.

We round the end of the alley and make it back to the pop-up market without another incident. Eyes to the sky reveal a few Fallen watching us. For whatever reason, they chose not to intervene, which is more disturbing.

Paxton nudges my arm with his and points down the row of vendors. At first I'm not sure what he wants me to see, but there it is, a lady with a kid, maybe a teen, setting up a table.

She sets jewelry on stands, then places a crystal ball behind them. The ball radiates and yields a colorful backdrop for the jewelry to shine, giving the merchandise an ethereal glow.

Athena approaches, asking about the necklaces and making small talk. The teen hangs back while the lady engages Athena in conversation.

Demons hover around each person, including Athena. Small ones fly around her head, implanting thoughts.

A hand on my arm pauses my steps before I have a chance to intercept the demons.

"Just wait. Let it play out. We won't let anything happen to her." Paxton waits with me, and we watch the exchange take place.

Athena walks away with a necklace and a smile on her face. Which is at odds with the stern look that comes across as part of her job.

"I want to talk to the teen. Sloan, you in?" Sloan shrugs, but approaches the table with me. Paxton and Tyler hang back and walk to another booth as people fill in the space looking for goods or services.

"So, how do you want to play this?" I ask Sloan as we maneuver around a couple of guys watching a display of fire wielders. Twirl it, swallow it, manipulate it so it dances. What the patrons can't see are the demons moving the flames around so they appear to dance and take shape.

Sloan's response is a raised eyebrow. "Right, got it. I take the lead and be my bubbly, people-loving self. You just stand there and scare them."

We pass artists, writers, musicians, dancers, and other artisans selling housewares, clothing and all kinds of stuff. There's even a booth with the name Lazarus across the banner. Apparently, for the right price, they can raise the dead.

Ugh, massive eye roll. That's not even original. Jesus brings the dead back to life, and demons attempt to copy him and fail. They can't even come up with anything original on their own. So lame.

A couple of people approach and admire the jewelry. While the lady is busy tending to customers, I draw close to the end of the table. The girl, dressed in jeans and a plain grey t-shirt, lays out new pieces.

I pick up a piece and run a finger along the side. A zing runs up my hand. Enchanted. Sloan picks up a couple of pieces, inspecting each one.

"Oh, this one is so cute. What do you think?" I hold it up for Sloan. It really is cute, but it won't be coming home with me.

She nods her head, playing along. "I like it." A small demon flies near Sloan's face, and she bats it away, but it comes right back to annoy her. Those demons push influence, typically toward bad decisions.

"These are so beautiful." I gush over each piece. "Did you make these?"

The girl startles at my question. Is she not used to attention? "Some of them."

A deep-blue stone catches my eye. "What is this one? The blue is stunning."

"That's lapis lazuli. It promotes wisdom, intuition, and truth." She fidgets with the necklace she's wearing. Interestingly enough, it's a cross.

"Wow, a beauty like this can do all of that. Which one is your favorite?" Make her comfortable. Don't scare her off.

She points to a black gemstone. "This is the black obsidian." And points to the necklace she's wearing. "It offers protection." There in the middle of the cross sits the stone.

"Is this a popular stone? Do a lot of people get this one?"

She tilts her head and leans against the table. "It depends on the person and what they're looking for."

"So you wear yours for protection? Do you need to be protected?" We don't have a lot of time, so I cut right to it.

The lady stops talking to her customer and looks over at us, but my attention remains on the girl.

She lifts a thin shoulder. "Everyone needs protection."

"Yeah, I guess you're right."

The little demon that's been pestering Sloan sits on her head. She flips her head as if fluffing her hair away from her face to get it off. I stifle the laugh that's bubbling up.

"Is your friend okay?" Her eyes widen at the scene Sloan is causing.

Sloan jumps around, batting at the demon. That's it. I can't hold it in. I double over laughing so hard it triggers a coughing fit. I finally catch my breath to respond. "She's fine, I promise. Just has her moments." Sloan walks off to take care of the little demon. It won't be bothering her anymore.

"Sorry about that. She cracks me up sometimes." Sometimes. Hardly ever, but sometimes.

The lady comes over and points to the necklace still in my hand. "Did you want to buy that? I can wrap it up for you, or you can wear it now if you'd like."

I am definitely not putting it on, and it doesn't look like I'll be getting any more information either. This was a dead end.

Sloan comes back with one less demon in tow. And not too far behind are Sookie and Cressida. They stop to admire the jewelry, and the lady turns her attention to them.

I place the necklace back on the stand. "It's beautiful, but I don't really have the money for it."

The teen lowers her voice and glances over her shoulder. "If you need it, I'll give it to you. I want you to be protected."

Oh, sweet girl. Here I am trying to help her, and she's trying to protect me in her own way.

"That's very kind of you. Is there anything I can do to help you?" I whisper out on a breath.

Cressida and Sookie are doing a good job keeping her distracted, telling her some tall tale from New Orleans about the origins of voodoo.

"Me? Oh, no, I'm fine, but thank you for asking." She peeks back at the lady.

"Are you sure? Because I sense something's going on." Maybe she doesn't need my help, but I don't think I'm wrong.

"Look, it's all good. Just upset today is all. Do you want the necklace?" Her response this time is terse.

She shutdown, and I won't be getting anymore answers. So far, this is a bust. "Let me think about it, and I'll let you know. I'm going to keep looking around. Thank you."

Once we're out of earshot, Sloan whispers, "She's hiding something."

"Yeah, she is. But the question is, what? Either she needs help, or someone she knows does." I throw my hands out and hit a demon. "Now what?"

These stupid demons, there's so many of them. But if I kill one with this many around, they'll all start attacking.

Paxton and Tyler examine medieval weapons at a nearby booth. Dressed in leather boots to the calf, a long blue shirt over tight pants and a gnarly beard, the Viking holds out a dagger for Tyler to inspect. I've never met a Viking, but this guy looks authentic. He towers over the guys, and his biceps bulge through his ripped shirt. Kind of makes me want to check out the weapons, too.

Dax and Roz catch up with us at a booth selling herbal teas, oils, and lotions. "We have found nothing, and no one has seen the two we're looking for. What did you find?" Roz slides in next to me to sniff a bergamot scented candle.

The market is busy with people filling every square inch of the space. The demons make it even more crowded.

"Nothing really. The teen at the jewelry booth was hiding something, but she shut down when I pressed her about it. There's probably a story there, but nothing I can do if she doesn't tell me."

Roz motions to the end of the street where Athena joins Wesley at a booth. "As interesting as this has been, I don't think we found what we're looking for. Let's check in with Wesley and see if they're ready to leave."

A pulse moves through the crowd, a beat of energy that shifts the atmosphere. Every hair stands on end. This operation is about to go sideways real quick.

Demons emerge from the shadows they created. Too many to count. Demonic power thickens the air, and people look around in confusion.

Demons by the hundreds attach themselves to each person, feeding lies, deception, and greed. The once calm patrons turn on one another, vendors accuse their neighbors of sabotage, disputes transform into altercations. Havoc breaks out.

Exactly what the demons planned. The crowd is a screaming, unruly mass of anger. Belligerent individuals fight each other and knock others over.

This is nothing but a distraction meant to keep us focused on where we really need to be. "Come on, we need to push through this crowd and get inside that warehouse. Whatever is going down must be big enough to create a diversion to keep us distracted."

It's a challenge to push through the crowd. I jump over a table when it crashes in front of me. Vendors yell out and try to protect their merchandise.

Two guys each grab a sword from the Viking's table while he's distracted with breaking up a fight. Others see them and think they should do the same thing. Tyler and Paxton take in what's happening and move in to break it up before someone gets killed.

This is such a mess. We need to get out of this and find where the actual operation is going down. As bad as this is, this isn't where we need to be.

Chapter 18

Sloan

The Fallen abandon the street bizarre in an elegant action as one unit and swoop down over the warehouse behind the booths, disappearing from sight. Whatever the Fallen are planning is more concerning than the all-out riot they created here at the market.

Our team shoves through the crowd to reach the end of the street. We're jostled around by the sheer number of people unaware of what's taking place around them.

Once clear of the mob, we grab our weapons and follow the path of the Fallen.

We arrive to demonic enforcers blocking our entrance to the warehouse, which only confirms my suspicions.

Next to the Fallen, demonic enforcers are the best of the best as far as demons go.

Standing next to Grace, we face off with a nasty demon known to prey on the vulnerable.

The demon searches for every negative word ever spoken against me and every perverted deed done. Long-abandoned thoughts unfurl from the hidden corners of my mind. Images from a bitter past violently assault my mind and break through the tight control forged out of necessity.

I throw up barricades meant to deny these attacks entry and wield my sword with precision. From the outside, no one would ever suspect the terrors replaying through my mind while I battle the demon enforcer.

It takes longer than it should, but after the demons are dispatched back to hell, I'm left wrung out. Psychological warfare is vicious, but we prevail by the truth of

Who we belong to. His Light and love overcome the darkness every time, as long as we don't lose focus.

The Light hovers and infuses me with strength needed for the task at hand, and I pause for a brief second to give thanks.

We join the rest of our team at the basement entrance. The metal door is fastened shut with a thick chain and lock. Like that's going to keep us out.

Wesley, Miles and Athena join us, slightly out of breath. Wesley pauses with hands on his hips. "We got your message, but we had to break up several fights and chase down a few thieves. When backup finally arrived, we turned it over to them. Thanks for giving us a heads up on the demonic activity. We would have never known what caused the outbreak otherwise."

"We think it was meant as a distraction to keep us from this warehouse. We need to get inside before what we came for goes missing." Dax nods his head in my direction.

I pull out a couple of long pins, which resemble needles, and after a quick manipulation the lock releases with a snick. Bolt cutters not needed.

"Make sure your comms device is on, and spread out. Let's find out what's so important it needs to stay hidden. Wesley, we'll go in ahead of you and take care of any demons or Fallen that stand in our way. Stay behind us as you search." Roz nods her head at the door. Dax opens it and runs inside, Roz right behind him.

No one is guarding the entrance from inside, so we split up at the two openings leading off the main entrance. Grace and I hang right, with Paxton, Tyler, and Athena behind us. We pair off like that until everyone is inside.

A pulse of evil permeates the air as we walk down the narrow hallway.

Two demons guarding a door ahead turn at our approach.

"I wonder what lies behind door number one?" Paxton calls out. He and Tyler peel away to engage the demons. I follow while Grace stands guard with Athena.

Athena motions to the other door that lies beyond this one. Grace shakes her head. "We have two demons guarding this door. Let's clear this room first and see what we've got."

If she goes off on her own, I won't stop her, but there's something on the other side of this door they don't want us to see.

The comms device goes off in my ear. "We made it to the center of the warehouse, and we're hiding behind some crates. Where are you?" Roz's voice echoes through the device.

Grace responds, "We've encountered two enforcers guarding a door. We'll neutralize the threat and assess what's inside."

"Copy that. Lots of activity going on. We'll stay hidden and see what plays out. Let us know what you find."

"Will do."

Grace joins in the fight when she realizes we need more help. Enforcers are the elite fighters, and we've already encountered more tonight than I've met in my lifetime. We're holding our own against them, but it doesn't get us behind that door.

With the four of us fully engaged, we fight at full capacity. It shouldn't take four of us to bring down two demons, but the Fallen knew what they were doing by having two enforcers guard the door.

Together, Tyler and I assist Grace and Paxton in dispatching the last demon keeping us from whatever is behind that door. With a wisp of ash, he fades from existence.

Paxton reaches the door while I put my sword away. Not surprising, the knob doesn't turn. I reach for the pins in my pocket to pick the lock, but Tyler beats me to it.

Enough already. What is with this guy? I don't need or want his help. Every time I turn around, he's there. Not sure what he's trying to prove, but it's irritating, and he's getting under my skin.

He's not earning any medals with me. I won't allow myself to be distracted by Tyler.

Tyler and Paxton enter first, followed by Athena, Grace, and myself. I monitor the hallway in case the enforcers have backup.

"There's nothing here." Grace turns around, surveying the postage stamp sized room, with hands on her hips.

Athena uses her flashlight to check the dark corners of the room. "Why would they guard the door to an empty room?"

"They wouldn't," I answer. "Check the floors and walls. Don't rely on what you see."

I haven't made it this far in life by relying only on appearances. What is hidden will emerge if you look beyond the surface.

I release my senses to get a feel for the room. And there it is. Something lies beyond that wall.

"Grace, check that corner over there." I nod to the corner off to the side.

She gets down on the floor and presses against the bottom of the wall. The wall depresses and releases, moving outward.

Athena removes her gun and stands at the ready as the others move behind the open wall.

"We've got kids and teens that were locked up over here," Grace speaks over the comms device, her tone urgent.

"The main part of the warehouse is being used as an auction site." Roz breaks in. "They're buying and selling humans like cattle. Some of them are young. Kids and teens, but we've got some adults, too. We need to move in before they vanish."

Wesley cuts in. "Athena, I've called for backup. Can you secure and protect the kids where you are?"

"On it," she responds.

"We dispatched two enforcers. What kind of numbers do you have?" I ask, needing to assess what we're up against.

Dax's voice comes over. "There's about twenty buyers and sellers along with two organizers, but the place is crawling with Fallen and demons. We won't make it out without additional numbers. We've got more coming. Once they arrive, we'll move in together. We can't risk going at it alone."

"We'll make our way to you." I motion to Athena. "Will you be okay on your own?"

She gives a sharp nod. "Go on, I've got this. I'll try to get information from them while we wait for backup."

As we leave the room, two burly men approach from the hallway. No doubt coming to collect their merchandise. Little do they know, they won't be walking away with any.

"Hey!" the bald guy yells out. "What are you doing back here?"

"We could ask you the same thing." Paxton pulls out his sword. The guy laughs and pulls out a gun. They both do.

We can't fight guns with swords. There's nothing that says we can't use guns, but in a situation like this, it's not the best way to handle it. Someone will wind up dead, and it won't be me.

Paxton and Grace take a step back, luring them forward while Tyler and I advance. Again with this guy.

"What's with the guns? Afraid of a little hand-to-hand?" I lift my hands to show I don't have any weapons.

"You can't be serious." The guy with a neatly trimmed beard on my right laughs. "Sure, we'll play your little game, but winner takes all." He tucks the gun behind his back.

"Nuh uh, drop the guns and kick them to the side." They hesitate, unsure of what to think of me.

"Drop your weapons first. And how do we know you don't have any more hidden?" Bald guy asks.

"I could ask you the same." My brow arches. I have no doubt they have more weapons, just as we do.

We stand off facing each other, but their curiosity wins out. Challenge accepted, and all visible weapons drop to the floor with a clatter and get kicked aside.

This is what I need. Nothing like bare knuckles and no weapons. It's raw and real and dirty.

It's a contest to see who will make the first move. They'll break first because they want to prove they can beat a woman.

The guy with the beard lunges forward. My palm shoots out, and I duck low before he even moves a finger. He lets out a string of curses. "You broke my nose!" He covers his nose with his hands.

His face contorts, turning purple, then he drops his hands. Blood drips from his nose onto his shirt. He comes at me full force while Tyler handles the other guy, even though I can take care of these two guys on my own.

His fists fly, and I dodge and weave, but his eyes are teary and he can't see well. A well-placed uppercut and it's lights out for this guy. His body hits the ground with a dull thud. That's gonna leave a headache.

Grace waves her hand. "It's fine, we'll use our expertise on the Fallen and demons. But good show."

Tyler continues to spar with his guy. He's just messing around and wasting precious time we don't have.

"Backup has arrived. Let's move," Roz calls out over the comms.

Tyler lands a knockout blow that finishes the fight without breaking a sweat, and we race to the center of the warehouse, grabbing their guns on our way. No point in leaving them there for when they wake up.

"Police, freeze! Nobody move!"

No one listens. People scatter like roaches, scurrying in all directions. Demons create more chaos by feeding frantic energy into the atmosphere.

While the police are busy chasing after suspects, we fight our own battle against demons and Fallen.

Grace and I fall in next to each other with ease and no Tyler around. I couldn't have asked for a better partner. God knew what He was doing when He paired us together.

At some point, Tyler and Paxton fight alongside us. We dodge humans and bullets while fighting demonic forces.

It's not an easy feat to avoid criminals running and fighting like a disturbed nest of fire ants. If I could, I would take them down, each one, with my bare hands. Not one of them deserves to live.

Holding innocent men, women, and children captive against their will. Selling them for profit as if they're products to be used and then later discarded. Treating them as nothing.

I understand God wants to give each person a chance at redemption, but if He sees my heart, He knows I wrestle with it. But I won't fight Him on it. I will obey and leave their sorry souls for Him to sort out and redeem.

It doesn't mean I won't met out a little punishment of my own. I know the evil that resides in their hearts. I know what they're capable of. The damage they do. The lives they destroy.

Maybe I can push them toward a change of heart. Maybe a little nudge with my sword. Or my fist. I'm not picky. Heck, I'll even use a gun if it will help. Nowhere in any of the texts I've read, said I couldn't.

As a man runs past, my foot pops out. He trips and skids face-first across the concrete floor. He must have been running at full speed because he slid for a distance. Good. My heart does a happy dance. I may have even let a smirk slip. My night just got a little brighter.

"Sloan, stop messing around and help me with this demon." Grace catches my attention. A demon pops up right behind her, and I slash out with my sword.

My leg back kicks as another person tries to run past. He smacks the floor with his chest and wheezes out a breath. That should keep him busy for a moment while I deal with this Fallen.

Our team battles tirelessly against demons and Fallen swarming the warehouse. Police pursue the traffickers as they try to make a run for it, aided by the Fallen giving them cover. The task force rounds up the innocent caught in the middle, but with so much chaos and confusion, some are bound to be taken.

My job is to take out demonic forces while the police handle the rest, but the demons keep multiplying.

The sword drops from my hand before the pain hits. The Fallen sliced through the muscles and tendons in my forearm, rendering my arm useless. Pain sears through my arm, but worse, the sliced muscles prevent my dominate hand from working.

My sword lies idle on the ground next to my boot as blood pours from the wound. The Fallen laughs as he makes his move.

Grace blocks the blow meant for me. My left hand snatches another weapon from the ether just in time to block another blow. I may be down one hand, but I'm not finished.

My right arm can move, but my hand is dead weight. The pool of blood at my feet grows larger with each beat of my heart. We heal quickly, but severe blood loss is deadly. I don't have much time.

Gunshots ring out. On instinct we duck, but continue to fight. Pain flares in my thigh, and I stumble but catch myself.

As Grace distracts the Fallen, I fall back and take a running leap into the air. My sword lands mid-chest at heart level. The Fallen vanishes in a cloud of smoke.

Grace collapses to the ground, holding a hand to her chest. I drop next to her. "I think I was shot," she gets out between breaths.

"Here, let me see." Sure enough, entrance wound in the back, exit wound through the chest. "Why didn't you say something?!"

She scrunches up her face. "I don't know, maybe because we were busy!" She tries to yell out, but it comes out breathy.

"We both need to get to the clinic." I hold up my right arm for her to see and then look down at my thigh to see blood from a hole. Guess I got shot, too.

"OH. MY. GOSH! Why didn't *you* say something? I had no idea you were injured. I didn't see it happen." She's not loud, but man is she angry.

"Hey!" I yell out to Paxton, who is the closest to us. "We're out."

He dispatches a demon in a puff of smoke then notices us huddled on the floor.

His eyes widen, and he falters for just a moment at the sight of blood. Not gonna lie, it's a lot.

"Go, we've got it. We'll catch up with you later." Paxton turns back to the fight as Tyler removes the head from a demon. He glances briefly in my direction, hesitates for just a moment, then returns to fighting. That moment of hesitation spoke more than any words.

Back at the clinic, Grace and I are both brought back to emergency surgery. Both of our wounds are life-threatening. Grace with a collapsed lung and possible other internal damage from the gunshot wound. My severed muscles and tendons require surgery to mend.

My eyes blink open to a dim room and Elizabeth in the chair next to the bed. She's asleep, her head tilted at an odd angle.

I'll give it to her, she's persistent. I have nothing against her. It's just a general distrust of most people, but she's always been gracious with no agenda.

I place my hands down to scoot myself up in the bed to get more comfortable, but pure agony shoots up my right arm and a grunt escapes before I can mask it. That was a stupid move.

"You're awake." Elizabeth gets up to help me. "How are you feeling?" She pushes the button on the bed to elevate my head.

"Like the tendons in my arm were sliced open." The announcement is a slight whisper.

She bobs her head. "Okay, stupid question. Grace is still in surgery, but she should be out soon. I asked them to move her to your room after she's out of recovery so you could be together."

"Thank you for that." It comes out scratchy.

"Here, let me get you some water." She moves to the table and pours water into a cup, then adds one of those bendy straws.

The cool water helps.

"You don't have to baby me. I should be good to go in a few hours." I don't mean for it to come out harsh, but it sounds that way. She doesn't deserve my snark.

She frowns at my tone. "Oh, I know, but you're just coming out of anesthesia and you're still a little groggy. Once they bring Grace in and I have a chance to see her, I'll leave you two to catch up."

"Thank you. I appreciate your help." And I do. She's only ever been compassionate. Maybe a little clueless, but kind nonetheless.

Voices from the hallway enter the room right before the door cracks open. Paxton peeks his head through. "Hey, we just got back and wanted to check on you and Grace. Can we come in?"

Not sure I can handle his energy right now, but I give an imperceptible nod. Elizabeth stands up when Paxton and Tyler walk in.

Tyler's solid form fills the doorway. Once Grace's bed rolls in, there won't be enough space for all of us. And I'm fine with that. Grace is the only one who needs to be here, anyway.

"Since you have company, I'll go. I'll check on you and Grace in a little bit." Elizabeth gives my blanketed foot a squeeze on her way out and nods to the guys.

Paxton takes the vacated seat as Tyler leans against the wall across from the foot of the bed. His broody scowl firmly pointed in my direction. He folds his arms across his chest and crosses his feet at the ankles. He gives off bored vibes, but his laser focus proves otherwise.

"What in the world happened? There was so much blood I wasn't sure who was worse off." Paxton scoots to the edge of the chair, waiting for my response.

I give him the recap of what went down. At the mention of Grace, his attention narrows. Those two are so obvious.

I'll be glad when Paxton and Tyler go back home and Grace and I can get back to our normal. We don't need them and their interference. Grace and I have a good thing going, and I don't want Paxton doing anything to mess with that.

As for Tyler, he can go on back home never to return. Those dark shadows he carries around only mean trouble, and I have enough of my own.

Chapter 19

Elizabeth

Paxton and Tyler take up a whole lot of real estate wherever they go. Sloan can handle those two by herself, time for me to duck out.

When Mom called to let me know both Grace and Sloan were in surgery, I jumped up from my nap and snuck down to the clinic as fast as I could. Yes, it goes against Roz's orders, but she doesn't need to know.

Plus, there's no reason why I can't check on Angel since I'm already here. At least she's something positive I can focus on since I'm at a loss for what to do about Mark. His entire attitude toward me has been off, and I can't figure out why.

Anyway, that's an issue to deal with later.

For now, I choose to focus on Angel. She needs extensive care for the foreseeable future. It'll take time for her health to improve, and the baby's as well. All I want to do is wrap her in my arms and make all the pain from her past disappear. If it were only that easy.

A quick rap on the door before I poke my head in. Mom sits next to the bed, trying to coax Angel to eat. I step in and close the door softly behind me.

"Hey, Mom. Hi, Angel. You look good today." She watches as I enter her space, still uncertain of our intentions and motives. At least she doesn't appear to be afraid of me. That's a good sign. "How's she doing, Mom?"

"Hi, my baby. We are eating, but it's going slow. I'm not sure this is a favorite." Her mom radar goes on full alert. She tilts her head to the side. "Are you on your way home to rest?"

Not sure what she sees, but I can't look that bad. She doesn't need to worry. I'll go home after I check on my favorite people.

I nod at the bowl on the tray. "What is that? Soup?"

Mom gives a quick nod. "It's chicken soup. Something light to start out with, but she's not interested." She lets out a frustrated sigh, and Angel stares right through me, as if I'm not even standing here.

"Don't worry, the food here is great. I think you'll like it." Maybe my enthusiasm will catch on.

"Brenda will be here soon, and she'll work with her." Mom shakes her head. "It's just going to take time. She trusts no one, and that's understandable. All we can do is encourage her and give her unconditional love. And we'll need to have loads of patience."

"Has she said anything?"

"Not a word." Mom waves her hand in Angel's direction. "This is it." No reaction from Angel.

I lean over and give Mom a hug, thankful to have her in my life. "I'll leave you to it. I need to get out of here before Roz sees me. I'll fix us something for dinner later tonight."

"Sounds good. I'll see you at home." Mom is back at the house staying with me, along with Mark's parents. My relationship with her is finally on the mend after so many years apart. Once Mark and I get married, she will go back to one of the apartments at The Cave.

It's amazing what honest communication will do for a relationship. At some point, Mark and I will need to sit down and have a heart to heart. Once we're both rested, we should be able to discuss our future without emotions running high. Or whatever has him so standoffish toward me.

I stop in one more time to check on Grace and Sloan. Paxton and Tyler left while I was gone, leaving the two of them in the room.

"They told us we can go home in a few hours. We're under strict orders to rest for the next couple of days." Grace sips a beverage from a straw as she flips through the channels on TV, finally landing on a cooking show.

"Yeah, there seems to be a lot of that going around. I guess if the team gets called out again, they won't notify us."

Sloan shakes her head as she finishes eating a sandwich. "Not likely."

"Alright, girls, both of you are doing just fine and on the mend. I'm heading home. See you soon." They wave as I walk to the door.

There's only so much I can do to escape the reality that is my life right now. My body went past the point of exhaustion, and now I am paying the price for it. I'm not too proud to confess that my tank is empty. And maybe I can admit that Roz was right.

When I walk in the house, Mark is in the living room visiting with his parents. As much as he's trying to avoid me, I didn't expect him to be here. I hesitate at the threshold, unsure of where to go in my own home.

"Uh, I'm just going to go up to my room and let you talk." I awkwardly motion up the stairs and stumble over my words.

"Oh, nonsense. Come join us." Charlotte motions to the space next to her on the couch.

I shake my head and back my way to the stairs. "Thank you, but I still need to rest. I'll fix dinner in a little bit."

"No need. I have a casserole baking in the oven. You just rest." She gives me a gentle smile, fully aware I'm trying to make an escape.

As soon as I enter my room, I close the door and collapse. My body flops back onto the bed, and I slam my eyes shut. I could not be more awkward if I tried.

Mark didn't even look at me, much less acknowledge me. How did we get to this point? We were about to walk down the aisle, then the underworld happened. What occurred between then and now to change how he feels about me?

Tiger bounces onto the bed and walks across the comforter to my side. "You have to talk to him." She lies down and snuggles next to me, knowing I need it but won't ask for it.

"I know that. He's the one avoiding me, not the other way around. What is going on with him, anyway? What happened to the sweet, gentle man I fell in love with? I know you won't answer that, it was a rhetorical question, anyway."

"Talk to him."

"Ugh." I take my shoes off and curl up on the bed. "Maybe once I'm rested, I can handle everything a little better."

What seems like only a few minutes later, I wake to the tantalizing scent of yummy garlic bread and voices drifting from downstairs. A glance at the clock tells me I was out for a couple of hours. Tiger is nowhere to be seen. I stretch my arms and rise from the bed to join the others.

Mark will be downstairs with his parents, and I need to take a moment to compose myself.

Charlotte is an amazing cook. The wonderful aroma drifts through the house, but I doubt I can eat a bite. My stomach churns as questions about my relationship with Mark swirl around.

Those heated looks of affection and longing are nowhere to be seen.

No, now, his eyes are haunted and cautious, no longer the expression of love and passion.

What if he's having second thoughts? What if he no longer loves me? That thought alone leaves me with a deep ache of loss. A hollowness already taking up residence.

Mark, his parents, and my mom are sitting at the table eating. Chicken casserole, salad, and garlic bread cover the center of the table.

"We didn't want to wake you in case you were getting some good rest." Mom gets up and goes to the kitchen for a plate.

"Come join us, dear. The food is still warm." Charlotte motions for me to sit at the empty chair next to Mark. He won't even look in my direction, just stares at the plate and moves the food around with his fork.

"Thanks, but I'm not hungry. I'm going to fix a cup of coffee for now. I may eat a little later."

Mom's face falls at my announcement. "When was the last time you ate?"

Excellent question. Honestly, I don't know.

Without providing an answer, I shake my head and walk to the coffee nook and keep myself busy by making coffee.

His presence enters the room before he does. I don't even need to turn around to know he's right behind me.

"Hey, um, can we talk?" he asks.

At the timidity in his voice, I place the mug down and face him. His hand kneads the back of his neck, and the expression on his face gives me pause. His brows knit together, leaving a deep groove between them. Whatever it is, he doesn't want to have this conversation.

Fine. Let's get it over with, but not before I have my coffee firmly in hand. I need all the reinforcements I can get.

I give a slight nod. "Sure, let me fix my coffee, and I'll meet you on the porch. Would you like a cup?" It's the least I can do, a peace offering if you will.

"No, I think I'll pass, but thank you." He shuffles to the back door.

After he walks out, I release the breath I was holding. My shoulders droop, and my head drops. Whatever he wants to say is going to change everything. Tension vibrates through my body.

I'm glad I didn't eat. It would have made a reappearance. Even the thought of coffee is making me queasy, but I'm not about to throw it out now. It's the only lifeline I have to anything good.

I have to find the perfect mug for this moment, as if my very survival hinges on it. Yep, and there it is. *Sip Happens*. It feels appropriate.

Armed and ready, I step onto the back porch and brace myself for the impending shoe drop. The silence is broken by lapping waves against the shore. A breeze drifts off the lake to ruffle my hair, which I haven't bothered to brush. It doesn't even matter. Mark probably won't look at me anyway.

I bring the mug to my lips and take a fortifying sip before sinking into the rocking chair. The view from my backyard never disappoints.

Too bad the man leaning against the porch rail is about to ruin it for me. The quiver in my gut urges me to run before he can fling his daggers, but he doesn't say a word.

Unmoving, like the statue in my garden, he acts as if he's unaware of my presence. But he'll talk when he's ready. Not one to use words carelessly or as a weapon, he'll take his time and choose them wisely.

He's the most magnificent person I know, both inside and out. Whatever he is dealing with has him shaken.

Another sip of coffee slides down like rocks, another moment of silence.

"I love you." Agony mars his voice as he finally breaks the silence. And if I didn't know him like I do, I would think he's lying. He doesn't even turn to face me. His gaze fixed firmly on the lake. As if he knows he won't be able to do this if he looks at me.

He breathes in deeply before proceeding. "I've given this a lot of thought. Not that I'm able to do much other than think. It's taking time for the venom to leave my body, and I'm not good for much of anything these days."

He braces both palms on the railing as if it's the only thing holding him up. His head bows. A need to settle this restless shake on the inside pushes me to force the rocker into motion. The sweet smell of coffee does nothing to soothe the unease.

"I think it's best to postpone the wedding. Indefinitely. There's no way to calculate a time frame right now to move forward with getting married."

And there it is. The other shoe just dropped, like a missile bound for destruction. Isn't that just like life? When things are going well, perfect even, that stupid shoe comes flying out of nowhere to crush it all to dust. Nothing like being blindsided by a random flying shoe.

The breath whooshes right out of my lungs, and there's no air to breathe in. The mug shakes in my hand, and I drop it onto the wooden side table before it falls to the floor.

"What did I do wrong?" With no air to fill my lungs, it comes out wobbly and disjointed. "I must have done something if you don't even want to be in the same room with me."

"I promise you did nothing wrong. It's me. It's not you." This time he turns to face me and leans back against the railing, hands braced on either side.

What did he just say? Oh no he didn't. My lungs fill with air, ready for a fight. This I can do. "Are you serious right now? Did you really just use the 'it's not you, it's me' line? No, I don't accept that. I deserve the truth." I stand up to face him.

He cringes and takes a step back. He actually backs away from me. "Remember when we were in the underworld?"

"Yeah, kind of hard to forget that." I fold my arms over my chest and wait for his explanation.

"Before we found you, or you found us, we were attacked. You were there, but it wasn't you it was an illusion. We were trying to find you, and then there you were. So breathtaking. All I wanted to do was get you out of there so I could hold you, but then you stabbed me. But it wasn't really you. It was a Fallen disguised as you."

He shakes his head, gaze moving back to the water. "I'm sorry, I'm not making any sense."

"Wait, so let me get this straight. I was there as an illusion, but it wasn't really me. And the illusion me stabbed you?" I'm not sure I followed his story.

"Yeah, that sounds about right, in the most condensed version. And now I have these nightmares, but they're not relegated only to night. It keeps replaying in my mind every time I see you. It's as if I can't separate the illusion from reality. My mind sees you, and every alarm in my body goes off. I see you as a threat even though I know you're not." His voice is thick with emotion, and his posture screams defeat. Arms limp at his sides, he moves further away from me.

At least now I have an answer. Unfortunately, there is no way for me to fix this. It could take years of therapy to undo the damage done in the underworld.

Even the glistening ripples of water on the lake can't bring me joy. "Wow. I don't know what to do with this." I've got nothing. I don't even want to fight anymore.

"And neither do I, which is why we can't get married. Not right now anyway. We can't even set a date for the future. I have no way of knowing how long it will take before I'm no longer afraid of you." Mark covers his mouth with his hand and wipes his lips. "And those words don't even sound right coming out of my mouth." His body slumps against the railing as if it's his only lifeline.

"Does Arden know?"

"He knows. He was there when it happened. He had his own illusion to deal with. We all did. None of us escaped."

I take a few steps down the stairs and drop onto the top step. My head falls into my hands.

"It doesn't help that the demon venom is still in my system. I have no doubt it's messing with my head. I'm okay as long as I don't see you. Or think about you."

A humorless laugh escapes. Of course, as long as he's not around me, he's fine. No wonder he can't be in the same room with me. He thinks I'm going to kill him. At least, that's what he sees in his mind.

He's right. There's no way we can get married.

A solitary tear traces a path down my cheek. The distant call of a bird does nothing to soothe me. My hands fist the hair at my scalp, and I pull tight until the sting registers. Anything to take away the ache within.

"Okay, so now what? What do we do?"

He clears his throat before he continues. "I'm going to leave the team. For now, I'll work directly with Arden on whatever he needs help with."

"But you're my Guardian. We're a team. What am I supposed to do?"

"I've thought about that, too. You can work at the clinic. It's what you did for years when you worked at the hospital. You are so good at it, and you love it."

Angry tears drip from my eyes. He's thought of everything. How perfectly perfect for him. We will live separate lives and just move on. It all sounds very clinical.

As if my heart is not involved. As if I'm not irrevocably attached to him.

What do they call it now? An "uncoupling"? As if it's that easy.

How does one go about it? Living when it feels like you're dying inside?

You know what? This is all his fault. He made me believe in love, that I could have it all, with him.

I stand up and dust off my pants. Without looking back, I walk the rest of the way down the stairs and stop. "Okay." It's all I say before I walk to the lake and turn right and keep walking. The sun will go down soon, but I don't care. Maybe I'll get lost.

I don't even know what to feel right now. How I wish I could feel numb, but that's not at all what I feel. Too many feelings. Too many emotions. Like a tidal wave surging up and over to take me out. Pummeling wave after wave.

His words, like a physical blow, their weight unbearable.

Heartbreak. That's all I can come up with. Everything hurts. It all hurts. Too much.

The pain of rejection cripples me again. As if I am held underwater and can't take a breath. I struggle to find air, but there is none to be found.

Not once, not twice, but three times to endure the agony of rejection. The shame of being discarded over and over and over again. My dad. Lucas. And now Mark. The one man I thought I could count on.

How much pain can one person endure before it breaks them? How many times do I experience rejection before I finally give up? The pain, it's too much, it's suffocating. No one just gets over something like this.

Is it possible to stop time? I need everything to stop right now. I need the world to stop spinning so I can get off and catch my breath.

My foot snags on a root sticking out of the ground, and I tumble forward, barely catching myself before I faceplant in the dirt. This is my life. I roll over and sit up.

Sparkles from my diamond ring catch my eye in the fading sun. A symbol of love, meant to be forever. How very short forever is.

I remove it and examine it, remembering the day he proposed. Valentine's Day. It's only been a month.

That's it. We rushed it. We should have waited.

My hand tightens into a fist around the exquisite ring nestled in my palm. The edges of the diamond cut into my skin, and I squeeze tighter to feel the pain. The dam breaks. I lean forward, my face to the ground, and weep at the unfairness of it all. It wasn't supposed to be this way.

How many days has it been since I stood in my bedroom ready to step into my wedding dress and start a new life with Mark?

Is this it? Is this how it ends?

"Why, God? Why?" My voice echoes and rolls over the water. But no answer returns.

A groan from the very depths of my soul escapes the confines and is released to anyone who will hear. Which would be absolutely no one.

Such a ball of messy emotions being pummeled by my tight control like a whack-a-mole.

By the time I gather those emotions in a tight ball and stuff them in a dark corner, the blackness of night cloaks the sky. It's fitting. The sliver of moon sheds little light. And I don't have my cell phone to use the flashlight app.

It's fine. I don't want to go home right now, anyway. I would stay out here all night, but the temperature is dropping, and I'm not dressed for a chilly night out in the woods.

The stuffiness in my head muffles the surrounding sounds, giving the illusion of safety.

I can't go back and face everyone. The pity in their eyes. The questions.

I don't mind the solitude. *Hello, old friend.* This I remember. It's familiar, and I can go back to it again.

My fist opens to reveal the elegant ring, its tattoo now marking my palm with a bloody imprint. No, gorgeous ring, I will not be putting you back on. Time to hide you away and forget you. I shove it into the pocket of my pants where it can no longer mock my pain.

Chapter 20

Mark

I destroyed her. Not with fists, but with words. Helpless to protect her from my very own utterance, she shattered like shards of glass from a carelessly thrown ball through a window, then locked those emotions down tight and wandered away. Head held high, she strode through the trees and out of view. No doubt to fall apart in solitude.

She's not the only one devastated by this turn of events. Not one single part of me wants to be separated from her, but I can't be around her either.

The love I have for her has not changed, only grows more with the dawn of each new day. There is no one else for me but her, and the bitter truth of it all is I can't be near her.

There is nothing I won't do to conquer this fear and get my life back. And once I do, if she will still have me, I will fight with everything I have to show my commitment to her, to us.

Left standing alone on the back porch with nothing left to lose, my hands rub down my face, and I groan out in frustration. The scratch of unshaven whiskers bristles against my hands.

We should be on our honeymoon right now, walking down the beach hand in hand, discussing our future, not walking away from each other.

My face tilts to the heavens, the bright sky in profound contrast to the shadow of bitter grief blanketing my soul. "Lord, I can't continue like this. The pain is unbearable. We need your help. Please heal my mind to see Your truth, and send peace and comfort to Elizabeth. Encourage her heart. We won't make it without you."

The back door scrapes across the threshold. "Mark," Mom's voice cuts through my desperate plea to the only One who can bring healing to this desperate situation.

She says nothing further, only wraps her arms around me and holds me close. Knowing I don't need to be brave for her, the tears tumble over, and I fall into the loving embrace.

"We don't have to leave. We can stay as long as you need us." She pulls away and studies my face.

As much as I want my parents to stay, I'm a grown man and should handle this on my own. "No, Mom. It'll be okay. Eventually. You and Dad have a life to get back to at home. And one day soon you'll be back for the wedding, I promise." Now, my primary purpose is to make those words come true.

"You know we'll be praying for both of you. It won't always be like this. God will bring healing, and you will have a wonderful life together." She squeezes my arm and walks back inside.

Left alone to trudge through these somber thoughts, I consider the immediate future. Life without Elizabeth. Life without my team. I have to remind myself it's only temporary. Mom is right. It won't be this way forever. It can't be. I won't let it.

My gaze follows the path Elizabeth took when she left. She doesn't want to see me right now, and I get it. Not after the way we left things. Old me longs to go after her, but it kills me that I can't.

"Lord, please be with Elizabeth. Help her know she's not alone."

After an hour of waiting around Elizabeth doesn't return. I need to do something. I can't sit around here all day.

When I walk back inside, Mom and Dad are in the kitchen feverishly whispering but stop when they see me.

"I'm going to head out for a bit, but I'll be back to bring you to the airport when it's time for you to leave." I need a moment to pull myself together.

Dad pats my shoulder. "Don't worry about us, son. Do what you need to do, and we'll be here when you get back."

***

Weighted feet carry me to the library inside The Cave. I had no destination in mind when I set out to clear my head, but this feels right. Books, some of them hundreds of years old, have their own sordid stories to tell. Maybe one will soothe the disquiet within.

But there is only one book that holds the answers for which I seek. Only one that can truly quell the ache inside.

My feet set a path to the wooden bookcase tucked in the very back corner. An often unused portion of the library, it sits secluded from the rest of the world. I discovered a hidden door in the bookcase a few months back. Every boy's dream . . . a secret passage. All the times I've been in this particular spot, no one else has wandered back here. I haven't shared this discovery with anyone, and for now, it's all mine.

The passageway opens to a set of stairs on an upper level. I secure the bookcase closed behind me and ascend the creaky wooden stairs. Anticipation fills the air with each step.

This is the one place I can disconnect from everything and be with the Light. My own private sanctuary. A space to breathe.

At the top step, I twist the knob and open the door. The musty smell of old books and dust wraps around me in a familiar embrace. Everything is just as I left it the last time I was up here.

When I entered this room for the first time, it was stacked with boxes of old books and long-forgotten, broken furniture shoved in a corner. With a little TLC, I was able to clean it up a bit, fix and rearrange some of the furniture, and unpack the boxes.

A mini library within a library and my personal refuge from the storms of life. The breath I didn't even know I was holding flows out unencumbered. I secure the door behind me, solidifying my privacy.

The old world style baroque armchair greets me like an old friend, and I sink into it and lean forward. I rest my elbows on my legs and cradle my head in my hands. Tremors roll through my body as the scene replays in my mind of the agony

I alone caused Elizabeth. I never want to be the one to cause her distress. My only desire is to bring her happiness. To share in all the joys life will bring and help carry the load during dark times, but never be the one to cause her grief.

After a few hushed moments, I straighten and reach for the book on the side table. It was a brilliant find. A Bible almost one hundred years old, tattered and weathered but still holding strong.

I treat it with care and open it with a delicate touch, seeking words of solace, hope, and healing.

"Father, lead me in your Word and open my heart to hear You. You alone hold the key to life. Please lead me, I pray."

Led to open Psalms, the thirty-fourth chapter, I turn the pages. And as I read, the fourth verse strikes me in the chest. I feel it deep in the marrow of my bones. "I sought the Lord, and He heard me, and delivered me from all my fears."

"Father, please free me from these fears that plague my mind." It leaves no question. My job is to pray and trust Him. He will deliver me from all these fears in His perfect timing. He is intimately aware of the fears that torture me. The ones I cannot even understand.

The rest of the time is spent reading and praying only to stop when the alarm on my phone sounds, reminding me to bring my parents to the airport.

When I return later, I track down Arden. He can either provide me with some nugget of wisdom, or he can put me to work. Either is fine with me.

It was difficult leaving my parents at the airport to catch a flight home. Mom cried as she hugged me. Dad prayed over me, then gently led Mom away.

God blessed me with the best parents. I miss them already and almost told them to stay. It was on the tip of my tongue, but I couldn't bring myself to say it. This thing with Elizabeth is more than I can handle on my own, but I would be using them as a crutch instead of dealing with it head on.

Arden is in his office pouring over documents when I finally locate him. He glances up from his reading when he notices movement in the doorway. His eyes are drawn and weary.

"What can I help you with?" I pull up a chair and sit down in front of his desk.

He leans back with a sigh and throws the pen onto his desk. "Just going over some correspondence from our international offices. We're trying to figure out how to get a hold of all the trafficking organizations popping up around the world.

No sooner does one get shut down than two more take its place. Honestly, it's the same with all the crime, murders, evil. It doesn't stop, which means we can't stop. Some days it's so overwhelming. Insurmountable even."

"Is there something I can take off your plate? I'm available." I cross an ankle over my knee.

"Yes, but I still want you to rest as much as possible. Don't get sidetracked with busy work, your job right now is to heal. Completely." He glances around at the piles neatly stacked on the desk.

He gathers several files and hands them to me. "But since you insist, these are requests. Please review them and reply. I trust your wisdom. Just notate your response."

I reach across the desk and take the files from him. His gaze is contemplative as he watches me. "Let's get together later. We can work on some light training. I think it will do us both some good to get our muscles moving."

I tap the files against my hand and stand from the chair. "You got it."

Back in the library, I tackle the files from Arden. The work is nothing complicated, just time consuming. No wonder Arden is overwhelmed.

We meet later that evening to spar. It feels good, but I quickly tire, and Arden takes notice. "Here, let's have a seat." He points to the bench against the wall and hands me a water.

"Thanks." I guzzle it back without stopping until the bottle is empty.

Arden stares off at nothing in particular, his gaze unfocused. "What else is going on? This is more than being overwhelmed."

He shakes his head as if to clear it, then looks at me. "It seems that after all these years Brenda and I will be parents."

Parents. At his age. He and Brenda aren't old really, but they must be in their late fifties.

He chuckles and sets his water down. "I can see by the look on your face that you're surprised. It's not what you think. She's not pregnant. Brenda wants us to take Angel in, maybe even adopt her, if it's possible. And I agree with her that Angel will get the best care possible in a stable home, and Brenda will be the best mother. It's what we've always wanted, it's just happening in a different way than we expected. I thought our time had passed, but God saw it differently."

"Well, then, congratulations are in order. I'm happy for you." Unfortunately, this situation is not that simple.

After a few moments of silence, I ask the question running through my mind. "What about the baby?"

"Yeah, that's the part we've been discussing. Angel is too young to take care of herself, let alone a baby. We also don't know if she even understands that she's pregnant. Brenda hasn't been able to get her to talk. Whether that's because of the trauma or simply fear, we don't know yet. Angel needs our full attention and focus to help her heal. We think adoption of the baby will be best for everyone."

"That makes sense, but it's a tough situation all the way around." My face breaks out into a huge grin. "I hope you're ready for this, Pops."

He shakes his head, but his grin is wide. "I don't think for a second this will be a walk in the park. But Brenda and I are able and willing to give Angel everything she needs. Brenda plans to quit her job, and I will need to be available more. It will mean changes to our normal routine and way of life."

Arden leans back, getting comfortable. "I'll be looking for someone to help me with daily tasks." He shakes his head before I can respond. "No, it can't be you. Your life won't always be like this. You'll be joining your team again soon. You and Elizabeth will get married, and your life will be busy. But I will gladly use your help until that happens."

Speaking of my team, a few of them walk toward us as Arden and I finish our conversation. The numbers have dwindled now that Grace and Sloan are down for a few days, but the New Orleans team stayed on.

Elizabeth is absent, but Roz may not have her back on the team yet. It couldn't hurt to ask, though.

"Where's Elizabeth?" I haven't seen or heard from her since I watched her walk away earlier today. I know she doesn't want to hear from me, but surely someone from our group has spoken with her.

They all glance at each other but shake their heads.

"We assumed she was with you all day. Why? What's going on?" Roz goes on alert.

I have no desire to make a group announcement that I've indefinitely postponed the wedding. As much as I don't want to discuss it, they need to know.

I briefly describe my experience in the underworld that brought me to this point, along with the discussion with Elizabeth earlier.

Each of their faces displays what they think about the situation. Roz is horrified, Cressida is heartbroken, Sookie looks like she wants to take my head off. I should probably sleep with one eye open tonight.

Dax gives nothing away. He simply assesses me, silently asking if I'm okay. Of course, I'm not okay. None of this is okay, and I don't know when it will be.

"I'll text her." Roz walks away with her phone in hand, typing out a text.

"Come on, let's spar for a little bit." Arden begins to speak, but Dax raises his hand. "Don't worry, I'll go easy on him, and I'll make sure he gets to bed early."

Arden nods and watches as we plod to the sparring mats.

Roz strides up to us. "She texted that she's fine, but she hasn't responded to any of my other questions." When I turn my head to look at Roz, Dax takes that moment to throw a punch that I fail to see or block. It glances off my chin and causes me to stumble to the side.

I lift my hand. "My fault, I took my eyes off the fight."

Dax raises his hands to show he paused. "I'm sorry. I was already mid-strike when you turned your head."

"Thank you, Roz, for checking. Please don't let her shut you out. I'm not able to protect her right now, but I would appreciate it if both of you will guard her until I can do it again."

Dax moves to stand next to me. "You know we will."

"I think I'm done. I'm going to get a bite to eat and go to my apartment. Thank you for sparring with me."

Dax pats me on the shoulder. "Take care. I'll see you tomorrow."

Alone in my apartment, I settle into the silence. It's deafening with no one around. It never bothered me before, but right now it couldn't be more grating.

I pull out my Bible and read through Psalms thirty-four again, focusing on verse four, "I sought the Lord, and He heard me, and delivered me from all my fears."

"Lord, please free me from all my fears. Remove this irrational fear that I have when I'm around Elizabeth. I can't do this, but You can."

That's how I spend the rest of my night. In prayer.

Chapter 21

Elizabeth

Roz and Grace blow up my phone. I'm fine, but I don't feel like discussing any of it or answering any more questions.

They can't fix this, or make it better.

Sitting by the lake in the dark last night, I did a lot of thinking. If Mark can step back from our team, then so can I, but it will be on my terms.

It's time to go back to how life was before. Before Mark. Before learning my fate as a Light Bearer. It was safe and sheltered. I didn't have a lot of friends, and I was okay with that. Fine even. There was no worry about my heart being crushed or torn apart. I kept my head down, did my work, helped people who needed it, and that was enough for me.

So far, I'm zero for two on walking down the aisle. Didn't learn that lesson the first time. Nope, had to try it again.

When Mark popped up, I wasn't even looking for a relationship. I was good, content even.

Time to take a step back and re-group, find a new way forward.

The Light nudges me, but I ignore it. I need to figure this out on my own. It's my fault for opening myself up again.

Time to figure out what my future will look like going forward and make it happen.

With keys in hand, I lock the door behind me. It's been too long since I've seen Andromeda or had my favorite cup of coffee from her shop.

One foot into the Miracle Beanery and the intoxicating scent of coffee permeates every cell, like an old friend wrapping me up in a warm hug. See? Coffee is the best friend.

Andromeda squeals when she sees me step inside. She runs around the counter and launches her lithe frame into my body. I catch her with ease. All of that training really paid off. Before she would have knocked me over.

"Ah! It's good to see you. Where have you been? I didn't think you would drop off the face of the earth when you went to work for Triton Security."

I duck my head and groan. "Yeah, neither did I. It's good to be back in here. I've missed you." And I mean that. She's a good friend with no messy interference where it's not welcome.

"Have a seat anywhere you like. I'll bring your favorite and come sit with you. I hired a new part-time employee, so I can come and visit with you for a few minutes." When she turns, her skirt flares out and her bracelets jingle.

She's so bright and bubbly. So unlike me. If only I could be bright and bubbly, too. I don't think I could pull it off, though. Not for very long anyway.

The leather armchair next to the fireplace beckons me to stay awhile. Sitting here next to the fireplace is one of my favorite places to be. Surrounded by coffee and books.

My purse buzzes, but I don't bother to take out my phone and look at it. I open my bag and pull out a book I've been wanting to read but haven't had the time. The plan is to stay here for several hours since no one will think to look for me here.

I've only just started in on the first chapter when Andromeda stops at the table with two glorious cups of coffee in hand. "You are literally one of my favorite people, but today you are definitely number one."

"Well, I'm honored, and I'm not above bribery. I hope this keeps you coming back. Alistair will bring us some pastries in a minute." She settles on the leather couch next to my chair and props her feet on the table. "It's so nice to put my feet up for a little bit. Thanks for the excuse to take a break."

"You are very welcome." I clink my mug against hers and take the first magnificent sip of divine goodness. This. This right here is what I needed. I relax further, sinking deeper into the chair. Any deeper and I may become invisible. Wouldn't that be nice?

"Andromeda, you are truly an artist. I want to be like you when I grow up."

"Darling," she says with a twist of her hand and dangling bracelets, "this world would be a very dull place if we were all the same. You are uniquely you for a reason, and don't ever try to change who you are. That would be a tragedy."

Alistair drops off two croissants, gives me a wink, and walks away.

Andromeda tosses her hand in the air. "He's a total flirt, just ignore him. These almond croissants are from the bakery up the road. They will melt in your mouth. I can't eat these every day, but I will indulge now and then."

She passes the plate over. The first bite is buttery and sweet. The almond paste is subtle and one of my favorite flavors.

"So good." I let out an unlady like groan.

"I know. That's why I get my pastries from there. My specialty is coffee, not food. I leave that to the experts."

She places her mug down. "So, how are you doing? And don't tell me 'fine'. I want to know the truth."

If I can tell anyone, it's Andromeda. What I can't tell her about is being a Light Bearer. So, I take the safe route. "I don't know that I'm cut out for Triton Security. I'm thinking about putting in my notice."

"Oh, does that mean you would go back to work at the hospital?" She rests her arm along the back of the couch and shifts her body to face me.

That's not something I know the answer to. "I'm thinking about just taking some time off." And here comes the big bombshell. "Maybe even adopt."

She squeals and claps her hands. She jumps up and hugs me. "You would make an amazing mom. I just know it."

Brenda mentioned she and Arden were looking into adoption for Angel's baby, and the words blurted out before I could stop them. I told her I may be interested in adopting the baby. This was before Mark blindsided me with his announcement.

I haven't discussed it with him, and I'm glad I didn't. It looks like this will be a solo venture. The more I think about it the more it solidifies in my bones. I want to be a mom. It wasn't until I was around Mark's family and saw how wonderful it could be that I decided I could have that for myself.

The baby needs a loving home, and I can be the one to provide it. I don't have to work, and the baby would have my undivided attention.

"I'm still thinking about it. No definite decisions have been made." I let out a sigh of frustration. Everything is up in the air, and I'm waiting for it all to fall and settle. "I don't know. If I make any permanent decisions, I'll let you know."

"Please do. Don't fall off the face of the earth again. I don't think my heart could take it. Here," she reaches for my mug, "let me get you a refill."

I wasn't planning on telling anyone I was thinking about adoption, but Andromeda doesn't know who I work with. She won't say anything.

After a few minutes, she drops off another cup of coffee. "I see you have a book, so I'll leave you to it. Stay as long as you like. I'll check on you in a little while."

I settle in and lose myself in the unfolding story of secrets and romance. A former FBI agent burned by her handler, forced to rebuild her life and forge a new path. She pivots her career to a private investigator determined to bring justice to cold cases, breathing life into investigations gathering dust and long forgotten by authorities.

Andromeda refills my mug a few times, but I'm left in my own little bubble, following the story of betrayal. Something I can relate to.

It's early afternoon before I emerge from my book haze. Probably because I need to go to the bathroom.

When I finally look at my phone, I cringe. So many missed calls and text messages. The safest route is to text Mom, and she can let everyone else know I'm still alive. It's a cowardly move, but I don't care. I have nothing to say.

My next shift to watch over Angel starts in a couple of hours, and I want to stay on that rotation. That's one thing I'm not willing to walk away from, but if I'm going to be on time, I need to get home and get a shower.

Andromeda gives me a hug before I leave with a promise to be back soon.

I arrive at Angel's room right on time.

Grams is the only one sitting with Angel when I walk in. She is sleeping peacefully while Grams works on a crossword puzzle.

"Hey, how's it going?" I place my bag down next to the couch.

"Quiet as always. She still hasn't said anything since the day she first woke up. The doctor wants her to get up and walk around. We need to get her out of that bed. Maybe you can help with that after she wakes up and gets some food in her. She still doesn't seem interested in food." She sighs and lays down the crossword puzzle.

"Thank God for Brenda and her never ending patience. It looks like this is going to be a long road." Grams watches me with eyes that see way too much.

"I know. None of this is easy. There's no textbook way to deal with this."

When Grams stands up, I give her a hug. Thankful she doesn't ask me any questions, although she probably wants to.

"The girls are fixing dinner tonight. I need to get going." Before she walks out the door, she turns back to me. "It won't always be this way, you know. Don't make any life-altering decisions in the midst of heartbreak. Trust me on this." She gives me a wink and walks out the door.

I've heard that before. But sometimes it's the only thing that makes sense. Sometimes changes have to be made.

When I walk over to check on Angel, her eyes are open and she's watching me. "Hi there. Let's get some food for you."

I press the button for the nurses station and wait for them to respond. "Yes? Do you need something, Grams?"

"It's me, Elizabeth. Can we get a tray of food for Angel? Maybe some ice cream and macaroni and cheese?" I give her a wink.

"That sounds like an interesting combination."

She's not wrong. "Just trying to find something she will actually eat. We need to get her interested in food. I want to get her up and walking later if you want to come by and help."

"Sounds good. I'll have that tray to you soon." She clicks off the speaker.

"Angel, we are going to try some food, and then get you out of this bed to walk around for a bit. But don't worry, we won't go too far in case you get tired."

She gasps in horror, eyes wide with fear. What in the world did I say to scare her? Then I notice her hand on her swollen belly. The baby must be moving. It won't be long before he or she makes an appearance.

How frightening it must be for someone who doesn't understand what's going on.

I move to the bed and perch next to her. "Nothing is wrong. You are safe, and you are okay. Brenda told you there is a baby in your tummy. The baby is just moving right now. It's a natural thing for the baby to move, and you've done nothing wrong."

"Let's take some deep breaths." I breathe in slowly and breathe out slowly, hoping she will mimic my movements.

After a few minutes, she calms enough to slow her breathing. "Do you mind if I place my hand on your belly?" She stares at me with eyes wide, full of fear and the unknown.

With a slow motion, I move my hand toward her belly in case I need to pull it back quickly. No sense in scaring her further.

She allows me to lay my hand against her abdomen, and I keep my voice calm and reassuring. "What happened to you before you came here — that's why there is a baby. That is not your fault. You did nothing wrong." The baby moves at the sound of my voice, and my gaze widens in surprise. A small smile crests my lips.

"What do you think, when the time comes, I adopt your baby and take care of it for you? Would that be okay?"

Maybe it's my imagination, but she gives the barest, most imperceptible nod. I'll leave it for now. More than anything, I want her to know she is safe.

The nurse brings a tray of food in. Two bowls of ice cream and two bowls of macaroni and cheese. No, it's not healthy, but we need to get her interested in food. Interested in anything really.

I take a bite of the ice cream and encourage her to do the same. She's hesitant, but picks up the spoon and gets the smallest amount. She places the spoon in her mouth and stops. Her eyes widen, and the smallest smile appears.

They've been giving her broth, crackers, and bananas. Mild and gentle foods, but she hasn't been interested in any of it. It was time to switch it up.

"It's good, isn't it? Now, we can't eat like this all the time, but it's okay to have a treat now and then."

I sit with her while both of us eat small bites of food. She even tries the macaroni and cheese. She didn't eat all of it, but she ate. I could just hug her for the effort, but that would cause her to panic. Small steps, but this feels like a huge win.

"Now, how about our next big adventure? Let's get out of this room and walk around." She still doesn't respond, but I watch her eyes, bright with excitement.

Encouraged by her bravery, I buzz the nurse again to see if she can take a walk with us. I hold my hands out to Angel and let her take the lead. I let her reach for me in her own time. The nurse walks in and helps Angel up.

We are holding her up, but it will be up to her to move around. We don't want her stuck in this room or in this bed. She's finally free, and she needs to feel like it.

We inform her of where we will touch her to help her walk and emphasize it's only until she can walk on her own. When she's strong enough, we won't have to help her walk.

It's a slow process, but we go down the hallway and loop back around for the room. It's a lot for someone who's been in bed for so long.

One of the male doctors' rounds the corner and heads straight for us while looking down at his tablet. Angel freezes on the spot. This is the first man she's seen since she's been here.

I release one hand on her side and position myself in front of her. "Excuse me, could you please go back until we can get back to the room?" I keep my voice soft and low.

The doctor looks up at my voice. At first he's confused, but then he sees Angel behind me. He nods his head and hurries back where he came from.

Once he's out of sight, I ease back to Angel's side. She's frozen in fear. We've kept her in a safe bubble with the same people, and it was too soon to spring a male doctor on her.

"It's okay. He's gone. You're safe. He's not going to hurt you. We are going back to the room." We basically carry her back to the room and get her settled.

"You've done such a good job. I'm so proud of you. You can rest now." I walk back to the chair and sit down. "I brought a book. I can read to you if you're up for it." She responds only with a blank stare.

Overall, it's been a success. I text Brenda to share the good news. She's thrilled and can't wait to see her tomorrow.

Angel rests fitfully through the night, but I'm there to soothe her and even read to her at one point.

Brenda arrives early the next morning with a tray of food for all three of us to share. She's hoping that if we eat with Angel, she will be more interested in eating.

Angel regards Brenda but doesn't say anything. Based on her eyes, she's happy Brenda is here.

We eat breakfast, and I fill Brenda in on our adventures. Angel picks at her food, but she eats.

"Have you thought any more about what you mentioned to me the other day?" Brenda's attention focuses on me.

The adoption. "Yes, I'm still interested, and I know you will need an answer soon. There isn't much time."

"What about Mark? Is he ready?"

"I haven't discussed this with Mark because he's postponed the wedding. Indefinitely. I have to move forward with my life. So, his opinion about this is irrelevant."

She gasps, and her hand covers her mouth. "Oh my gosh, I'm so sorry. I had no idea. Are you sure this is something you want to tackle on your own?"

"I'm thinking about stepping away from my duties here, and I'm financially stable. I don't need to work. The baby will be well cared for and loved. I also talked to Angel about it last night. I think it's important that she has a say in it as well. I want her to be comfortable with it."

Brenda contemplates the situation. A single woman wanting to adopt a baby. It's not that unusual.

"Have you prayed about this?" she asks.

"Uh, no, I haven't." I haven't prayed, and I haven't discussed it with anyone. I don't think an off-handed remark to Andromeda counts as a discussion.

"This is a huge life-changing commitment. You need to pray about it and know that this is what you're supposed to do. If you try to do something outside of God's will, it will get messy."

She's right, but I don't want to admit it.

I haven't prayed about any of it. I've been too hurt and angry. And if I'm being honest, I want to make my own decisions. There's no reason to wait on God to tell me something I don't want to hear. And no, I haven't asked Him about leaving my team either.

I'm afraid I won't like His answer.

Chapter 22

Mark

Over the next couple of weeks, I help Arden with busywork he doesn't have time for. I'm able to relieve some of his workload so he can take the time to get a room prepared for Angel. They need the room ready for her to move into as soon as she is released. She's doing well getting up and even eating, and the medical team will release her soon under supervised care. The clinic is fine, but it's not a good long-term solution. She needs a home with space to make it her own.

Brenda will have Arden visit Angel in the hospital to help her get acquainted with him. It's an enormous risk, but she needs to get used to seeing men around and to know she's safe. And she will. Eventually.

Heading back to the library, I get a text from Devon saying he wants to meet for lunch today if I can spare the time. I don't think Elizabeth has spoken with him since we've been back from the underworld, and that's got to be disconcerting for him. She definitely hasn't been by to see him.

His recovery has been slow, but even so, it's still faster than mine. Some days it feels like I'm trudging uphill through tar with a gorilla tied to my back. It's painfully slow.

Devon and Gage are already seated at a table in the far-left corner when I walk in. I stop and fill a tray with food and join them. "How's it going?" I take the seat across from Devon.

"Physically getting stronger each day. What about you? I heard about the demon poison, that's tough. Recovery can take a long time." Devon reaches for his coffee mug, takes a sip, and leans back in his chair as if settling in for a long conversation. Gage picks at what's left of the food on his plate with a bored expression.

"I'm getting better. Not used to being sidelined for so long. Today I have a bit more energy. So, Dax and I will take advantage of it and meet later for some strength training." I take a bite of the stacked turkey sandwich and wash it down with some water.

"What about Elizabeth? How is she? We've only texted a couple of times, and that's it. I don't know if she blames me for what happened, but I can understand if she does." His forehead wrinkles and the fine lines around his eyes become more pronounced.

Gage puts down his glass with a loud thunk. "She can't blame you for that. It wasn't your fault. You're just as much a victim as she was."

I shake my head and place the sandwich back on the plate. "I don't think she blames you. She's kept her distance because she's afraid it might happen again."

The light in his eyes dims a little. "Have you found anything that might keep it from happening again? I can't live with the possibility of being used as a portal to the underworld . . . again."

"I need to find the journal that has the information about people or objects being used as portals. I don't remember which journal it is, but I'll do some digging and see what I can find." It's not what he wants to hear. I know he wants a straightforward solution, but there may not be one.

"I was hoping you'd found an answer already. It's arduous living with this burden." His dejected tone stirs my heart.

I fold my hands under my chin. "I know. I need to devote more time to research and see what I can find. Have you heard any more voices since we've been back?"

He shakes his head. "Not one. Nothing. Not even a feeling. I've been spending regular time with the Light, and I've discovered a depth I've never known before. I'm praying there is no more portal. That it's gone."

"Gage, have you noticed anything different with Devon?"

He levels his gaze at me with determination. "Actually, he's more calm, centered even. Before, he would be the one to dive headfirst into a situation and ask questions later. He's not like that now. Believe it or not, I was the more rational of the two of us."

A chuckle escapes before I can stop it. "I would never have expected that."

Devon's lips tilt up at the edges. "God has given me a second chance, and I won't waste it. I want to be a part of Elizabeth's life, but never at the cost of her safety. If you can find a way to make it happen, I would be forever grateful."

"You've been the most important person in her life. Ever since your death, or what she thought was your death, she's missed you desperately. Until recently, she's felt very much alone in this world. I know she wants you back in her life, and I'll do what I can to make it happen."

Devon's face lights up with a full smile. At first, I think it's because of my words of encouragement.

"Hi, everyone," Hannah greets our table. "I'm a few minutes early, but I didn't think you would mind."

Gage stands up and removes his tray from the table. "Thanks, Hannah." He gives her a nod and leaves.

She must sense my confusion at his abrupt departure. "I told Gage I could use Devon's help with some of the housing issues that have come up recently. Gage had a meeting scheduled with Arden anyway, so the timing worked out."

Hannah must not notice how Devon looks at her, but his gaze is attentive in a way that suggests more than friendship. I wonder what Elizabeth would think about this development.

To have her friendship again. To sit down and talk with her and watch her facial expressions as we discuss this. My hand rubs the ache in my chest. Her absence is causing physical pain. I miss her with a fierceness that burns within me.

Pushing the tray aside, I stand up from the table. "All right, you kids, I'll leave you to it. Devon, I'll let you know as soon as I come across anything that may be beneficial."

He stands up to shake my hand with a firm grip. "I appreciate your help."

I lean down and kiss Hannah's cheek before I leave. She squeezes my arm when I walk past. When she tries to catch my eye, I don't respond.

Since there is nothing I can do right now to help myself, I'll help Devon in any way I can. What I need is access to his family journals.

I've texted and called Elizabeth a few times to check on her, with no response. I doubt she would respond if I were to ask for some of the family journals.

A violent punch to the shoulder greets me as I step into The Cave. "Come on, old man, let's train." Dax is already striding away while I rub my shoulder. Under normal circumstances, it would not faze me. It goes to show how much damage was done while I was in the underworld.

He puts me through the paces, but I don't quit. Sweat pours down my face, and I'm barely standing when we're done, but it's the farthest I've come since returning. He knows just how far to push me without breaking me. Although he brought me right to the brink.

"Let's go grab a bite to eat." He slings his arm around my shoulders, and I almost collapse from the weight of it. I'm barely standing as it is.

He must sense the instability he created because he quickly removes his arm.

"Wish I could, man, but I've got some errands to run." I won't fill him in on my plan of breaking and entering. He would probably volunteer to be my wingman. Which I would normally welcome, but on the off chance I run into Elizabeth, I would like to speak with her. Even if just for a moment. If I can be around her for a moment.

We don't need an audience for that. Things are awkward enough as it is.

No one knows where she's been. Based on what little Hannah has seen of Elizabeth, she's barely even home to sleep. Calls and text messages remain unanswered. We're all worried about her.

I'm more than worried. She's pulling away from us. Away from me. Even though, in a way, I pushed her to it. But it was only meant to be temporary, never permanent. Only until I can get myself together. Until I no longer have these panic attacks when I'm around her.

Until I can love her the way she deserves to be loved. And I can't love her that way while I'm still afraid of her.

"Anything I can help with?" Dax's words cut into my thoughts while I stare at nothing. He slaps me on the shoulder, getting my attention.

"Nah, man. You go ahead. I know the team is heading out soon, and you need to get ready before you go." The team is being sent out on a mission for a few days, minus Elizabeth and me.

Part of me feels like I'm letting them down, but the other part is fully aware that I would be an unnecessary liability.

"If you're sure. I'm only a call away if you need anything." His gaze does not leave mine, making sure I understand he means what he says.

I give him a nod of agreement. Once he's satisfied, he leaves to meet with the rest of the team.

Now, for a little B and E.

This may completely backfire. Elizabeth could be home. She could very well stab me for being in her personal space uninvited. I shudder at the memory of it happening before and almost back out. But if I can help Devon and Elizabeth mend their relationship, I will brave a panic attack. Or any other attack.

Part of me wants her to be at home just so I can put eyes on her and know she's not in a downward spiral. The other part hopes she never realizes I walked into her safe space unannounced. I know very well that she doesn't want me here.

When I walk through the door of The Cave, it opens to Elizabeth's hidden office. So technically, I'm not really breaking and entering.

The door closes behind me, and I glance around the empty office. Elizabeth doesn't come in here much by herself. She likes her comfy chair by the window in the living room. This office is just a holding place for the journals and books and for easy access to The Cave.

With hands on my hips, I bow my head and pray. "Lord, I need help. Please show me what I'm looking for. Help me find an answer for Devon. For Elizabeth. For myself." When I finish, I approach the first book case and scan over the journals.

The first time I looked through these journals, they were completely blank. Most likely, the words were hidden until the Light revealed them to me. Now, I need the Light to reveal the answer we need.

With so much history in this small space, I get lost in the pull of the old journals. What seems like only minutes to me could very well be hours later, something niggles at my ears, and I stop what I'm doing.

"What are you doing here?" The voice takes me off guard.

I jump and drop the journal I was reading, unaware anyone had come in.

Tiger sits primly on the desk watching me.

"You scared me. How long have you been sitting there?"

"Long enough to know you are completely absorbed in what you're doing."

I stand up and stretch my back. I've been sitting hunched over a pile of journals for who knows how long.

"How is she?" If anyone knows the truth, Tiger will.

"Not so good. She's planning on walking away from it all. She wants to go back to her isolated life because she thinks it will protect her from getting hurt again. But we both know that's not living. That's hiding, and it's no life at all. Especially not the life God has for her."

I fall back into the chair and brace my elbows on my knees, clasping my hands together. She's spiraling and letting the pain take over. What have I done? What can I do? My hands are tied. "It was never my intention to hurt her."

Tiger hops down from the desk and approaches me. "I know that, and I think deep down she knows it, too. But she's scared – scared of being rejected again. She's making decisions without thinking them through. She's reacting to the pain."

"How do I help her?"

"Get yourself healed, then pursue her as if your life depends on it . . . because it does."

A thump followed by a scrape resounds from upstairs. She's home. My time has run out. It's time for me to go.

Tiger sashays to the bookcase and paws a book on the second shelf. "You'll want to bring this book with you."

I reach for the journal and pull it out. "Thank you. For everything. Keep an eye out for her, please."

I pull open the door that leads back to The Cave. "You know I will," Tiger responds before I leave the room.

Journal in hand, I make my way to the library and my hiding spot, ready to dig in. Hushed tranquility encircles the room when I walk in. It's a welcome reprieve. I turn on the lamp next to my chair and settle in.

The journal I have in hand is a few hundred years old and mostly legible. Leather worn by time creaks as it opens. A tribute to the lives gone before us and a path to guide those who follow. I pull my personal journal from the side table and jot down notes as I read. Something in here will give us what we're looking for. It may not be an exact scenario of what we are dealing with, but there will be something useful. I hope I don't miss it.

Several hours in, I take my time to read carefully, being thorough in my search. The Light flutters as I flip the page. I read through it once, twice, even three times. Not sure I completely understand what I'm reading. It's so simple. Too simple.

With an idea in place, I schedule a meeting with Arden and Devon. I pray this works.

Chapter 23

Elizabeth

My hand freezes on the chair. Someone else is in the house. I pause and wait, but the sensation passes, and I continue to shove the chair out into the hallway. I'm on a mission to clean out the upstairs guest room and move the furniture into my upstairs office. The office that people can actually see, not the hidden one.

Tiger rounds the corner as soon as I clear the doorway.

"Oh, it's just you." She must've been the one I sensed in the house.

"You don't sound thrilled to see me." She jumps onto the chair I just moved.

"It's not that." I swipe the sweat from my forehead. "You know what? Never mind. It's fine." I'm not even going to start with her. She was the one I sensed in the house. No reason to have a discussion about it. Besides, her presence is comforting, but I'm not about to tell her that.

"You hungry? I was about to stop and fix something to eat." I need to take a break before I move all of this into the office and rearrange the setup in there.

In the kitchen, I fix a simple salad, and Tiger gets a can of tuna. The back patio is the perfect spot to enjoy some afternoon sun while we eat.

It's been nice having time to myself. To work when I want and rest when I want. There's no time clock to punch, no one telling me where to go or what to do. I set my own pace.

Why didn't I try this sooner?

With all the calls and text messages I've been receiving, I finally put my phone up and only check it periodically. Everyone wants to talk, ask me how I'm doing, make sure I'm okay with the wedding being called off. No, I'm not okay, and I'm not discussing it with anyone.

"You need to be careful not to get stuck in your own head. God gives wise counsel if you seek Him." The fork pauses on its way to my mouth, and I look at Tiger. She hops off the porch and saunters into the woods, leaving her tuna behind.

She wants me to pray, and I know I should, but I need some space right now just to be.

Looking out over my backyard, I remember I wanted to plant an herb garden several months back. Maybe even try my hand at some vegetables. I pull out my phone and look for someone who can clear out a space of land and bring in some dirt.

After lunch, I make the call.

The guy I speak with lets me know he had a cancellation and can bring his crew tomorrow. Excited to have that task marked off, I go back inside to finish clearing out the guest room.

***

The last few weeks fly by. The newest addition transformed my backyard, and I am pleased with the outcome. Tiny plants all nestled into their new home. I can't wait for them to grow. Fresh herbs and vegetables, all from my very own backyard. Time to experiment with some new recipes.

The room is finally finished. My plan to keep the upstairs office changed, and I moved the desk to my bedroom. There was a perfect spot for it next to the window. It's all coming together. Only needs a few last-minute touches.

I lean my shoulder against the post on the back porch and take a sip of coffee from a mug inscribed with *Trouble is brewing*. A contented sigh escapes. Domesticated life suits me.

The sun barely crests the horizon, casting its pink and yellow glow to release the night's hold. I'll never tire of this view. The way the sun glints off the water, the mountains with their majestic peaks in the background. A bird soars above the water, gliding effortlessly on the wind.

I tilt the mug back to finish the last sip of coffee and walk inside to get my purse.

It's time for my morning coffee and conversation with Andromeda. We meet each morning for coffee and the latest news. Plus, it keeps me from being a hermit. See? I'm getting around people.

As I reach for my purse, my phone buzzes with a text from Grace. Again. I glance at it before I shove it in my purse with no intention of responding.

But this text stops me.

Grace: Grams isn't acting like herself. I'm really worried, and I wasn't sure who I should reach out to. Do you think you can come over and check on her?

Me: Sure, I'll be right over.

Yes, I've been avoiding Grace, but there's no hesitation in my response. Grams isn't young, and she's been going full throttle since finding out she's a Light Bearer. If Grace thinks something is wrong, then it would be wise to stop by and check.

Going over there is the right thing to do. Maybe it's nothing, and I can turn around and come right back home. But if it's something serious, I would never forgive myself if I just blew off Grace's concern.

I pull up to the grand Victorian about thirty minutes later after nearly losing my vehicle in the pothole - laden driveway. It's a hazard. One day, someone will go down the driveway and will never be seen again.

"Knock, knock." I let myself in the front door and walk down the hallway past the staircase. "Where are you?"

"Back here. Come to the kitchen," Grace calls out.

Grace is pouring a glass of tea when I walk in and is the only one in the kitchen. "Where is Grams? What's going on?"

"She wanted to get something from the basement but hasn't come back up yet. I'm glad you're here. We can go down together." She grabs my arm and drags me to the door.

"How long has it been since she went down there?" Concern for Grams' health weaves a taut cord in my chest. Worry mounts as the list of possibilities ticks through my mind.

She tugs me down the stairs. "Long enough to be concerned." The stairs are a beautiful polished wood that belongs in the foyer of a grand home and not in a basement.

Once at the bottom of the stairs, I glance around what Grace called a basement. This is not like any basement I've ever seen. Victorian furniture fills the space and could be used as an extra living room for company. Windows set high against the ceiling give the only clue that this could be a basement.

The door at the top of the stairs creaks as it closes, which isn't creepy at all, then the lock clicks.

"Um, Grace, please tell me you have a key." She pivots away from me and moves to a vintage sofa tucked against the wall. An elegant victrola stands regally next to the red and gold sofa, and for a moment I wonder if it still works. But that's not why I'm here.

"Grams, where are you?" I don't see her, but she could be at the other end of the room.

Grace leans back on the couch and tucks her legs underneath her. All too casual for a crisis. "Grace, what's going on? Where is Grams?"

"Okay, promise not to get mad." She holds up her hands with an air of innocence she does not pull off.

Nothing good ever comes from a conversation that starts that way.

"What is going on? I want the truth." My hands land on my hips as I face her fully. The tips of my ears get hot, and my gut tightens.

"I may have lied a tiny bit about Grams." She pinches her thumb and forefinger together and scrunches up her face. "Don't worry. She's fine. She went to the grocery store to pick up what we need for dinner tonight."

The tips of my ears are just the beginning. My neck and face get too warm, and my skin prickles. Little pricks of light swim through my vision as anger takes over.

"What is the real reason I'm here? And why have you locked me in your basement?"

She stands and places her hands out to her sides. "What was I supposed to do? You won't answer any of my calls or texts. You're avoiding all of us. You're pulling away. You're never around when I sneak into your house. I was desperate." Tears fill her eyes, and her lower lip quivers.

A little of the anger melts, but not enough for any of this to be okay.

"And you thought this was a good idea?" My voice rises with the heightened emotions. "Lying to me? Locking me in the basement so I'm forced to talk to you? Not cool." I pace along the oriental rug to keep my hands from reaching out and grabbing hold of her.

"Look, I'm not saying it was a good idea, but I didn't know what else to do." Her shoulders lift as if to prove her innocence, but all I see is red.

I stare at Grace in indignation, who looks blessedly ashamed now. "What was your plan exactly?"

"Well, I was going to give you time to calm down, then I was going to find out why you're pulling away from all of us. Then convince you we need you, and you need us." Her bubbly personality is replaced with one of urgency, and regret laces her tone. "You can't just walk away. We're family, and family doesn't give up on each other."

Well, okay, she's got me there. But locking me in the basement is not okay, and she won't get a pass from me on that.

At least I'm safe, and I can call for someone to get me out if I need to.

"Grace, there are things about my life that I will not discuss with you. Sometimes people need to deal with things on their own." I fold my arms across my chest, ready to leave.

"But that's just it. You're so used to being alone you don't even realize you have us to talk to, to lean on. You don't have to go through anything alone."

"I'm ready to go." I'm not discussing my life with a teenager.

She moves to block my path to the stairs. "No, not until we talk about this."

Raised voices from the basement door float down. I can't make out what is being said, but whoever it is sounds angry.

"Grace, move out of my way. We are done here."

The door flies open, and Roz barrels down the stairs with Sloan on her heels. "Liz, are you okay?" Roz asks when she reaches the bottom of the stairs.

"I'm fine, just aggravated and ready to leave. Wait, did you know what Grace was planning?"

"No, I most certainly did not. I would never have gone for this. I stopped by to pick up a book that Grams left for me on the kitchen counter. This one," she throws out her thumb at Sloan, "was leaning against the basement door looking all too guilty. When I started asking questions, she told me what Grace planned," Roz huffs out with hands on her hips.

"Hey, it wasn't my idea." Sloan raises her hands in defense.

"No, but you participated by closing and locking the door. That's enough." Roz lets out a frustrated growl.

All three focus back on me as if I'm a caged animal ready to pounce. "Well, I've had enough for one day. Thank you, Roz, for unlocking the door for me. I'm leaving now."

Grace reaches for me as I walk past her, but I shrug off her hand. "Please don't hate me."

I stop at her words. "Grace, I don't hate you. Yes, you lied to me. I was worried about Grams, and the way you went about this was all kinds of wrong. I'm not happy with you right now, and I may not speak to you for a while, but I don't hate you. I need some time."

Her voice reaches me as I walk up the stairs. "I know you're hurting, but don't shut us out. Please."

My feet pause as I reach the door, but I don't turn back around. "I hear you. I promise not to shut you out. But don't call me today. And maybe not tomorrow either."

I exit the house and shield my eyes against the brilliant sun. No doubt Roz is giving them an earful and probably doling out punishment.

All the anxiety and tension drain out, leaving me depleted.

Roz finds me outside leaning against my car as I stare at the flower garden, trying to calm down before I get behind the wheel.

"I wasn't down there long, but I'm glad you showed up. If it came down to a fight with Grace to get out, no doubt she would probably win. I just wanted to leave." I fold my arms across my chest.

Roz leans against the car with me. "Are you kidding me? It's the least I can do. The girls have been sidelined. No more missions for the foreseeable future. If they can't be trusted to make decent decisions, then they cannot be trusted out in the field."

The scene I picture causes the tips of my lips to curl up. "I bet Sloan is having a fit."

"You know it." Roz shifts her feet. "They will also do all of your chores at home for you. I told them to give you a week to cool off before they show up."

"Thanks, Roz."

She nods her head in acknowledgement. "And you know . . . revenge is not a bad idea either. I'll help you come up with something good."

"I don't know. How do you pay someone back for lying to you and locking you in a basement? A very nice basement, I might add. Nicer than my house." I kick a rock against the ground.

"You let me think about that."

"You know, I hate to admit it, but Grace is right. I have been pulling away. I've thought about leaving the team and just walking away from it all." Maybe I should talk to someone.

"I've noticed. I wanted to give you your space, give you time to come around, but I'm worried you'll walk away if we push you too hard. I didn't have anything as elaborate as Grace planned, but I was going to talk to you."

She chuckles and lifts her face to the sky. "She loves you. We all do. You aren't just part of our team. You're family. When one of us is hurting, we all hurt."

"I'm just trying to figure out what to do. Nothing is working out. The wedding has been called off, Mark can't stand to be in the same room with me, and I allowed myself to become so exhausted that I was a liability to our team." I drop my hands to my sides in frustration. At myself. At the situation.

"Mark has not given up on you or the wedding. He's trying to heal so he can be the man you need him to be. That man is madly in love with you, and this is destroying him because he's scared to death of you"

"It just all feels so final. That this is it. That it won't get any better than this." And that's what it boils down to. That this final.

"That's the enemy talking. God does nothing halfway. What He starts, He finishes. When you get home, I want you to look up Philippians chapter one verse six. Meditate on it, and ask the Light to lead you. When you start feeling like you're going off the deep end, call me. Don't let it get to this point where you feel you have nothing else to live for."

With a deep breath, I allow her words to penetrate through the pain. "You're right, I will. And I'm turning my phone off for the rest of the day. I'm not ignoring anyone, but I need silence right now."

"I get it, and I'm sorry Grace ambushed you to force a conversation. I'll be having a discussion with her about boundaries later."

"I don't agree with the way Grace went about it. Or that Sloan went along with it, but she's right. I shut myself off, and I was spiraling." I push off from the car and dig the keys out of my purse. "I'll look up that scripture when I get home. I think what I need right now is a good cup of coffee and a hot bath."

"Before you go, I found out from Arden that we have no positive ID for Angel. IT has done all they can, running her photo through every database available. She's a Jane Doe."

"I can't say I'm surprised. We don't know the entire story, not until she tells us, if she even knows."

With no positive ID for Angel, we're unable to locate any family. She has no one.

No one but us.

"We'll take care of her." Roz walks to her car but turns before getting in. "And take care of you. I'll check on you tomorrow, and call me if you need me."

Before I get in my car, I give her a quick nod. I send a text to Andromeda since I missed our morning coffee. She doesn't need to worry.

I'm not looking forward to the drive home, but I need that coffee and a hot bath like something fierce. My limbs shake with the fading adrenaline of worry and anger.

Once I've settled in the bath with a glorious mug of coffee and my Bible, I look up that verse in Philippians.

"And I am certain that God, who began the good work within you, will continue His work until it is finally finished on the day when Christ Jesus returns."

I close my eyes and let the words sink in. God will not quit on me or give up on me.

Mark hasn't quit on me, even though it may feel like it because he can't be around me. Why does love have to be so complicated?

No, what I did was quit on him before he had the chance to do it to me. And that's not fair to him. I abandoned him when he needed me most. He needs me to fight for him and to fight for us. And what did I do? I walked away. I didn't answer his calls or texts. I ignored his attempts to check on me.

I will never admit to Grace that she got through to me with her little stunt. But she did. I'll let her sweat a little bit. She and Sloan can clean my house and run my errands. I think I might enjoy that very much.

Getting back into God's Word is nourishment to my anemic soul. I look up some other scriptures to meditate on.

In James it tells me I should see my difficulties as an opportunity for joy, because it produces endurance, and then, through that endurance I become stronger. But honestly, I would rather it just be easy. I don't want the difficult times. This scripture pushes me out of my comfort zone. But it pushes me to where God waits to help me, if I will let Him.

I've come to understand that this life in God is not an easy one or a safe one. Not in the way I would think of safe. My soul is safe in His hand for heaven and eternity, but my comfort is not. We work so furiously to be safe, happy, comfortable. But what if that's not how we're supposed to live our lives? To live a safe life seems like a good idea, but what if that's not what it's all about and we miss out on the adventure of a lifetime?

So many places in scripture it says, "Do not fear". I know I can trust God with my life. Even if I don't trust anyone else with my heart, He alone is trustworthy.

What about Mark? Is he worthy of my heart?

God seems to think so. So, I will trust Him. There are mysterious promises found in the Word of God, and maybe I won't understand it all this side of eternity. I will trust Him with my heart, and I will trust that He knows best for my life. I trust that there is no pain in my life that will ever be wasted. I trust He can bring good from it no matter what happens.

To live my life afraid of ever experiencing heartache is no way to live. It's inevitable. Difficult times will happen at some point, but is it bad to want a break from it, too?

Jesus, please heal my heart. Help me accept your words over my life and not the lies of the enemy. Please heal Mark, both mind and body. And thank you for the family you have given me. They may not be related by blood, but they are my family. And please forgive me for not coming to You sooner with this.

CHAPTER 24

MARK

Buzzing from my back pocket pauses my steps as I approach the door to Arden's office. We're meeting to discuss a potential solution regarding Devon. I'm a little nervous. This might work, but I don't want to get everyone's hopes up if it doesn't.

Worst case scenario? We all end up back in the underworld. A shudder runs through my body at the thought, and sweat breaks out on my forehead.

We need this to work.

Before I walk in, I pull out my phone.

My Love: Hi

With only one word, my heart stutters before finding its rhythm again. It's been weeks since I've heard from her, and now she's texting without me having to prompt her for a response.

I'm torn. Everyone is waiting for me to let them know what I've discovered, and now Elizabeth texts for the first time in weeks.

If she's reaching out, that can only mean one thing. She wants to talk. And I want nothing more than to hear her voice.

Reluctantly, I place the phone back in my pocket and walk into the office. I'll text her back when I can give her my undivided attention. She deserves that and so much more.

I hope this doesn't take long.

Arden sits behind his desk speaking with Dax and Roz while Hannah stands off to the side, flipping through a book.

"Thanks for coming in to share with us what you found. Devon and Gage should be here in a moment. Please have a seat." Arden motions to the chairs around his desk.

"Thanks. I really hope this works, but I'm not sure how long it will take to find out." I take the seat next to Dax and breathe in a shaky breath. My knee bounces, and I rub my hands on my jeans.

"There is no pressure on you. We're thankful for your time and dedication in looking into this matter." Arden gives a tense smile.

Devon and Gage walk in and shut the door behind them.

"Okay, let's get this show on the road," Gage announces to the room as he takes the chair closest to the door.

Devon wanders next to me and sits down. He leans over and whispers, "I know it doesn't seem like it, but Gage is worried this will be a dead end."

"He's not the only one," I mutter in response.

Hannah places the book back on the shelf and joins the rest of us.

Arden nods to me. "Okay, Mark, the floor is all yours. We're curious to hear what you've discovered."

Every eye focuses on me. The nervousness I felt earlier, now magnified. "I hope I haven't wasted anyone's time by having you all come here. And really, it seems too simple."

Roz speaks up, "And that's usually the way of it. We seem to make things way more complicated than they need to be."

I face Devon. "Based on what I've found, there is something used as an anchor in order to open a portal. It can either be physical, like an object on the person, or even something as simple as a scar. It can also be attached to a memory or a thought, and once it's triggered, it serves to open the portal."

Devon lets out a sardonic chuckle. "I have lots of scars, memories, and thoughts. How could we possibly pinpoint it to the exact one?"

I have given some thought to this. "I think I may know. What is the one thing you felt you couldn't trust God with? Something you were afraid to give to Him?"

The room remains silent. None of us can do for Devon what he needs to do for himself.

He hangs his head. The weight of it all rides on his shoulders. It goes back before being taken by Leviathan. To the years before captivity.

The stakes are high. None of us will have a moment of peace until he gets this right. This doesn't just hang over him, but over each one of us as well.

He releases a deep sigh, completely deflating before us. "The only thing it could have ever been. Elizabeth. She was my responsibility. It was my job to protect her. I kept her from this life to protect her, and all I did was fail her. Epically."

He shakes his head and stares at his open palms. "She deserved so much better than what I gave her. I've let her down every step of the way."

"No, you didn't," Hannah speaks up from behind Devon. "She knows you love her. That's more than she can say about her own father. So, now, you make it right. There's no place safer for her than in the hands of her heavenly Father. Let your hold on her go."

"Your job is to love her, be there for her, and let God protect her." That much I know, from my own experience. "Forgive yourself. This will free you from the responsibility that you can never meet. The expectations you had for yourself, to protect Elizabeth and keep her safe at all costs, were expectations you were never meant to carry."

"I know you're right, but I don't know how to let her go." He glances over at me. "You sure there's not an easier way to fix this?"

I shake my head. Sometimes the most simple answer is also the most difficult.

Hannah rests a hand on Devon's shoulder. "Let God do what He does best. He will take care of her. I trust that."

"Devon, you need to seek God's forgiveness for trying to take control, and you have to forgive yourself. The guilt is eating at you. God will help you, and He'll give you peace about it. Don't carry this guilt anymore. The enemy has used it against you. I agree with Mark. I believe this is the weapon the enemy used against you." Arden gives him a head nod. "You know what you need to do."

Dax and Roz stand and quietly leave the room. I stand next to Devon and place my hand on his shoulder. "We can't do this for you. This is between you and God. Allow Him to wipe away the guilt and set you free. But you also need to forgive yourself."

We leave the room to give Arden and Devon some privacy. I sure hope this works.

I fully believe that somehow Leviathan used Devon's guilt as an anchor and was able to pull the trigger at just the right moment to cause the most damage. And he almost won.

Now that I'm out of the room, I can breathe. I've been itching to text Elizabeth back. The whole time I sat in Arden's office, I wanted to pull that phone out and stare at the one word text she sent. Who would think that there would be so much hope in that one word?

I escape to my secret hideaway in the library. No one needs to see me grinning like a goofy teenager.

As soon as I secure the door behind me, I grab the phone and sink into my chair.

Me: Hi, it's good to hear from you. How are you?

She doesn't answer right away, and my excitement shifts a little. I waited to text her back, but only because I knew I would not be able to concentrate in Arden's office.

I need to be patient. I pick up the old, worn Bible from the end table and open it up. Only God can help Devon release Elizabeth to His care. It's the safest place for her to be, and once Devon realizes that, he will experience true freedom.

With head bowed, I say a prayer for Devon.

Off and on I check my phone, thinking maybe I missed her text. Still no response from Elizabeth. She'll text back when she has time, but I was hoping it wouldn't take so long.

About an hour later, I head downstairs to the cafe for a bite to eat.

Back in my secret library, I'm flipping through some of the files Arden gave me when my phone finally buzzes. Anticipation races through my veins. I fumble with the phone as I pick it up, nearly dropping it.

My Love: I'm okay, but I've been better. I know it's hard for you to be around me, so I thought maybe we could text.

Me: I would love that.

My Love: I'm sorry for going silent on you. I was hurt and scared, and I was trying to protect myself.

Me: I understand that. I don't ever want to do anything that would hurt you.

My Love: Can I call you? Would that be okay?

Me: I would love that.

My phone rings a few seconds later. "Hi."

"Hi." The sound of her voice is something I never want to take for granted. "Is this okay? It won't bother you?"

Bother me? Is she kidding? "Let's try it, but I don't think it will be a problem." I need this to work. For right now, it's my only connection to her.

"I need to apologize. I abandoned you when you needed me most, and I'm sorry for that. All I wanted to do was protect myself, but I should have been there for you instead." The pain in her voice reaches out to me, beckoning me to ease her burden.

"You didn't abandon me. I don't want you to feel like you did. I'm the one who needed to step away, but only long enough to heal so we can be together. I'm sorry I ever caused you to doubt my commitment to you, to us." I rub my chest to ease the pain.

"So, I've kind of made some decisions that will affect you, and I feel like maybe we should discuss it. I kind of got lost and didn't think there was a future for us anymore. And so, I sort of leaned into that when I made some of these decisions." I can picture her, bottom lip tucked between her teeth as she waits for my response.

Troubled by what she said, I'm feeling a little uneasy. "What happened?"

She blows out a breath across the phone. "Well, it all culminated when I was locked in the basement . . ."

"You what?" I fumble the phone and catch it before it hits the floor.

"It's not what you think. It was Grace and Sloan," she rushes to reassure me. "But anyway, I was going off the deep end. I allowed the voice of the enemy to convince me you didn't want me."

"I'm scared to ask where this is going." This doesn't sound good.

"You still plan on marrying me, right?" she asks, a little uncertain.

Uh oh, time to put my game face on. "Absolutely. I'm going to marry you. There's no doubt in my mind." This is the one thing I'm certain of.

"Well, you might get a package deal." Her voice is a little hesitant.

A package deal? What does that mean? "Okay. I may need you to elaborate on that."

"I may have told Brenda that I would like to adopt Angel's baby." Silence rings through the phone after the word baby. My mind needs a moment to catch up.

"Wow, okay. There's a lot going on with that statement. I might need just a second to wrap my head around all of this."

She wants to adopt a baby. Now. Not in the future.

Don't get me wrong, I'm glad she's finally talking to me. I take a few deep breaths and ask God for guidance. This would be the worst time to say the wrong thing and hurt her or push her away.

"You want to adopt Angel's baby. In a way that doesn't surprise me. You have a connection with her. But are you sure you're ready for this right now?" We aren't even married yet. I figured we would adopt eventually, but not before we got married.

She pauses before answering. "To be honest . . . I haven't prayed about it. I was hurt and haven't talked to God for the last several weeks. I was hoping you would pray with me about it since this will affect you, too."

I release the breath I wasn't aware I was holding. "I will always pray for you and with you. You don't even have to ask. I pray for you, and for us, every day."

A frustrated huff comes through the phone. "I should have been doing that, too. Maybe then Grace wouldn't have felt the need to lock me in her basement."

"Uh, yeah, we should circle back to that, too. But first let's pray. We need God's guidance for this and for our future."

I lead us in prayer. For healing. For guidance. For our relationship. We pray together and for each other, something we should have been doing long before now. That falls on me. If I'm going to be the leader of our home, then I need to step up.

"Thank you for that," she says. "I really needed it."

"No reason to thank me. We should have been doing that from the beginning. I'll do a better job going forward. Now, how about you fill me in on this getting locked in the basement thing? This is the first I've heard of it."

She proceeds to tell me how Grace lured her to the house. I can't believe Grace would do such a thing, but apparently she did, and with Sloan's help. I'm thankful Roz showed up when she did. I only wish she had been confident enough in our relationship that she could have come to me with this.

I plan on having a little talk with Grace and Sloan myself. What were they thinking? I never thought I could be disappointed in them, but they proved me wrong.

"So, what are your thoughts about adopting a baby this soon? Is it too much for you?" she asks.

"Honestly? I'm okay with it as long as that's what God wants for us. What will you do about our team? What will that look like for you?" She needs to view it from all angles.

"That's something I'm not sure about. How will I balance being a mom and a Light Bearer? I'll need to pray about it. I don't have any of it figured out. In the heat of the moment, I blurted out to Brenda that I'd like to adopt the baby, but I don't have a plan." She sounds a little uncertain now.

"Okay, we'll pray about it. God has an answer; we just need to know what it is."

"Yeah." She hesitates. "I should let you go. It's getting late." Her voice comes through softly.

I could talk to her all night, but this was a step in the right direction. "Thank you for reaching out to me. Can we talk again tomorrow?"

"Yes, I would like that. Good night, Mark."

"Good night, Elizabeth. I love you."

"I love you, too."

When I put the phone down, I realize the weight on my heart has shifted. With that one phone call, I feel lighter. Hopeful, even.

***

The same torment plays on repeat every night. The scene from the underworld arrives in full force, causing my skin to heat and prickle. Sweat breaks out across my forehead. The stench of hell permeates into every pore, leaving a sludgy film. There's no getting away from it.

Lord, please not this again. I can't bear to relive it.

And there she is, beautiful Elizabeth strides confidently toward me. A stealthy swagger aimed in my direction. That glorious smile of hers firmly in place. She's a sight to behold, and my relief at seeing her is immediate. Finally. We found her, and now we can get out of here and go home. The sooner we make our escape, the better.

My feet can't get to her fast enough. She's the reason we left our lives behind, knowing with every certainty we might not make it back alive. She's worth it. Always.

I will always come for her. She doesn't even need to ask.

Her form holds steady as I draw near. Unlike before when her form would shimmer and shift.

Her smile glows brightly, and relief washes over her at the sight of me. She lifts her hand, and I jerk back, waiting for the sharp blade to strike.

But it never comes.

No, this time her arms raise and slide around my neck. Her embrace, a welcome respite to the hollow feeling of being stabbed by the one I love the most.

Confusion about how this dream is playing out courses through me. This isn't what happened.

"You came for me." The awe in her words fills me with pride.

"I will always come for you." Joy floods every part of me.

"Mark?"

"Yes?"

"I love you." Those words silence every fear.

"I love you, too. More than you know." My hand glides through her hair.

"Let's go home." She reaches up and places a kiss on my lips. Yes! This is how it should have happened.

As my eyes blink open, my bedroom comes into focus. Relief and peace replace fear and anguish. My heart is calm, my soul is quiet.

Hope glides through my veins. Could this be what I've been praying for? Can I finally be around Elizabeth without panic paralyzing me?

Chapter 25

Elizabeth

My phone buzzes from the counter behind me as I finish fixing my second cup of coffee. I flip it over to see who it is.

Mark: Good morning! Are you home?

Me: Yes, I'm about to go into the backyard to water my plants.

Mark: Do you mind if I come over?

Me: Are you sure that's a good idea?

Mark: Do you trust me?

Me: Of course, I do.

Mark: I'll see you in a little bit.

A flutter of excitement fills me at the thought of seeing Mark again. Even but for a moment to see his face. At this point, I'll take what I can get.

I set the phone down on the counter and lean back against the island as I sip my coffee. Sun streams through the windows as stillness quiets my soul. I may not have all the answers, but that despondent feeling is no longer trying to strangle me.

Ever since Mark and I prayed together, I've been more centered . . . more calm. It goes to show I can't neglect the Light nor ignore my relationship with God. It doesn't work. No matter what I'm feeling, I need to spend time with Him.

I walk to the backyard and survey the garden. The herb garden is thriving. Each of the tiny plants peek through the soil, proof that life will continue to flourish no matter the circumstances. I would never consider myself a farmer, but there's just something so satisfying about having a garden to tend. There's nothing like fresh herbs in my dishes, and it only serves my creative side to develop new recipes. Freshly caught fish topped with a sage brown butter sauce, so perfect it will melt in your mouth. Yes, that will be next on the menu.

"Hello?" Mark's voice startles me out of those thoughts as he walks from the side of the house into the backyard.

"When did you get a garden?" Wearing jeans and a T-shirt that hugs his form, he strides confidently toward me. His biceps bulge beneath the sleeves, straining for freedom. I miss those strong arms wrapped around me. Holding me close. Protecting me. Loving me.

I turn off the water, and he remains at the edge of the backyard, those eyes following my every move. "Maybe a few weeks ago? Although, I've always wanted one. It's mostly herbs though, with a few vegetables thrown in."

"I bet you love it." He pulls his hand from behind his back and produces a large bouquet of wildflowers. Blue columbine, wild bergamot, blue aster, and California poppy thrown in. The mix of flowers spills out of the brown paper wrapped around them. A bow made of twine secures it all together. I love the way he thinks outside the box.

"Thank you. These are beautiful. Much better than plain old roses." He moves a little closer, his gaze cautious as he watches me. I can't tell what he's thinking. What lies behind those eyes that capture my heart?

He hesitates for a moment before finally closing the short distance between us. Panic dampens the lighthearted moment, and I hope this isn't a mistake he will later regret.

He leans closer, but hesitates again. Testing the waters, maybe? His hand touches my cheek, and his eyes scan every inch of my face as if remembering all the times we shared.

My battered heart hopes he doesn't change his mind, but I let him go at his own pace, knowing he needs to make the first move. It would be devastating to have my advances rejected.

Finally, his head tilts toward me. His lips brush delicately, almost reverently, as they join mine. The kiss is tentative at first, seeking acceptance, but quickly turns into more. So much more. I lean closer, not able to get close enough. I've missed this. I've missed him.

The kiss grows heated, and it's easy to get lost in the passion. Wait, a minute.

I jerk back and gaze into his eyes. "Mark," I whisper. "This is okay?"

His smile is brilliant and bright. He picks me up and twirls me around. "More than okay!"

He releases me, and I slide down against his body. He picks up where he left off. A kiss so intense and hungry, but before we get carried away, he leans back and takes a breath.

"You have no idea how badly I've wanted to do that. I have missed you so much." His forehead touches mine, and he closes his eyes.

Still struggling to focus after that kiss, I try to pay attention to what he's saying. "But what happened? What changed?"

He shakes his head and laughs. "I think it had everything to do with us praying together. It was the key to releasing the fear that had consumed me. Something shifted when we did that. And it will be something we continue to do going forward. Prayer together is not an option."

I lean my head against his chest and breathe in his scent of wood and leather. His firm hold reassuring. He leans his cheek against the top of my head, and we stay like that, staring out over the water.

Before long I pull away. "I should go put these flowers in some water. Why don't you come inside?"

Once inside, I fill the vase with water and add the flowers. The cascade of colors brings life to the white granite on the kitchen island. "Thank you, Mark."

"You're welcome. And there may be some more news." He leans both palms against the counter.

"What kind of news?" I can't imagine it being any better than this.

"We may have found what caused Devon to be used by the enemy as a portal to the underworld. Time will tell, but I'm pretty confident we figured it out."

"You really think it's something that can be fixed?" A spring of hope ignites. Hope that my relationship with Uncle Devon can be restored.

Mark nods his head. "I believe so." He reaches his hand out to hold mine.

"So, I may get Uncle Devon back, too?" It's all I could have hoped for.

"Yes, I believe so." He nods his head again, and pulls me to him. We sway together, dancing to our own rhythm. "You think we can schedule a new date for the wedding?" He pulls away, grabbing both of my hands in his. His thumbs rub against the back of my hands, stirring all kinds of feelings. The gentle hum between us is steady.

"You don't think we should give it some time?" I would hate to rush it this time and have everything fall apart – again.

Then again, that may just be fear talking.

He definitively shakes his head. "I'm ready. I don't want to wait another day, but more importantly, I want you to be ready. If you're not, we'll wait."

All that could go wrong, and the dangers ahead, flit through my mind like a jittery hummingbird. "I'm nervous. What if something else happens?"

"Oh, I can guarantee something else will happen. If we wait for the perfect time, we'll never get married, but it's your call." He pulls me closer and wraps his arms around me.

My arms reach around him to hold him tight. "If you're confident you want to do this, let's find out when your family can make it here so we can plan it."

He leans back, searching my eyes and places both hands on my cheeks. "You mean that?"

The corners of my mouth lift in a smile. "Yes." He places a gentle kiss on my forehead and releases my face.

I check my phone to see the time. "It's almost time for me to go sit with Angel. Brenda was going to bring Arden by sometime today to introduce them. The rest of us plan to be there to lend Angel our support. We want her to feel safe."

"That's a good idea. And since we're talking about Angel, do you know when the baby is due?" He leans against the island and crosses his arms over his chest.

I lean my hip against the sink. "We're thinking maybe a few weeks, but there never is a solid date on when a baby will arrive. They come when they're ready."

"Are you ready to be a mom?" There's no challenge in his tone, just curiosity.

A breath blows out between my lips, and I play with the hem of my shirt. "I wish I were more confident, but I don't know that I'll ever be completely ready. I want to be a mom, but I never thought I would have the chance. Now that I do, the thought is a little scary, but it's what I want."

"Then let's do this. We can provide a loving and stable home for a baby who needs it." No hesitation.

I love his confidence. Maybe it will seep over and encourage mine. "How do we balance being a Light Bearer and Guardian with being parents?"

"Let's ask others who have done it before. We can even talk to Brenda and Arden. I believe there's a way we can balance both." He steps in front of me and wraps his arms around me. It's as if he can't stop touching me now that the fear is gone.

"I love your certainty." I snuggle deeper into his embrace, thankful to have this closeness with him.

"Go spend time with Angel, and let me get in touch with my family so we can set a date. I'll see you later today?"

I lean forward and place my lips against his, delighted I can do this again. "Sounds good. See you soon."

***

Angel's first time meeting Arden was uneventful. She stared at him and leaned farther into the bed, but there was no screaming and no meltdowns. Maybe, with all of us girls present, she felt safe. That was the idea anyway.

Arden spoke to her and explained who he was. He offered her a safe space in his home with Brenda, an olive branch of sorts. He was so sweet and gentle as he spoke to her. Overall, it wasn't a awful experience.

Angel still doesn't want to speak. The only way we can tell what she's thinking or feeling is through her eyes and if she nods. We watch her face for subtle clues. When she feels like she has something to say, I believe she'll talk.

More than anything, we want her to know she's safe, loved, and cared for. I pray that one day soon she'll be able to smile and even laugh.

Brenda and I share the shift to watch over Angel. She wants to observe Angel and see if she's unsettled after meeting Arden. But so far she appears calm.

I pull out one of those adult coloring books along with color pencils from my bag. The thought behind the coloring book is to see what, if anything, will encourage more interaction from Angel. To get her interested in something. We each have rotated, bringing different things in with us to stimulate her mind in positive ways. Grams did cross-stitching, Mom brought in elementary word games, Sloan did make-up, Grace would tell stories with Angel as the heroine.

Little by little, we have offered her insight into a world without fear or threat. A safe space for creativity and new experiences.

Brenda and I both work on a page from the book as well. It's kind of therapeutic. Nothing more stressful than deciding which color scheme to use. Angel's brow furrows in concentration as she fills the lines with color on her page.

We don't know her level of education, or even if she can read or write. There's still so much we don't know, and just as many concerns for her future.

Brenda has been working hard with Angel, and it's been very small steps with little progress to show for it.

It will be good for her to get out of the medical clinic and have space of her own, but Brenda doesn't want to rush it. All part of those small steps.

Angel focuses on the page in front of her and turns the page to get the right angle. "Oh, Angel, that's beautiful. I love those colors." She selected a butterfly and thoughtfully chose shades that go well together. Deep purple, lavender, subtle shades of blue. She has an eye for color.

An imperceptible lift at the corner of Angel's lips is the only clue she's pleased with the praise.

My eyes meet Brenda's, and there's a twinkle in her eye and a slight grin crosses her face.

Content coloring together, we each settle in with our own works of art. I'm rounding out the edging of a flower when the ground beneath my feet vibrates. I glance up in alarm and catch Brenda's gaze as she drops her pencil.

Another rumble shakes the ground. I place my pencils and artwork on the table. "Brenda, stay here with Angel." Before I even make it to the door, a loud boom vibrates through the air, and the ground rolls, throwing me off balance and into the wall.

I glance back to see Angel wide-eyed, watching Brenda as she moves to sit on the bed next to her. Brenda nods her head in my direction as she takes Angel's hand in hers. "I'll keep her safe. You be careful."

With a nod of agreement, I peek out the door and watch people race down the hallway past me. My stomach somersaults and dips as I secure the door behind me and follow the others.

My feet follow the rush of bodies as I catch up with one of the nurses. "Hey, what's going on?"

Her head jerks to the side as if she just realized she's not alone. "I think we're under attack. We'll leave some staff here with the patients while the rest of us gear up."

We emerge into The Cave to frenzied activity spilling from every corner. I have to get changed into tactical gear for added protection before being thrown into the fray of whatever is about to hit. As I'm changing clothes, the earth rumbles and shakes beneath me again. Whatever barriers we have in place for protection may not hold much longer.

Roz runs right into me as I exit the changing rooms. She backs up after I bounce off of her. "I didn't know if you would still be here."

Coincidence or not, she's a welcome sight. “Roz, what in the world is going on?” The ground rolls again, knocking me off balance.

“It's nothing I've ever experienced at The Cave, but we're under attack.” She marches into the heart of The Cave, and I rush to follow.

“What do we do?”

“What we always do. We fight. They will breach our protective barriers soon, and we need to be ready.” Her stride is steady and sure, and I try to mimic her posture, whether I feel it or not.

The reality of our situation sinks in. This is bad. So bad. I need Defender.

A resounding boom ricochets through the air. Debris and rocks fall from The Cave's ceiling, landing around us. A rock narrowly misses my head just as I duck out of the way.

“I'm so glad I found you.” Mark runs toward us as he dodges the falling debris. “I came as soon as I got the text alert.”

Relief at the sight of him steadies me. “I left my phone in the room with Angel. Mark, I need Defender.”

“Yes, you do. Close your eyes.” He places both hands on my shoulders.

“What? Right now? We don't have time for that.” He can't be serious.

"Close your eyes." His voice leaves no room for argument. I do as he says and close my eyes against my better judgment.

"Now, I want you to picture Defender. Do you see it?"

"Yes." The vision I have is of Defender floating in front of me, just like the first time we met.

"Now, I want you to reach out and grab it." My hand lifts and wraps around the hilt. My eyes pop open in wonder at the solid form in my hand. Defender sits nestled in my palm.

"It's that easy. Now, you will have Defender whenever you need it." He backs away.

I gaze in wonder at Defender, then turn my attention back to Mark. "Why didn't you ever show me this before? It's easy enough."

He shrugs his shoulders. "You have to be in the right head space. Plus, it's nice to be needed, but I'd rather you be safe and able to defend yourself."

"That's sweet. Let's move." Roz shoves past us further into The Cave.

"We're here. We made it." Grace runs up to us out of breath with Sloan striding up beside her. "We just got the notification."

Oh, good, my two least favorite people right now. Mark slides his arm across my shoulders and pulls me into him. A form of solidarity. I'll accept it.

Roz gives them a hard look. "Fine, we need the numbers. But as soon as this is over, you're back on the sidelines."

Grace bobs her head in acknowledgment as Sloan turns around and marches away.

Gurgles and splashing emerge from the lake as water bubbles up from the surface. A geyser erupts, then another and another as the lake turns violent. Storm clouds build inside The Cave as lightning strikes out in anger, seeking a place to land.

We are under attack.

Chapter 26

Elizabeth

"They plan to invade through the lake," Marks says as he makes confident strides to the lake, the storm brewing around us. "We need to head them off."

Light Bearers and Guardians around us follow him. Grace and Sloan, Roz and Dax, a solid line with him. So many willing to follow where he leads.

"We need to do more than be on the defense. This is our home turf. Let's show them what happens when they dare to invade our home." Shouts of agreement rise up around us.

Pride for this man of mine wells up with such intensity it surprises me. He's mine. How dare the enemy try to take this from me. I'm done being a punching bag for the darkness that seeks to destroy me and my family.

No more! We are getting married. I'm done waiting, and I won't let this invasion stop us.

Defender vibrates in agreement, warming my palm. This stops now. I'm tired of being the target.

As we near the lake, I raise Defender in defiance. Flames engulf the blade, and excitement tinges the air. Weapons all around me rise in solidarity. Fierce determination lines every face.

This is our home, our space, our safe place. This demonic aggression against us will not stand.

Darkness descends across the lake, dominating The Cave. Waves roil and writhe in anguish, growing in agitation. The earth breaks open and cracks beneath our feet, creating a divide all the way to the lake. Inky blackness creeps along the newly formed crevice, hissing as it moves.

And just that quickly, doubt slithers through my mind. How do we fight this?

The lake explodes as demons and Fallen spill through from the underworld. Ready or not, it's on.

Demons ride the waves onto the shore while Fallen take flight above us. Way too similar to what happened at the breach, but no visible hole to the underworld to close. Shadows emerge from the water as if ghosts rising from the grave have come to hunt. They waft through the air and take flight.

The Cave is now invaded by the darkness. How did this happen? We have barriers in place to prevent this.

Lord, please lead. Show us what to do here. And please protect us all.

Clashes, grunts, shouts ring out around us. A demon steps from the mist and lunges forward, almost taking me by surprise. A moment sooner and I would have been gone.

Defender swings about, catching the demon across the shoulder, dropping his arm from his body. The arm holding the weapon that would have surely ended me. There cannot be another moment of distracted thought.

I swing Defender at the midsection, slicing clean through and upwards to the neck. Black sludge spills out at my feet. No time to focus on the gore as so many more emerge from the bowels of hell.

Fallen fly up and then swoop down as they make their move.

But they don't attack. They fly around through The Cave, almost as if they're searching for something.

No time to figure out what they're doing, another demon leaps in front of me, oozing a slick substance from its skin.

"Watch out," Grace grunts out as she kicks a demon off of her sword. He turns to ash as she swipes at another one. "That demon secrets poison. Don't let it touch you."

That's just great. Poison.

It lunges at me, but I jump out of its reach. A drop of poison lands on my sleeve and sears a hole right through.

Defender ignites. A rush of flame leaps from the sword, and the demon erupts in flames. It runs through the sea of fighters screaming and hissing as it dissolves.

Good to know the poison is flammable. That was a close call.

Ghost-like shadows hover above us while the demons continue their assault. I've never seen these creatures, so I have no idea what problems they will cause us.

"Watch out for the wraiths," someone calls out while I battle two demons.

My body flips around to attack the closest one while the other takes advantage of my distraction. Claws scrape against my side, tearing apart the reinforced material of the tactical shirt, leaving a gash under my ribs.

Mark reaches out with his sword and takes off the demon's head. He goes right back to battling his own demon which he quickly dispatches.

No sooner do we get rid of one than three more show up. We're at a severe disadvantage if the angels don't show up soon. They have to know we're under attack.

A few of the Fallen above us change course and zero in on our group. I watch them out of the corner of my eye while trying not to get myself killed.

Why single us out? Is it because of me? Seriously, guys, I'm not that special.

Torn between watching what the Fallen are doing and the demon in front of me, I'm unable to concentrate on what needs my attention most.

Just as a Fallen reaches me with sword raised, Zebulon blinks in front of me with a smile then disappears with the Fallen. Gone. The Fallen that was there is just gone. Taken by one of our angels.

Thank God they showed up.

It's strange. I don't see the angels above us, but they show up right before an attack and take the Fallen with them. A sneak attack by the angels? Yes, please!

"Mark, do you think this is like the breach? Should I try to close whatever portal they opened in the lake?" I ask after killing off another demon. This one left its mark, a nasty cut to my leg.

Mark offers a grunt as he fights off a giant of a demon with horns protruding from the sides of his head. He's massive and putting up a decent fight against Mark's strength.

"I don't know, but it's worth a try. If it doesn't work, it doesn't work, and we can try something else." Mark takes the opening and finishes off the demon right as two more pop up.

"The wraiths are on the move," Grace calls out as she and Sloan fight back to back.

Shadows lower and drift closer. "What exactly is a wraith?"

"It's not a physical attack but a mental one." Roz grunts out as she does a roundhouse kick. "They cause depression, paranoia, suspicion."

And just when I thought things couldn't get any better.

With the disturbing thought of wraiths lingering in the back of my mind, I commit to close whatever portal has been opened up. Just as I aim Defender at the lake, flames shoot forward and throw me off balance.

I land awkwardly on my side. Hard. A cry escapes past clenched teeth. The scent of something burning reaches my nose as heat covers my head. I jerk my head around. My hair is on fire!

When I fell, I landed next to the black sludge creeping along the open crevice in the ground. Based on my stellar assessment skills, I can concur that it will burn if you land in it.

"A little help here!" It's not aimed at anyone in particular. I'll take anyone's help. I can't put out this fire on my own unless I make a run for the lake and jump in. Except for the fact that demons are emerging from the lake, and I would be running straight toward them.

I roll around on the ground, but it's not my body on fire, it's my hair.

Grace leaps over the black sludge and throws herself on top of my head. Hard.

My skull cracks against the ground, and I see stars. Literal stars. Little white dots shoot around my vision. "Oww!"

"Sorry, it was an emergency. No time to be gentle. But good news, your hair is out. Bad news, you've lost most of your hair." She jumps back up and takes out a nasty demon sneaking behind Mark.

As I roll myself over, the scent of burning hair lingers in the air.

With Defender aimed at the lake, my goal is to stay down. My hope is that being low to the ground will keep me mostly out of sight.

Defender flares and flames blast from the sword to the lake. A few screams fly out as the flames take out anything in its path. Whatever was in its path is now disintegrated.

That's not going to work. You're going to lose. You will lose it all this time.

The odds are stacked against us. We can't possibly defeat our enemy. A tear escapes as hope dwindles. Defender's flame slows to a trickle, and the demons continue their rise to the surface.

"It's the wraiths! Ignore whatever thoughts you're thinking. It's not real," Roz reminds me.

The wraiths! I had forgotten that quickly. There's no way to keep up with it all. It's just too much. My head hurts. My side hurts. And all the other numerous injuries.

God, if you don't do something, we won't make it. I'm not sure how much longer I can do this. Please help.

Defender flares to life, reigniting the flame to shoot across the lake. Hope stirs again, and I let Defender do what it does best.

A few of the Fallen shift above us and fly away. Aimed right for the clinic.

The clinic. Angel is still in there. My heart pounds unsteadily. There's no way Brenda can fight them off.

Pain forgotten, I launch from the ground and all-out sprint to the clinic. An explosion rocks the ground, splitting it open beneath me.

I tumble in and catch my back on a sharp edge. Pain sears my skin as it slices open. Thankfully, the fall is short, and I land with Defender right beside me. An unwelcome hiss meets my ears as I try to get my bearings.

I place Defender in the loop of my pants and look up to see how far I've fallen. It's not far to the top. The fissure is shallow enough I may be able to climb out. The sizzling and hissing grow closer. I'm running out of time.

It's dark and hard to see anything at all. My hands slide against the rock, but there's nothing to grab hold of. There's got to be a way out, something I can use to climb out.

That dreaded hissing sound is right next to me. I have to move. Now!

The ledge is just out of reach, so I jump up to catch hold of it. All that does is jar my already aching head and now my back. My boots land in the sizzling sludge, smoking instantly on contact. Not good.

I'm officially out of time, and running out of options. My chest tightens, and negative thoughts swirl through my mind.

With shaking hands, I frantically grope against the rock until I find a small ridge to grab. With everything I have, I pull up, feet sliding against the rock seeking purchase.

Please, God, I need help.

My foot catches on something, and I push up, able to crawl the rest of the way out.

I roll, bounce up, and run for the clinic, hoping I'm not too late. But when I run through the entrance of the clinic, my hope falls, and I stagger back a step.

It's too late. I'm too late.

The clinic sits in shambles. I'm not even sure where the hallway should be. With tears streaming down my face and anger coursing through my veins, I climb over debris in the direction I need to go.

When I finally reach the room, or where it used to be, I call out for Brenda. The door is leaning against the wall, so I peek inside.

Brenda is pinned against the opposite wall and can't move, but she's alive. She lifts her head and lets out a cry as she sees me reaching in.

"Brenda, can you move at all?"

She shakes her head, and tears fall. "My legs are under the wall, and I can't move it."

She turns her head, and blood trickles down the side of her face into her eye. She tries to lift her arm but lets out a cry. "I think it's broken." In breathy rasps, she hurries to get out the rest of it. "And they took Angel. I couldn't do anything to stop them. The room exploded, and the wall fell, trapping me here. Two beasts came in. It was nothing I've ever seen before. Angel screamed and fought them with everything she had, but she was too weak and no match for them. They took her, and I couldn't do anything but watch." She lets out a sob.

"Let me see if I can move the wall enough for you to scoot out." I bend down to grasp the broken edge, but Brenda's voice stops me.

"You have to go after her. No one else knows she's missing. Someone will come by soon enough to help me, but there's no one to help her. Leave me, go after her." Tears track down her cheeks.

I'm torn. There's no way of knowing how bad Brenda's injuries are. They could be life-threatening. But what about Angel? She won't survive if we don't get her back. And fast.

"Okay, if I see anyone on my way, I'll let them know you're here. Hang tight. Help will come, I promise." More tears escape before I can stop it. I don't want to leave her here, but she's right. Someone has to find Angel.

God? I know I keep asking for help, but we really need it. All of us. Not just me. Help me find Angel and get her back. Send someone to help Brenda. And help us end this.

I climb over the broken door and out into what used to be the hallway. Muffled cries for help from every corner of the clinic reach my ears. How will I know Angel's voice?

I close my eyes and focus on the Light. It has to guide me. I can't just go running off without a lead. There's no time to waste going in the wrong direction.

Go straight.

My eyes open. Straight leads back to the heart of The Cave. With renewed determination, I scramble over the remnants of the clinic and continue forward in fervent prayer.

My heart falls when I claw my way out of the clinic into The Cave. It's completely unrecognizable. Our home has been destroyed. If this war doesn't stop soon, there won't be anything left. And maybe that was the whole point of it all. But part of me feels like they were looking for Angel. Maybe that's just a bonus. A way to really stick it to us. Or me.

Whatever it is, we don't have much time, if any.

In the chaos of fighting, how do I find Angel in this mess?

And right after that thought, two actual angels catch my attention. Fiercely fighting against two Fallen.

Instinctively, my feet carry me in their direction. I'm scanning the area for any glimpse of Angel when I spot a small shape on the ground near them.

Nothing more than a lump on the ground, but I know it's her. Not moving. I race for her and get knocked sideways for my efforts. My body hits the ground, but I jump up quickly.

I swing Defender at my opponent and let loose all the anger brewing inside. This demon should have left me alone. He never stood a chance.

With the unwanted distraction finished, I regain my focus and turn to the slight form on the ground. My feet stumble at the blood pooling around Angel. Her blood. So much blood.

Given the very stressful nature of her pregnancy and her young age, it's possible she's hemorrhaging. She could die. The baby could die. They may not make it.

Defender drops to the ground as I fall next to her. There is nothing I can do to help Angel. Even bringing her to the clinic won't help. The clinic is wrecked. Only God can save her.

I place my hands on either side of her face and pray. Hard. I beg God for mercy. The Light flares in my hands as I lift up Angel to the only One who is able.

As I plead with God to heal Angel, a cry rings out as an angel tumbles from the battle in the air. The Fallen he was fighting flies directly for Angel. Or me. Not sure which one of us he's after. Not sure it makes any difference.

I grab Defender while remaining crouched over Angel. There is no other option but to protect her, even if it's the last thing I do. And it very well may be the last thing I do.

As the Fallen nears, he slows to a stop right above us. Defender, clasped firmly in my grasp, is ready for the attack. The Fallen sneers at me and laughs. "Do you really think you can defeat me?"

No, no, I really don't, but I know the One who can. There's no point in saying any of it out loud. I simply raise Defender and bow my head.

"God, please help."

Defender flares to life, and the handle warms in my hand, but I don't look up. I keep my head bowed over Angel as my free hand rests on her head.

A shout rings out in the distance. Not a shout of pain or of war. No, this one is different. It's a shout of something more.

Another shout. And another. Shouts ring out together.

The sound moves me to raise my head and look up. Nothing could have prepared me for what I see. A dome of fire completely surrounds myself and Angel.

Fire pours from Defender and has created a perfect shield around us. A Shield of Fire.

The Fallen above unleashes his fury against the shield, but it holds. Nothing he throws at it penetrates the shield.

"Thank you, Jesus." Our cover.

As the shouts continue all around, someone cries out, "Lift up your shout of victory! Lift up your shout of victory! Lift up your shout of victory!"

It's a crazy declaration because we are losing. Big time. Our clinic is decimated. The Cave is destroyed. Angel is barely alive, and we are grossly outnumbered in this fight.

But in it all, I sense a stirring deep in my soul.

Hope.

"Lift up your shout of victory!" The cry spurs on a wave of shouts. Each cry echoes through The Cave answering the cry before it.

I unleash my shout to join with the others as faith stirs hope within me. A battle cry of victory.

But the shout does more than stir faith and hope. It urges more demons and Fallen to furiously attack our shield of safety. The dome of fire that has been holding back the darkness creates a desperation in their fury.

As they continue their assault, the shield cracks. Like a delicate eggshell, each strike adds a fine line through our shield.

My fear is that they will break through at any moment. Our shield of fire isn't holding.

But the shouts of victory continue to rise up around me. Stronger. Resilient. And with it, an overwhelming desire to join their chorus despite what is happening above us. As the cracks in the shield multiply, creating a webbing of cracks, my shout of victory rings out again to join with the others.

A multitude of voices merge as one voice, a roaring thunder rolling through The Cave.

A lone, majestic voice breaks through, rending the atmosphere, "Heaven has been waiting for your shout and is responding!"

The sound of roaring thunder rushes back and forth, creating a whirlwind. A vortex of sound and fury spinning up waves of blowing wind. Rushing faster and faster until it completely obliterates the shield of fire surrounding me and Angel. The shards from the shield scatter into millions of sparkling crystals illuminated by a brilliant light.

Our shield is gone, and we are now fully exposed to our enemy.

The violent force of the shattered barrier breaks forth as dawn, dispelling every demonic being. Shafts of light reach every part of The Cave and the darkness vanishes. The glory of God fills the space, cleansing and refreshing every battered soul.

Angel weeps beneath me, and I drop Defender to cling to her. I gather her in my arms and rock her back and forth. "It's going to be okay. You're going to be okay." I reassure her with every breath.

I place my hand on her swollen belly, but the life that was there this morning is already gone. And my heart shatters all over again. An innocent life who never made it into this world.

I lay my head next to Angel's and mourn the life I will not meet on this side of heaven. A keening sound surrounds us. At first, I think it's Angel, but then I realize the deep, mournful sound is coming from deep within me. A bitter wail of loss and grief mixed with the solace that we made it through.

Angel is alive, even though the baby is not. We will need to cope with the loss at another time, but right now my focus is on Angel. She's still not out of danger. The amount of blood she has lost is potentially fatal.

I pull back to get a look at Angel. Expecting to see fear, but that's not what I find. Not at all. Her big eyes meet mine.

"You came for me." Nothing more than a soft whisper. And it's the most beautiful sound.

Chapter 27

Mark

One moment she was next to me and the next, she was gone. She took off, but I couldn't follow. Not with demons launching a direct attack against me trying to get to her. It was all I could do to protect her.

And through it all, somehow she managed to catch her hair on fire. I don't know how she finds herself in these situations. Thankfully, Grace came to her rescue, almost finishing her off in the process. It's truly a miracle Elizabeth has survived as long as she has.

Now that the demonic attack against us is over—for now—I need to find her.

Total devastation everywhere I look. Nothing left untouched. The lake has settled to its normal calm, albeit notably darker and murky.

How do we fix this? Our safe haven. My home.

With hands resting on my hips, I turn in a circle and take in a deep breath that brings an immediate stab of pain.

My hand automatically goes to my side. At the feel of sticky wetness, I look down to find an open wound. Well, one of many.

Yeah, now the pain is kicking in as the adrenaline subsides.

I need to find Elizabeth, and then we can head over to the clinic for stitches, repairs, or whatever else we might need.

I'm not the only one looking around trying to figure out where to go. Everything is unfamiliar.

A large split in the ground runs through The Cave leaving a deep gouge right through its core. Bending over, I peer down to gauge the depth and find that it's not a bottomless void. Although if someone were to fall in, I bet it would be an unpleasant surprise.

While scanning the crowds for Elizabeth, I steer clear of the ruptured earth, not wanting to fall in myself.

"The clinic is gone. There's not much left. The wounded have nowhere to go," Dax mumbles as he walks next to me.

My feet come to an abrupt stop. "What do you mean 'the clinic is gone'?"

"What I said. They destroyed our clinic. People are digging through the rubble now, looking for anyone who may be under the debris. Let's go help." We pick our way over the broken ground in the direction of the clinic.

What if that's where Elizabeth was headed when she took off? "Yeah, I'll go with you, but I'm looking for Elizabeth."

I run right into the back of Dax as he halts right in front of me. "She's missing again?" he asks as he faces me, ignoring that I just ran into him.

"Not like that." I know he's referencing what happened at the breach, and the time she was missing for three months afterwards. "I can feel her. I know she's here, just not where."

He shakes his head and continues walking. "She has got to stop disappearing."

"Don't I know it. It would make my life a whole lot easier. I'm surprised I don't have a head full of grey hair at this point."

As Dax continues his walk to the clinic, my gaze snags on a form on the ground. A mound, really. Nothing distinctive but enough to leave me curious, so I make a path for it.

A huddled mass comes into view. My heart quickens and my feet hustle. I fall to my knees and wrap my arms around her.

But I wasn't expecting two bodies. I peer down and see Angel tucked under Elizabeth. Protected.

And blood. So. Much. Blood.

"How bad is it?" I whisper in her ear. I don't want to alarm Angel or scare her.

Elizabeth lifts her head, and tears track down her cheeks. My heart drops. She didn't make it.

She offers a despondent smile. "The baby didn't make it, but I believe Angel will recover if we can get her immediate care. Will you help me get her to the clinic?"

"Of course." Angel is safely wrapped in Elizabeth's arms, and it causes my heart to patter. "Angel, would it be okay if I lift you up and carry you? Elizabeth will be with us the whole way."

She gives me a slight nod of her head as tears drift down her face. I bend down and ever so gently remove her from Elizabeth's care and stand up. She weighs nothing.

I wait for Elizabeth to join us before we make our way to where the clinic used to be.

"Dax was telling me there isn't much left of the clinic. I don't know if anyone is available, but let's head that way."

"Oh, my gosh." Her hand touches her forehead, leaving a bloody smear. "I forgot about Brenda. She was trapped under a wall when I left. She insisted I go after Angel and leave her. I hope someone found her and was able to get her out. So, yeah, there isn't much left of the clinic. But I can help Angel if I can get access to supplies. One way or another, we'll get her the medical care she needs."

Elizabeth gently touches the hole in my side. "It looks like you need a little medical attention as well."

A sardonic laugh escapes. "I think we all need aid, though I'm not sure we'll get it."

Not sure if I should even mention this, but maybe I should. "Umm, I hate to bring this up, especially right now, but do you know that most of your hair is missing?"

She lifts her hand and touches what's left. "Uh, yeah, I forgot about that, too." She drops her hand back down to her side. "I probably look like a freak, and there's nothing I can do about it. Honestly, I'm just thankful we survived."

"Me too. And I don't care whether or not you have hair. I still love you."

"Good to know."

We join the masses as we stagger in the same direction. Either looking for help or looking to help.

A laugh breaks out as I think about that zombie movie.

"I'm scared to ask why you're laughing at a time like this." Elizabeth's hand lands on my back and warms me all the way through.

"We look like walking zombies."

She looks around and laughs. "You're right. But we're alive. We made it. Look at this place, though. It's completely destroyed."

A woman greets us at the entrance of where the clinic used to be. "We have only one small section left open with minimal damage, and we are only taking the most critical cases. A separate triage area is being set up where the sparring mats used to be."

Elizabeth walks up to her and whispers, pointing to Angel in my arms. I look down, and her eyes are closed. Whether she's just resting or passed out from blood loss, I don't know.

"Okay." She motions for me to follow. "Watch your step. We'll take her back right away. Elizabeth, you will stay with Angel during the procedure. We need the help, plus she'll have a familiar face when she wakes up."

"Do you know if anyone helped Brenda?" Elizabeth asks. "She was stuck under a wall."

"Yes," she nods. "She's in surgery now and will need time to recover, but we are confident she's going to make a full recovery."

Once they take Angel back to the only space that's usable, I search for any way to help while I wait.

I team up with Gage and Devon, and we clear away debris to make a level path in the clinic.

Devon's voice breaks into my thoughts as I shove a wall out of the way. "I can't thank you enough for the time you spent looking for a solution to help me. And I just want you to know I've been putting in the time, and I'm working on letting go of the guilt of failing Elizabeth. She's in much better hands with the Lord than anything I could ever do. All I've done is hold her back, and I don't want that for her. She's blessed to have you in her life." He throws a hefty chunk of rock to the side.

"I'm relieved to hear it. Elizabeth needs you in her life."

"Thank you." He slaps me on the back and gives my shoulder a squeeze before returning to work.

With so many of us pitching in, we're able to clear out hallways and additional spaces that the clinic can use for the time being.

It's going to take time to get everything back in order at the clinic and in The Cave. The sheer amount of work that's needed is overwhelming.

Arden stops by after leaving Brenda's side for a moment. "I've got reinforcements coming from the other divisions. Some have already arrived. We've got a triage area set up in The Cave. I know you guys have been working hard, but I want you to take a break and get checked out."

Arden grabs my shoulder before leaving. "Mark, you're in charge for now. I'm stepping back to take care of Brenda. I took care of getting reinforcements here. You can handle the rest. I trust you." He slaps me on the back and walks away.

Stunned. He just handed over the reins of the Northwest Division to me and walked away.

Not that I blame him one bit. Brenda needs him, and he needs her.

My heart races at the responsibility placed before me. This is huge. He could have chosen anyone, but he chose me to fill his shoes, even if for a short period of time.

Wow. So now what?

Gage punches me in the shoulder. "Come on, boss. Let's do what he said. We'll head to triage, then you can introduce yourself to the reinforcements."

Not long after, I find myself in the throes of delegation.

"Howdy, stranger." A familiar voice calls from behind.

I twist around to find our New Orleans team striding forward. "We heard the call for help, dropped everything, and got here as fast as we could."

"Thank you." I return the hug Cressida offers.

"I hear you're the one in charge. Point us in the right direction. We're here to help." Sookie offers an animated smile that sets my heart at ease.

"Thank you so much for coming. As you can see, we need all the help we can get." It's all so disheartening. The devastation is immense, beyond anything we are capable of taking care of on our own.

Cressida slides next to Sookie and surveys The Cave. "It definitely looks different from the last time we were here."

"No doubt." Gage places his hands on his hips, blood and gore covering most of his body.

The next few hours are spent fielding questions, going over a basic rebuild plan, and checking in with each team to make sure everyone is accounted for. I even meet with Grace and Sloan, and delegate some of the more menial tasks to them I don't have time for. Sloan has a mind for strategy, while Grace has enough energy to light up a whole town. Plus, it will keep them out of trouble and away from Paxton and Tyler, who are now working on repairs at the clinic.

If not for Dax, Gage, and Devon, I would be drowning. I don't know how Arden does it all.

Finding a quick break, I look for Elizabeth while I have a moment. I need to lay eyes on her, even if only for a second. Just seeing her face will ease some of the burden.

"There's my bride to be." She's sitting on the floor with her back resting against the wall, eyes closed. Given the room shortage, Angel and Brenda are sharing a small room. I imagine it's a relief for both of them to be together anyway they can.

"Hey, we haven't been here long. I was just about to leave to find you." She gives a small but tired smile. She looks as worn out as I feel. As we all feel. But that small smile she just gave brightens all the dark of the day. "I helped with my nursing skills as much as I could, but they need so much help."

"What about Angel?" I ask.

"She's as good as can be expected at this point. With the amount of blood loss, she needed a transfusion. She's finally talking, which will make it easier for us to communicate with her."

My attention moves to Arden, sitting at the end of Brenda's bed. I reach over and shake his hand. "Arden, how's Brenda?"

"She's in and out. It'll be a long recovery, but she's a fighter. Had some internal damage and a few broken bones, but she will mend." He nods his head in Elizabeth's direction. "We've been discussing things. Obviously, Brenda won't be taking care of Angel for a while."

Both Angel and Brenda are still asleep, so I take a seat next to Elizabeth on the floor and fill Arden in on the restoration efforts of The Cave.

"I can't tell you how much it means to me that you're able to handle this while I take some time away for Brenda." Arden's relief is evident in the sag of his shoulders.

"It's not just me. We have a lot of help. Which is good because we're going to need it." I pick up Elizabeth's hand and lace my fingers with hers. "Before the attack on The Cave I spoke with Dad, and they'll be here this weekend. Not sure it's the best time now, but I still want us to get married. Especially after what happened today. I don't want to wait any longer. There will never be an ideal time to plan it out. So, let's just do it."

It's not a fancy proposal. I already did that, but with the way things are going, if we don't get married now, I worry it may never happen for us.

"Sure." She shrugs her shoulders.

Uh oh. What does that mean? Did I just make a mistake? I thought it made sense. And she doesn't want anything extravagant. Oh boy, I may have just blown it.

"Are you sure you're okay with it? Even after everything we just went through?"

She shakes her head and glances up at me. "No, you're right. Planning something hasn't worked out so far, so let's just do it. Small and simple. It's all we need."

"As long as you're confident this is what you want. It will only be the wedding. We won't be able to take a honeymoon right away. There's too much to be done here, not to mention both Angel and Brenda need full-time care." Not gonna lie, I'm bummed about the honeymoon, but it can't be helped. *That* we will need to plan for. We can't run away right now with all that's going on. Too many people are depending on us.

She lays her head on my shoulder and squeezes my hand. "We shouldn't wait to get married. We have only now. This right here is what matters."

She reaches up to wipe her eyes. "Hey, are you okay? What's wrong?"

"Now that the adrenaline is wearing off, it's hitting me that the baby is gone. He or she didn't even have a chance. They killed her . . . or him. I just feel like maybe it was a girl." She cries against my shoulder, and all I can do is hold her. I can't take this pain away. It's not something I can fix. So, I give her this, a moment to mourn.

"I'm sorry, my love." A tear escapes at the cruelty and sheer hatred of the Fallen. At the tiny life lost. And for what?

God, grant her Your peace and love and comfort.

I lean over and place a kiss on the top of her singed hair. "We're not promised tomorrow. Whatever time we have left here on this earth, I want to spend it as your husband."

Angel stirs in the bed, and I take that as my cue to leave. I don't want Angel uncomfortable with me around, so I'll give her some space.

"I'll spread the word to the others that we'll get married this weekend. I'll check in with you a little later. I love you." I rise from my position on the floor.

"I love you, too." Before I leave the room, she calls to me. "And Mark? I can't wait to be your wife."

And those words give me wings. I feel like I can do anything.

We're getting married.

It's finally happening.

Chapter 28

Elizabeth

Despite the gore covering his body, Mark leaves the room with a contented smile on his face. A smile I put there. My battered heart does a little happy dance.

Angel stirs awake, and I get up to check on her. As I pass Brenda's bed, Arden reaches out and places his hand on my arm.

"I'm sorry that Brenda and I won't be there for the wedding. I hate to miss it, but please have someone take lots of pictures for us, or maybe even live stream it for us. It will almost be like we're there." He removes his hand, and his tone turns serious. "Since I'm staying here with Brenda, I'll keep an eye out for Angel, too. She'll be comfortable with Brenda here in the room with her." A slight crack in his voice hints at the strain he's under.

He's trying so hard to keep it together. "Thank you, Arden. I wish you could be there too, but I understand. And don't forget, you need to take care of yourself, too." The dark smudges under his eyes reveal deep exhaustion and hint at the worry for his precious wife.

I lower to the edge of Angel's bed and take her hand in mine. She opens her eyes, and when she sees me, she gives me the faintest of smiles.

"Hi there. How are you feeling? How is the pain? Do you need anything?" Probably too many questions to ask right off, but I don't want her in pain.

"It hurts a little." It's a soft reply, but I couldn't be happier she's finally communicating with us.

"I have something you can take that will help ease the pain, but it won't make you sleepy." It's important for her to know that she has control of her body.

She nods her head and accepts the medicine I hand to her.

"Think you might feel up to eating a little something?"

She gives a small nod.

"Good. It's not much, but I was able to find some soup."

I fix her some water. "Here, this is so you can take the medicine." I hand her the cup so she can hold it herself. "Drink some water first."

She looks so much better and even has a little color to her skin. She finally realizes we're here to help, and she can trust us.

After we both finish eating, she leans back against the bed and sighs, then turns her head and looks at Brenda's still form on the bed.

Wanting to put her at ease, I explain, "She's okay, just resting so her body can heal."

Angel faces me again. She hasn't acknowledged Arden, but she knows he's there. I consider it a win. He hasn't interacted with her, letting her set the pace.

Her face morphs from calm to somber. "I'm sorry," she whispers, tensing with the statement.

"Sorry? For what?" What can she possibly be apologizing for?

"The baby . . . is gone. I wanted you to have the baby." Her bottom lip trembles as she utters the words.

And the one thing I've been really good at avoiding with Angel has now been given a voice. I've been able to compartmentalize it into a box to deal with later, but it's unavoidable. Angel needs reassurance. And maybe so do I.

I make sure my face does not reflect the turmoil playing hockey in my gut. With her hand firmly clasped in mine, I hope to give her reassurance.

"Please don't be sorry. The evil you witnessed today is set on destroying us, but you *survived.* And that's something to rejoice about. We can mourn the loss of the baby, but there is nothing for you to be sorry for. I'm just glad you're here with us."

For whatever reason, God's plan did not include me bringing home a baby. My womb and arms remain empty, but I will focus on the blessings I do have and trust in God's plan for my life. Doesn't mean I'm not devastated, and I'm sure I'll bawl my eyes out later when no one is around. The loss will be there for a long time.

"Would it be okay if I give you a hug?" I want nothing more than to wrap my arms around her and comfort her.

She watches me but doesn't respond. I don't want to force anything on her she's not ready for.

"It's okay. Maybe another time." I smile so she knows I'm not upset.

She returns the smile, then looks away as if gathering courage. "Can I go to the wedding?" Her gaze finds her lap, and she fiddles with the blanket. "I heard you talking about it."

"Let's see how you're doing first. I'm not sure if you'll be physically up for it. But if so, I would love for you to be there. Maybe we can work something out to make it happen."

She nods her head, and I sit with her for a while before she drifts off again.

This whole time Arden hasn't moved an inch, but finally allows himself the freedom now that Angel is asleep. It must have taken a huge amount of discipline to be that still. "Thank you again for agreeing to take Angel in while Brenda recovers, but are you sure it's a good idea now that you're getting married this weekend?"

"It will be fine. It's not like we're going on a honeymoon right now. Besides, we still have Grace, Sloan, Grams, and my mom to help. Angel is familiar with all of us. We'll make it work so Brenda can concentrate on getting back to full strength."

It's time to go home and turn the nursery back into a guest room for Angel. I'll get the girls to help me rearrange the furniture. It's the least they can do to help me.

I'm still furious with both of them, and I'll use that to my advantage. And I won't feel guilty about it for a second. I wonder how long I can hang it over their heads. Oh yeah, I plan to use the basement thing to my advantage for a long time.

Hours later, I get Mom to take a break and sit with Angel. The housing situation is a mess. A lot of the apartments were damaged and need to be rebuilt. What apartments are available will be used to house the other divisions here pitching in to rebuild.

She's been busy rearranging apartments and lodging. I'm sure she'll be happy to take a small break and sit with Angel.

***

The door to the nursery cracks open as I push it forward. The beautiful sanctuary I worked so hard to create. My hand glides along the blanket lovingly placed across the bed rail of the precious baby crib.

I slide into the glider next to the window and hold the stuffed bear to my chest. The dried lavender bouquet Mark brought me for our first dinner together lingers in the air from the vase on the dresser. Every little touch in this room, planned to perfection.

Every single detail meant for a little one to enjoy as I snuggle the precious babe to my chest.

The first tear falls. I got ahead of myself. I planned without prayer. I made a decision and asked God to bless it. But how could He bless something that wasn't His plan in the first place?

The baby was never meant to come home with me but to go to her heavenly home.

"It's perfect."

Startled, I drop the bear, and it tumbles to the floor. Mark hovers in the doorway. I never even heard his footsteps.

Battered, bruised, and dirty, he walks in and kneels next to the glider. He places his hand over mine. "Sorry, I didn't mean to startle you. Your mom told me where I could find you. But as I was saying, it's perfect, Elizabeth. Any child we bring home here will be blessed."

His hand squeezes mine. Our hands. Both covered in dried blood and who knows what else. My eyes meet his. So tender, full of love and compassion.

Another tear tracks down my cheek, and he swipes it away with his thumb, giving the utmost care.

I shake my head. "I have to turn this room into a guest room for Angel."

He looks at me quizzically. Oh, that's right, I didn't tell him. I really need to work on this communication thing with him.

"Yeah, so about that. I kind of told Arden that I would take care of Angel until Brenda was able. Especially since I have a medical background. I hope you don't mind." It will be an awkward situation for sure, with us getting married this weekend and all.

His face turns thoughtful, and he's quiet for several moments before he speaks. He needs time to process what I just threw at him, although I wish I knew what he was thinking in that brain of his.

"Why not let her stay in the guest room down the hall and leave this room as it is?" His question surprises me. He rolls with it like he wasn't just thrown a curve-ball when he was expecting a fastball down the middle.

"Well, I was thinking she may be more comfortable right across the hallway from my room. That way she won't feel so alone."

He strokes my hand with his thumb, back and forth in a rhythmic pattern, soothing my mess of tangled emotions. "Or you could ask her which she would prefer. Maybe show her both rooms and ask where she would be more comfortable."

"You're right, I could ask her. But what if she doesn't know what she wants?" My body leans toward him seeking his comfort.

"Then she changes her mind." He shrugs as if it's no big deal. And he's right, it's not.

It's not a permanent solution anyway, only until Brenda is ready to bring her home.

He leans forward until his forehead presses against mine. He breathes me in, and I take a moment to savor this. The heartache of not filling this nursery has lost some of its sting. Some, but not nearly enough.

There will be time to grieve, but right now I only want to make a safe and inviting space for Angel. To rejoice in our victory, not dwell on our loss.

God is good. He always is, He always will be. He can be nothing but good, whether we understand it or not, does not change who He is.

Mark leans back so he can look into my eyes. "Why don't you go get a shower, and I'll help you rearrange this room if you really want to."

"No!" I didn't mean to shout that. "I mean, yes. Yes, to the shower. No, to the help. If any furniture is getting moved, Grace and Sloan will do it. All of it. And anything I can think of for the foreseeable future."

He laughs and pulls me in for a hug. "That's my girl. I like it. Go get cleaned up. And maybe you can get Sloan to fix your hair for you before the wedding." He reaches up and pulls at a few of the long strands that survived. "I'll use the bathroom downstairs to shower, and then we can get something to eat. I'm sure we can find something in the kitchen to throw together."

"Sounds like a plan. I could really use a hot shower. I haven't even looked in the mirror to see what's left of my hair. I'm kind of afraid to look." I kiss Mark on the cheek and walk by, leaving him standing alone in the nursery.

The aches and pains from the battle have kicked in full force. Stab wounds and cuts are already starting to heal, but that doesn't mean it doesn't hurt.

The hot water soothes my tight shoulders. I move my neck from side to side to work out the soreness. Grimy water pools at my feet before washing down the drain.

Too bad the water can't wash away the tender disappointment of empty arms. Sorrow escapes the confines of my heart in the solitude of the shower. As the tears flow, I ask God for help because I don't understand. What do I do now?

The heavy weight of it all hits me. Unable to hold myself up any longer, I slide down the shower wall to the floor and cradle my head in my hands. The tears come in a mighty torrent until I'm heaving.

It hurts. It hurts beyond words. The grief cascades, and I allow it to flow instead of holding it in.

"God, I can't do this on my own. Please help me accept this."

Having a baby of my own was right there for me, but then it was taken away. And I've been left with nothing but a vapor of what could have been.

I'm not sure how much time has passed, but the water turns cooler, chilling my overheated skin from the travail of sorrow.

Rising on shaky legs, I turn off the shower and step out. The pain isn't completely gone, but I feel lighter, able to carry on.

There's a wedding to prepare for, a future husband who loves me, a young girl who needs me.

Joy weaved with sorrow.

God never promised life would be easy. Actually, He said times would be hard, and we would experience difficult seasons. But He promised He would never leave us.

I wipe the condensation off of the mirror with my hand and stare at my reflection. The mirror doesn't lie. My hair is awful, and my eyes are red and swollen.

When I finally arrive downstairs, I find Mark at the stove. "Hey."

He pivots to face me and drops the spoon. He walks over and gathers me into his arms. He doesn't say a word, just holds me. He allows me to lean on him as he holds me up.

He pulls back, grabs my face in his hands, and kisses my forehead. "Hey, you trimmed your hair."

I reach up and run my hand along the jagged edges. "Yeah, it was weird having some long strands while the rest of it was short. It's temporary until I can get Sloan to work her magic and make it look decent."

"You okay?" His eyes scan my face.

My eyes are bloodshot, and he knows I've been crying. "No, but it will be okay. I trust that in time, it will be good."

"It will be. You'll see." His smile is tender as he releases me and turns back to the stove.

"What smells so good?"

"That would be our dinner. What you smell is bacon. We're having mac and cheese with BLTs. I hope you're ready to eat because everything is finished." He plates up the food and brings it to the kitchen island.

"Wow, I think I'm getting the better end of the deal in this relationship." I accept the plate from him as he sits down next to me.

He takes my hand in his. "You may think that, but we both need each other. There will be times when I'll need you to be the strong one, and I will do the same for you. We're in this together. No more trying to do things on our own. That has obviously not worked out well for us."

He prays over the food and then we dig in. A moan escapes after the first bite of food. "How in the world does this taste so good?"

He chuckles. "Because we were starving. When you get hungry enough, you'll eat just about anything."

"Rabbit is good, Rabbit is wise."

"Wait a minute," he drops his fork with a clang. "Did you just quote a line from Twister?"

I give him my biggest, cheesiest grin.

He jumps off the stool, picks me up, and twirls me around. "I'm so glad you're mine."

When he finally sets me down, he doesn't let me go. He leans forward and gently places his lips on mine as I melt into him. What starts out as light and innocent quickly turns passionate. The kiss sets off a torrent of butterflies in my belly and tingles my toes. Every nerve is a live wire. Before we get carried away, he pulls back, breathing heavily.

"I am so glad we're getting married in a couple of days." He walks back to the island to pick up his dishes. He leans against the sink and bows his head, trying to pull himself together.

Me? I'm a little stuck. I know I should move and pick up dishes or do something, anything, except stand here like a statue. He's right. We need to get married, and soon.

Chapter 29

Mark

Grace and Sloan bring Angel to Elizabeth's house the next day. She was released to rest and heal at home. It seems a bit soon, but what do I know?

Sloan carries Angel up the stairs with ease. Angel weighs next to nothing, so it's not a difficult feat. She treats Angel with a tenderness not often seen where Sloan is concerned. I wait downstairs while Elizabeth shows Angel both bedrooms and lets her decide what room she wants.

Hannah moved out to give us extra space. She's sharing an apartment back at The Cave with Sookie and Cressida while they help us get back up and running.

Reinforcements have taken over the majority of available apartments. All the divisions have sent in backup to help us rebuild.

My parents made it in and are staying in the downstairs guest room. My brother and sister, along with their families, will arrive later tonight but will stay at a hotel. We will have a full house for the wedding tomorrow.

We're finally getting married, but I'm not wild about the accommodations with all the extra guests. It's going to make for a very awkward honeymoon.

We simply can't leave right now. There's too much to be done and too many people relying on both of us.

I'll move over the rest of my things tonight and spend my last night at the apartment, freeing up much needed space for someone else when I leave.

Elizabeth walks down the stairs after helping Angel settle, and I set down my Bible when she pads into the room.

"Hey," she meets me with a kiss, "where are your parents?" She's precious wearing a ball cap so that it covers her hair.

"They're in the kitchen. Mom insisted on making everyone a huge dinner tonight. Dad is her sous chef and has to do everything she tells him." That gets a laugh from both of us. Knowing my parents, it's a game between them. I just hope they're not making out in the kitchen. If so, we might never eat dinner.

I can't wait for us to have that. All the domesticated stuff we can do together like fix dinner, work out in the garden, take road trips. I want it all with her.

"I'm glad they're here. It'll be good to see the rest of your family."

I place my hands on her hips and draw her a little closer. She instantly softens in my arms. "So, how did it go with Angel? The girls getting her settled?"

She slides her arms around my neck. "Yes, they brought some of Grace's smaller clothes over from when she was a little younger for Angel to wear. That way, she gets to decide how she wants to dress. Sloan brought over some sweats and t-shirts from The Cave with the Triton logo on them." She lets out a laugh. "Those two are so opposite. Anyway, Angel picked the room at the end of the hall. I think she wants to have a little space. I told her we'll keep her door open and the bathroom door open at all times, and once she's completely healed ,she can move about the house freely.

"Until she's more stable, someone will get her up and down the stairs. We have a wheelchair for her to use. That's our solution, so she can attend the wedding. I'll let her decide whether she wants to eat in her room or eat her meals with the rest of us. This is unfamiliar territory, not only for her, but for us as well. I want to make the transition for her as easy as possible."

"And you're doing a great job. It will be an honor to call you my wife tomorrow." My lips caress hers, just a whisper of a touch and linger there. She sighs and melts even further. I love that I have that effect on her.

The stomp of feet down the stairs breaks apart the kiss.

"Okay, we're heading out. Angel is asleep. She picked out the most adorbs pajama set to sleep in. Pink with little sloths on them and lace at the hem of the pants and sleeves. She was so happy. I left the night light on in the bathroom and in the bedroom. So she should be good for a little bit. There's a bell on the nightstand she can use in case she needs you." Grace says all of this with the energy of a sugared-up toddler, using hand motions to explain everything.

Sloan simply says, "I'm out," and walks out the door.

"We're heading out to meet the New Orleans team for pizza night. We'll see you bright and early in the morning to help you prepare for your big day!" She gives me a quick hug and shares a longer hug with Elizabeth. "And for what it's worth, I'm really sorry about the whole locking you in our basement thing."

"I know," Elizabeth replies and leaves it at that, but she adds a small smile to ease the sting of remaining at arms length.

Dinner is a loud, chaotic affair. With all of my family, Hannah, Dax and Roz we make a loud bunch. Mom made spaghetti with salad and homemade rolls. Man, my momma can cook, but so can Elizabeth. I'm one very blessed man.

Angel decided to stay upstairs and eat, but Hope, my niece, brought her meal upstairs to eat with her so she wouldn't be alone. She's a sensitive soul.

Angel is doing really well despite everything she's been through. Much better than we could have expected or hoped for. She even explored the bathroom and the upstairs floor with Elizabeth.

She wants to make sure Angel understands she can get up and move around on her own, that she's not limited to a certain part of the house. Her only limitations right now are her health and her strength, and Elizabeth is determined to help her get it back. Well, actually, better than she was before. Healthy, vibrant, at peace, healed and whole.

Mom brings out a berry cobbler for dessert and sets it down on the table as Dad follows her with a tub of ice cream. "Thank you, Momma. I think I should try it first to make sure it's edible."

"Oh, stop." She slaps my hand as I reach for the spoon in the cobbler. "Just for that, I think you should fix a bowl for each person before serving yourself." The look she gives me lets me know she's not playing.

Dang it. Now I'll be the last to get any. If there's any left.

Roz accepts the bowl I place in front of her, but before she digs in she whispers to Elizabeth, "I didn't know Grace and Sloan were meeting our friends from the New Orleans Division for pizza until you mentioned it to me. We need to keep Tyler and Paxton away from the girls. I'm not comfortable with two eighteen-year-old guys hanging out with two sixteen-year-old girls. I really thought we wouldn't see them again for a long time, so we had nothing to worry about."

"I think Tyler just turned nineteen, but I don't think you need to worry about him and Sloan. Sloan does not want to be anywhere near him. But we definitely need to keep an eye on Grace and Paxton. Have you seen the way they look at each other?" Elizabeth takes a bite of the cobbler, and her eyes close as she lets out a moan. My mouth waters at the sight. Pushing thoughts of Elizabeth aside, I need to hurry and get this dessert served so I can eat mine before the cobbler gets cold and the ice cream melts.

"Let's keep the girls occupied in any other place than where the guys will be. They can even pitch in to help us with Angel. I'm sure we can keep them busy enough and away from the guys until they go back to New Orleans." Elizabeth sets down her spoon and takes a sip of water.

"Let's do that." Roz points her spoon in Elizabeth's direction. "Starting tomorrow, we'll keep them so busy they won't have time to hang out. Once they turn eighteen, though . . ." Roz lifts a shoulder, and her face turns somber.

I finally sit down with the last spoonful of cobbler and dig in. This. This right here makes eating dinner first worth it all. I could be stuffed as a tick and I'll still want Mom's cobbler.

"Yeah, once they turn eighteen, we'll have limited influence over who they hang out with or even who they choose to date. Kind of scary. And they aren't even my kids." Dax joins in. He pushes his empty bowl away and pats his stomach. "Momma C, that's some mighty fine cooking. You're welcome here anytime."

"Dude, not your house, and that's my momma." I give him a hard glare, which he completely ignores. "But yes, the food was excellent, Mom, and you are welcome here anytime because it will be my house starting tomorrow." The smug smile I aim at Dax does not go unnoticed. Nobody gets dibs on my momma and her cooking except me, but I'll share her with Elizabeth. And maybe my dad.

"You boys are too much. And I'm glad you enjoyed it because you can both do the dishes for me." Oh, she's good.

My dad stands up from the table. "And that, my boys, is why I'm a very lucky man." He reaches for Mom's hand and helps her up from her chair. "Shall we go for an evening stroll?"

She takes his hand and allows him to lead her to the back porch.

"I guess we should get started on the dishes." Dax takes Roz's plate and gives her a kiss. "Why don't you and Elizabeth go relax? The men have this."

"You don't have to tell me twice." She hops up and leaves the table.

I lean over and kiss Elizabeth. "I'll join you in a little bit."

"Okay, but I'm going to fix some coffee first." She walks to the coffee nook and gets the coffee started. "Anyone else want coffee?" she calls out.

Several answer back with a "yes."

It still remains a mystery to me how anyone can drink coffee at night unless they are actively trying to stay awake.

It's not long before everyone goes their separate ways for the night. I hate to leave, but I also can't wait for tomorrow to get here.

I pull Elizabeth into the hidden office for a moment alone with her before I leave. "This is it. Your last day as a single woman. Any regrets?"

Her gaze finds mine as she leans into me. "Regrets? Yes, just one."

That stings a little. I was hoping she would say 'none'.

"Don't give me those sad, puppy dog eyes. My only regret is that we haven't been able to do this sooner. It feels like wasted time." She snuggles a little closer.

I know what she means, but we finally made it. Now we just need to make it down the aisle tomorrow.

I don't linger long. It would be so easy to stay, and my resolve is slipping. With a final hug and kiss goodnight, I slip out the door and go back to The Cave to spend my last night as a single man.

Chapter 30

Elizabeth

Soft light rouses me from a dreamless sleep, and I stretch my arms overhead with a wide grin. It's my wedding day, and I'm determined to make it down the aisle this time.

A bounce on the bed induces a scream from my lips before I can catch it, even though I know who it is. Tiger shouldn't take me by surprise, but she does.

"Oh, my gosh! I wish you would stop doing that!" I throw off the covers and hop out of bed, ready to get this day started. The wonderful aroma of freshly brewed coffee fills my lungs, and my taste buds beg for a caffeine fix.

Tiger spins in a circle on top of the comforter looking for the right spot to curl up. "You startle too easily."

"You haven't exactly been around very much. I've forgotten you're supposed to be my guide." I walk to the bathroom, use the facilities, and try to brush down the burnt hairs on my head. My hair is ruined, and I don't know what to do with it.

"Just because you don't see me doesn't mean I'm not around. I stayed with Angel last night and watched over her. Even Roz was able to sleep while she sat with her." Okay, that was sweet.

"Thank you for that. I'll go check on her. Wait, maybe I should get coffee first. Yeah, definitely coffee, then Angel."

It's no surprise to find Charlotte puttering around the kitchen. "Good morning, do you ever sleep?"

She turns from the stove as I walk to the coffee nook. "Of course, I do. I just want to make sure everyone has fuel for the day." She hands me a new coffee mug in the palest shade of pink with *Bride* written in gold cursive lettering.

My heart does a happy dip. "Thank you." We wrap our arms around each other in a lingering hug. I rest my head on her shoulder and take a moment to thank God for this woman.

"Now, get your coffee and head upstairs. The girls will be here soon to get you ready. And don't worry about a thing today. We have it all covered." She pushes me toward the coffee nook and turns back to the stove. "I'll bring breakfast up to you and Angel shortly."

Coffee in hand, I march back upstairs to check on Angel. The door to her room is closed for the first time since she arrived, and I'm a little concerned. It should remain open at all times. I tap lightly on the door, "Hey, it's me. Can I come in?"

"Yep, just a second," Roz calls from the other side of the door.

A moment later, the door opens and Roz beams. "We have a surprise for you." She steps back so I can peer into the room.

Angel is sitting on the side of the bed in a beautiful pale green dress that highlights her eyes. The dress is a little large for her frame, but it doesn't take away from the lovely, shy smile on her face. The first one from her I've seen.

"She wanted to get dressed up for the wedding. I told her we have all day to wait, but she insisted." The slight grin on Roz's face lets me know it wasn't insistent, but more of a request.

"You look lovely, Angel, and I'm so glad you'll be at the wedding. I hope you're hungry, Momma C will be up with our breakfast shortly."

I turn to Roz. "Why don't you go downstairs and fix a cup of coffee? I can hang out with Angel while I finish my first cup."

"Thanks, I would love a cup. I could smell it all the way up here." She walks to the door, but before she leaves, she turns back. "We had a real good night last night. I think Angel slept all the way through, and I was able to sleep on the recliner in the corner." She pats the door frame and makes her way to the kitchen.

"That is such good news. I'm so glad you were able to rest." I sit down in the recliner and watch as Angel shifts on the bed to face me.

"Thank you," she says in that small voice. It's as if she wants to say more but hesitates. It may take some time, but she'll learn she's allowed to speak her mind.

"You're very welcome." I settle back in the chair and drink my coffee. "Did you walk around a little this morning?"

"Yes, Roz helped me." She slides off the bed and rises to stand. "I don't want to lie down all the time." She smooths her hands down the front of her dress in a nervous fashion.

"And you don't have to. You just need to take it slow and build up your strength. I'm so proud of you for the progress you've already made."

"Knock, knock." Roz and Charlotte come in with two trays of food and set them down on the dresser. Charlotte notices Angel standing up. "Oh, look at you out of bed. Would you rather eat at the table downstairs?"

I glance at Angel and raise my eyebrows. It's up to her. She's not a prisoner in this room.

She gives a slight nod in response.

"Okay, let's move breakfast downstairs. We can eat at the breakfast table." We move Angel and the food downstairs.

Charlotte prepared her famous cinnamon rolls, bacon, yogurt with berries and granola, and sliced banana. Before I dig in, I fix another cup of coffee.

"Can I have some?" Angel asks as I lift my mug for a sip.

I'm proud of her boldness for asking and surprised she wants to try it, but I don't see why not. "How about I fix you a cup the way my mom used to fix it for me when I was younger? She called it coffee milk. It's mostly milk with a little coffee and honey. If you like it, we can always add more coffee later."

I warm up some milk in a mug, then add a little coffee and a touch of honey to sweeten it. I find a pale blue mug with flowers and butterflies in the back of the cabinet and present it to Angel with a little flourish. "Ta da."

She smiles and takes the offered mug. She sniffs it first before taking a sip, and her face lights up instantly. "I like it."

Roz chuckles. "I bet she does. You'll have her addicted to coffee by next week." She breaks off a piece of cinnamon roll and stuffs it in her mouth with a moan.

"I don't see that as a problem." I shrug my shoulder in response and pop a piece of bacon in my mouth and hum in delight. "Charlotte, can I keep you here?"

"Oh, just call me Momma C like Grace does. Everyone else is starting to do the same. And you have me, as often as you want me. I'll come whenever you call." She smiles before taking another bite of food. Calling her Momma C will be easier than calling her Mom like she originally requested. That would have been too confusing with my own mom.

Before long, the house is abuzz with mega doses of estrogen. Mom, Grams, Grace, and Sloan arrive with travel bags in hand, loaded down with makeup and hair essentials. Mark's sister Margaret, and his sister-in-law Sophia, with her daughter Hope, join us a little later. My room turns into a bridal spa. They hired a couple of ladies to do our nails, while Sloan and Grace work on hair and makeup. Angel loves the attention and is mesmerized by the nail polish.

She deserves to be pampered. Hope sits next to her and shows Angel some videos on her phone.

Sloan trims the mess of hair on my head, or what's left of it, removing the scorched parts. She's doing a great job of making the haircut look intentional.

Grace pulls my wedding dress from the closet. I haven't looked at the dress since the last time it was waiting on my bed for me. Today is an opportunity to put all of that behind us.

Mom interrupts my thoughts as she slips into her own dress. "Devon will meet you downstairs at the back door. He doesn't want to risk anything happening again. He would rather be around all of us while he's with you."

Speaking of putting things behind us. There are too many negative emotions attached to that day that I don't want to dwell on today.

My goal is to get down the aisle without incident and marry the only man who can put up with me.

"Okay, take a look." Sloan turns me around to face the mirror. She's given me a cute pixie cut, and the makeup is subtle, not overdone. Like me, only a more glamorous version. I won't be gracing the cover of any magazine, but I'm confident Mark won't turn around and run away. At least Sloan didn't have to shave my head.

"Sloan, you did a beautiful job. Thank you." She nods her head and moves her attention to Angel, where Grace finishes curling her hair, leaving it to hang in loose waves.

Charlotte walks in carrying a tray with veggies, hummus, pita, fruit, and cheese. She brought drinks for us earlier. A blood orange mojito mocktail so refreshing I could imagine myself sitting on the beach drinking it.

"Charlotte, you have to stop. No more serving us," Mom fusses in a sweet voice.

"Oh, don't worry, that's it. The guys are downstairs getting ready, so I'm staying up here."

"Good." I get up from my chair. "Come sit down and let the girls do your hair and makeup for you."

"You know what? I think I will." She grabs a drink from the table and slides into the seat in front of the mirror.

I fix a small plate of food and watch the ladies in the room who mean the most to me. They gathered together to celebrate this new chapter in my life, and I'm overwhelmed by how very blessed I am. The only one missing from the festivities is Andromeda. I wanted to invite her, but I could not explain away anything supernatural if it were to occur.

What happened last time is on everyone's mind, even though no one has mentioned it. They've all rallied around me, and they won't leave me alone for a moment. I wouldn't be surprised if they all try to walk me down the aisle to make sure I get there in one piece.

A laugh escapes as that vision plays out in my mind. That would be funny.

Angel's head bobs, and I know she won't last much longer. "Why don't you climb up on my bed for a little bit and rest so you'll be able to make it to the wedding." She starts to protest, but she doesn't have much fight in her. She's out as soon as her head hits the pillow.

She would be so upset if she were to miss the wedding, and I don't want to take that from her. If she can rest now, she'll feel better later.

While Angel rests, we talk quietly and finish getting ready. There is no better way to spend the time than enjoying snacks, getting mani-pedis, and girl talk.

A quick rap on the door pauses our conversation. "You ladies decent?" Dax calls through the door.

That wakes Angel up, and she rolls to sit. Roz cracks the door but doesn't fully open it.

"I was sent to inform you that everything is ready. It's go time." He kisses Roz on the lips and walks away.

This is it. It's finally happening. Giddy excitement flutters in my belly like little hummingbirds taking flight.

"Let's get you into your dress." Mom hops up while Grace brings the dress over. They help me step in and get me buttoned up. I slip on my shoes and take one last look in the mirror.

Bright eyes sparkle back with happiness. A quirk of my lips hints at the impending adventure that awaits.

"Come on, Angel, I'll carry you down." Sloan reaches out for her.

"I want to walk," Angels protests.

"I'll make you a deal. I carry you down the stairs, and then you can walk. Once you're strong enough, you'll be able to manage the stairs on your own. Maybe we can practice this week." Sloan places her hand out for Angel, and she accepts.

We make our way down to the back porch, and I sneak a peek out the window. The sun will set soon, but it's still plenty bright out. Twinkle lights are wrapped around the trees and hung around the gazebo. They will click on once the sun begins to fade. Potted plants and flowers line the gazebo with about twenty chairs spread out in front.

Sookie, Cressida, Paxton and Tyler stand around with the guys chatting, waiting for us to take our places. All except Uncle Devon, who lingers on the back porch all by himself.

Roz and Mom stay with me near the back door, while everyone else goes outside. They walk to the gazebo and take their seats.

When I step onto the porch, Uncle Devon faces me. "You look so elegant, Elizabeth." He leans down to kiss my cheek but pulls back at the last second. He's scared to touch me, and I don't blame him.

Mom and Uncle Devon lock eyes, and something unspoken passes between them. I'm not a fan of secrets, but I'm not wasting time on that today.

Mom hands me the bouquet of spring flowers. "It's time. Shall we do this?" She puts out her elbow for me to take, but Uncle Devon does not.

"I'll walk with you down the aisle, but if you don't mind, I will not touch you."

"I get it, and thank you for that. It's probably best for now." He gives a tight nod. I understand what he's thinking. He wants so much to give me a hug right now, but he's afraid. That hint of fear taints the day, but I won't allow it to have control over me.

Dax holds up his phone at the front of the gazebo and pushes play. A sweet melody flows through a portable speaker on the ground.

Mom and Uncle Devon escort me down the aisle to my future. Mark has not taken his eyes off me since I stepped onto the porch.

I'm only about twenty-five feet away, when he bows his head, his grin wide and visible. When he lifts his head, I'm only a few feet away and the sheen of tears in his eyes tells me all I need to know. He's barely holding it together.

The minister we met with before clears his throat to begin the ceremony. Mom kisses my cheek, and Uncle Devon slaps Mark on the back. They each take a seat, leaving me and Mark together at the front.

Roz accepts my bouquet I hand her, and Mark takes both of my hands in his in a reverent hold. "You're stunning," he whispers. A tear tracks down his cheek, but he doesn't move to wipe it away.

Me? I cannot wipe this ridiculous grin off my face. I want to laugh and jump up and down. We finally made it! We're really here.

There was no official plan for us to write our own vows. It would have been nice, but who had the time? We keep it simple and do the whole 'repeat after me' thing.

Pastor Terry takes a moment to address us. "Scripture tells us the 'two shall become one'. It's God that does the joining, the oneness. Too many marriages fail today because they don't understand the significance of unity. Often, the husband and wife will continue to live their lives as individuals—doing their own things, making their own decisions. Not understanding that they are no longer separate but one. The relationship between husband and wife has a pattern. It should mimic the relationship of Jesus and His church body. Jesus, the head, and us as His body. He cares for, provides for and loves each of us. Leading us to follow after Him.

"Mark, understand that you and your wife are one. You may be the leader of the home, but you can never abuse that position. And Elizabeth, understand that your unity is under the head of your husband, just as unto Christ. The supreme thing for you both to always remember is you're under the headship of Jesus. If, as husband and wife together, you always consider Jesus first, your relationship will be solid."

It's a sobering thought to be united as one with another person. No longer thinking only about yourself but literally in union, as one, no longer separate. In Ephesians, the Bible calls the wife to submit to the husband as if unto Christ, and for the husband to love his wife as Jesus loves the church. Both hold an incredible responsibility to love and submit as you would for Jesus out of loving devotion.

The command is simple, choose the other over yourself, but it's not easy when we are naturally selfish people.

So many enter into marriage lightly without a clue how to do it properly, only for it to fizzle out in the end. Marriage isn't easy. It's an enormous amount of work and concessions on both sides. Most marriages fall apart when one or both are motivated by selfish ambition. You can't be selfish and have a successful marriage.

Marriage is a sacrifice. If you're not willing to do that, then there's no point in getting married.

With full knowledge and acceptance of this, Mark and I aren't taking it lightly. We hold our vows dear, as if they are treasures to protect.

Throughout the whole ceremony, Mark and I consider each other as we pledge our lives to one another.

"It is my honor to present to you, Mr. and Mrs. Mark Armstrong." Cheers and hollers erupt. "You may now kiss your bride."

The joy I feel is mimicked on the face staring back at me. Mark wastes no time in dipping me backwards to place a lingering kiss on my lips.

"We did it," I whisper.

"We did it," he whispers back as our friends and family gather around to congratulate us.

"Let's get this party started!" Dax yells and throws his hands in the air. He pushes a couple of buttons on his phone, and the music changes to something more upbeat.

Picnic tables are decorated for the reception, and once the food is delivered, it gets spread out on the tables. Twinkle lights click on as the sun sinks below the horizon, leaving final golden rays to linger across the lake, adding its own sparkle to the descending dusk. A breeze drifts up from the lake, cooling my skin.

"Here, taste this." Mark leans forward with a fork full of chicken fettuccine for me to try.

A smile forms. "You know you don't have to feed me." But I take the bite, anyway. I mean, he is handing me one of my favorite foods.

"I know that, but I want to."

After a few more bites, Mark gets up and stretches out his hand for me to take. "Would you care to take a spin with me?"

Ready to follow him anywhere, I place my hand in his.

Eventually, the party and music fade, and everyone gathers around talking and sharing stories. No one is in any particular hurry to leave.

Between our trip to the underworld and this latest attack, we were hit hard and left reeling. It's a pleasure to sit back and relax for a day before getting back to work again. We have no guarantee of tomorrow, and it's best to take advantage of the blessings while we can.

I glance over to check on Angel. She and Hope are sprawled out on the grass looking up at the stars. How long has it been since she was free to gaze at the stars? She deserves moments like these and so much more.

"Cake time." Sloan walks out with the wedding cake, with Grace following close behind carrying the groom's cake. A two-tiered wedding cake covered in real flowers is set down on the table before us. Grace places the groom's cake next to it. A single layer of chocolate decorated with a toy sword and shield.

Grace hands Mark the knife and takes a step back. "Please don't smash cake in my face," I plead as Mark slices into the creamy white frosting.

He smiles and gathers a bite onto the fork and raises it to my lips for a taste. "I'm not going to do that to you." I take the bite he offers, and flavors of almond and raspberry burst in my mouth.

"Wow, that's good." I give Mark a bite to taste, and he moans his pleasure.

"Oh yeah, that's gonna be good with a cup of coffee in the morning." Mark laughs at my declaration of wedding cake and coffee for breakfast.

Even after everyone is served, there's still enough cake left over. Now I'll be dreaming about breakfast.

"We have a surprise for you." Roz walks over to us with an envelope in hand. Grams follows behind her with a huge smile.

I should be concerned when Grams is involved.

Chapter 31

Elizabeth

Mark shrugs his shoulder and shakes his head, just as thrown off by this surprise as I am. He opens the envelope as everyone gathers around.

He pulls out an invitation on cream-colored card stock with flowers embroidered along the border.

It reads:

You are cordially invited to spend three luxurious nights at Casa de Grams, where you will be waited on hand and foot. A magnificent, world-class swimming pool highlighted by majestic floral gardens awaits your enjoyment. Cast every worry aside, as all will be provided for your stay. Simply Enjoy.

Mark clears his throat and sets down the invitation. "What about all the work that needs to be done? We can't leave that for someone else to do."

"Yes, you can," Gram says with hands on her hips, "and you will. Nothing's going to fall apart for three days without you. Besides, you have plenty of help. Now, if you'll follow me, your chariot awaits."

Mark opens and closes his mouth, but nothing comes out. We weren't expecting anything. Especially not a getaway for a few days.

"You'll have the house all to yourselves. Grace and Sloan will come by to prepare every meal. They will text you when the food is ready, and will set the table for you and leave. You won't have to see them or hear them." Roz smiles widely at the picture she painted for us.

I sneak a peek at Grace and Sloan's reaction. Grace is beaming, but Sloan is completely poker-faced. No doubt this is part of their punishment, and I couldn't be more pleased with this form of sentencing.

"And if you need anything at all, text Grace or Sloan and they will take care of it for you." Roz nods her head toward the door.

We follow her through the house as the rest of our family and friends gather at the front outside. They line the walkway with sparklers in hand to send us off. At the end sits a limousine with the driver holding the door open for us.

This is all so unexpected, and better than anything I could have imagined. We planned to stay here in the house and get back to work tomorrow, but this is hands down so much better.

Mark takes my hand and spins me around, leaning me into a dip. He kisses me soundly as the others cheer him on. Once I'm righted, I sway a little and lean against him as he guides me to the limo under sparkles of light.

The pure joy dancing on Angel's face as we pass her lights me up inside. Today has been amazing, and her happiness is the icing on the cake.

We wave to everyone as we step into the limo. I lean against Mark as the limo takes us to Grams' Victorian home. "You know, we don't have any luggage."

He places his arm around me and whispers, "I really don't think you'll need any." His lips tickle my ear, and I giggle like a little kid.

Only a few days ago we were fighting for our lives, and now we're married. It feels wrong in a way, that I shouldn't be this happy so soon after the devastation we survived.

But I refuse to feel guilty for being happy. I'm well aware of how quickly things can change.

The limo makes it down Grams' driveway without incident. She must have trimmed the brush and leveled the driveway just for this.

The fresh scent of flowers permeates the air as we enter the grand Victorian, no doubt from the lovely gardens on site. Rose petals line a path up the stairs.

"When did they have time to do all of this?" I ask Mark, his hand on my back guiding me to the second floor.

"I'm sure they had help in putting this surprise together."

The petals lead us to a set of closed double doors. Mark opens them and then sweeps me up into his arms. A laugh escapes as he walks me across the threshold.

He lets me down gently, and I survey the room while still wrapped in his arms. The room is gorgeous. A king-size bed covered by a fluffy duvet takes center stage in the room, with more rose petals on top. Directly across from it is a grand fireplace flanked on either side by windows. To the right is a full bathroom with a claw-foot tub.

"Looks like we have luggage." Mark points next to the wall where two small suitcases sit next to each other.

"Wow, they really did think of everything. I wonder which one belongs to you and which one is mine." I nod at the suitcases on the floor.

"There's only one way to find out." He lifts them both onto the bed and unzips them.

I cover my mouth with my hand while Mark places his hands on his hips. We both start laughing at the same time. It's obvious who they belong to.

His suitcase has no less than ten pairs of boxers and probably twelve pairs of socks, one t-shirt, a pair of running shorts, and sweatpants.

Mine has several sets of lingerie neatly folded, a few panties, two t-shirts and one pair of shorts.

"Honestly, it's better than nothing." I laugh as Mark pulls out a pale blue lace nightie hanging from his pinkie.

Mark holds up the lacy garment. "I would be fine with nothing, but this is good, too."

A shy smile crosses my lips as I take the nightie from his hand and place my lips on his. "Give me just a moment."

No idea where that boldness came from, but it flees as soon as I close the bathroom door behind me. I take a deep breath to relieve some of the pressure building in my chest. Why am I so nervous? It's Mark. Kind, gentle, caring, understanding. I'm safe with him.

Two new toothbrushes sit on the counter with toothpaste. Yes, I should definitely brush my teeth.

Once my teeth are brushed, and I use the facilities, there's not much else I can do before I need to go back out there. A glance in the mirror reveals the wedding dress. That I still have on.

There's no way I can get out of this by myself. Not with all of the buttons.

I pull open the door to find Mark leaning against the bedpost only in his dress pants. He frowns when he sees me. But I'm completely distracted by the abs he has on display.

"I didn't expect you to still be fully dressed."

A small laugh escapes, and I walk closer to him. "I may need a little help to get out of the dress."

I turn my back to him. He runs his hands up my hips and moves them to my back where he fumbles with all of the buttons. "Do you plan on wearing this dress again?"

"Not planning on it. Why?"

He rips the back of the dress apart, and buttons fly across the room and ping against the hardwood floor.

"There you go."

"Yeah, I guess that's one way to do it."

"Too many buttons," he growls in my ear.

His hands linger against my hips, and I turn my head without turning my body. "You can help me with the rest."

He leans down and kisses my exposed neck. "It would be my pleasure." He trails kisses across my bare shoulder and slides the cap sleeves down my arms.

The nervousness fades as we get to know each other on a completely different level . . . as husband and wife.

***

The decadent scent of coffee rouses me from a blissful sleep. I inhale deeply and sigh with a stretch, my hand bumping into a warm body along the way. A smile forms as I slide against Mark. He wraps his arm around me and snuggles deeper in the bed.

I poke him in the side. "There's coffee."

He grunts but doesn't say anything, eyes still closed. It's sad that he would choose sleep over coffee. I slip out from under his arm and slide soundlessly out of bed.

I reach for Mark's shirt and pull it on. I open the door and there sits a tray on the floor with a carafe of coffee, two mugs, cream, sugar, and spoons. A slice of wedding cake is perched on a delicate plate next to the carafe. They remembered. A little drool escapes from the corner of my mouth just thinking about it.

I slide the tray into the room and close the door. It's best not to pick up the tray. I don't trust myself not to spill the contents all over the floor. Kneeling down, I fix a cup of coffee then slide back into bed.

My head leans against the headboard, and I sip the lovely brew. Bright light peeks through the shades, hinting at a late morning. I flip my phone over to check for messages and find two.

One is a picture of Angel with Hope eating breakfast together. Angel looks like a completely different child. She's vibrant and full of life, and I am thrilled to see her act like a normal young teen.

The second text is from Grace letting us know that breakfast is ready and warm in the oven.

"Shouldn't you be resting?" His voice is all grumbly but so inviting.

"There's coffee." I smile as he slides his arm around my waist and buries his face in the curve of my hip, giving it a little nibble. Okay, maybe the coffee can wait a few more minutes.

An hour later we walk downstairs for breakfast. "We should sit outside next to the pool. It's too beautiful to be stuck inside," I suggest as I pull the food out of the oven. Pancakes with bacon, and I add the slice of cake to the tray.

"Works for me," Mark responds, taking the bowl of fresh berries from the island and following me to the outdoor patio.

"As far as honeymoons go, this one is pretty nice." Mark fixes a plate and hands it to me.

I take the offered plate from his hand. "Thank you. And I agree. It's simply stunning here. A few days away, but still close to home, was the perfect compromise."

I set the plate down on the patio table next to a tropical bouquet of flowers in a blue and white vase. "Would you like a cup of coffee? I'm going to fix another one."

"Yes, thank you." He fixes his own plate while I take care of the coffee.

"Here you go." We both take a moment to relax in the beauty before us. The gorgeous pool surrounded by pristine gardens offers us a little slice of paradise without the inconvenience of a long trip.

Such a thoughtful gift. And all the special little details our friends planned out for us, including a bottle of champagne chilling in the fridge.

"I really wanted to take you on a honeymoon, but I couldn't justify a trip with all of the work and leadership that's needed right now." Mark reaches for my hand and kisses it. "I'm glad our friends and family didn't agree."

"Me too. With everything we've been through, we really needed this." I picture Sloan and Grace dressed in maid uniforms slaving away in the kitchen and laugh out loud. "Besides, Grace and Sloan still have to make up for the basement incident, and this is an excellent form of community service. I'm not diabolical enough to come up with a form of payback on my own."

"Maybe after this you can accept their apology and give them some grace." Mark takes a sip of coffee and finishes his slice of bacon.

"I have forgiven them, but I'm not so sure I can trust them right now. Forgiveness? Yes. Forgetting? Not so much." I finish the berries on my plate and push away the rest of the pancake. My eyes close, and I lean back in the chair, basking in the sunshine.

The scrape of Mark's chair across the stone tile has my eyes popping open. He stands and presents his hand to me. "Care to take a leap with me?"

My lips lift at the corners. "I'll go anywhere with you." I place my hand in his, and he pulls me from the chair. He walks me to the edge of the pool.

"We don't have our swimsuits." Still wearing his button-up shirt, I grace him with an impish grin.

"You know, somebody forgot to pack those. I guess we'll just have to make do." I laugh as Mark jumps into the pool, taking me with him.

We push up from the bottom and break the surface, a goofy grin plastered on my face. "Heated pool. I was afraid it would be freezing."

Mark pulls me into his arms, and I wrap my legs around his waist. "Remind me to thank Grams for making sure the pool is heated." His lips find their way to my neck, and I melt against him.

Tangled together, we make the most of our time in this isolated oasis.

Epilogue

Angel

Two weeks later.

Run!

Urgency yanks me awake, and confusion fogs my mind at the crushing weight on my chest.

NO, not this again! Please.

Swollen eyes flutter open against the glare of a bright bulb dangling from the ceiling.

The weight hasn't moved, making it hard to breathe.

Wait . . . if he isn't moving . . .

I only hope he's finally dead, and this isn't a dream.

Run!

The voice. I recognize that voice. I've heard it before.

I want to run, believe me, I do. I've tried so many times before, but nothing ever worked. And I always paid the price.

The dead weight on my chest pulls me from those thoughts. With a desperate need to take a breath, I shove and scoot, shove and scoot, and slide out from underneath.

Finally, I can breathe. The deep breath I take brings with it the nasty smell that coats the air. With heavy arms, I push up, and my bleary eyes scan the room.

My room. What an awful thought.

A room that's been mine for too long.

But I know now, it won't be mine forever.

A bed pushed against the wall. A small nightstand holding only a broken locket. *The locket he gave me as a promise to take care of me when Mom sold me for her next high. He lied.*

The boarded-up window gives no light and no hope for escape. And the locked door. Always locked. *But this time, it's not locked. I have a way out.*

Run!

That voice again. The One I've become familiar with, full of light and love. This Voice does not lie.

I lift my hands and rub my eyes, but the jingle I'm used to doesn't sound. I look down at hands no longer chained to the bed. *I'm not chained to the bed because He unlocked it. The One attached to the voice made a way of escape for me.*

My bare feet slide onto the cold floor. The torn, dirty gown lies next to his clothes in a messy pile. I glance back at the still form on the bed. He hasn't moved. *And he will never touch me again.*

Shaky legs carry me forward to the pile on the floor as a shudder runs through me. I bend down, but decide to pick up his dirty gray t-shirt instead. It's cleaner than the gown he makes me wear, so I pull it over my head.

He still hasn't moved, but I sneak another peek at the man on the bed to make sure.

On wobbly legs, I bend down again and dig through his pockets. My hands shake so badly they're almost useless. *But they aren't, my hands are strengthened.*

If I get caught he will probably kill me. And I'm okay with that because living is so much worse.

Run!

I was ready for death, and even welcomed it, but that Voice called me, drawing me.

I'm trying, I am, but I can't move like I need to. It's so hard to shake off whatever he gives me.

I like it, whatever it is, because once he gives it to me, I feel nothing. I don't have to think about where I am or what he's doing to me. I even beg for it. I'm not ashamed to admit it. But right now, I'm moving too slow.

But as I watch this now, my mind is clear and open to the Voice. No longer stuck under the fog of what he gave me.

My hands move through his pockets till I find what I'm looking for . . . keys. I tighten my fist around them to keep them quiet.

Fear that he may attack at any moment shoots through me. *I watch myself inch toward the door on bare feet.* One eye on the door, one eye on the still form. *So full of fear, but I was protected the whole time by the One who was saving me.*

The doorknob is cold and smooth in my hand as I turn it, checking to see if it's locked.

I don't know why I bother. It's always locked. *But this time, He went before me and unlocked the door.*

Surprise runs through me as the knob turns in my hand, and the door opens.

I tiptoe into the hallway and push the door behind me, turning the knob gently so it doesn't make any noise. But a small sound from somewhere in the house makes me pause and hold my breath. *The noise I didn't recognize then, but I do now, was the flutter of angels wings.*

I don't dare make another sound. Now, I stand in the hallway, out in the open, no longer hidden.

My fingers open, and I stare at the palm of my hand. So many keys. I need to choose the right one and lock the door so he can't get me. *And He knew I would never make it on my own, so He came to help me.*

It takes a few tries to find the right key, but I could cry when the key slides in and locks the door. I take a breath and relax, but only for a moment.

Someone else may be in the house, so I don't have time to waste. I slip down the hallway as quiet as I can, and look for a way out.

I don't know where I am. There's only this hallway with a couple of closed doors and then a messy room with chairs and a couch.

A door stands on the right. I peer around the wall and look into the room, but no one is in here.

Run!

All I want to do right now is find the One that voice belongs to. How I long to run to the safety of His open arms.

I sneak to the door and turn the knob, but it's locked. It doesn't need a key though, and with a turn of the latch it unlocks.

Darkness surrounds me as the door swings open, and I walk out wondering if any of this is real. I secure the door behind me, amazed at what just happened.

I take a deep breath of clean air for the first time in what feels like forever. I'm free. *And He set me free!*

But now what?

I always dreamed of leaving, but never made it this far.

As I step off the concrete to the gravel below, the rocks bite into the bottom of my feet, yanking me back to the task at hand. Soft light from the moon helps me see the dead grass that covers the yard. *But is it the moon? I look up and see an angel hovering above me. Not the moon, an angel.*

A large tree is on my left with a truck parked under it.

A truck. An idea pops up.

Don't know where I am or where to go; I just need to leave while I can.

Tall grass crushes under my bare feet, making more noise than I want while I limp to the truck. When I reach the door, I pull on the handle, and the door lets out a loud groan into the quiet night. My hand freezes on the handle, and I jerk around, hoping no one heard.

With no time to waste, I hop in and glance around the dirty inside.

Barely able to see over the steering wheel, I can only reach the pedals by sitting on the very edge of the seat. I hope I know enough to get out of here, and that's all I'm trying to do. After a few tries, I find the right key and with a horrible noise, the truck rumbles to life. Someone had to have heard that and will come for me any second. It's now or never.

He was guiding me all along – the One Elizabeth prays to. I've heard her, and the others, pray over me.

I pull the handle down and push the pedal on the right. The truck moves back so fast it scares me, and I slam my foot down on the left so hard I knock my head into the steering wheel when the truck jerks to a stop.

Okay, that could have gone better. Don't push so hard. Got it. I try again with much less force, and the truck backs through the grass. With a softer touch, I move the handle again a few times and press the left pedal until the truck wiggles forward. In slow jerks and stops, the truck bumps onto the gravel drive. It's dark and I can barely see, but the moon shines just enough to light the way.

Somehow, I make it to the road, but now I need to decide. Should I go right or left?

And for the first time, I get to decide.

I turn the wheel to the right and hope for the best. A flutter moves inside my chest.

And as the truck rushes forward, light threatens the darkness. Evil chases me, but there is an angel guarding me. I see it all.

I watch as I lift my hands from the steering wheel and close my eyes. The truck slams into the ditch, and that's all I remember.

But I continue to watch as the angel battles against the dark flying demon. Mark and Dax jump out and rush to help as other demons try to get me. Roz and Elizabeth climb into the truck to help me.

All the things from that night I was never aware of. God allowed me to see it as it played out.

I owe Him my life. The God that Elizabeth and the others have told me about, I owe Him my everything.

My eyes open, and I glance around. I'm safe. I knew it before I opened my eyes. My room. The one in Elizabeth's house. The one she so lovingly put together for me.

Movement at the end of the bed scares me until I realize it's Elizabeth's cat, Tiger. She walks over and curls up on my lap. She nudges my hand with her head for me to pet her. I run my hands along her soft fur and think about the dream. The truth of that night. Seeing what really happened changes everything.

"God, if you can hear me, I want to thank you. I owe you everything, and I want you to have it. It's not much, but I give you everything I am and all that I have."

A flutter grows, and love fills me. I don't even know how to explain it; I just know it's love. My eyes close to the warmth flowing through me.

I'm filling you with my Light. You will never be alone.

It's the voice I've come to recognize. Excitement flows through me. "Am I going to be a Light Bearer like Elizabeth and Grace?"

No, my daughter. You are going to be a Guardian. You are going to help others, like yourself, find freedom and hope.

"Yes, I want to do that."

Good, there's much for you to learn, but if you keep looking to Me, I will guide you every step of the way.

"Yes, I will."

This is so exciting! I need to tell someone.

I jump out of bed and rush down the stairs, so thankful I can get around on my own now.

Elizabeth calls out from the living room when I run past into the kitchen. "Hey, sweet girl. Where are you running off to?"

I turn back to the living room. She's sitting in what she calls her 'comfy chair' sipping coffee with her Bible open on her lap.

"Oh, can I have some coffee milk with extra coffee, please?"

She laughs and sets her Bible on the table. "Of course, and you can tell me all about what has you in such a hurry this morning while I fix it."

And I do. I tell her all about the dream and how God showed me He was with me the night I escaped. She finishes my coffee milk, but when she turns and faces me, tears run down her cheeks.

"Is it okay if I hug you?" She always asks me if it's okay and will only hug me if I give her permission. I nod my head and welcome her embrace. This time, I even wrap my arms around her.

When she steps back, I continue. "And there's more. God said He filled me with His Light, and He's making me a Guardian."

"Oh, wow." More tears spill from her eyes, and she wipes them away.

"You want to hug me again, don't you?"

She nods her head. "I do, but I just hugged you, so it's okay. That's just. . . Wow! A Guardian, that's such a tremendous honor. Sloan will be a good person to shadow, but she'll need to take it easy on you at first."

I point to the coffee mug still sitting on the counter. "Can I have my coffee milk now?"

"Oh yes, of course." She hands it to me, and I take a bug gulp. So good.

"Good morning." Mark walks in and stops when he sees Elizabeth. "What happened?"

She fills him in on everything I just told her while I drink from the warm mug. My mug. The one she gifted me. It even has my name on it. My new name, Angel. The name I treasure and will use as my own.

The names he called me didn't belong to me. I don't remember my name from before, and I don't want to. That's not who I am.

Mark turns his attention to me. "A Guardian. What a blessing and a privilege. If you have any questions or need any pointers, just let me know. I would be happy to help."

I smile and nod my head at him. "Thank you."

Elizabeth fixes a cup of coffee for Mark and hands it to him.

"What are you girls up to today?" Mark asks before taking a sip.

"Grace and Sloan are on their way over. We're taking Angel shopping for clothes." As soon as she finishes speaking, they both walk in.

"And that's my cue to go. Ladies, try not to get into any trouble today." Mark kisses Elizabeth and waves as he leaves.

Elizabeth fills them in on everything that happened in my dream.

Sloan's gaze drifts over me from head to toe and nods her head as if she's decided something, and says, "We have a lot of work to do. Let's go."

Grace throws her hands in the air. "Wait a minute. What about shopping?"

A flutter of peace and contentment floods my soul. This is what living feels like. I won't waste a minute of it.

The End . . . until next time.

A Note from the Author

Thank you so much for taking time to read Shield of Fire. Out of all of the books you could have spent time reading, you choose this one, and I am humbled. If you enjoyed the book, would you consider leaving a review? Book reviews are important for authors, and we need them to stay alive. No, not literally. But book reviews carry weight and help other readers find our books.

The very beginning of this book is based on a dream, and I knew I had to write her story. Millions around the world are suffering under the abuse of labor and even bought and sold for their bodies.

According to A21, "An estimated 50 million men, women, and children are enslaved right now-more than at any time in history." The numbers are staggering, but what can anyone do about it?

Organizations like A21 are actively working to stop slavery and human trafficking. Check out their website for ways you can help https://www.a21 .org/index.php

Or look for local organizations in your area for ways to help locally. Together we can help those who can't fight for themselves. If you see something, report it.

This was a difficult book to write, and I shed many tears over Angel and her situation. And for those like Angel who haven't found a way out.

Certain stories have a way of gripping you tight, and they won't let go. This was one of those stories.

Be a voice for the voiceless.

Switching gears a bit, some of you may be wondering what happened between Grace and Paxton, and Sloan and Tyler. Don't worry, it wasn't time to tell their story just yet. But there will be a third book coming soon that will focus on Grace, Sloan, and Angel, and maybe even a little more of Elizabeth and Mark.

Yes, you heard that right, Forged in Fire will be a trilogy! I am currently working on Book 3, so make sure to follow me on Instagram or Facebook for the latest news and updates.

You can follow me on goodreads:

g

goodreads.com/author/show/21694840.A_L_Evans

and my Amazon Author page here:

a https://amazon.com/author/author_alevans

You can follow me on:

f facebook.com/

instagram.com/

Acknowledgements

Writing is a very solitary journey, and for those of us who are self-confessed introverts, we must be very careful not to turn into hermits (it can happen). Thankfully, I have a few friends and family members who keep me grounded and prevent me from falling off the deep end. Mostly anyway.

Now for the monumental task of giving thanks to those who helped me along the way.

First and always, all praise to God, my Heavenly Father, for giving me this story to write. Thank you for sending your son Jesus and for the gift of Holy Spirit. You are the very breath that I breathe and my every heartbeat.

Jessica P, you did it again. You proofed, critiqued, and asked the tough questions all while growing another human. Thank you for all that you did to help bring this book to life.

Thank you to all of the beta readers and proof readers who helped me cross the finish line.

I want to give a shout out to my home Bible study group. You are such an inspiration to me. Thank you for your prayers and support. I'm blessed to have you in my life.

And thank you, the reader, for your time. You could have read any other book, but you spent your time reading this one. I am truly thankful.

Also by

A L Evans

Forged in Fire - Book 1

Book 3 in the Forged in Fire series is coming soon!

About the author

A L Evans is no wilting flower, but in the hot, humid South her hair can get a bit frizzy. Born in New Orleans, she calls Louisiana home with her family, and one very unsociable cat named Oakley. She has a full-time career in the finance industry and works on her writing late into the night. Answering what she believes was a prompt from God, she began her writing journey later in life, late perhaps, but right on time. She writes stories that weave the supernatural with themes of purpose and grace. When not balancing numbers or plotting the paranormal, she can be found in the kitchen flirting with new recipes by adding her own twist, often with more success than her cat's attitude suggests.

You can follow her on:

f facebook.com/

instagram.com/

You can follow on goodreads:

g

goodreads.com/author/show/21694840.A_L_Evans

and Amazon Author page here:

a https://amazon.com/author/author_alevans

www.ingramcontent.com/pod-product-compliance
Lightning Source LLC
LaVergne TN
LVHW090555110826
845146LV00001B/135